THE

PURPLE HAND

Waid Woodruff

Published in 2011 by AuthorCloud Publishers

Authorized Edition

Published by AuthorCloud Publishers
P.O. Box 302, Kaslo, B.C., Canada VOG 1MO
(503) 545-8930
www.authorcloud.com

ISBN-978-0-9866241-0-0
ISBN-4781849237611

This novel is dedicated to

Sergeant Alexander Shearer, "Uncle Alex"

He was

The Toughest Man Alive

And to all fallen law enforcement officers

*"... Those friends thou hast, and their adoption tried,
Grapple them to thy soul with hoops of steel...."*

William Shakespeare

Hamlet Act I, sc. 3

Author's Note:

The Purple Hand is a period piece. It takes place in Hollywood during the late summer and fall of 1962. The back story begins in August, the month Marilyn Monroe was found dead in her Brentwood home.

That fall, President John Kennedy challenged Nikita Krushchev to turn around a fleet of Soviet ships carrying missiles to Cuba and to remove the missiles already on the island: the Cuban Missile Crisis.

Also, during this period, the inner workings of the Italian Mafia were relatively obscure, especially so in the west, even though motion pictures had depicted gangsters as far back as 1904 (*The Moonshiners*). The "first" modern gangster film was Ben Hecht's *Underworld* (1927)—shot from the gangster's point of view. The movie won Hecht an Oscar for original screenplay. The first 100% talkie crime film produced was *The Lights of New York* (1928); and, in 1931 *Bad Company* was shot. It was the *first* to feature the gangland massacre on St. Valentine's Day.

The early gangster actors: Edward G. Robinson, James Cagney, Humphrey Bogart, Paul Muni, and George Raft were cast in such films as: *Little Caesar* (1930); *The Public Enemy* (1931); and *Scarface: The Shame of a Nation* (1932). Brian de Palma remade the film with Al Pacino in the title role of *Scarface* (1983).

In the 1950s, "gangsterism" was being portrayed as the Mob, an "organized" crime organization. Abraham Polonsky's *Force of Evil* (1948) starring John Garfield began the string of such films.

Today, *Omèrta*, "made man," and "wise guy," are well known. Francis Ford Coppola's three-part gangster saga *The Godfather* (1972, 1974, 1990)—written in collaboration with Mario Puzo, the author of the best-selling novel of the same name—was about a Mafia dynasty (Corleones). It gave the public insight to the "secrets" of a crime *family*. The term "family" replaced the specific words "Mafia" and "Cosa Nostra."

Despite the disclaimers of LAPD Chief William H. Parker and FBI Director J. Edgar Hoover in the late 1950s and early 1960s, the Mafia was indeed a major force in organized crime, and often vendettas, such as the one that forms the context for this book, extended across geographical boundaries and generations.

Today, we live in a world where many criminal "mafias" exist.

*   *   *

The City Hall with its 434-foot distinctive tower was the tallest building in Los Angeles until 1964. Police officers working a foot-beat or driving a patrol car did not carry wireless radio equipment. They relied on themselves and each other for assistance; their lifeline was their car radio and/or a Gamewell box that housed a landline to their division's front desk.

When cops, all males, (except for Juvenile Division, Jail Division, and various vice operations), "ran" persons for wants and/or warrants they were subject to the whims of those persons they had stopped. Often officers waited five minutes or longer to receive the results; their requests went through a tortuous circuit: first, to Communications Division, put in writing, then placed in a sealed capsule and sent via a pneumatic tube to the second floor: Records and Identification Division. A clerk manually searched the files, documented the findings, and returned the written data through the tube. Meanwhile, the true law-abiding citizen was often put out; however, the wanted criminal knew what the results of the records check likely would be. Patrol cops were vulnerable during the wait, and they knew it.

A Code 3, lights-and-siren, situation, often found the unit losing speed due to the extra "drain" on the black-and-white's (patrol car's) battery. Uniformed officers carried six-shot .38 caliber revolvers with six-inch barrels, and only 158- or 200-grain ammunition was allowed. Many carried a .38 snub-nosed revolver as a backup. Shotguns were stored in the trunks; there were no cell phones, computers, or GPS systems. This was prior to the Miranda Supreme Court decision and DNA tests.

Suspects had many tags, usually "asshole," but not "perp"; and, there were no fancy "sidewalk stars" on Hollywood Boulevard, only "wannabe stars."

For those interested in *kenpo* check out www.kenpokarate.com

All factual errors my fellow officers are bound to discover, including insidious typos, are solely mine, attributable to mild senility.

One typo, meant to bring a chuckle, *was* left in Chapter 24.

Prologue

Leonardo Brunetti was eight, too old to cry, but he couldn't help it. His pa was dead, gunned down last night. He squatted on the slush-covered curb, not caring that his trousers were getting soaked. It was Christmas day and it was snowing. There were presents under the scraggly tree, but he just couldn't open his. He covered his face with his arms and sobbed.

Three years ago Ma and Pa had taken him from Sicily. Pa had told him they had to leave because Il Duce, Benito Mussolini, was trying to wipe out all the Sicilian families. Pa didn't say why, only that they had to take advantage of an escape route provided by the boss of bosses of all Sicilian families, Don Vito Cascio Ferra.

Pa had said it would be a big adventure. Leo hadn't thought so and hadn't wanted to go. He'd liked living in Trapani and playing bocce ball with Pa and his friends.

Leo shuddered. They never should've come here. He remembered how Ma and Pa had tried to make him feel good saying they would live in America's east side with other Castellammarese families. The big move had been scary, and he'd puked on the rolling ship soon after leaving Marseilles, France, more than once, too.

He missed his playmates on Via Francesco Crispi in Castellammare del Golfo. They all understood each other. Here, he still "rassled" with American words. Everything sounded wrong, unmusical, but still, he was learning the lingo good enough.

With Pa gone, Ma had to find work. Leo didn't know if they would stay in Brooklyn, a section called Williamsburg. He'd never seen Ma so upset. He didn't like it. She wailed, crying she wanted to be close to her brother and his family, the Simeti's. They lived in a four-flat Brownstone in an area called "Hell's Kitchen."

It sounded scary.

It had been five years since Pa was buried, and Leo now knew about the Mafia. He also had caught on to the ways of Americans, learning the ropes so to speak, but the Kitchen was a tough neighborhood. The kids along West 47th Street still fish-eyed him, staying away because his pa had been a Mustache Pete. They were leery of skinny Nino Simeti, too. They all believed he was nutso because of his wild-ass violence and unpredictability. Everybody called his cousin, "Crazy Nino."

Adding to the neighborhood kids' anxiety was knowing that Leo's pa had been cut down by the infamous Angelo Sancia, whom everyone called The Purple Hand.

Since the move, Leo had been envious of the other kids on their block. Too often, he pictured them with their pas laughing and eating cotton candy while strolling along the Coney Island boardwalk, or playing catch in Prospect Park, and going to the zoo, like he and Pa had often done. Ma never took him anywhere, she was too busy working in the garment district.

Leo was left alone, a lot. He felt alone too.

Anger over the loss of his pa grew, as did Leo's size. He was beginning to realize he could bully his way into a quasi-friendship with the other boys. He saw they were afraid of him, and he kept it that way.

He liked being feared and not being challenged.

School was a drag, he hated it. One day he got so fed up he kicked his teacher's ass. It got Leo expelled. *Fuck 'em all.* He might not have Pa no more to teach him things, but Leo would get by.

Within weeks, he and his cousin, Nino, who was six years older, were running errands for Tommy Lucchese, a crime boss who had the smarts to take advantage of a war between two other bosses.

Leo, while gulping a Coke at a soda fountain near the Brownstone, told Nino, "Mustache Pete's brung it on themselves fighting over who the hell is supremo. Made it damn easy for Lucchese."

"Yeah, fuckin' Masseria rubs out Maranzano then gets his own ass hit, s'posedly by some Italian an' Jew gunners."

Simeti's words stirred a fury within Leo's gut. He thought of the so-called Jew hitter who killed his pa.

He remembered his pa telling him how important families were: "We Sicilianos gotta stick together, 'cause no one's gonna look out for us, but us. An' if we don't sticks together like a family we looks weak. Jus' remembers that Leo."

The Sicilian loyalty code was dead to many Italians, but it was in Leo's blood. He would honor it even though the younger Mafiosi Simeti's age thought it was stupid. They killed only those who stood in the way of making money. But to Leo, settling a vendetta was more important than making money. Besides, long ago he had vowed to find the Guinea-Jew killer of his pa, and to rub out his yellow ass.

The Purple Hand

"Y'know I'm always looking for one a them fucks, Nino."

"I knows, Leo—the shits losin' your ol' man like that—was jus' trying to stop th' yella cocksucker from quittin' th' family." Simeti slurped his drink. "Remembers—I was there when Uncle Bruno, your pa, gots hit, an' that cocksucker who done it didn't look like no damn Jew-boy to me. Th' fucker coulda killed my skinny ass, too. 'Stead, he jus' stares at me real hard like an' then he splits."

"Maybe the yellow fuck didn't shoot kids. Y'were what, fourteen? Think y'would know him if y'ever saw him again?"

"Hah. Y'bet. I'll never forgets *that* frigid fucker's face."

When Leo turned eighteen he moved to Chicago and got a job driving for a mob capo in Cicero. From that underboss he heard about the rival gang wars that raged before he was born. Leo also learned that a "Little Joe" was an execution method for loan-shark debtors, welshers, and others who failed to pay up. Four slugs, double deuces, in the skull, often coated with garlic juice, each bullet in two straight rows followed by the word being put out. The bosses wanted all debtors to know the consequences. Less deadly methods included the breaking of legs to ensure that the vigorish, "vig," interest money, was paid on time.

Leo was drawn to the bloody violence; it'd excited him ever since he'd bullied the neighborhood kids into accepting him. He'd learned soon enough to stay away from the tougher kids—he didn't wanna look weak. He enjoyed being a "leg breaker," as long as he had a couple of other muscles with him; and within a year, he and his pals were doing Little Joes for the Cicero boss.

But Leo's ultimate goal was to become a stand-up guy, a made man. Only jerks worked nine-to-five. By his twentieth birthday, he'd double-deuced a half-dozen chumps, made his bones, and went through the life-committing blood ritual with the dagger, like crazy Nino Simeti had.

On an early August day in Los Angeles Leo got a call from his cousin. Nino was in Tucson at Joe "Bananas" Bonnano's pad and getting ready to fly to San Diego. He wanted Leo to pick him up in Pacific Beach at "The Bomp" Bompensiero's house.

Leo was damn curious why Nino had come west. While driving north in his yellow Cadillac convertible with the top down, Leo asked Nino, "What brings you out west?"

3

"Had packages for Bananas and The Bomp from Lucchese."
Two bosses, two days. What's up?

Leo's cousin slouched on the black-leather seat chewing gum, blowing big pink bubbles, and sucking them in before the whirling wind plastered them onto his long Roman nose and caved-in cheeks.

A few highway miles of bullshitting about their boyhood days in the Big Apple as sons of Mafiosi got Simeti talking and Leo learning more.

Leo glanced sideways when cousin Nino said, "Joe Banana's gots his eyes on LA—says Little DeSimone's a cream puff."

"No wonder the don's never seen around." Leo tore the cellophane from a fresh cigar and let the wrapper fly away in the rushing air.

Keeping his eyes on the highway, he pressed the red hot lighter against the cigar's flat end and tasted the harsh smoke, his mind working.

Simeti said, "Yeah, Tommy Lucchese says his gambling ops are fuckin' weak. His boys're stupid too."

"Pio's one a them, Nino. The capo thinks he's smart—being big in porno flicks and strong-arming, but he can't control his boys neither. 'Slick' Pio wants to take over the south-side rackets 'n' run all the books in town."

Leo knew "Momo" Giancana had "convinced" Frank DeSimone that his underboss, Dante Pio, needed Leo's extra muscle. That was the reason given for why Leo was in Angel Town. Actually, he was an ear for Momo. Leo now realized that Nino was doing the same shit for his boss.

Now he knew why his cousin was sent to L.A.

"Nino, y're gonna like the west-coast weather, and the extra vig."

"Ya gots that right. Hey, Leo, when we gets to Long Beach find me a car dealer. I wants some classy wheels like this here Caddy."

"How about waiting for a 'sixty-two Thunderbird—the new Landau model?"

"Longs th' Bird's cherry red. Gots me four large burnin' a hole in my pocket. But they can sit there a few more weeks."

About a month had passed when around noon, Leo, about to enter the Continental Club in Hollywood, heard his cousin yelling, "Hey, Leo. Leo—hold up—gots somethin' y'gotta hear."

Twisting back, he saw Simeti climbing out of his fancy red T-Bird.

When his cousin caught up to him he said, "Unfuckinbelievable."

They went inside and found stools in the dimly lit bar. Simeti soon unloaded what he'd discovered.

The Purple Hand

Two Compari-and-Sodas later, Leo was squirming on the bar stool.

"Y'know, Nino," he was removing a limp newspaper clipping from his billfold, "I've carried this," he placed it on the counter, "wondering if I'd ever be so dumb-fuckin' lucky to find the chump—'n' you did."

"I remembers my ol' man tellin' me th' so-called Jew hitter really was a Guinea name a Angelo 'Pinky' Sancia," Nino said.

"Yeah, you told me the yellow fuck helped Sammy Purples' Jew gang in Detroit's booze war." Leo had hated the non-Sicilian Guineas till he learned all Italians called each other that when they didn't like someone. "'N' everyone calling his ass The Purple Hand . . . just 'cause he was s'pose to be so damn fuckin' ferocious."

"Hell—youse are more ferocious than that cocksucker ever tho't to be." Simeti slid the clipping toward Leo. "I also gots me an ol' picture a him." He patted his trousers pocket. "That's why I knows it's th' fucker."

Leo signaled for another Compari. "Twenty-eight years—no Pa." He belched. "Yellow fuck's gonna be *finito*, 'n' soon."

Chapter 1

Neall Haley sat with his back near the swinging door entry to the kitchen, his chosen spot in the Italian restaurant ever since he'd met the lithe waitress several months ago. He was nursing a beer waiting for eleven o'clock when the blonde Lissa Renzo would end her evening shift.

Across the dining room in a corner booth sat a suave looking gangster with a tall and showy brunette. They often came in for a nightcap. Twin thick-necks always accompanied the older mobster. They hunched at a nearby table and occasionally looked Haley's way. They knew he was the heat. He knew they were killers—he had no real proof.

Screw them.

Roosting in a place frequented by Mafiosi was not the wisest thing for a cop, but pretending to ignore them had seemed safe enough. He'd observed that they left Lissa alone although they did check her out. He might be risking his neck, but she was well worth it. The gorgeous woman had stolen his heart.

He had plans that Labor Day night—his twenty-sixth birthday—his blood rushed in anticipation, bathing him with titillating warmth contrasting with the cool Oly he held.

The French door to a rear courtyard and numerous motel rooms, part of the Hollywood Riviera del Palme restaurant/motel complex, swung wide, catching his eye. The opening was filled by a swarthy mobster. He stepped inside, brushed off the dark blue lapels of his single-button Italian-cut coat, and glanced at his large gold wristwatch. Haley had become familiar with Brunetti's nightly routine.

He had just come from Number 8. The prostitute who occupied the room had told Haley she serviced Leonardo Brunetti nightly at nine. From her, Haley surmised that the corpse found a week ago with its head drilled like Swiss cheese was the lousy meathead's dirty work. No proof, besides, it had gone down south of Hollywood; the Wilshire Division homicide dicks had caught it.

A month earlier when Brunetti first appeared, she'd told Haley that he was a Sicilian called "The Beak," and that he had arrived from Chicago. She didn't miss much at "The Palms."

He'd noted the overgrown hood's high-bridged nose, it took up a large part of his craggy face. The moniker fit, Neall Haley had decided.

To avoid eye contact with the huge Sicilian, he focused on the tiny bubbles rising in the schooner before him, but he sensed the Nose moving closer, he could smell the cologne.

Haley looked up warily his elbows staying on the table. His left hand slipped to the magnum revolver beneath his jacket.

The Beak stopped beside the table, dwarfing it.

"Hey bull, I wanna talk to ya—in private—tomorrow at that booth," he pistol-pointed to the far corner where the suave gangster sat cozily with the attractive brunette. "Three sharp!"

Haley glared up, his left hand now on the gun butt. "Forget it."

"Huh, your fuckin' future ain't important to you, Haley?"

Haley was surprised by Brunetti's agile maneuver in spinning away; more so, that he knew his name. The lousy meathead might have heard it from the suave gangster. Lissa would've told Number Two if he'd asked her, like she'd told Haley the underboss' name: Dante Pio.

He watched Brunetti amble across the green carpet and sit opposite the twins thick-necks. They were tearing apart small loaves of seeded garlic bread while devouring piles of fettuccini smothered in a creamy white sauce. Brunetti didn't look back; he did nod to the underboss.

Moments later, a hand softly touched Haley's shoulder.

"I'm ready."

He jolted to his feet, but when he saw Lissa's startled look he said, "Uh, my mind was elsewhere, hon—sorry."

He resisted asking her if she knew why Brunetti wanted a meet with him. Haley did not want to risk spoiling their night together. Why would she know anyway? If she didn't have the answer, she might try to find out. Her questions could make the meatheads nervous.

The thought unnerved him. No harm must ever come to his woman. He'd asked her why she worked there and she replied that the boss was good to her and the tips were better. She seemed happy. He didn't push it.

He trailed her car the eight blocks to her Gardner Street apartment, parking and waiting until her blue Pontiac pulled into the carport space assigned to her unit. He'd about decided to ignore the brazen challenge, but Brunetti's tone had Haley feeling uneasy.

Her abode was now his second home. In the months they'd dated, he knew where she kept most everything, except for the bedroom where she'd gone. He had yet to experience the pleasure that room promised. His choice. Lissa had never stopped him when his ardor increased, but he wanted their first intimate time to be special.

He reached into a cupboard, retrieved two stemmed glasses and a bottle of Cabernet. He slid open a peninsula counter drawer. Taking out a corkscrew, he uncorked the bottle then set it aside, allowing it to breathe. Stepping to the hi-fi player, he selected several LP albums, including vocals by Ella Fitzgerald and a Duke Ellington platter.

Ella's *The Nearness of You* was winding down when Lissa emerged through the bedroom door wearing a teddi, her toenails a matching pink. She knew his wish.

"Happy Birthday, Neall."

What a present!

He spun to the counter and poured the wine, nearly spilling it.

I'm acting like a damn schoolboy.

When her body leaned against him he forgot about the Cabernet.

Haley awoke to sunlight streaming through the bedroom window. Lissa, snuggled beside him in the crook of his arm, still slept. Her rose-petal fragrance lingered in the mid-morning air. He didn't want to disturb her but his right arm had numbed—a small price to pay for what she'd given him. Their lovemaking had been long and unceasing, lustily physical at times, and caressingly soft at others. Always exciting. His heart sped every time her doe-eyed gaze cast upon him.

Oh how I love this woman.

He brushed a kiss across her cheek. She stirred and clasped an arm around him, a sleepy smile showing. He stirred, too, as her warmth, her musky smell, her deep murmurs, enveloped his desire.

A long moment later, his explosive release finally sated him. He stretched alongside her, he never wanted this to end.

Eventually, he rolled out of bed telling himself that nothing was going to mar this sunny late summer day—he would ignore Brunetti's blunt demand; even so, the huge meathead's ugly tone had Haley feeling antsy. Why did he want a sit down? What in God's name could possibly affect "his fuckin' future?" The question was irresistible. Haley had to find out.

First, however, he must make a trip downtown to Hill Street, and the Jewelry Trades Building. The engagement ring he'd ordered was ready.

The Purple Hand

He planned to follow Lissa home from work like he usually did on his night's off and say the words that would make his life an unending joy.

After showering, he downed a cup of freshly brewed coffee. At the door, he kissed her long and deep. "Hon, I'll drop by here this afternoon."

An hour later, he stood by his black Porsche in a public parking lot and opened the tiny blue box again. Damn if the stones weren't perfect: a one-carat cut gem with tapered baguettes on the sides—the diamonds' brilliance in the sunlight had dazzled his eyes. He snapped the lid closed and dropped the box into an inside jacket pocket.

He looked into the rear-view mirror and caught the satisfied glint in his icy-gray eyes before he slid on the Air Force style Ray-Ban glasses. He adjusted the shades and thought how he would drop to one knee that night and ask Lissa to be his soul-partner for life.

Slipping on deerskin driving gloves, he brought the sports car to life. His future looked bright. On the drive to Hollywood, however, his mood changed to one of misgiving. He had intended to drive to his Fern Dell rental pad in the Los Feliz district, but he couldn't shake loose Brunetti's threatening challenge.

Haley reluctantly headed toward The Palms on La Brea north of Sunset Boulevard. It was two-thirty, enough time to down a bowl of tomato bisque, crackers, and coffee. He sat at his usual table and more than once while eating he gave the foyer a surreptitious glance, his knees bouncing all the while.

He was surprised when Lissa breezed in shortly before three and whispered, "Hi lover—I'm filling in—Jan's sick."

Soon after, Brunetti strode through the front entry and went to the corner booth. He slid onto the red vinyl seat and looked at Haley, sneering. Using his trigger finger he waved Haley over.

Haley pressed on his knees, not budging. He didn't want to admit it, but the idea of sitting with the meathead had frozen him. *Damn it.*

Lissa apparently had seen Brunetti's gesture. "Aren't you going to see what Leo wants, Neall?" She sounded apprehensive.

Haley edged off the chair hands fisted, his right arm pressed against the magnum under his brown bomber jacket, and moved to the corner booth trying to match Brunetti's hard-eyed stare.

Lissa followed Haley.

Slouching onto the bench seat opposite Brunetti, Haley crossed his ankles to help steady his legs. The smell of cologne was familiar.

9

Beak Brunetti ordered Compari-and-Soda. Lissa looked at Haley.

"Just water," he said.

When Lissa turned away, Brunetti didn't mince words. "Here 'tis. My cuz done seen your ol' man driving a light-gray plumbing van over in Brentwood—"

"What the?" Haley, sucking in, sat taller, his ankles uncrossing.

"Yeah, 'Dago luck' my cuz says. He damn near ran into the van. The black 'stache is some different he says, but seeing your pa's left mitt sticking outta the window my cuz takes hisself a closer look. Some a your pa's pinky was missing."

Pop *had* lost part of his left pinky. What the—? Haley's mind spun. Then he recalled that his pop did have a project on the affluent west side.

Haley's legs began bouncing a staccato beat, he wrung his hands below the table, then pressed down hard on his knees.

What the hell is going on?

Lissa arrived and placed Brunetti's drink on a coaster and went to serve another table. Brunetti unfolded a newspaper clipping containing a half-tone photo. He smoothed out the yellowed article on the tablecloth and pointed at the photograph. "Lookie here, Neallie Baby."

Being addressed so familiarly by the hairy meathead brought goose bumps. Haley eyed the *Detroit News* article. It was dated October 28, 1930. The faded picture depicted two men, alleged gangsters, wearing dark double-breasted suits and dark fedoras. They stood by a black sedan. The stockier of the two, identified as Ari Sands, held Haley's gaze. The man resembled how Haley's pop might've looked much younger, but Ari Sands didn't have Pop's brushy mustache. Visualizing a '30's style pencil-thin black one on Pop nearly gutted Haley.

Brunetti tapped a polished fingernail over the photo caption.

"Like the slick shit in that fuckin' pix—your ol' man—he's missing some a his pinky. What d'ya think?"

Haley noted Ari Sands' left hand caught in a forward movement reaching out to a car door handle. Five fingers were visible, and the little one appeared shorter. Putting on a tough look, Haley shoved the frayed clipping back, but Brunetti's cruel deep-set eyes had Haley's full attention.

"That chump called hisself Ari Sands, a Jew name—but he's a Guinea outta New York. Name's Angelo Sancia. Pinky for short. He's your ol' man, Lonn Haley."

How does Brunetti know my pop's first name? Besides, Pop's Irish.

The Purple Hand

Brunetti worked on his drink and rattled off a tale that Haley, with trepidation, refused to believe:

"Five years after that pix was snapped, the hit on Dutch Schultz went down at The Palace Chop House in Newark—when Dutch run with Charlie 'the Bug' Workman. Yeah, your goombah pa was part a that, too," Brunetti belched, "before he split—his yellow ass vanished . . . 'til now."

He grunted and fingered a Dutch Master from a pocket. He slipped it from its cellophane wrapping and bit off the leaf-wrapped end. He turned, spat out the piece of tobacco, and licked the cigar. Mouthing it, he snapped a flame to a golden lighter, and puffed while slit-eyeing Haley.

Haley realized that Brunetti was savoring more than the cigar. Haley didn't smoke, but suddenly he wanted to. He pictured the flickering flame being put to a dried dog turd; the image didn't relieve his need; a cold snake slithered up his spine. The Palace Chop House name had rung a bell.

Brunetti set down the cigar, snatched a napkin, honked into it, and rasped, "The yellow fuck should never've split."

Haley's mind switched to his parents' Los Feliz home, to his pop's favorite room, the den, where a glass ashtray with The Palace Chop House logo owned a spot on a lower bookshelf. The small souvenir had been there ever since Haley could remember. He recollected when he'd questioned his pop's earlier life but had never heard this side of it.

Has to be bullcrap.

Easing in a deep breath he wondered how it could be? When that news photo was snapped, Brunetti, and probably his cousin, had to be boys. What were the odds? Hell, there were kids he'd gone to high school with, kids he no longer could name, and he'd graduated only eight years ago.

Couldn't be.

Yet, his pop had never talked about his early childhood, only that he had grown up in the "Big Apple."

What Haley had just heard was total bull, but apprehension flooded him. He jammed his knees together, his mind reeling.

No damn way is this true!

He wanted to believe that, he had to, yet he was unable to shake the black shroud suddenly enveloping his very being, or the memory of Pop in the den on the phone, not talking whenever Haley had entered.

So what? Parents did that.

He watched Brunetti knock down the last of his drink, followed by his thick lips drawing on the dog turd until its brown end glowed red.

"Yeah, back then your ol' man was Angelo Sancia." Smoke escaped Brunetti's twisted mouth. "He scrambled his ass like the rest of 'em for Diamond Joe Esposito 'n' Scarface Capone."

While talking, he waved to Lissa for another drink. "Pinky done climbed over tons a bodies—politicians, Mick gangs 'n' his own kind. Angelo Pinky Sancia, the smart-head fingerman called The Purple Hand— s'posedly 'cause he was some fierce fuckin' enforcer for Sammy Purples. Hah. All my life I been wanting that sonofabitch. Now I got his yellow ass pinned, 'n' I'm gonna have me some fun 'n' games."

Scowling, he leaned closer. "Yeah, Sancia done split the family— 'n' he shouldn'ta. Uh-uh—'n' 'cause he did, you're gonna play my l'il game, Neallie Baby, if you care about your pa staying healthy."

There it is! He believes his own bullcrap. Pop's life is on the line.

The bald threat had turned real. Haley itched to plug Brunetti if only to erase what he'd just heard.

Lissa placed a fresh tumbler of Compari-and-Soda before Brunetti. She pretended to ignore them, but glanced at Haley, frowning. He saw how Brunetti looked at her as she turned away. Haley bit down on his lip.

Be cool, don't create a problem—not where she works.

Damn, before the meathead had accosted him the night before, all he had wanted was to enjoy his birthday night with Lissa, but he'd just been screwed—royally so.

What a gift. A damn lousy one, too.

Brunetti gargled an oily laugh cut short with a sputter. He nearly choked and snatched the soggy-tipped dog turd from between his lips.

"What's so damn funny, Beak?" Haley got a satisfying get-even feeling saying the meathead's tag. But the claim and threat gripped Haley like a clamp on his withering balls.

"Like I told ya, Haley—" Brunetti coughed up mucous and tongued it onto the cloth napkin, eyeing the brownish glob like it was rat poison. "Your fuckin' future."

"You're no part of my future, only a small part of my today."

Apprehension swamped Haley. He didn't feel as defiant as he'd tried to sound. His mind, a gyroscope. He now realized the logo on Pop's company vans displayed the plumbing shop address in Glendale. Hell, a phone call to the business number would provide Pop's name. Brunetti or his cousin could've staked out the building and then tailed Pop home.

But connecting Pop to me. . . . Damn.

The Purple Hand

The day before, at his parents' house, Haley had enjoyed a birthday barbecue. Brunetti and/or his cousin must've spotted him there.

Sliding from the corner booth, Haley said, "You're full of crap, Beak. I'm not buying any of it."

Brunetti also stood, his eyes narrowing as he deftly stuffed the old clipping into Haley's jacket opening.

"I want you to have this l'il reminder. Think about your pa 'cause I'm gonna be speaking some serious shit next time we talk—'n' hear this—don't be telling your ol' man squat. Your trap stays shut, till I say fuckin' otherwise, or else—*capisco*."

Haley rushed to the men's room and puked up the tomato bisque. He splashed cold water over his face, rinsed his mouth, and swallowed tap water to dilute the acid burning his throat.

He left The Palms, not telling Lissa that he was going, his mixed emotions and roiling gut wouldn't allowed it. He raced the Porsche to his parents' home filled with morbid dread. He needed to look at a snapshot.

After viewing it, he sat for a moment, trembling, glad that his mom was grocery shopping, but knowing he had to leave before his younger sister came home from school.

Minutes later, after buying his first carton of cigarettes, Camels, he was in his own pad grabbing a half-empty bottle of Glen Livet. He dropped onto the recliner in his living room, smoked while drinking the Scotch straight. Whatever Brunetti had in mind, it wasn't good.

Haley had to tell Pop—his life was on the line. But could his weak heart take it? And if Haley told his pop, Brunetti's "or else" came into play.

"Damn it." Haley smacked a fist into a knee. Regardless if Pop was or was not an ex-hit man, how could he protect himself if he didn't know that Brunetti believed he was? Not alerting Pop wasn't right, but it could kill him. Not telling him could get him killed, too. The fear was sickening. Haley had to stop Brunetti and the damn cousin who had started this shit.

How much time was there?

The Beak wanting to play a "l'il game" must mean that Pop had some time. But how much?

The next mid-morning Haley awakened with a ripping headache, but knew his mind had been active. While asleep he had dreamt of an encounter he had witnessed earlier that year between a blue-suit and a psychotic vicious killer of women. The fight had been deadly; scared the crap out of Haley, but the dark-haired Montego had damn well amazed him.

13

Haley kicked off the light bed covers and stretched out on his back, contemplating. The more he rolled his thoughts the more he was convinced. Mike Montego was the right cop. He'd also be a damn competent partner.

Before that night's roll call Haley approached the FCU supervisor, his pal, Sergeant Brad Kozier, and presented a proposal that included Montego and Kirtland W. Deal as new partners. "Dealer" was an unknown, but Montego had shown a liking for the first colored cop to be assigned to the Sixth Division. Being the solo black in an all-white division also meant that Dealer would be more apt to keep his mouth shut were he to witness something he shouldn't have.

Haley had heard that the half-Mexican Montego had faced down more than one wise-ass cop because of the black man—not that Dealer needed it. He looked like he could handle himself . . . still, Montego had been there. *He's loyal.*

With no clear idea how to ensure the cop's support in the manner Haley wanted it, he had to gamble. Although his best weapons were his badge and service revolver, he realized that in order to use them effectively he needed backup, a partner he could both trust and rely upon to keep quiet. He'd had a good partner, but had lost him to promotion, and the relief man on the unit was transferring to Vice.

During the pitch to Kozier, Haley emphasized that no one had accepted Deal like Montego had. Haley also suggested to Brad that having both of them in the two-car squad along with Bobby Diaz, a dark-skinned Mexican, and two other qualified cops working the second car, would add effectiveness to the six-man Felony Car Unit.

"Times are changing in Angel City—especially in 'Hollyweird,' . . . and Brad, please keep my name out of this new partner thing," Haley said.

When Kozier agreed, it was frosting on Neall's belated birthday cake. He sat back, relaxing. He now had a solid partner in Mike Montego.

The next night, while sitting in roll call, Haley's mind was on his pop. Was he safe? Not till Brunetti and his cousin were aced. First, Haley had to identify and find the cousin; then come up with a practical way to off both meatheads while keeping Montego and Deal in the dark.

As luck would have it, Kozier had given Haley an arrest warrant for Leonardo Brunetti. Chicago P.D. wanted his ass. One meathead on the tray.

But what should I do about it?

Montego entered the room and spied Haley in the back row.

Wow—I forgot how deep blue Montego's eyes were. Penetrating.

14

Chapter 2

Mike Montego paused beside a banana palm, letting his eyes adjust in the twilight. A sudden rush of warm wind crackled the dry palm leaves in the lush Italianate courtyard. The air was stuffy and hot. So was he.

Where are you, Haley?

He searched the shadows behind the The Palms restaurant as Leonardo Brunetti, his target, ambled toward a lighted red door. It was one of many in a row of single-story rooms.

Montego's gut tightened.

As if for reassurance, he patted the *foreign* felony warrant tucked into his coat pocket. He was about to advance on the dark-suited goon when a flashlight beam blinked once from the far end of the building.

Haley!

Three sharp knocks cut through the air. Montego's gaze shot back to the oversized goon now facing a door with the number 8 on it. Brunetti was checking the watch on his right wrist.

A lefty.

The door swung inward to a petite woman with fiery red hair styled into a large bouffant. A low-cut white dress left little to the imagination.

The mobster stepped inside.

The woman stuck her head through the doorway, eyed Montego in the shadows on the path for a heartbeat, then quickly shut the door.

He rushed down the path to Haley. "Thought we were squeezing the big bastard between us? Some sandwich job." Montego let out a long breath noting that Haley was breathing hard. He'd been up to something—but what? "Brunetti's little gal friend saw me—I mucked up good."

"No sweat, Montego—we're cool."

This was Montego's first watch with Haley whose reputation preceded him. The street cops said he saw every motion you made, heard every word you spoke, but you would never know it by looking at his pale blank face. Some cops seemed convinced he could kill a person without blinking while telling you exactly what was happening two blocks down the street—that's if he told you anything. "Ice Cop" he was tagged. The troops respected him—claimed Haley handled bad-asses like a steel pick on ice.

Whatever.

"For what it's worth, Haley, after speaking to the older hood in the corner booth, our boy said something to the greasy goons chomping garlic bread at the next table—couldn't make out what they were jawing about, but they're sitting tight."

Haley loosed a Camel from a crumpled pack in his shirt pocket, dipped his head, and fired a silver Ronson to it. He inhaled a deep drag, then said, "Probably told the thick-necks to stay put while he gets his ass laid." His words sounded through a smoky cloud as he pocketed the lighter.

Montego shook off the sweat beads from his nose and chin. The heavy four-inch Colt revolver in the new hang-down rig on his left side was bugging him. Since learning only that day of his new assignment, he'd practiced hand-to-hand combat movements trying to get used to the stiff new shoulder holster he'd rushed out and bought. He wasn't used to it, and the stifling heat hovering at 90° didn't help.

Yesterday he was sweating in the blue wool LAPD uniform, today he was sweating in a lightweight sports outfit. Yesterday he worked patrol. Today he worked in plainclothes with a partner he knew only by reputation.

Slipping a finger beneath the leather rig-strap to ease the pressure on his left side, he continued to study his new partner.

Haley, the Camel dangling from his lips, looked toward the targeted door and yanked a nickel-plated .357 Smith & Wesson from under the right side of his sports coat.

Montego noted: *A lefty, too.*

Haley broke the revolver open. Using the ambient light from a nearby room window, he checked the six chambers while rolling the cylinder. The ash from the burning cigarette fell onto his jacket sleeve when he shoved the four-inch magnum into its leather home.

Montego was curious about Haley's bad-ass reputation. Did the guy chamber "hot loads" in the S&W? His blank face gave no clue.

"Shall we do it, Haley?"

"Uh-uh. Let the lousy meathead drop his silks then we'll take his hairy ass down." Haley drew more smoke in. The Camel glowed with life.

Montego finger-shifted the narrow strap on his rig, again.

Imagining Leonardo Brunetti, a mob killer wanted by the Chicago police, busted with his shorts hugging his socks was mildly amusing, but taking the huge bastard from a small room presented problems.

Was the stacked whore the only person inside with Brunetti?

"How do we make sure it's only our boy with the hooker?"

16

The Purple Hand

Haley swiped the sheen from his forehead, thin-lipped the cigarette to the other side of his mouth, and again pulled out the S&W.

"It's just them two." He pointed the gun barrel up and surveyed the shadowy courtyard. "And The Beak's larded ass can't make it through the rear window . . . no matter—he won't run."

Beak? Montego shot Haley a look. "And his chesty little friend?"

"Not a problem—she'll move out of our way." Haley's smoldering Camel stub bobbed as he spoke.

"Oh?" Montego, feeling in the dark, literally, studied Haley again.

"Bathroom's on the left when you enter—makes things tight. And Montego, watch your damn piece—my ass is first inside."

Haley took a last drag, let the weed drop to the grass, crushed it underfoot, and moved toward door number 8.

Montego ground his molars. He touched the writ in his coat pocket but left it alone. He wanted both hands free. Lifting the sweat-damp, white cotton shirt from his chest, he trailed his partner, grumbling silently.

Flexing his hands in anticipation, he loosed his own .357 magnum: a blue-steel Colt Python. He took a relaxing breath and drew on his hand-fighting regimen to center himself.

They stopped in front of the red door with Haley on the doorknob side. Montego took the hinged side thinking how every one of the hundreds of times he'd done this in uniform he'd always been on edge.

This time was no different.

Haley raised his right index finger against his pale thin lips and whispered, "Tonight, *Numero Dos* is about to lose one of his main men."

He rapped the red panel two times.

Almost instantly the door opened. The redhead, all breasts and hair, puffed on a cigarette in a black plastic holder. She flashed a worried smile at Haley, glanced at Montego, then scooted between them into the courtyard leaving a trail of smoke.

Haley slipped inside through the swirling smoke, his S&W pointed straight ahead.

Montego followed in one stride and half-crouched in the entry.

Brunetti wasn't there, but beyond Haley, Montego saw a navy-blue suit coat neatly draped over a high-backed lounge chair. A TV atop a lowboy played Rod Serling's *The Twilight Zone* theme. Opposite it was a made-up queen-sized bed with a blue coverlet.

He's in the bathroom!

Montego leveled his revolver at the cut-glass doorknob. The mobster had to have heard the raps on the door.

Seeing no hinges, Montego knew the door opened inward. It did. *Fast.*

Haley spun toward the opening.

A fully clothed Brunetti barreled out and slapped the S&W away. The magnum flew across the carpeting. He kicked Haley in the groin.

Groaning, Haley collapsed. Brunetti whipped a semiautomatic from a shoulder holster just as Montego whammed into him. Brunetti sprawled sideways, the pistol still in his left hand.

Haley, rising to his knees, scrambled on all fours after Brunetti who twisted, arcing the 9mm pistol toward Montego. Haley reached Brunetti before he could fire, foot-swiping the Italian's gun hand, knocking the piece free. It slid under the bed.

Haley yelled, "Shoot his ass!"

Instead, Montego rammed his 4-inch steel "snake" home, booted Haley's magnum away from the action, and sprang forward.

Brunetti shoved Haley from him, rolled and started to reach under the bed. Before he could grab his pistol, Montego wrenched the mobster up and backwards into the lowboy.

The TV slid off and landed on the carpeting with a flash and a poof.

The *Twilight Zone* was ended before it started.

"I've got him, Haley."

Brunetti, snorting bloody mucous like a winded horse, regained his footing, spit at the dead TV, and bull-charged Montego.

"You sonofabitch."

Montego, ready for it, side-stepped and grasped a handful of greasy black hair in one hand and Brunetti's holster strap in the other. Using the big man's own momentum he slammed him nose-first into the nightstand, toppling the lit lamp, killing the bulb. The glow from the bathroom doorway was now the only illumination in the cluttered room.

Brunetti, his light-blue shirt mottled with blood, struggled to his feet just as Montego dropped with his full weight onto Brunetti's back.

"You're busted Beak."

Haley hooked a handcuff loop around the mobster's thick wrist while Montego, gripping the right one, unfastened the Rolex making room for the second steel loop. They forced Brunetti's arms up and over, raising their prisoner onto a sitting position. Haley secured the second bracelet.

18

"Damn good shit, Tonto." Haley helped muscle their belligerent catch to his feet, then he went to retrieve his magnum from the entryway.

Haley had used Montego's nickname, yet the guy hadn't said it in a derogatory tone like some patrol cops had—but then only for a short time. Hearing the friendly tag suggested to Montego to begin calling his senior partner by his first name.

Montego drew a lungful of air, then hissed it out as if through a trumpet mouthpiece to dilute the adrenaline pumping into his bloodstream, a trick he'd learned to force more oxygen into his bloodstream.

Haley holstered his revolver and snagged Brunetti's pistol from under the bed. He popped out the full magazine, ejected the chambered cartridge, and secured the semiauto inside his waistband.

Montego slipped the golden wristwatch into Brunetti's front trouser pocket and during the pat-down removed the hair-oil residue on his hand onto Brunetti's clothing.

Brunetti, mouthing ugly slobbering noises, fought the stainless steel cuffs to no avail.

After running a forearm over his own wet brow, Montego gripped Brunetti by the arm and jostled him out the door where he spied the red-haired whore hunkered amongst azalea bushes near a corner of the building.

Although mostly hidden in the dim light, her swan-white dress had given her away, its skin-tight contours concealed no threatening weapons—at least not the deadly kind. Her statement wasn't required in a warrant arrest, but Montego was curious about her having smiled at Haley earlier.

"What's your name?" Montego asked.

"We don't need her info," Haley said, cutting off any response. "Let's haul The Beak's ass to our unit before other thick-necks show."

Montego had no problem with clearing the motel area.

The guy sure likes being the boss.

They marched the mobster through a side passage to the un-marked four-door Plymouth parked a block north on pine tree-lined Lanewood. Except for their tramping noises, the dark residential street was quiet.

At their unit, Montego opened the rear door and tossed Brunetti's suit coat over the back of the front seat.

Beak Brunetti suddenly bucked loose from Haley's hold.

Montego instantly clenched the nape of Brunetti's muscular neck and shoved him headfirst onto the back seat. The big goon twisted back, glaring at him in the reduced light.

"You just made a big fuckin' mistake, Blue Eyes." Then he shifted his dark look to Montego's blond partner and, spewing more blood, said in a growling voice, "Especially you, *paesano*."

"Paesano?" Montego glanced at Haley. "Thought you were Irish." He'd said it jokingly to play down the venomous tone in Brunetti's voice, but in the moon glow he noted his partner's mouth had pinched.

Haley grabbed his baton from the angled rubber-hose door sleeve. "Slide your hairy ass to this side, Beak."

Slamming the door, he strode around the car to the opposite side and dropped onto the back driver's side where he could "stick" Brunetti's legs should he kick up at Montego's head with his size fourteens.

Montego appreciated his partner not taking chances in case Brunetti had such an unkind idea during the drive to Hollywood Receiving Hospital.

When they rolled into the drive-through breezeway separating the small medical facility from Police Station Number 6 to its north, the sedan reeked of Leonardo Brunetti's blood, sweat, and cologne.

Brunetti received medical treatment, then was walked to the station. The PM watch lieutenant checked for a doctor's signature on the MT slip and glanced at Brunetti's taped nose. He nodded sagely.

Montego noted the mobster's deep-set eyes during the intake process: flinty in the now swollen sockets. But the acne-scarred Brunetti uttered nothing, simply glaring and dipping his head slightly as if to say, "Just you wait."

During the booking process, Montego reflected on the night's happenings: While he and Haley had nursed warm beers and waited for the expected arrival of Leonardo Brunetti at The Palms, one of several rumored Italian gangster hangouts in Hollywood, he had asked, "Haley, why did you call Brunetti 'The Fixer'?"

Haley was finishing his umpteenth Camel. Exhaling smoke, he gazed around the grass-green carpeted room. "Yeah . . . you've been cruising the streets in black-and-whites."

Montego, consciously rubbing a thumbnail, a result of nightmares; it helped him cope—he began doing it as a child—watched Haley stubbing out his cigarette while scrutinizing him.

"The Chicago prosecutor's homicide case against one of their local meatheads vanished along with their key witness—nearly the final fix, except the corpse had four twenty-twos planted in its skull. Brunetti blew it—they lifted his partial prints from the ejected brass casings providing enough points to make a positive ID."

The clanging of a steel-barred cell door confining Brunetti brought Montego's attention back to the small jail. With the goon behind bars, Montego left.

On his way out he stopped in the closet-sized anteroom to key open a wooden wall-mounted gun cubicle. He removed his firearm thinking that the best thing about foreign, out-of-state, warrant busts was the wanted guys couldn't bail out and beat the arresting cops back onto the streets.

Haley, finished with filling out the Arrest Report-Short Form, waited in the unmarked squad car for Montego and breathed deeply. Brunetti was out of action, the immediate threat gone.

I almost blew it tonight. What the hell was I thinking?

If he had killed the lousy meathead, he would never find the cousin-asshole who had identified Pop as Sancia to Brunetti.

Haley briskly massaged the back of his arms to remove the chill.

The sarge had provided him with a brief bio on Leonardo Brunetti, but the sergeant had no clue that would locate the finger-pointing cousin.

Haley dropped a hand to his aching balls—

The driver's door popped open.

Haley jerked his hand from his groin and quickly fumbled a Camel pack free, pissed that he now was chain-smoking—thanks to Beak Brunetti.

Montego tossed the Peerless cuffs onto the bench seat and keyed the V8 motor alive.

"Chicago PD should bury The Beak's butt pretty deep, Neall."

Haley snatched the handcuffs and shoved them into his waistband. He pulled a Camel free, but needed both hands to steady the damn lighter.

Taking a deep drag, he glanced sideways at Montego while blowing smoke out the open side window.

"Yeah, I suppose—unless The Beak fixes his own fix."

Gotta ID his meathead cousin, ace his ass—end this nightmare.

Leaving the leather shoulder holster rig on, Haley muted the TV's sound, poured a nearly full tumbler of Glen Livet neat, and dropped onto the tan La-Z-Boy recliner, his favorite chair. The darkness outside the bay window in his house matched his mood.

The dull gnawing in his innards not helped by the kick into his nuts had him touching his tender balls while he swigged the single-malt.

He thought how his academy classmates had referred to him as the "lone gray-eyed wolf." Several of his partners said he was one cob-tough cop—cold as dry ice. They'd tagged him "Ice Cop." It had stuck.

What a joke.

He realized he'd talked too rough to Montego. Not the way to earn his loyalty, and Haley sorely needed it. It had pissed Montego off, but a twisting gut had Haley playing the damn Ice Cop stint.

Admittedly, Brunetti's bullcrap story days before had Haley shook. He hurt emotionally. He should be acting corncob tough, instead he was behaving like a damn worthless chicken.

He was afraid to face Pop.

Not fair.

Chapter 3

Haley pushed in the footrest on the La-Z-Boy and went into the kitchen. He fixed a pot of coffee. While it brewed, he went into the living room and stared out the window. The sun had yet to rise; the grayness of the pre-dawn made the view indistinct, like his thought: how best to handle the crappy situation Brunetti had laid on him. Haley felt suffocated, crushed actually.

Admit you're afraid Ice Cop.

He must go down to the PAB and check some names at Records and Identification Division. It likely would be a wasted trip; Angelo Sancia or Ari Sands could well have never been to L.A. And to get any information out of NYPD without an ongoing case to fall back on would take clout. He had none, and if he did, there was a chance that it could backfire on him.

Should he pull up criminal info on the names, the data probably would be thirty years old, so what could he possibly learn? Even flying to New York on his own time and searching through newspaper morgues would only provide microfiche articles. Nothing substantive.

While in R&I he also would check out the name Lonn Haley. The thought of doing that brought a brief shiver. A Haley checking out a Haley might raise eyebrows. To make any criminal records check he would have to fill out a search request chit and also sign in on the records log. Still, he had to risk it. The other names, Sancia and Sands, on the request should help to satisfy the curious eyes of the clerk.

Haley, back in the kitchen, poured the coffee with second thoughts about doing a search for any type of criminal offense, it simply couldn't have occurred. Pop held a state and a city plumber's license so Haley doubted there could be anything serious or the licenses wouldn't have been granted; and no birth records because Pop was born in New York City. This Haley knew, and his parents' marriage certificate would prove nothing only that he wasn't a bastard. He snickered. His chest ached.

After he made the trip downtown he would face Pop and get some answers. He must think about how best to accomplish that so his pop had no choice but to respond. Haley also needed a plan to ace the unknown cousin when he found him; it would involve using Montego, but to pull it off Haley needed to get the cop into his corner. Then an ugly thought struck.

What if this isn't the meathead cousins bullcrap, but a mob thing?

*　　*　　*

Montego slogged up the slight grade on Temple Street toward the decades old Hall of Justice, a granite-block structure, its walls blackened with age. He pulled out his pocket Bulova: 8:45. Fifteen minutes until he needed to be in Superior Court. Appearances often were a waste of time, but this time the Deputy District Attorney had assured Montego the case would be heard.

He entered the marbled lobby to the combined smells of cleaning products, and coffee in paper cups carried by a potpourri of uniformed cops, defendants, and defense attorneys—male and female.

Drawing a bead on an opening elevator he flowed with the crowd, but the operator-controlled door shut when he was a step away. He stepped back and bumped into someone. It was his beach-town neighbor, a detective who also was his pal.

"Uncle Alex—going my way?"

His pal liked the "uncle" moniker, and their local cop chums in Manhattan Beach called him that, too.

Alex Strait, a six-foot homicide detective, with a "baby" handlebar mustache and a perpetual near-smirk grin on a narrow, rawboned face, was dressed to sartorial perfection, as usual. Today, he wore a beige two-button suit complemented by a thin blue tie.

The trim detective shook his head. "Not likely Officer Mon*tay*go. We have an interview up in High-Power." His jaw muscles rippled beneath weathered skin as he nodded to his partner standing nearby.

Montego had been in High Power three years earlier, as a rookie cop. He had been escorted by his mentor, Detective Eagon Quinn, into the gray concrete maze of holding cells with the "special-case" prisoners that were kept from the general prison population. His mind re-echoed the magnified sounds of the clanking steel and the humming murmurs of defendant-clients and their lawyer-counselors. It had been an enlightening exposure; the onset of his observing how slick attorneys wove blatant lies into "legal truths."

"The pusillanimous prick cut his common-law's face," Strait said.

Montego was used to Strait throwing out fancy words, like the one he'd just used for cowardly. Montego eyed Strait's shorter partner vying for an open elevator but getting edged out by the pressing throng.

"When's your partner transferring to the third floor?" Montego was referring to the Homicide Bureau. They handled the high profile cases.

Strait often groused about downtown leaving the fifteen divisions with the so-called non-romantic murders to investigate, yet he was assigned to Hollywood Homicide where high profile or "romantic" murders were not uncommon.

"Give it time, just keep your nose clean." Strait's eyelids lowered as he twirled a mustache tip with a flick of his manicured fingers. His manner and dress befitted the look of a British Army colonel.

"I heard that Tonto tangoed last night."

"Yep, but the dancer wasn't too friendly—got his beak busted."

Montego wanted to talk about his new partner, Haley, but resisted; this wasn't the place and there was no time. "Say, Mister Toughest Man Alive, are your bones up to running the 'Weave' Sunday morning or are the steep streets along the beach a bit too much?" He'd found out that "The Weave" had gotten its name from Strait. Over time the arduous street route had developed a reputation as a brutal training course for local joggers.

A bell dinged nearby. Glancing over, Montego saw Strait's partner set like a distance runner ready to go when the elevator door opened.

"Challenging the TMA? Best be ready. By the bye, do not expect *Señor* Brunetti to forget the nose shift you gave his scrobiculated visage." The natty older detective slipped past Montego and into the last space in the elevator. "He's got heinous cronies in 'Jollywood.'"

The brown-uniformed operator eyed Strait with a raised eyebrow as she slid the door shut cutting off what looked to be a full-fledged smirk.

Montego chuckled. Webster dictionary checking time. Again. He assumed the "S" word had to do with Brunetti's acne-scarred face. The words Strait came up with. On Sunday morning Montego would get even.

The next elevator arrived and Montego squeezed into a spot. While it whirred up the shaft, he mentally prepared for his upcoming testimony.

When his re-cross examination was completed, just before the noon hour, he promptly left the courtroom to show he could care less about the verdict; he didn't want his future cases tried before a judge who might think he wasn't being objective. Besides, seeing the glowering purse-snatcher who had resisted arrest slumped at the defense table wearing an arm cast and sling was satisfying enough, but better was the accumulating overtime hours that the court appearances provided. They became "Specials," days off to body surf, to play beach volleyball, and to party with his gal friend.

Montego crossed Temple Street, passed the City Hall, and headed for the eight-story Police Administration Building. Inside the institution-green PAB he rode the freight elevator up to Homicide Division. Two detectives manned the room during the lunch break; both wore white shirts. The one nearest the entry was handling incoming telephone calls. The farthest one, with a gray felt hat cocked back, was forty-four year-old Eagon Quinn. The bachelor sat at a four-person wooden table-desk.

The tall, solidly built detective-sergeant had been solving murders since the early 'forties, back when Montego knew his wavy hair to be carrot red. Now, partly due to his night law schooling, drifts of snowy white ebbed back from a widow's peak, a contrasting crown above his ruddy face.

Quinn had worn fedoras long before four robbery dicks had made themselves popular as the "Hat Squad." Perhaps unknowingly, but unlikely, Quinn was the reason that Montego had pinned on the gold-and-silver LAPD badge. He and Joe Whitehead, another homicide detective-sergeant, had often dropped by Montego's mother's small duplex on the weekends. He loved those Saturday afternoon visits, but years passed before he understood the true reason the detectives came by, when he realized his full-time working mother, a divorcée, had wanted them over.

She believed her only son needed trustworthy men in his life.

Eagon Quinn, seeing Montego entering the squad room, shoved back his barrel-backed chair, adjusted the fedora, and scratched his hairline.

"Mikey, what brings you to the third floor?"

"A Chicago goon called The Beak." Montego leaned against a table-desk across from Quinn. "Tell me about Leonardo Brunetti."

"I know you busted his beak," Quinn grinned. "Surprised me too. Those Mafia gunsels usually don't resist arrest. Something must've tweaked his nose, besides you." He grinned again and settled back in his chair. Yawning, he lifted a half-smoked cigar from a crusty tin ashtray.

"Brunetti jumped my partner. What's the scoop on this bad guy?"

"He's a hired gun—arrived about a month ago from Chicago. Originally, he's from Brooklyn."

"My partner mentioned another goon. Called him Numero Dos."

Quinn thumb-lit a blue-tipped stick match. Letting the flame settle, he said, "Interesting that your partner knows that. Dante Pio *is* the number two crime boss, a *capo regime* they call their underbosses. He answers to Frank DeSimone, the LA *don*—that's what the Italian Mafia families, gangs, call their top guns."

With a grin and a twinkling wink Quinn was letting Montego know he and the commander of Intelligence Division, the watchdog of organized criminals in L.A., were tight. The flame was now under the cigar's stub.

Quinn drew in, then blew out two near-perfect smoke rings.

Montego finger-stabbed the first one like he'd enjoyed doing as a kid on Saturdays during Quinn's visits.

Quinn said, "You might've seen capo Pio with a snazzy looking woman when you served the warrant on Brunetti. The gunsel does like the pretty ladies."

Montego remembered the well-groomed middle-aged fellow sitting snug-like with an attractive brunette who could've been the double of the First Lady, Jacqueline Kennedy. The statuesque woman, overly dressed for The Palms, had worn elbow-length black gloves and sparkling diamonds. Montego amused himself, thinking how the fancy woman was a gangster's gun moll—the thought now seemed a bit "Hollywood."

While on patrol, he'd never had a face-to-face with any gangster. At the time of the Brunetti bust, all he knew was what Haley had said about a Chicago murder case involving the guy named in the warrant, and his being a "fixer." Except for a Peter Falk movie, Montego knew next to nothing about criminal gangs, and much less about the Italian Mafia.

Quinn snagged Montego's attention back to real time. "The local underboss is moving into the southwest side by ordering the Ralph's market bombing that killed a box-boy. That was two blocks from where the owner of Acme Liquors was fatally shot. Me thinks that Brunetti and a cohort took out the poor bloke—we don't have enough to nab the gunsels, yet."

"I heard the Acme homicide was nastier than most."

"A stark warning. The victim's nails had been plucked and both his hands tattooed ugly with tire tread-marks." Quinn pointed at Montego's hands. "Upsetting you?"

Long ago, Quinn had picked up on Montego's nervous habit of rubbing his thumbnails. He quit messing with them.

"And I must tell you, Mikey, the Mafia has methods that would make a snake shed its skin and bare-belly it over hot lava to escape their clutch. They're not people to fool with."

Montego studied his mentor's stern face looking for a bit of humor, but saw none. Brunetti's personal threat in the prowl car popped into mind.

"You or Chicago PD got enough to put the huge goon away?"

27

"Who knows? The gunsel's cagey, for sure. Gave us *nada*. He's downstairs in a holding tank as we speak. Roy's talking to the Chicago boys now, readying things for tonight's red-eye to O'Hare."

Roy O'Brody, Quinn's long-time partner, matched his age. They were like brothers, more so since the early 'fifties when O'Brody began drinking too much. His son had been killed fighting in Korea.

Quinn glanced at the papers on his desk. "Come tomorrow morn we'll be dumping our pain-in-the-ass on the windy city's finest. Although, Leonardo Brunetti does have a knack for beating the legal system."

"You're full of good news."

Montego, realizing his mentor wanted to get back to his report, knuckled the tabletop and headed for the door.

Strolling out of the Glass House—its half-glassed walls in the lower prisoner holding areas had given the building its common name—Montego walked north up Los Angeles Street toward the historic Spanish Plaza. He passed the fancy wrought-iron gazebo and took in the piquant odors wafting from the Olvera Street *tiendas*.

He turned east toward the Union Railway Station with the Spanish mission tile roofs and stucco walls. When he stopped beside his four-year-old white-with-red trim Chevy pickup, the limited '58 Cameo Carrier model, he checked the vast area around him. Then he realized with some annoyance that he was reacting to the off-hand remarks from Strait and Quinn about the Mafia.

Montego's thoughts flashed back two summers to when he'd gone to see *Murder, Inc.* at the Paramount Theater. He'd asked Quinn if the mob character played by Peter Falk was a true portrayal and Quinn had replied, "It's no act, Mikey. The gunsels shoot first with no questions afterwards."

*   *   *

Leo Brunetti stood gazing through the glass encompassing the large holding cell. Soon he'd be back in Chicago. He'd thought the fix was in and he didn't have to worry anymore about the rap. Now, he'd have to make some new arrangements. He needed to do it without bugging Momo, the boss. Cousin Nino could do it.

Shoulda used him to begin with.

Loud hacking coughs brought Brunetti out of his musing. He growled and fish-eyed the punk on the other side of the glass-walled room.

28

The Purple Hand

Reaching to his chest pocket for a cigar and finding none pissed Brunetti off. The damn bulls had seized all of his personal stuff.

He dropped onto the wooden wall bench and stretched his legs out. His mind drifting, knowing he'd fucked up the previous night at The Palms.

While taking a leak in the motel's bathroom, he'd heard something and looked through the slight opening in the frosted awning window. He'd spotted Sancia's cop-kid coming toward the room door with that blue-eyed Montego. He hadn't seen the bull before.

Haley had to be up to something having a new partner.

The bulls had looked like they meant fucking business.

He had intended to mess with Haley before rubbing out old man Sancia, but had believed the two bulls were coming to shoot Brunetti's ass. He'd felt cornered, and had acted out of fear—he couldn't help it.

Stupido.

Had he killed the bulls, he would've been in deep shit with Momo.

And Haley's new partner. What was with that fucking bull, Tonto?

He could've shot my ass—but he didn't.

More loud hacking brought Brunetti's mind abruptly back to his confined situation. The punk now lay sprawled on the concrete floor. Brunetti had a mind to go kick the puke's smelly ass, but didn't need the trouble it would bring.

Brunetti wished Cootchie Goochie, the sexy redheaded whore, would be on the plane with him. He imagined grinding away on her bones while flying high all the way to Chicago.

Damn. He hated being taken from L.A. before getting to settle up with Pinky Sancia, but Brunetti damn well would be returning.

Haley and his old man are dead men. . . . Tonto Blue Eyes needs to be taught a fuckin' lesson, too. It don't matter that he didn't shoot my ass.

Chapter 4

Montego, in the Watch Commander's office, perused the Daily Assignment Board for Monday, September 10. He eyed the MID-watch listing: Unit F-1, KW Deal/M Montego—Day Off: N Haley. He learned that Haley regularly had Mondays and Tuesdays off. The third man working "Frank-One" would be his partner tonight. He looked forward to working plainclothes with Kirtland Wellington Deal, a classmate at the Police Academy.

The last three nights the felony unit had kept busy serving warrants, and there had been little discussion between Montego and Haley. But for Montego's tummy comfort, Haley was too hard to read. And the guy liked spouting orders. It reminded Montego of boot camp.

He had to set things straight with the icy guy. Partners must work as one, trust each other totally. Their lives could depend on it.

Upstairs he spotted KW outside the detectives squad room.

"Kay Dub—hold up—hey, some cool duds. Showing me up?"

KW Deal flashed a "pearlie" grin. They exchanged feigned punches and bantered about their new assignment before stepping into the home of the "brown-suits." They had twenty minutes until roll call began.

A jowly detective sat behind a scarred wooden desk close to the entryway, a filtered cigarette hung from his puffy lips. The night-duty dick, his white shirtsleeves rolled half way up his thick and hairy forearms, thumbed through the day's crime reports. A dog-eared *Argosy* magazine and a pack of Raleigh cigarettes completed the desktop picture.

Puffy Lips, his head canted toward Montego, eyes squinted to avoid the streaming smoke, grunted "Hello," ignoring KW as he continued riffling through reports.

Montego, about to ask if the detective teams had any warrants for FCU to serve, saw Strait come in from the Burglary Squad's room in back. He pointed to his table, the first of a row of three against which blond-wood chairs were uniformly placed. Montego figured Strait's partner had done it before signing out for the day. It'd taken a while to accept Wayne Nells' quirks, his militaristic manner. However, Strait liked his precise an formal partner, having more than once said, "Wayne's dependable."

Nells was the senior homicide dick in the division, and was slated to fill Quinn's spot downtown. Eagon Quinn had let it be known that he was pulling the pin on September 14, after an even twenty-five years on the job. It meant an open seat in Homicide, but too soon, Montego believed, to land the position he coveted.

He introduced KW Deal to Strait, having noted the big wall-clock: 5:55. "The TMA is working late tonight."

"TMA?" KW made a curious look.

"Meet the Toughest Man Alive," Montego said, grinning.

KW eyeballed the semi-smirking, mustachioed homicide dick now twisting back on his chair to open a metal file cabinet behind him.

Strait pushed off from the green file drawer, slamming it as his chair dropped forward. "Since you FCU gentlemen dropped by I'll give you a live one. Suspect is a Mister Paoli Salico. Word has it the worm is holed up in the old Saint Andrews Hotel."

Montego accepted the felony warrant. "A heinous charge?"

"Murder à la first—Salico's a hired gun for Mister Pio."

"Pio?" KW scanned the writ Montego held between them.

"Dante Pio." Montego pocketed the writ. "Local underboss, the number two Italian Mafioso. His muscles've been cutting into the gambling action on the southwest side."

"You're impressive, Tonto Montaygo." Strait half-smirked.

"Uh huh." KW nodded slowly, his upper lip curled. "Heard some peckerwoods have the neighborhood buzzing."

Strait looked from Montego to KW. "It also put Salico in a jam. We think he's the prick who bombed a south side market for Mister Pio—guess you heard about Haley and Tonto, our new mob squad, nabbing in *The Beak* last week?" Strait caressed his mustache.

"The Beak?" KW eyed Montego. "That the mobster thug you told me about in the hallway—the one who called Ice Cop a paesano?"

"Yep. An imported gun for Dante Pio, the capo regime—capo for short. He's like a captain or a lieutenant—an underboss to the local Mafia don, Frank DeSimone."

"Paesano, capo regime, Mafia don?" Strait arched an eyebrow. "My, my—Tonto the hopeful TMA is taking the mob squad job seriously."

Montego shrugged. "I guess Leonardo The Beak Brunetti thinks Haley's a friendly Italiano." He turned and put an arm across KW's shoulders. "Come on, my *ebon* paesano. It's roll call time."

*   *   *

Montego faced into the warm air whipping in through the unmarked sedan's windows as KW drove them away from the setting sun en route to the old hotel on Santa Monica Boulevard.

KW suddenly slapped the steering wheel. "Yo, F-Car cruising is kinda cool—for the most part—if we have no warrants to serve we can drum up our own work since assigned radio calls're kinda scarce."

"Yep, we're *kinda* on our own hard-eyeing the goings on out here." Montego watched the evening's peach-toned sky growing more intense through the smoggy haze as the orange sun edged lower behind them.

KW knuckled Montego's arm in a lighthearted gesture. "No damn way I saw myself wearing 'civvies' and chasing bad dudes in the uptown Sixth with a blue-eyed honky. 'Course your skin's dusty colored—count of your beach life, huh?"

Montego, blinking away smog-induced tears, turned from the window and drawled, "Riiight." The air-cleansing warm Santa Ana winds had died during the early morning hours and the basin between the Coastal Range and the Pacific had trapped the day's traffic and industrial fumes. L.A. was growing too fast, and nothing was keeping up. Not the freeways, not public transit—and for sure not the blue-suits patrolling the crowded streets, nor the dicks trying to nail the never-ending felons protected by crafty lawyers.

Whether his being a police officer in the City of the Angels made any difference or not, didn't matter. He liked the challenge. He touched the leather-backed shield clipped to his belt and rubbed the oval surface with its raised centerpiece of the monolithic City Hall, L.A.'s tallest building; on the eleventh floor his mother enjoyed a career with the Fire and Police Pension Department.

At Van Ness, KW drove the four-door next to a police motorcycle angled on a kickstand behind a Buick Roadmaster. A sullen-looking male with a crew cut sat behind the steering wheel strangling it.

Montego recognized the motorcycle officer penning out a citation, a "Greenie."

Barry Ruggles smiled and waved them off. Montego signaled back, pride filling him. Cops and firefighters were a large part of his growing up years—at least on Saturdays. He was too young to know that the city government under Mayor Shaw was corrupt—it was his love for Quinn and Joe Whitehead that had influenced him to be an L.A. cop when he turned twenty-one.

In 1950, William H. Parker took over as Chief of Police. The strict disciplinarian began to rebuild the sliding LAPD's reputation. In time, the department was attracting men and women from all over the country.

Even so, the "new" force had its problems, especially for applicants of color. The silent treatment and the "Tyrone" and "Rastus" cartoons taped to Montego's locker because of his friendship with KW Deal had tried his patience, but nothing daunted his admiration for the man; besides, only a few bigoted cops made it obvious to Montego's face anymore.

"S'pose we're the token seasoning, you think?"

KW's words took Montego back; he guessed what he was thinking.

"Yep, we're the spice cops." On their first day at the Academy he'd approached the recruit in the upper parking lot and had made a stupid goof. He'd asked him if he knew a black guy named Jordan Smith.

KW Deal had snarled, "Why the hell you asking me?"

The response jarred Montego. He had asked KW because the other classmates were white, except for one Mexican and himself, but he was half Scandinavian, his mother's side. Apologizing, and feeling the fool, he'd offered his hand. KW had ignored it.

However, he had pressed on. "Expected Jordan, a monster guy, to be here lining up with us recruits this morning. We 'spotted' each other in a weight-room when we were toning up for the fitness test—didn't think to exchange phone numbers."

Getting no answer, he'd pressed further, "Today, during our lunch break, I spent all my dimes dialing up every J. Smith in the phone book—had no luck."

KW, hands flexing, continued to scowl so Montego had given it a final press.

"Jordan always joked that the LA force lacked seasoning. He said its flavor needed balancing, and a hot peppercorn like him was just the right spice. And if we ever got paired up that in no time we'd be chronicled the Salt-and-Pepper Shakers of the illustrious El A Pee Dee, even though I was a mite cinnamon flavored."

KW had burst into a wide grin and reached out. They'd clasped hands, Montego taking in the depths of the man's sincere expression.

The acrid air blowing through the car window burned Montego's eyes; he brushed a finger along the thin curving scar on his neck below the jaw line, courtesy of a teen Mexican bully with a sharp blade. The memory reminded Montego of Jordan Smith saying, "I grew up scared 'cause of my skin color. Wasn't the only one felt that way—smelled the fear all around, everyday—that's why I pumped the heavy iron. Won't be scared anymore."

Montego, thanks to the knife-wielding bully, had also known gut fear as a boy, and had made a similar pledge.

After steering the Plymouth south at Western Avenue, KW said, "Ever learn why that Jordan dude never showed?"

"Nope." Montego settled back in the bench seat, glanced at KW's solid profile and smiled, glad that the athletic man handled his role so well. *Jordan Smith and me, we would've been a great team*, but he liked KW; he wasn't as sure about his pale blond partner.

In a serious tone, he said, "Now see what's happened?"

KW's head snapped about. "What d'ya mean?"

"What d'ya mean, what d'ya mean? Got myself teamed up with your Jim Brown look-alike butt—probably have to play catch-up ball from now on, too."

"Damn right." KW chuckled and smacked Montego's arm. "That boy's playing some kinda football."

At Santa Monica Boulevard, KW eased to a stop for the red light. When the light flashed green he turned into the peach-turning-to-dark plum evening.

"Surprise me none if Jimmy makes MVP again this year—"

A thunderous explosion rocked their car. KW hit the brakes.

"What the," they both uttered.

Shattered bricks, glass shards, and wood splinters rained onto the four lanes, pieces of it landing on their unmarked car.

"Crap's flying all over the place," KW exclaimed.

"Up there." Montego pointed to the third floor at a light-colored cloud billowing from a cavernous hole in the age-stained St. Andrews Hotel. The rest of the red-brick structure, like many erected in the 1920's, looked intact. "Front wall's blown out."

KW sped the plain prowler through the collecting debris, the right front tire running against the curb. He stopped at the Sears' entry across the street from the hotel.

"Store windows are blown out." Montego, snatching the hand-mic from the dash clip, radioed, "Six-Frank-One—major explosion." He gave the Radio Telephone Operator the location and requested several RA, rescue ambulance, units, a fire engine company, emergency utility crews, and police backup for crowd control, ending with, "Show this unit Code Six." They were now off the air. The RTO handling the Hollywood radio frequency would show their unit out for investigation on her status board.

Montego yelled to KW, "Building looks solid—I'll see what's what."

"Got the street situation," KW shouted back, already waving people toward the Sears store's raised entry porch.

Montego, fearing that hurt people were inside, raced into the fusty hotel, passing several men reeling out the hotel bar's street-side doorway clutching beer bottles. He bypassed the self-service elevator and bounded up the creaking stairs three at a time, checking the occupants coming down for injuries. Most looked confused or scared. None were bleeding.

The third floor was an unsettled haze of whitish, powdery grit. The hall lights were out, but twilight filtered in through the gaping hole in the wall fronting the street. He pulled out his handkerchief to cover his nose and mouth. He rushed door-to-door along the central corridor. Dirty white dust swirled up from the threadbare carpet with every step. He knocked on and opened the few closed doors. At one, he heard groaning inside. He entered to see a tenant rubbing his forehead. The man wearing underwear was groggy but otherwise didn't appear hurt.

He had the guy don trousers and then helped him out into the hall where gas fumes were apparent. A woman was fumbling for the self-service elevator call button.

"Don't touch any switches! I'm a police officer." He flashed his badge. "Take this man down the stairs and outside—as fast as you can."

Entering the last room at the front across the hall from the explosion site, he heard a hissing sound. Holding his breath, he found a gas heater and turned it off. Once out of the room he cleared his lungs and looked for any signs of a fire. The remains of the interior lath-and-plaster walls across the hall were nothing but dangling bits. He swore he'd seen smoke, but no longer was certain. Nothing was burning.

If not a gas explosion, what was it?

A bomb?

He used his handkerchief to wipe the fine granules from his eyes and proceeded into the corner room where the detonation had occurred.

Inside, the remaining pieces of the age-yellowed ceiling, walls, and planked floor showed signs of a thick residue. Blood mixed with plaster and slivers of wood. A glob of it clung in a sinewy shred to an exposed floor joist. The hairs on his arms prickled.

Carefully, he stepped on overlapping boards and piles of rubble to search for any occupants.

He moved toward a twisted piece of metal stuck into a small section of the hall wall still standing: part of a bed frame with coiled bedsprings hung from jagged ends of exposed lath. Dark reddish goop oozed from it.

Twisting back, his foot kicked up a chunk of broken plaster. He looked down at a partial human hand and three deformed fingers. Blinking, he saw it was attached to a torn and bloody singed forearm sticking out from a length of turned wood—the upper part of a curved table leg fixed to a tabletop of gray-marbled Formica.

He lifted it, his gut churning. Mingled in the crumbled masonry and broken matter meshed with mattress stuffing, was black-matted hair, and something slick and grayish with a bowed shape—*bone!*

A repulsive wave surged in his chest, escaping as an acrid gasp. The gross remains were unidentifiable. Something powerful had done this.

Shaken, he stood, letting the tabletop drop. It struck a strip of cracked-pine that popped up to expose a dust-coated gray metal object.

A semiautomatic pistol!

Ululations from a siren pierced his ears. He left the gun and gore and moved to the yawning chasm in the front wall. He looked down at the littered street. An engine company had arrived. KW was with the gathered spectators in the Sears entry alcove.

"Kay Dub—call out a Whiskey Unit."

KW spun about, not seeing Montego.

"Up here."

KW spied him.

"Get the dicks rolling."

KW waved and rushed to their unit to radio the RTO and have her inform the Communications Division dispatcher in the PAB.

Montego eased back into the musty hallway. He no longer smelled gas fumes. Breathing more easily, he trod down the stairs. At the second floor landing he came upon an elderly couple clutching each other, appearing disoriented. He helped them out and across a pair of streetcar tracks to join the group of gawking and chattering onlookers.

Over the dying wail of a siren he hollered to KW, "Dicks coming?"

"Yo, RTO confirmed it."

Just then a heavily chromed Harley-Davidson bike screeched up. It carried the stocky bike cop they'd passed by earlier. The fun-loving Barry Ruggles unsnapped his white Bell-Toptex helmet and twanged, "Howdy Montego, Dealer."

"Hey, Bear. You helping out with these lookie-loos?"

"Just for you, Tonto." Ruggles, also known as "Hubba Bear," dismounted the big bike like it was a thousand pound blooded stallion. His polished knee-length Danner boots skimmed the black leather saddlebags as he sounded the small and chromed "Ooga horn," capturing the attention of the gaping onlookers.

"Hubba Bear do love to entertain a crowd." KW chuckled.

"More so since marrying Momma Mary, our night watch RTO."

"Bit the dust? Yo, why'd you have me call out the brown-suits?"

"We've got us a crime scene on the third floor. Found what's left of a man's head and arm—by a semiautomatic pistol. I'm betting it's what's left of Paoli Salico."

KW frowned. "You saying the warrant's been served?"

"Looks like."

KW grunted. "Effective retribution, I s'pose."

Montego located the battalion fire chief and advised him of a probable homicide scene at the blast site. He next searched out the public utilities crew chief and apprised him likewise. Then he returned to their Plymouth sedan to get the detective's ETA from Momma Mary just as a plain green four-door came to an abrupt stop a few yards from him.

A rawboned and sartorially dressed man scrambled out.

"Uncle Alex—why're you here?"

"I heard the RTO say 'Frank unit' and 'Saint Andrews Hotel,' and knew it was you donkeys. Sheesh what a mess." Alex Strait stepped over a broken brick and stared up at the jagged hole in the hotel's wall.

"Join me if you want to see a real mess." Montego led his pal up the stairs. "Explosion was localized. My guess, a stick or two of dynamite packed in flour did the deed."

Strait cast him an odd eye.

"That's what it tasted like."

Chapter 5

Montego arrived at work on Friday surprised to find that Haley had taken a Special. That meant an enjoyable shift working with KW.

Before roll call Montego went into the dicks' squad room to see Strait about the human remains found at the bomb site, but the Status Board indicated that Strait was in the "field."

Montego read the note tacked to it: "Montego—C-Strait after R/C."
Alex is working late, again.

When roll call ended, he and KW went to the Homicide table.

Strait, sitting alone, narrow-eyed Montego then looked at KW.

"Dealer, you ought to know what a keen palette *Señor* Tonto has. Our lab detected wheat flour and traces of nitro. Not to bore you with the chemistry, it was dynamite, likely a couple sticks of Hercules Dynagel—can be purchased at your local hardware store. By the bye, packing it in flour added nothing to the blast."

"So, the evil doer isn't a powder monkey." Montego hadn't missed Strait's semi-smirk. "Pro bomber or not, it sure wasn't tossed up three floors and through the front window. Tell us, TMA, what triggered it?"

"Mister Salico's weight on the bed—must've set off a pressure fuse hidden between the coil springs and the mattress." Strait stood, lifted his coat off the pedestal rack, and slipped into it. He pointed at the case folder. "Prints from his severed fingers matched those in our fingerprint file."

"Kinda blew his cool, huh?" KW elbowed Montego.

Montego shook his head feigning disgust. "What's your take on it?"

Strait seemed delighted by KW's remark as he put the Salico folder into the file cabinet. He nodded toward the empty chair across from him.

"Wayne thinks a southwest-side gang is retaliating. If he's right, the Italian mob will have them for lunch." He raised the green desk blotter and slid out a folded paper. "Got an arrest warrant here for another one of Mister Dante Pio's imported gunslinger pricks: Gordon Riffelano. It came in today's mail from Miami."

Montego scanned the writ and handed it to KW. "Up to going to the Classi-Chassi? Maybe my snitch can help us find this bad guy?" He winked at Strait who knew of his informant, a strip-club bouncer, and had warned him that informants often learned more from cops than they divulged.

The Purple Hand

KW handed the arrest warrant back. "Gotta hit the head." Over his shoulder he called, "See you in the breezeway, Tonto."

Strait reached under the blotter again and retrieved a small ID photo. He held it out. "I almost forgot—here. Riffelano's mug shot." He lowered his voice. "Been meaning to ask. How's it going with Ice Cop?"

Montego took the photograph and went with Strait to the doorway.

"Strange guy—likes doing things his way, for sure." He hesitated to say more, but he trusted Strait. "Haley called the shots when we busted Brunetti. Said the guy would head for a room in back soon after he got to The Palms. When Brunetti arrived, Haley told me to wait and tail the 'meathead,' his word, into the courtyard where we would make a sandwich pinch. Then he split—but he didn't show and the goon went into a motel room."

Strait paused at the doorway and slid his magnetic Dyno-taped nameplate to the "Off-duty" slot on the Status Board.

Montego waited at the head of the stairs until Strait neared and they were on their way down.

"When I told him that Brunetti was with a whore, he said she'd move out of our way. Sure enough, when the goon knocked she opened the door in a flash, smiled at Haley, and rushed out past us—like it had been scripted."

Strait, arching an eyebrow, paused on the mid-landing.

Montego added, "And he described the motel room to a tee."

"I would advise Tonto to stay on his toes around Ice Cop." Strait skipped down the steps and into the lobby. Turning toward the rear hallway he said, "Keep your nose clean."

Montego stopped at the front counter where he briefly kibitzed with the desk officer, his landlord, David "Rosy" Rosenbloom.

Joining KW at their unit parked in the breezeway, Montego held out the mug photo.

KW eyed it then returned it. "Thug's a mean looker." He fired up the prowler and headed to *The Boulevard of Renown*, the world-famous neon-lighted roadway. "Maybe Riffelano's the reason Haley took a Special tonight."

"Not Ice Cop." Montego was curious, however.

KW drove into the small lot behind the strip club and remained behind the wheel while Montego went to the smudged fire-exit door and pounded on it. He recalled the late afternoon he'd responded to a radio call,

"459 Report," at an upstairs apartment where a TV had been taken in a burglary.

At first blush, he'd thought the female victim's clothes had been taken, too. She'd claimed to work at the Classi-Chassi as an exotic dancer billed as Rhonda Reddi. She had looked ready when she had answered the door wearing only red bikini panties and a purely innocent expression. She'd commented that it was her normal attire when alone at home.

Curious, he'd later gone to the strip club to watch her dance around a chrome pole. Backstage he'd met Marc Story; the bouncer had gotten into a minor jam with a Prince Albert can filled with marijuana. Montego had learned this from Rhonda. A talk the next day with the arresting narcotics cop got Story a pass. A valuable snitch was born; a curiosity appeased.

The metal fire-door grated open, brassy music blared. Story stood there, four inches taller than Montego's six-foot-one frame. Story was "repped" to be a "touch psycho" in a down-and-dirty brawl, and Montego had no doubt that the bruiser could handle himself.

"Hey, Officer Montego—how they hangin', man?"

Montego backed off the stoop giving Story room to step out and join him. The tanned, black-haired guy with a Dean Martin curl came off like he wasn't very bright. Montego accepted it as his cover.

"Marc, I need to tap your smarts."

Story looked around the parking lot, eyed KW, glanced toward the street, then said, "Inside. Don't wanna see nobody hurt, s'all."

Montego believed that Story meant he wouldn't rat out anybody if he thought it risked getting a chum blown away. Stepping up and into the dim, stale-smelling, warm passageway, Montego queried his snitch.

Soon he rejoined KW. "Riffelano likes the chickies. Story says he's a john in a 'pomped-pimp's' tally book. He suggested checking out the Cinegrill for a skinny black guy with a Little Richard pompadour."

KW snorted. "Eboneezer Slick—Bony Slick."

"For real?" Actually, Montego had heard about KW's black snitch.

"Me, lie to Tonto?" KW entered traffic on the famous roadway cops called "The Boulevard," and headed toward the historic landmark, hotel, The Roosevelt.

Montego watched the bustling evening pedestrian action along the broad walkway until the historic landmark came into view. Most of the transplants appeared seedier, he thought. Lost souls seeking some kind of success in "Tinsel Town." Tourists were easier to spot.

The Purple Hand

KW steered the sedan south at Orange Drive and right into the parking lot behind the hotel. He buzzed the valet with his badge and found a spot next to the west-side hedgerow.

Montego eyed KW. "You handling Bony alone, *mi amigo,* or must I assist you with your pomp-haired snitch?"

KW lowered the radio chatter. "Can talk to Slick Bony without your salty-*ass*istance, wiseacre." He switched off the ignition and spun away. "'Sides, squeezing the skinny out of a black man is way too difficult for you *fey* white boys." He made a rumbling sound, backwards-kicked the driver's door shut, and pranced away casting a "gotcha" look over an exaggerated swinging shoulder and a straight-hanging arm.

"Hey, that's good—I'm impressed, officer." Montego figured that had he gone into the lounge, too, the pimp-snitch would've clammed up.

He sat back and gazed at the glow in the early night sky above the hedgerow. It emanated from overhead security lights a block south at Hollywood High, his alma mater. During high school he'd resided with his mother. Before that, in the Valley; then, thanks to Eagon Quinn, while in junior high, he'd boarded in Torrance with a Japanese family, the Konos.

That had come about during his final year in elementary school because of the Mexican bully. Montego rubbed a finger over the thin scar below his jaw. Paco, a 14-year-old, held back two semesters in school had given it to him while pressing him against a picket fence bordering his weekday "foster" home. It'd started as a taunt because Montego had a Hispanic surname and couldn't speak Spanish. Paco was showing off to his *chicano* buddies, but then he'd gotten carried away.

When Quinn saw the wound, he'd convinced Montego's mother to let her son live with the Kono family when the school year ended.

Every Saturday following the knife-cutting incident, Quinn had driven Montego to the Torrance residence. There, he had undergone a regimen of hand-fighting techniques: *kenpo,* an Okinawan martial arts form. His confidence grew. On the last day of school, as luck would have it, Paco's gang had trapped Montego in a field a block from his foster home.

Paco had rushed at him waving a switchblade, but a move by Montego had knocked the blade to the dirt. He'd grabbed it and lashed upward, slicing into Paco's chin and nose. It'd sent the bully and his rag-tag gang into fearful flight.

A slamming car door brought Montego alert. He blinked away the boyhood memory and looked around the parking lot. The area was quiet, but danger lurked in places seemingly safe. He'd had several experiences and had handled them. Even overseas in the army barracks where cultures clashed; and, the times he couldn't retreat, he was careful how far he went, always remembering Paco. Montego applied the same rule as a cop, most times.

During Brunetti's bust, he'd held back even though his irritation with Haley's tactics had Montego wanting to take it out on the big goon; and, it was obvious that Haley had wanted him to shoot Brunetti.

Brunetti's verbal threat came to mind as did Quinn's parting words when Montego had left the PAB the next day: "Pio's gunsels probably gave the local street gangs a choice. Go along and make a few bucks or refuse and buy a full mag of slugs. It'd be that simple."

Would face-to-face encounters with mobsters increase with Haley?

Montego heard his partner whistling an upbeat melody.

He must have gotten a solid lead.

KW plopped behind the steering wheel and stopped warbling.

"Had to stroke Slick's bone before he'd *come* across."

"Aagh. OK, spit it out." Montego shook his head in mock disgust.

"Riffelano," KW keyed the ignition, "AKA Gordo, be bald, rotund, and most cruel. Bony's afraid of the thug, but he likes the easy bread and Riffelano has no problem shelling out two C-notes for a pair of hookers and three hours roll-around time on Tuesday nights."

"Where's the playpen?"

"Knickerbocker. Since Haley's off on Tuesdays," KW waited for a private ambulance to scream past, "it'll be Tonto and me snatching the bald thug with his C-notes' bulge." He turned a somber face toward Montego. "Bony Slick claims Gordo *comes* at midnight and splits at three."

"Aagh, again. Tummy's growling. I need an early Seven—some food. How about Big Spike's?" The tag for Tiny Naylor's drive-in across from The Palms had stuck with him ever since his car-cruising days. Like his classmates, their take on the popular drive-in's name was "tiny nail," so, the high school teen crowd chose the antonym: Big Spike's.

KW nodded and drove toward La Brea as Montego's thoughts turned to the sit-down he planned to have with Haley the next night.

Even with the windows open, the zestfulness of everything-on-it cheeseburgers and salted fries from their Code 7 meal break had lingered satisfyingly in the police unit until end-of-watch.

"A slow Friday—log's a two-liner."

"You eyeballing the carhops has gotta be worth a line on our log." KW, chuckling, neared the two-story orangish-rough brick police station. "Should be fun *come* Tuesday." He smugly tapped his fingers on the wheel.

Montego printed EOW on the DFAR, Daily Field Activities Report. He sensed his partner had something more to say, so he waited before keying the hand-mic to notify Communications. When no words came, he radioed, "Frank-One, end of watch."

Rolling up the side window KW abruptly said, "Tonto want to meet my woman's politically motivated daddy, one Rudolph Forrall?"

"I'm not into politics." Montego retrieved his briefcase.

"But the snappy little lawyer wishes to gaze upon those deep-blues of yours." KW's tone sobered. "Before you busted Brunetti, Rudy had a memorable meeting with him and another thug."

"Tell me more." Montego turned off the radio, his interest piqued.

The day before, curious about the Italian mob, he had stopped by the Manhattan Beach library and found *The Brotherhood of Evil*. The non-fiction book described the 1957 FBI-led raid in Apalachin, a small town in western New York, when a caravan of law officers busted in on fifty-eight Mafia bosses from all over the country gathered at Joseph Barbara's large estate. Among the many Mafiosi netted was Frank DeSimone, in his first year as the L.A. crime boss. He'd succeeded Jack Dragna, after being his *consigliere*, attorney.

"Prefer to let Rudy do the talking," KW said. "He heard about your thing with Brunetti from Yola—my fault. Bragged some to my woman about you and Haley." He slowed the sedan and pulled into the city-owned garage and auto service lot behind the Juvenile Unit building.

The mention of Haley's name had Montego rubbing the back of his neck. "I did read that Forrall is running for the Eighth District seat. Sounds like Dante Pio might be involved in some lobbying." He didn't mention that his girlfriend's uncle was the incumbent city councilman, Eugene Preston.

KW killed the lights and the motor.

Montego signed both their names on the DFAR and retrieved his briefcase from the back seat, thinking about the mob's strong-arm moves on the southwest gangs in Preston's fiefdom.

"And why am I meeting your pretty fiancée's illustrious father, Mister Rudolph Forrall, Esquire?"

"Dunno. Two o'clock tomorrow, OK?"

"Never knew barristers worked on Saturdays."

Chapter 6

Montego paused in front of Forrall and Associates on Crenshaw when KW touched his arm. "S'pose you know Yola's dad is an activist type, kinda— friendly with a lot of people in a *lot* of different places."

"Why doesn't that surprise me?" Montego had caught the inference.

They were greeted inside by a pleasant receptionist, her steel-gray hair tied back severely from her soft brown-black face. She showed them into the moderately sized and well-appointed law library. Volumes of law books filled the ceiling-high wooden cases on three walls. A long, square, polished mahogany table took up the center of the room in line with a large gold-framed print of Winslow Homer's *The Fog Warning* on the end wall.

Yolanda Forrall, KW's fiancée, rose easily from one of the eight dark leather chairs around the table. She was around five-seven, shapely from top to toe. Montego had met her at the Division's last Christmas party. He'd liked her warm casualness then; today she seemed different, rather formal. She wore a navy blue knee-length skirt and a white, high-necked, jacket-blouse favored by Vince Edwards, star of the popular prime-time television show, *Ben Casey*. Like the actor, she left the collar open.

The young woman smiled at him, a hint of warmth showing, and then, with a graceful turn to her right, she said in a voice as smooth as her milk-chocolate complexion, "Officer Mike Montego, please meet my father, Rudolph Forrall."

On cue behind her, a small-framed man with features similar to hers and about her height stepped into the room. His coloring, however, was much darker, almost eggplant in shade. Forrall's pearl-gray gabardine, three-button suit, and vest complemented his skin tone. A silky bright-blue handkerchief billowed above the left breast pocket, matching a silk cravat perfectly tied with a large Windsor knot.

The lawyer glided toward Montego, his slender hand extended; a large blue sapphire cufflink ringed by gold filigree sparkled.

"Please call me Rudy. May I call you Mike?"

Montego shook his hand, hesitating before responding, "OK . . . Rudy."

44

A glint on Forrall's vest caught his eye. On a thick braided gold chain dangled a Phi Beta Kappa key. The small symbol of high academic achievement had served the man's purpose.

Montego accepted the offer to sit, enjoying the cool richness of the leather beneath him.

Yolanda brought an ornate silver carafe and placed it in front of her father. She then went to retrieve two personalized porcelain cups and placed them appropriately on the polished table.

Forrall poured steaming coffee into Montego's and KW's ceramic cups, ending by filling his daughter's and his. He offered cream and sugar while exuding a confident mien, albeit a bit supercilious, Montego thought, waving off the additives while taking in the aroma of the fresh brew. Yolanda's formality now made sense.

How long will Kay Dub tolerate his future father-in-law?

"Kirtland might have told you, Mike, that I am seeking the Eighth District seat on the city council, or perhaps you might have read it in the *Metro* Section of the *Times*." Forrall's practiced smile gleamed, exposing an even row of small, very white, teeth. The politician-lawyer edged along the table opposite Montego.

"The reason I am seeking . . ."

Like a student in a lecture hall, Montego listened to Forrall talking about poverty and the plight of the black folk in North America. The words reminded him that extremism where perspectives narrowed and people wore invisible blinders and earplugs meant conflict, or worse, anarchy. Inevitably, it meant law enforcement involvement. Even though the blue-suits might win the battles, they'd never win the war. Cops could sense a change coming, and more and more they were letting their fears be known in the squad cars and in the locker rooms, but couching their comments in ways that wouldn't make them assailable, even by their partners. Cops rarely used words like "cultural revolution," but in private they boldly voiced how fewer and fewer citizens on their beats treated them with respect. The more conservative cops especially hated the situation. He resisted joining in, his strict upbringing kept him from speaking politics or race relations; but, he knew that it made the job tough for KW.

Montego tried to keep his personal views to himself, striving to treat the public the same as he treated his fellow officers. He had responded to the overt bigotry, however, when it touched his friendship with KW.

Montego knew he was sensitive to his own mixed heritage. Besides, he'd been influenced by what he'd learned from his "big brother," Kenji Kono.

Six years ago when "Kenny" joined the LAPD, he was the first Japanese to do so. Today, he headed the Physical Fitness Unit at Training Division. Kenny had told him, "Bigots who act out their prejudices actually are hiding from their own fears." Montego valued Kenny's reasoning.

Hey, who's lecturing whom?

He glimpsed KW grinning above his cup as if reading his thoughts. During their Academy days, KW had explained about the way his black neighbors viewed their lives and their futures. He'd sounded like Jordan, who had made similar comments when they were working out together in preparation for joining the LAPD.

Montego let his eyes answer KW's grin as Rudolph Forrall wound down his monologue.

" . . . and, democracy requires social equality and respect for all individuals within a community."

The man sat across from him beside his lawyer-daughter.

"Now to the issue that brought us together," Forrall said. "Some time back, a pair of rough-looking men approached me claiming that they supported my campaign. It was Russell, my manager, who alerted me to be wary of them. So, I had him do some checking. Knowing I always make every effort not to associate with any unseemly people, he suggested that I apprise Kirtland," Forrall glanced at KW, "and Kirtland told me that you might have had contact with one of these men while on patrol." He returned his gaze to Montego.

Hesitating briefly, Montego slid Brunetti's mug shot across the table. "I brought a photo of an individual fitting the description Kay Dub mentioned." He glanced at Yolanda sipping her coffee. Showing it was not against LAPD policy; he was unsure about revealing a name, but believed that KW had already apprised his future dad-in-law.

Forrall's tongue-tip moistened his lips while he studied the image. "Yes, yes. What can you tell me about him?"

Montego pointed at the small picture. "Leonardo Brunetti was extradited to Chicago where he'll be tried for Murder One." He paused to wash down the cool coffee, not about to say to a likely future city official that the guy was a mob enforcer involved in an Eighth District bombing and two homicides. He hoped KW hadn't. Publicly, Chief William H. Parker claimed the Mafia didn't *operate* in L.A.

Montego looked at KW. "Kay Dub might have told you more."

"Kirtland did happen to mention your encounter. I believe he called the man Beak Brunetti." Forrall appraised KW with a Chesire cat smile.

Montego, relieved, still hoped KW hadn't said too much to Forrall.

"Well, Mike, I won't take any more of your off-duty time." Forrall stood and proffered his small, manicured hand, his gaze intent. "I assume I no longer need to be concerned, and I do appreciate you coming to see me this morning. What you have just told me shall remain confidential."

Montego had counted on that, having already flirted with the idea of symbolically retaining the attorney with a dollar to ensure his closed-mouth. He'd only met with the high-profile barrister because of KW.

Was I wise?

Chapter 7

The sun was settling over the tree-lined horizon as Montego drove. He adjusted the mirror inside the pickup so he could see the bright emerald-colored eyes of Julie Preston. Outside mirrors kept the following traffic in view. Sunlight shone through the rear window igniting her long coppery strands. They were like fingers of fire. It set off the bewitching face of "Strawberry Gal."

In the months they'd been dating, he had yet to tell her the tag.

She'd think it silly.

Until he'd met Julie, Sunday afternoons had given him a sense of dread and loneliness, a feeling that had carried over since he was a child, when week after week he was wrested from his mother's warm arms, a time when his heartrending sobs poured into nightfall.

Not this Sunday evening, not with Julie snuggled beside me.

Often, on their drives into the Angeles Crest mountains, he'd find a secluded spot and spread out their "love" blanket, her word, to share an intimate interlude. He thought of it more as a lust blanket. The urge was upon him now because her hand was stroking his inner thigh. Even so, it contrasted with his tumbling thoughts about his new partner, Neall Haley.

The night before, they had been swamped backing up radio cars so there had been no "sit-down." In fact, there had been hardly any words exchanged between them. They even had missed their meal break. Not settling matters had left Montego feeling a bit uneasy. At home, when he'd crashed, his sleep had been sketchy.

"I hope you won't mind if I'm a mite quiet this evening, especially if your father and uncle get into politics or religion." He sighed. "For sure, I'm no Puritan." They were on their way to her parents' Elizabethan-style mansion in Laurel Canyon for a celebratory dinner.

She pinched his thigh. "Your upbringing was little different from mine. Didn't your guardians in North Hollywood tell you 'golly' and 'gee' were slang words for God and Jesus and never to be spoken when upset?"

"Jeez, you're right," he teased. "I tasted a lot of green Palmolive before I learned to say '*Tanto peor*' which, you now know, is Spanish for 'so much the worse.'" He'd learned not to use any profanity when angry around the foster home, so deciding to cuss in Spanish he'd gone to the

48

school library and perused an English-Spanish dictionary. Away from the foster house he'd practiced swearing out loud until eventually, *"Tanto"* became his habitual cuss word. The foster parents accepted it as "funny."

"And now your friends call you Tonto."

"That came about because 'tanto' sounded like tonto."

"Maybe I should call you Tonto. It comes from the Spanish verb *tontear* meaning foolish."

"Only when I'm around you." He brush-kissed the tip of her up-tilted nose, and quickly had to correct his steering on the curving road. "Hey, will I get to see your little curtsy tonight?"

She pinched his leg again, but harder. "It's only a slight bow—you know I hate it, but Daddy likes it." She glanced at him. "OK, when I was little, I thought doing it was cute, but not after I turned eight. I love Daddy dearly—you know I do it only to keep him happy."

He considered the behavior odd, but let it go.

They neared the Preston's manor. Time to put on the darn dog and pretend to be at ease with her highbrow parents; he was uncomfortable around them. Although they treated him genially, he wasn't convinced they accepted a cop as a worthy beau for their only daughter. Julie had never mentioned what their expectations were regarding her future husband, but he was sure they had very definite ones.

He didn't think too far ahead, he'd made the marriage mistake once while serving Uncle Sam in West Germany. He'd thought he knew what love was, but found that Cherli had only wanted a ticket to Hollywood. Now, with Julie, he had trouble trusting his feelings. He didn't want to make another mistake. When he bedded her it was out of lust, a purely physical feeling. He wasn't sure it included love, but her warmth satisfied.

He had learned that she had been brought up with strict decorum. Her parents expected her to curtsy whenever serving their houseguests. It bothered him, but he also saw that both of her parents paid her lavish attention. They covered the lease on her studio-apartment below his pad, bought her an Austin-Healey sports car, and took care of her graduate school tuition at UCLA where she studied interior design. He could imagine how she would decorate his attic apartment if given the chance, but he liked how his attic abode, "The Pelican's Perch," looked.

"I really appreciate you getting tonight off. My parents insisted that I celebrate my aunt and uncle's silver anniversary with them." She stroked up his thigh. "Uncle Gene chose the entrée: corned beef and cabbage."

49

Her wandering fingers excited him. The upcoming meal didn't.

"I expect the dinner topic will include golf with his buddies at the Wilshire Country Club, but in the library afterwards, it will be politics."

He smiled, his interest in civic affairs *had* piqued since learning that Rudolph Forrall sought Eugene Preston's city council seat.

Montego decided not to mention his earlier meeting with the "kinda" activist lawyer.

He steered onto the up-curved driveway and immediately smelled boiled cabbage. It disturbed the piney fragrance in the shade-cooled canyon, killing his arousal from Julie's mischievous fingers.

Taking Julie's hand, they climbed the several marble steps, passing between a pair of Corinthian columns.

Suffer through this for her sake.

After the fast-pace run with Strait that morning, Montego had kicked back for most of the day reading the *Times*. For sure, he intended to stay relaxed this evening.

One concern he had was his attire, but Julie assured him that his blue blazer and light-gray slacks perfectly fit the evening dress code. He seldom wore formal clothing and possessed only two dress-up outfits for court appearances and now for his new plainclothes assignment. He had bought the suits at a cop's discount from Cooper and Kramer's on Santee in the garment district. His other suit, a beige lightweight-weave jacket and dark-brown gabardine trousers, was in his bedroom closet hanging under tissue paper fresh from the Hollywood Professional Cleaners. They had removed Brunetti's blood-spatters, also at a cop's courtesy discount. More bloody nights like that and he likely would be spending an entire paycheck at C and K's for another sports outfit.

Passing through the vestibule they stepped into an expansive great room where the slightly built Eugene Preston stood. The councilman had wispy gray hair, receding broadly, a sour, pinched face and a sanctimonious expression. His weak chin tucked above a white silk ascot matched what Montego imagined a typical Victorian preacher might have looked like.

He shook the politician's limp hand, mostly grasping fingers, and noticed the man's gray eyes wince.

Julie had guessed correctly. The dinner topic was mostly golf at the Wilshire Country Club. He didn't play the game and tried not to look bored.

The moment Aunt Martha finished her cherry pie and dabbed a napkin to her blush-pink lips, the brothers stood as if cued by a spark.

The Purple Hand

The women rose in unison. Montego eyed Julie, stifling a snicker.

Ted Preston pointed. "Shall we gentlemen take our repose in the library—leave the ladies to their kitchen tasks?" He wore a white turtleneck and a wine-colored blazer with six golden buttons. A colorful embroidered crest was mounted on a breast patch pocket. Montego assumed the crest had to do with the family surname.

Julie had told him their wealth had come from a series of patents her father held for a plastic molding-extrusion machine. Ted Preston, though, chin up, claimed the family's good fortune was a blessing from the Lord Jesus Christ.

At the Valley home, Montego had been drenched in a pool of religion. He'd since rebelled to the formalized side of it. He'd stopped going to church when he began feeling like a hypocrite. He had nothing against religion per se. Most people needed a faith supported by a congregation. He had his belief, but to be proselytized like he had been as a youth had turned him against organized religion. Attending services where the pastor had the congregation shaking hands of the people around them often had him greeting people who had screwed him over, like the auto mechanic who'd billed him excessively for a simple brake job and the next Sunday smiled at him like it'd never happened.

Forgiveness. Tough to reconcile.

Montego's loafers sank into green carpeting when he followed the brothers into the library. The carpet matched the green leather inlay adorning the top surface of a large double-pedestal desk angled across the far corner of the masculine-decorated room. Its cherry-wood facing depicted an intricate intarsia of Christ's Last Supper. Above a red-and-black bricked fireplace with an accentuated smoothed ash mantel hung a large ornately framed Warner Sallman's sepia-toned portrait of Jesus.

Easing down onto the familiar burgundy-colored leather armchair he again felt dwarfed by it. He'd been inside the house several times, the first time he'd sat in this same chair. That was when Julie's father had studied him with aplomb and said, "You are here because I wish to get better acquainted with the young man *currently* dating my *only* daughter."

The feeling had been more nerve-wracking than Montego's first time on the witness stand in Superior Court. The man turned him off.

Ted Preston lifted a silver dish with chocolate-covered mint wafers and placed it on the round table next to his brother. Sitting beside it, he said, "Gene, are you still being pressed about the proposed liquor ordinance?"

"My yes, Teddy. They simply refuse to accept my adamant no. I must say, they are doing everything they can to test my resolve, and I can't abide them anymore."

"What we are referring to, Michael, should interest you. In my brother's district certain people are seeking a change in alcoholic beverage licensing. The group intends to increase the number of local liquor-serving establishments, apparently hoping to attract the nightlife crowd—"

"And a most undesirable bunch, I dare say," Eugene Preston interrupted. "Oh, I quite understand how many of our human race tend toward debauchery," he paused, "but we have more than enough bawdy saloons in my district. Why the evils such places attract—"

Julie's appearance in the opened double-doorway stopped him. She carried a silver platter with a matching carafe and three porcelain cups and saucers.

"I believe each of you take your coffee black." She set the carafe next to the chocolate wafers and filled their cups. "This Guatemalan blend is rather robust—like the three of you." She returned the carafe to the platter and handed out servings of steaming brew.

Ted Preston looked the proud father while his daughter performed her little task. When she moved behind Montego and placed a hand on his shoulder close to his neck and squeezed gently, he realized the brothers' verbal exchange had tensed him. Until he worked with Haley, he wouldn't have connected the "certain people" to the L.A. Mafia crime organization.

Montego slid his fingers over hers as her father's eyes stayed focused on his daughter. She withdrew her hand and glided to the doorway, where she turned and bowed slightly. Montego winked. The doors closed.

Why is she still under her dad's influence?

Ted Preston turned to his older brother. "Gene, the argument for the proposed liquor ordinance, as I understand it to be, is that the growing population in the area justifies—"

"Yes, the Coloreds are moving in," The councilman dabbed a small napkin to his thin lips. "And I must say, their kind simply cannot handle such gross temptations."

Montego tasted his coffee and tried to enjoy its flavor, but the room atmosphere was getting claustrophobic.

Eugene Preston peered at the dish of mints. "It's really a shame, too. Our nicer neighborhoods are rapidly going downhill. The street corners are becoming hangouts for those people." Breathing in deeply, he assumed a squared shoulder posture. "We must not allow them to degrade our areas. Why, one can just see how the hoodlum goings-on are contributing to the unwholesome yearnings of their uneducated kind."

Montego steadied his cup, heat rising from it, and deep inside him. He was unable to fight the urge not to stick his nose into the discussion any longer.

"You're saying that certain people, the local mob actually, want more liquor outlets believing it will draw Blacks into your district—"

"Now there's a bright young man, Teddy," Eugene Preston interrupted again. "Parker needs more officers of his making. He's thinking quite properly. Just ask him. I would venture he knows how those Coloreds loiter on the street corners, gambling and drinking, even urinating. Doing filthy sex." He glanced up at the Christ portrait. "Can you imagine how it would be if there were even more sleazy saloons?" He dropped the now wadded napkin onto the table beside him.

Montego covered a big sigh with a cough and put down the cup, realizing what Dante Pio was hoping to accomplish on the southwest side.

Eugene Preston snatched a mint. "I am certain our young officer here can attest to the way those darkie women parade around on the sidewalks barely clothed, and such wild get-ups, why it's just appalling." The politician mouthed the chocolate wafer and chewed while staring at the print of Jesus Christ above the mantel.

"Yes, Michael. What *do* you think?" Ted Preston's left hand rested on the old Bible on the small table alongside his chair, his arched fingers drumming the leather cover.

"I am not sure that I can give you a knowledgeable answer, sir." Montego squirmed in the oversized armchair, upset for allowing himself to get involved. His focus went to Ted Preston.

The man's fingertips went from drumming to flipping the Bible's worn binding. His head turned to his brother. "Similar gatherings by my darkie employees occur outside my Pacoima plant. I must admit I have seen them shooting dice on the sidewalk after working hours."

Montego pushed his toes deep into his loafers and flexed his calves. *The brothers feed each other's bigotry.*

Eugene Preston palmed two more mints, sizing them up before popping both into his mouth. He licked his fingertips, chewed, then said, "Why, just last week," he swallowed, his Adam's apple bobbed, "I was on a district tour and I had my driver stop by a group of Colored men sitting around drinking—rolling dice. I told those boys to go find themselves a decent job and quit loitering. Why, they just sneered at me and kept their gambling and hollering foolish gibberish."

He stood, squared his narrow shoulders again, walked stiffly to the fireplace, and placed a hand on the mantel. "Yes, if I had my way, I would see that type kept out of our decent neighborhoods. I don't wish to affront your guest here, but the police are simply not stopping the violent conduct of those savages." He thrust out his chin, and again gazed at the Sallman print.

Montego, his stomach tight, drew in a deep breath and expelled it under pressure to draw the brothers' attention. He no longer could resist not being involved. Knowing he was about to shoot himself in the foot, he spoke in a serious tone, "Councilman Preston, I assume you represent all of the people in your district?"

"Why yes—of course I do." Eugene Preston withdrew and unfolded a monogrammed handkerchief and squeezed his hands into the white cloth.

"Well, tell me, sir, what does one's skin color have to do with a gang of mobsters pushing for passage of the proposed liquor ordinance? Are you suggesting that Blacks are more prone to drink alcohol, to gamble, and to play the rackets than *you* whites?"

Eugene Preston, stony-faced, turned to face him, his thin eyelids lowered. "Why, I am truly surprised at you, young man—accosting me this way. You, an officer of the law—of all people—should know that Coloreds simply do not handle their liquor at all well. And as long as I chair the Planning and Zoning Committee that ridiculously liberal ordinance will never see the light of day—and those people pressing me can just be damned. They are nothing but a gang of moronic hooligans."

Montego sprang to his feet, not caring that he had startled the brothers. "Obviously, those so-called moronic hooligans believe they can take advantage of the residents in *your* district, hoping to lure them into gambling away their money on rigged rackets. Have you considered that most of those good folks are trying to better their stations in life? And in doing so, many are being stretched to the point where they're one paycheck away from losing their homes—and if that happens, they will be destitute on the streets. It's cops like my partner and me who must deal with the results first hand. I might agree with you about the liquor ordinance, *sir,* but I do not agree with your myopic characterizations."

The Purple Hand

The pasty councilman clutched a golden candleholder on the mantel with one hand, appearing to steady himself while he blotted the chocolate-smudged handkerchief to his forehead with the other.

Pivoting, Montego glared at Ted Preston pressing his fingers down on the Bible. "My partner is black, and I know he's proud of his heritage. Believe me, it doesn't affect how he serves the citizens of Los Angeles— the same people your public-servant brother swore to represent without prejudice, without bigotry—*and* with his hand on the Holy Bible."

He spun and took a quick step to face the slight councilman head on. The man stumbled backwards into the wrought iron firewood tray.

"My partner puts his life on the line every time he goes into your so-called decent neighborhoods, and he doesn't take the time to consider the person's skin tone. He is out there exposed, like all cops, protecting and serving people of all colors—whenever necessary."

Montego stormed to the library entry, grabbed the brass handles and flung both doors open. Tempted to bring up Rudolph Forrall's name, he twisted back, but instead he said, "See this," he touched his chin, "a shade darker than your Gothic white—that must mean that I do not belong here in *your* decent *white* neighborhood."

He marched into the kitchen, interrupting the three tasking women.

"Julie, I'm leaving—you ready to go?"

She froze for an instant before quickly untying her frilly apron and apologizing hurriedly to her frantic-looking mother and open-mouthed aunt.

Snatching her clutch purse from the sideboard, she scurried toward the front door with him.

Barely a step ahead of them, Ted Preston, his face livid, opened the door, scowling. "Julie, my dear, I think you should stay."

Montego, holding onto her upper arm, rushed her through the doorway. She didn't resist, to his relief.

He drove down the dark canyon road, doubting that he would ever enjoy the taste of chocolate mints again. He felt a slight regret, knowing most likely that he'd never be invited back to the Preston home. That didn't matter, but what it meant to Julie, did. It upset him that he had lost control.

They drove west with traffic along Sunset through Beverly Hills toward the ocean.

Julie stared out the window. She had been silent since they'd left.

"Julie, I'm sorry I blew up and rushed you away like I did, but your darn uncle infuriated me with his bigoted remarks."

"I'm sorry, too." She sniffed and dabbed her moist eyes in a hankie. "Uncle Gene can be exasperating."

On Vista Del Mar, approaching the Pacific, she placed her hand on his leg. Her forgiving touch and the bright late-summer moon's glittering path over the rippling phosphorescent waves took his mind off the bigoted brothers. He eyed her briefly. The lunar reflection cast a radiant glow on her face, adding an allure to her fine features. He pictured her familiar contours while her soft fragrance caressed him. Life with her was great. That's what mattered.

He reflected on their times of passion when she absorbed his fierce gentleness with liquid intensity. But when their fervor subsided into warm tenderness, her mood would turn quiescent.

Last Wednesday night, while snuggling in bed, she had commented, "I do love playing house with you, but sharing your bed goes against my upbringing. I feel like I'm sinning."

Flustered, he'd gazed into Julie's green eyes searching his and said, "I want to afford a nice house before starting a family." That was as close to a commitment as he could offer.

He knew what she'd wanted to hear, and maybe he was in love, yet the words of commitment stumbled on his tongue, never crossing his lips. All he could say was, "It's not a sin to make love unless you think it is, and I don't." Then he'd skipped to, "You know that I've gotta make my stripes, reach detective grade. That's my main goal–for the both of us."

Also, he wasn't sure she fully understood his job, and he didn't want to frighten her. But he knew the truth. Prowling the streets in a black-and-white confronting drug-dazed crazies out stealing to support their growing addictions, often brandishing firearms, was making the job more dangerous.

He would never say, "I won't risk our children not having a dad." That wasn't being fair. Obviously, detective work was safer, and without having to say it, she seemed to understand and be placated.

OK, I'm being selfish, but I want to be a homicide dick.

How much did her parents, especially her dad, have to do with his reticence to commit himself? He didn't know, but after this evening, he'd likely blown any civil relationship with the austere man.

Tingling caused by her fingertips now circling his inner thigh, her signal for intimacy, had him grasping the wheel. Her disconcerting words about love and marriage the night before faded.

The Purple Hand

She nibbled at his earlobe, then blew lightly.

"Can we take a walk down by the surf?" she murmured.

In the rearview mirror he glimpsed the side of her high cheekbone in the ambient moonlight and felt a flutter from her teasing tongue.

He caught a quick breath. "Down there OK?"

Without looking, she whispered, "Perfect." Her nibbling continued.

He angled the truck to the curb and quickly slipped out of his sports jacket. He jogged around to her door and clasped her hand before tugging out the love blanket from behind the seat. Anticipation of what was to come suffused him. Balmy air pockets carrying misty night sea smells added to his thrill.

Barefoot, they wound their way down the succulent-covered slope, aiming for three sentinel palms silhouetted on a dune above the shoreline.

They kicked up sand along the surf's snaky edge as they darted sideways each time a "ka-whumping" wave sent a scalloped edge of foam surging toward their toes.

When they reached a secluded site on the cool, quilted sand, he spread the blanket and lifted her willing body. He spun them about holding her close, lightly blowing into the hollow between her neck and shoulder, her long hair brushing his face.

He dropped to his knees and set her down. She undid his trousers and leaned into him. Their lips touched and opened. A rushing charge coursed through his body. He unbuttoned her blouse, unhooked her bra, and lay her back to savor her soft breasts. In time, he tasted his way down the smooth flesh, pausing for moments, then proceeding slowly downward.

Her fingers had been tousling his hair lightly—but soon they were clawing urgently.

Sliding up onto her hot body, he moved rhythmically and watched moon crystals dance in her eyes. Her throaty squeals and his rapid breaths fused with the roaring jet plane soaring low out over the night sea.

When the intensity of the moment subsided, he saw in the moon glow the familiar look on her face, the expression that said she had sinned.

He'd seen it too often.

Chapter 8

Montego spent most of Tuesday in court waiting to testify, only to have the defendant cop a plea; but it meant overtime.

He left the courthouse too late to run the Griffith Park trails so he drove straight to the station. Getting to work early would give him time to kibitz with Strait, and being seen by the detective-lieutenant, and jawboning with the teams working the various crime tables in the squad room was good exposure. It might be a bonus when the time came to fill a detective vacancy. His new plainclothes assignment made rubbing elbows easier.

Nearly 1700 hours, yet the squad room was a hive of activity, and he craved to be a permanent part of it. The open transoms failed to clear the air of cigarette and cigar smoke, a mainstay of diligent investigative work that he'd gladly contend with.

A detective coming in from the burglary squad room in back was smoking a Sherlock Holmes-style briar, it added a sweetly different mix to the hazy air.

Montego slid a chair next to Strait, nodding to Wayne Nells who was busily writing a report on the opposite side of the table-desk.

"Kay Dub located that Florida mobster, Gordon Riffelano," Montego said. "The guy is supposed to be getting serviced by two whores at the Knick tonight. We plan to snatch his ass there."

Strait leaned back, a knee pressed against the under edge of the table for balance. "Lucky man—I got a call this morning about that prick. Dade County Sheriff says he's as mean as they come." Dropping forward, Strait said, "I must tell you, we think he was Mister Brunetti's accomplice on the south-side murder."

Montego slipped the writ from his pocket and scanned the Florida criminal code numbers: FSS 782.04. "Murder One. The guy's no virgin." But a felony was a felony, or it was until the Brunetti bust. That goon had proved that special skills were needed when nabbing Italian mobsters.

On the way out of the squad room Montego gazed into the captain's glass-walled office. The skipper was talking to an auto-theft detective with whom Montego had once had words about KW. The dick spotted him causing uneasiness in Montego about getting a spot at the Homicide table.

Downstairs, he bought a Milky Way bar from a vending machine.

The Purple Hand

At 1810 hours, he entered the roll call room surprised to see KW sitting on the front row bench next to Bobby Diaz, a member of the other FCU team. KW usually sat with him and Haley along the rear wall.

"Yo, Tonto. Guess I'm going to be missing out on the Gordo bust. Ice Cop's here. 'Bad' Bobby D and I are working Frank Two tonight."

The disappointment on KW's face showed. Just then, Haley entered the room heading for the back row. Making a sympathetic gesture to KW, Montego nodded to Bobby D and went back to join his partner.

"Surprise, surprise. What gives, mi amigo?"

Haley glanced at him. "I decided to make up for the Special I took."

Montego didn't press, still he was curious. Friday nights usually had a lot of action, although the last one had been rather slow.

The watch commander called roll while the field sergeant passed out the DCIs, daily crime information sheets. The briefing session ended with a weapons-and-ammo inspection. Montego took the occasion to watch Haley empty his weapon and saw the six cartridges in his open hand.

Regulation—what did I expect?

Fifteen or so minutes later they strolled through the Knickerbocker Hotel lobby, past the restaurant entry on their way to the rear parking area. After reconnoitering they agreed they knew the landscape well enough. They paced up the north side returning to Ivar Street where they jay-jogged over to their curbside unit.

Montego, settling back in the passenger seat, focused on the hotel's main entry. He wondered if there was enough time to clear the air with Haley on how they would operate in situations like this one. Just then a Yellow Cab pulled up in front of the hotel. The cabby scurried to the passenger side to open the door. Montego recognized the character actor climbing out.

Taking the distraction as a clue, Montego decided to hold off confronting Haley.

"Kay Dub's snitch says Riffelano will be alone."

Haley took a drag on his cigarette, seemingly preoccupied.

Tanto, the guy was living up to his reputation—but he played things too close to his chest, and he was a bit too salty. However, Montego wanted this assignment and if Haley were to put the stink-eye on him, it could put him back in uniform. The Felony Car had him assisting the dicks by serving their arrest warrants, like the one in his coat pocket. FCU kept him in contact with the brown-suits, important for getting into the dicks' bailiwick.

59

Still, he must clear the air if he and Haley were going to be a team.

"How do you want to handle this Riffelano guy, *partner*?"

Haley, glancing sideways at him, tossed his cigarette butt out the side window. "We'll bust the lousy meathead after he's done banging the Bobbsey twins—at EOW."

Montego shifted about. Some cops he'd worked with didn't like taking the initiative in sticky situations, but not Haley. He decided things fast—maybe too fast. How often was he wrong? Returning to the hotel before end-of-watch meant overtime. Was that the reason? It held little appeal. Why not make the bust now? When Montego's stomach growled, Haley glanced sideways at him, again.

Did I see a slight smile on Neall's face?

"We could grab the goon climbing from his vehicle at midnight—deny him playpen time."

Haley's eyes squared on Montego. "That how you wanna do it?"

Montego heard agreement in the even-toned reply, but Haley's look was void of meaning. Something was on the guy's mind. Did he think it would be an easier bust after Riffelano finished playing with the prostitutes, expecting the goon's guard to be down.

"Your call."

"Good." Haley started the motor and wheeled the prowler south to The Boulevard and east into traffic.

Montego caught Haley's mouth curving into another near smile.

"There're better things to do in the meantime, Tonto."

"Working overtime's fine—I'm off the next two." Like most cops, Montego preferred two consecutive nights off. On Wednesdays evenings, he practiced kenpo at the Kono's dojo, then saw Julie, and on Thursday nights he attended a criminology class. Last Thursday he'd worked because Sergeant Brad Kozier had insisted that he needed Montego on the shift.

Taking in the dry-warm evening air, Montego visualized the next night lounging with Julie in the Perch, a ritual following his workouts with Kenny and Yoshi, but his mind still tossed about how to deal with Haley. The guy did seem to be looking at nothing while seeing and hearing all that was going on about him.

They'd cruised another two blocks when Haley peered at Montego.

"You care if we take an early Seven?"

"*No problema.*" Good. Finally they would talk over a warm meal and clear the air about the Brunetti bust.

At Gower Street, Haley braked for a red tri-light.

"Tonight, I want you to meet my parents and my teenaged sister, Missy. I also have another younger sister and a brother, but they both live out-of-state."

Montego, recycling what he'd just heard, realized that no way could he talk about the Brunetti bust in front of the guy's family.

Haley thumbed his lighter and lit a Camel while the prowler leaped ahead on the green light. Smoke whipped out the open side window.

"Missy'll like your blue eyes."

He turned right into a short driveway belonging to a modest Spanish-style house and killed the V8. He climbed out but waited for Montego to come around the sedan while scanning the neighborhood.

Typical of a cop.

They crossed a corner of the lawn to get to the front porch. Before reaching it the outside light came on, the door opened and a wavy-haired man sporting a trimmed graying brush mustache greeted them with a smile. He was several inches shorter than Montego, about Haley's height.

Haley said, "Mike Montego—my pop, Lonn."

"My pleasure, sir." Montego found his hand clamped in a vise-like grip. The man's strength was impressive.

"Call me Lonn, I'll call you Mike?" His query, a near-hoarse tone.

Montego, smiling, nodded as Haley, already through the entry, said, "Pop's a pipe twister." Haley quickly turned away.

A blonde woman and a pretty teenaged girl appeared in the foyer. Lonn placed an arm around the woman's slender waist. She nearly matched his height. She had a short hairstyle that reminded Montego of Doris Day, the actress in the movie, *Pillow Talk*. It framed her high cheek-boned face. The woman, who had to be the mother, had light-gray eyes and creamy colored skin. It was obvious where Neall Haley's complexion came from.

"Dear, our son's new partner, Mike Montego," Lonn said.

She offered her hand. Montego took it gently. She held his firmly, smiling, and saying, "Please call me Irene." Her warmth drew him in.

"And this is our youngest daughter, Missy." She held her hand out. "But the Sisters at her school call her Michelle. Missy is a senior at Immaculate Heart High School."

Missy Haley beamed a bubbly smile. Her smooth complexion was like her mother's, but her eyes were a very dark brown much like her father's, only larger, yet they had her mother's almond-shape.

61

"Hi, Officer Mike." Missy left her mother's side, grabbed his hand and pumped it vigorously, causing her long black curls to dance over a blossoming figure.

Neall Haley stepped back into the foyer and clasped his sister's shoulders from behind. "Take it easy on him little Sis—that hand protects my hide." Glancing at Montego, he spun Missy around and kissed her forehead.

Montego, struck by the loving gesture, observed the sparkle on the parents' faces turn to genuine pride. He warmed with the thought of having his own children one day. Perhaps with Julie.

They moved into the living room.

He noted the Baroque furnishings in the Spanish-style house. The home's decor suggested that the father had a successful business, and his straightforward manner clearly came through. It had to attract customers, and keep them, too.

"Let's not waste your forty-five minute lunch break—Code Seven I believe you call it," Irene's smile was engaging. "I hope you boys are ready for a bite of home-cooked food?"

"It's why we're here, Mom. My partner's stomach's been growling like a timber wolf," Haley said. Missy giggled. Haley left the room before Montego could read the guy's expression, assuming he had one.

Montego was concerned that they had not requested or received approval for Code 7 from the communications dispatcher, but figured Haley had gone to a phone to call in their location and status.

Lonn, grinning slightly, gestured toward a rough-plastered archway. "This way to the feasting table, Mike."

Missy grasped his arm and led him to a made-up rosewood table covered by a fine damask lace. A bright silver chafing dish occupied the center. She pointed to the setting next to her place.

"Sit here, Mike. Momma's seat is across from Daddy."

Montego sat on the tapestry-padded chair to the right of Lonn, now taking a seat, realizing his partner had planned this. Why? Was this why the guy wanted to bust Riffelano at EOW—why he was working tonight?

Ice Cop is a strange guy.

Light jazz blew through the doorway. Haley appeared soon after. He sat across from Missy.

"Charley 'Bird' Parker?" Montego asked. He got a nod from Haley.

Missy brushed against Montego's arm.

"I love Elvis, especially when he sings, *Love Me Tender*."

Irene entered holding a silver vessel filled with steaming rice and green beans.

Montego's stomach growled, again.

Missy giggled, again.

He quickly made an "Oh well" face.

Irene took the end seat and the Haley's bowed their heads.

Montego glanced at his partner. Praying didn't fit with his thoughts about the icy guy.

"Dear Lord," Irene prayed, "we thank You for genuine friends and ask Your blessing of this food to the good of our bodies. Amen."

The simple mealtime prayer was quite familiar to Montego.

Lonn lifted the chafing dish lid revealing steaming stroganoff. He filled the plates passed to him while saying, "Mike, how about John Glenn orbiting Earth last February in under six hours?"

"It was amazing, and the Telstar satellite flying around in orbit."

"All these space ventures and possibly a trip to the moon," Irene said. "Can you believe—?"

"Mike, do you really think we can fly all the way to the moon?" Missy interrupted, quickly covering her mouth with a napkin in response to her mother's frown.

"President Kennedy claims we will, and before the 'Seventies, too."

From time to time as they ate, he caught his partner sly-eyeing his father. On one occasion Haley looked about to speak, but said nothing.

Lonn refilled his plate. Replacing the chafing lid, he said, "I think Sandy Koufax might have another no-hitter in him."

"It'd be quite a feat. Say, from what Neall said earlier, I take it you're a plumber. I'll tell Mother—that's if you do small house repairs up on Mulholland." Montego hadn't said "my parents" because he didn't think of the fire captain, Steve Buckingham, his mother's know-it-all husband of ten years, as his father.

"No job's too small or too far away—our company motto."

"Pop's being humble," Neall Haley said flatly, not looking up. "He's got a crew retrofitting a fancy mansion up in Mandeville Canyon, besides two subdivisions in the San Fernando Valley." His tone was harsh.

Irene glanced at her son, then she smiled at Montego. "My husband started Professional Plumbing Systems seventeen years ago, after the war."

"Yeah, before the war he lived in the Big Apple," Neall Haley said. "What did you do back then, Pop?"

Montego stiffened. His partner's tone had turned caustic.

Lonn raised his head, leaving food on his fork. "Oh, a little of this, a little of that, son." His grin seemed tentative.

Montego realized he'd stopped eating and was rubbing a thumbnail.

"You must've done something." Haley didn't look at his father. "How'd you make a living?"

Irene's expression to her husband seemed to say, *What is going on?* She then turned to her boy with a puzzled expression.

"Your father was a plumber's apprentice. You knew that."

Montego noticed Missy ignoring the exchange.

"Do pipe work at The Palace Chop House, or was it your hangout?" Haley then eyed Montego. "There's a glass ashtray in the den from the joint—must be a treasure—been in there ever since I can remember."

Irene glanced at her husband, then back at her son. "Neall, it's just a small souvenir he kept." Her voice was soft.

"What—stowed in his duffel bag while he fought in Europe?" Haley let out a deep breath, then guzzled some water.

"It was a keepsake—and your mother kept it along with my other personal belongings here at home." Lonn turned to Montego, "I met and married Irene while living in London." He gave his wife a sidelong glance, smiling. "After Neall was born we moved stateside—before the war started in Europe." He looked at his son "Yes, Neall, while in New York City I did have pals, and The Chop House *was* one of our *hangouts* . . . the ashtray's a memento of that time, that's all."

"Your pals—were they Black Irish, like you?"

"Neallie, what's that got to do with anything?" Missy said sharply.

"I *really* don't know, Sis. Curious is all."

What Montego knew about genetics reminded him that hair and skin coloring didn't necessarily follow directly from parent to child.

To ease the tension, he said, "Missy, how's high school?"

She put down her fork, snatched the napkin, and dabbed her lips. "Good, now that I'm a senior."

"When do you graduate—February, or next June?"

The teenager, her brown eyes sparkling, glimpsed her mother.

"June—and you must come to the ceremony, Mike. You'll get to see the new car Daddy's buying me—"

"That's *if* you keep getting straight A's, and new to you—not a *brand* new car." Her father smiled and took a drink of his coffee.

"I know, I know." She turned to Montego. "Isn't that the coolest?"

He nodded. "Are you planning on going to college?"

"USC. That's the deal for the car. So I can drive to the university."

"How do you get to school now?" He knew he was being a bit nosy, but he still wanted to ease the tension he sensed around the table.

"Momma usually drives me—except on her play days."

"What Missy means," Irene frowned at her daughter, "is that I have a weekly bridge party that I like to attend."

"That's what I meant. On Momma's *card playing* days I walk home with my girlfriend, Shirley. She lives up the street." Missy smiled at her father. "Sometimes, Daddy will surprise me and pick us up."

Lonn also smiled as she continued, "Mike, you must come to my birthday party, too. It's next month on the fifth—a Saturday. Promise me?"

From the time they had left the Haley home till 0230 hours, Montego and Haley backed up patrol units, including several "Prowler now" calls, and a 211, a robbery of a liquor store. He'd wanted to ask Haley what was going on between him and his dad, but held off. It wasn't his place to inquire. He did say, "You have a wonderful family, Neall. I always wanted a sister. . . . When Mother remarried, she was forty, and well into her career, so no kid."

Haley, wordless, parked across the street from the Knickerbocker.

Montego fought to not let the guy get under his skin.

"OK, partner. What's going on with you?"

Haley remained silent for several minutes, then, "Been on edge, but things should be cool now that Brunetti's gone."

"Cool?"

"Lissa working where Brunetti hung out made me nervous. It's bad enough that Dante Pio and his thick-necks hang out there."

Montego accepted that. "Before we busted the big goon you said you were sidetracked, then you described the room layout and told me what the whore would do. How'd you know?"

"Been going to The Palms most every night that Lissa worked—weeks before Brunetti showed his hairy ass. When the killings started on the southwest side, it made sense that he was involved. Nancy told me that he was a cock-hound and liked jumping her bones."

"Nancy? The stacked redhead?"

"Nancy Gooch. Old flame—cheerleader from Marshall High."

"You, a blue-and-white Barrister? We Sheiks played you guys in the Western League."

"You look like a *sheikh*, too. Only you're missing a 'stache and a goatee." Haley cracked a slight grin and lit a fresh Camel. "Yeah, I was in Nancy's room alerting her when she saw the meathead on the walkway. Damn near got my ass stuck crawling out the rear window."

"Explains your breathing so hard."

Haley eyed him. "Nancy's dream was to be a movie star." Smoke drifted from his mouth. "I lost contact with her when I left for boot camp—Fort Ord. After my discharge, I joined the LAPD. I soon found out she'd gotten her glory-bubble popped on a sleazeball's casting couch. He had her doing porn flicks in a pad above The Strip." He sighed and took a deep drag on the cigarette. "One step from the grimy streets. Damn sweet kid too."

Haley's rare show of emotion gave Montego pause.

"Cheerleader to hooker—tough." Montego opened the car door. "Sit tight. I'll check the hotel."

Haley watched Montego crossing Ivar Street toward the hotel.

I'm screwing up, upsetting Mom and Missy in front of Montego—stupid. Why am I feeling so suspicious about Pop? Hell, I checked him out the best I could through the system. Nothing bad.

Unable to dig up Pop's birth record didn't matter; Haley's British birth certificate showed that his father was a plumber. What else could be checked?

As far as Ari Sands went, there was nothing, but then Brunetti had indicated the name was an alias. Angelo Pinky Sancia wasn't in the criminal files either, but he might never have been busted. Civil records documented he was born in New York City in 1911, and reported "missing in action" on December 7, 1941, during the infamous Pearl Harbor attack.

Unable to absolutely prove that his pop wasn't Angelo Sancia had Haley bollixed; it was why he had been provocative at the dinner table. Why had he tried to draw Pop out in front of Montego? Did he want his new partner to think twice about Pop being a straight-arrow?

Haley sighed. Pop had been damn cool. But then he always was.

Is Angelo Pinky Sancia truly dead? Is the Italian mob looking for the ex-hit man, too, or just Beak Brunetti and his cousin? It's bullcrap—Pop's not Angelo Pinky Sancia. . . . Pop—don't be an ex-hit man.

Chapter 9

Montego surreptitiously checked the registration book after distracting the sleepy-eyed clerk by asking for information about renting break-out rooms for a planned conference.

Accepting a brochure, Montego returned to the prowler.

"Our boy's playpen is up on the fourth floor. Registration shows a G. Riffelano. His vehicle's a '62 Eldorado. I saw no bodyguards lingering."

"Any vehicle ID?"

"Got it here." Montego opened his field notebook, grabbed the mic, and ran the license number.

They waited. When the RTO radioed back, "No wants or warrants" and verified the make and year, they exited the four-door and headed for the hotel.

Stillness blanketed the opulent lobby. In the rear parking area they found the Cadillac. Montego tried the car doors—locked, and the black hood felt cool to the touch. He checked the other cars in the area, confirmed they also were unoccupied and that their hoods were cold.

"No bodyguards." He scanned the area slowly to reaffirm his earlier observation.

Haley checked his wristwatch. "We'll take down Riffelano when he comes out to his Cad." He moved to the rear exit.

Montego, biting on his lower lip, preferred to grab Riffelano leaving the room when the goon likely would be less alert. But now wasn't the time to debate tactics. Focus on the bust. Montego checked the time on his Bulova as he moved closer to Haley who was lighting a cigarette.

Smoke boiled from Haley's mouth when he said, "I expect lard-ass to be packing on the right side, low under his coat. . . . It might get hairy."

Montego faced him.

How in the heck? OK, maybe Nancy-gal told him.

"How're we doing this, Neall? If Kay Dub's snitch is right, we've got ten before our boy shows."

Haley moved to one side of the doorway. "Right here. It's late, so no bystanders—it's why we waited. Stand there. I'll yell 'Police' and buzz the meathead." He flipped open his jacket, displaying the badge on his belt. "He'll turn my way—and 'Gordo' might get funny—so stay out of my line of fire." He took a last drag from the cigarette, dropped it on the pavement and ground it underfoot. "And this time I'll stay off my keister."

Faking a chuckle, Montego pulled out Riffelano's mug photo again: round bald head, porcine eyes, small and empty. A puffy face, thick lips, rough-textured like sausages. Ghoulish, the fat guy also looked like he enjoyed inflicting pain. Plucked fingernails and tire-tattooed hands circled in Montego's mind. The guy's looks alone suggested he wouldn't go easily.

The sleek Eldorado held Montego's gaze. How would this bust go down? He sensed sweat beading on his chest. One never could tell when dealing with the other side. Other side—*tanto!* Earlier that year, in bloody hand-to-hand combat, he'd killed a crazy. The District Attorney had deemed the death justifiable homicide—but the vivid memory never faded.

Hugging the wall opposite the door from Haley, Montego shoved the small photograph into a coat pocket, and withdrew the Colt Python. He opened and rolled the cylinder to check the six 158-grain rounds, his thoughts on the Academy range-master, another of Mother's cop friends.

Art Dougherty had taken Montego to the Mojave Desert during his awkward teen years to learn reflex shooting by targeting on empty tin cans that Art threw into the air or sent careening off rocky slopes. Like an older brother, he had preached, "Remember, Mike, at night the tendency is to shoot high—so aim low."

With most handguns, Montego had the confidence to direct the bullet to where his trigger finger pointed; with the Python, it didn't matter whether he extended his arm or kept his elbow tight to his side, he'd learned how to counter recoil and shoot accurately either single- or two-handed.

He holstered the blue-steel 4-inch and sucked in the cooler early morning air. The warm Santa Ana winds had subsided, but the stale industry and auto-exhaust odors prompted him to exhale sharply.

Mentally ticking off time, he shrugged his shoulders and worked his fingers. He tried to visualize the upcoming scenario, hoping for a quick and cooperative takedown. His eyes traced the lines of the black Caddy.

The bad guys sure liked the flashy toys.

He heard the hotel door swinging open and simultaneously Haley's low voice rasp, "Gordo!"

Montego glimpsed Haley's magnum already up and Riffelano's left hand raising an automatic across his body.

Freeing his revolver, Montego shouted, "Police—freeze—"

Two deafening blasts shook Montego.

Riffelano's gun-hand jerked up, his dome-bald head snapped back, but his body spun toward Montego.

Ears ringing, Montego crouched.

Two more shots blasted, one came from Montego's Colt Python.

A slug ricocheted off the concrete wall with a resounding *sping*.

Riffelano landed on his back, his head smacking the pavement just outside the doorway a body-length from Montego.

Haley rushed up, his magnum pointed down at the unmoving body. He kicked the weapon loose from the mobster's death grip.

"Damn, he was fast."

"He died fast, too." Montego realized that Gordon Riffelano had failed twice to aim low. His first shot an instant too late, narrowly missing Haley, the second fired reflexively in death—*nearly hitting me.*

A bloody spot like a middle-eye was centered above the bridge of Riffelano's nose. Montego knew the hole was not from his piece. The emerging splotch on the mobster's immense chest showed where the bullet from the Colt Python had struck: next to a visible red logo of a Lucky Strike cigarette pack halfway out of a shirt pocket near Riffelano's stilled heart.

Squaring up, Montego inhaled the acrid air, blowing out harshly as he jammed his revolver home. He willed himself to be calm and replayed the event frame-by-frame. He wasn't paying attention when the goon came through the doorway. Exactly how things had gone down was not that clear, but Riffelano had gotten funny like Haley had claimed, and also like he had said, the goon's pistol had appeared low on his right side. Not sure about the still reeling mental images, Montego eyed the slim blond called Ice Cop.

"Neall, you didn't call out 'Police' or badge the guy?"

Haley smoked a dozen Camels during their extended watch while enduring the officer-involved shooting protocol imposed by department regulations. The OIS investigators had him retelling the tactics they had employed.

He didn't reveal knowing Riffelano packed low on his right side; Nancy had clued him about that.

The tedious process along with the bullcrap Brunetti had dumped on him had Haley tossing around second-guesses. Why hadn't he listened to Montego and taken the fat fuck upstairs in the hotel hallway outside the room? Had he chosen the rear exit because he wanted to kill a meathead, any meathead? Had he played Ice Cop to scare off Brunetti's cousin, hoping to remove the threat against Pop? But if the threat was a mob thing. . . ?

Waid Woodruff

*   *   *

Leo Brunetti hung up the pay telephone in the narrow inner hallway of the old Chicago courthouse, turned and shuffled ahead of the uniformed guard into the prisoner holding area, his leg chains dragging on his ankles.

After the steel-barred door clanged shut he sat on a bench along with the other jail-garbed defendants waiting to be arraigned. He pondered his situation. His cousin had just confirmed that the "apple was cored," code that the fix was in. He snorted knowing he would beat this fucking rap, too. By arraignment time he'd know if there'd be a damn trial or not.

He sat with his back against the concrete wall, picturing being in the Riviera del Palme motel room balling the hell out of sexy Goochie. The sight of the redhead with her big tits bouncing on top of him had his roscoe brick hard and ready to spit.

While massaging his boner through the cotton trousers, his pleasure was interrupted by the haunting words: "You're busted, Beak."

The barred door creaked open and another defendant had his leg chains removed before he headed out to the courtroom.

Brunetti's boner died, but not his anger.

He again saw himself in Hollywood, but this time he was getting even with Blue Eyes. He touched his bandaged nose.

That muthafucker. Gotta put my mitt into that pretty face—smash it.

Yeah, and also have me some fun and games with Neallie Baby.

Best of all, however, would be when he took out old man Sancia, the yellow fuck would see it coming too . . . it would be slow and painful.

Chapter 10

Five hours of fitful daylight sleep left Montego dragging. Released from the shooting scene, he and Haley had made their way down Vine to the 24-hour Brown Derby Coffee Shop. Haley, pasty-faced, had said nothing. Montego had his own concerns. What he had done nauseated him.

He mentally repeated his answers to the questions asked by the OIS investigators, the Officer-Involved Shooting dicks from downtown, but his version never varied, even though his thoughts wavered.

Over cups of black coffee he'd accepted that Riffelano was already dead when the slug from the Colt Python entered the mobster's heart, yet *spinging* sounds still echoed. Riffelano hadn't been gun shy—a bit of comfort—and Haley's quick and deadly accurate headshot was impressive.

The guy had been right by opting to take Riffelano at the rear exit; bullets caroming off the concrete walls, particularly the 9mm Largos from Riffelano's Beretta would've penetrated the hotel's interior walls and could have hit an innocent person . . . *had the goon been able to draw his pistol.*

Considering that Haley had made the best choice caused Montego to think Haley had good reasons for his actions, but a clearer understanding of how the guy thought for future tactical situations was needed.

Montego replayed the events in his mind, and other than being a too-close call, the shooting had been clean. But overlaying his thoughts was the Brunetti bust and Ice Cop's actions on that night. Had Haley wanted to kill both Brunetti and Riffelano?

Haley's words, "Gordo might get funny—so stay out of my line of fire"; and, the whirling vision of Riffelano's "three-eyed" face added to the mix of spinning thoughts in Montego's mind. Further misting through the mélange was the in-depth interview by the OIS sergeant in the hotel lobby.

What had Nick Karos, the lead detective, determined?

Yesterday's surprise dinner with the Haleys also had Montego thinking. He'd actually enjoyed it, but a meet-the-family meal?

Meanwhile, they were on relieved-from-duty status pending the Shooting Review Board's decision. Being RFD with pay didn't matter that much, but being cleared of wrongdoing did.

Donning swimming trunks, Montego jogged down to the hard-pack and watched several surfers in the crashing waves. His mind was still on his deadpan partner and their violent contacts with two mobsters. In last night's case, Haley had not called out "Police" nor badged Riffelano, and Montego's comment had only gotten an unintelligible mumble.

They'd come close to being shot; not something to think about.

To counter a sudden chill Montego sprinted down the sloping sand and along the surf until he felt warm. Then he raced into the foaming tide. The cold, salt-and-sand gritty water grabbed his attention. He swam out past the breakers and stroked north. Catching several big waves he body-surfed, eventually riding a large one to shore, his mind finally free of the shooting.

After a long shower he was more centered. Since Julie had classes, he would spend the day perusing his forensic science text book. He had a test tomorrow night at L.A. City College; other cops and cop hopefuls were in his police science class. The instructor was an LAPD sergeant.

It was six in the evening when Montego drove to the Kono's residence. On the cobblestone drive he shut off the V8 and stroked the rabbit's foot charm hanging from the ignition key chain. He gazed at a long koi pond alongside a winding pathway that led to the *dojo*, the training building, hidden by lacy varied-colored foliage.

Two acres of Oriental landscaping encompassed the homes of the elder Konos, their grandson's small family, and Kenny's mother. His dad, Nao, had been killed in the Vosges Mountains of eastern France during the Second World War. He'd fought with the 442nd Regimental Combat Team. It was comprised of Japanese-Americans.

An owl's soft hooting alerted Montego. He slid off the truck's seat and slammed the door. The loud gesture was a form of politeness that he'd arrived, even though he knew his presence was known the moment he had opened the large wrought-iron entry gate.

Yoshi, the elder, had taught him to listen. "Hear what others miss." It had helped Officer Montego. Sauntering to the dojo, he heard his huaraches squeaking and his sweatshirt brushing against his skin. He realized people heard the chirring sounds of crickets, if they thought about it, and most people heard their own breath escaping when sighing, but how many listened to the sounds of dry leaves rustling, or to a gentle breeze? He heard such sounds, but Yoshi and Kenny heard when a leaf fell nearby.

Montego eyed the guest house with its traditional oriental roof and up-turned corner eaves. The dragon's-blood-red trim still bright like it was during his Academy days and rookie months following his divorce. It had been a period of anger and sorrow. The Konos had once again taken him in;

their wise words had helped him to overcome his bitter disappointment at a failed marriage.

As he closed on the dojo, a meadowlark "chupped" nearby.

The training hall was treated like a shrine. Perforated paneling and woven-reed wall-matting helped to mute the vocally explosive *"Kiais"* that accompanied specific thrusts, kicks, and blows of the sparring fighters.

The elder stood stoically at the entry beside his grandson, Kenny.

"Michael-san is punctual as ever." Yoshi bowed.

The three smiled and bowed to each other. Montego bowed again to the elder who returned the honor with a lower bend. Once erect, Yoshi said, "This evening we concentrate on directed energy." The trim man slipped out of his red-gold slippers and preceded Kenny and Montego inside.

The owl hooted again.

After a series of warm-up katas, sparring began. The movements progressed to the free *kumite* kata or contest form: *Shinken Kumite,* literally "real sword" kumite. Yoshi watched closely as utmost care had to be exercised to halt the blows and kicks inches short of the mark.

Moments into the kumite a meaty face with a bullet hole flashed in Montego's mind, followed by echoing gunshots. His instinctive reflexes slowed. He feared he would fail to measure his blows and immediately stopped. He bowed to Kenny, turned and saluted Yoshi.

"Sensei-san my mind is not alert. Please accept my apology." He stepped away, bowing once more to the grand master, and again to Kenny.

The elder and Kenny knew about the shooting, but said nothing. Montego could see the understanding in their eyes. They continuously exhibited the utmost patience. He had not developed the Kono men's serene self-control, and often was reminded of it in the dojo. The tough lessons had begun with the sensei advising, "Learn to train your *shin*, your heart, Michael-san, and practice this much-revered art with honor. *Nichidu takara*: life is the most precious thing, my son."

Yoshi's words brought a brief, but sharp, pain to Montego's gut as he left to shower. Riffelano's wide-open dead eyes with a bloody third between them, rolled around inside his mind like red dice.

Before leaving, Yoshi and Kenny asked Montego to join them in the main house for a cup of steaming green tea.

When Montego stopped to close the entry gate, a horned owl with a small rodent in its talons, swooped low through the headlight beams.

Three times. An omen?

73

Chapter 11

Standing outside The Palms Montego pulled on the fob attached to his Bulova, the watch a memento from his father. The luminescent dial read: 9:10. Montego expected to catch Haley inside, figuring the guy would be nursing a brewski and jawboning with the gorgeous waitress, Lissa, during her free time.

Montego had met Lissa the evening they were waiting for Brunetti to show up, just before the bust. She'd worn a sarong-style waist-skirt and a flowery blouse, its tails tied below her shapely breasts. Her looks and outfit complemented the Italian décor.

He recalled her cheery greeting sweetened by a sugary voice as she regarded him brightly, but only long enough to be polite and then her brown-eyed gaze had rested on Haley.

Stepping inside, Montego paused, the dinner business was good. Lissa, came up, smiled, and pointed to the table near the kitchen, the one where he'd sat before. He nodded toward the kitchen area. "Neall in there?"

"No." Faint lines creased her brow. "I read about the shooting in the paper. It said he was all right—he's OK, isn't he?" The bright red rosebud nesting in her honey-blonde curls enhanced the blush of her cheeks, but her doe-brown eyes lacked the sparkle he'd seen on the previous occasion.

"He's fine, Lissa. Hasn't he told you about last night?"

"I haven't seen Neall today." She glanced toward the corner booth.

He didn't look where she'd glanced. "How about an Oly?" He sat.

Curiosity won out. He casually took in the corner booth. Dante Pio was sitting with Jackie Kennedy's look-alike. She obviously had a thing for elbow-length gloves. A balding, long-nosed man holding the hand of a familiar looking woman with medium length styled red hair sat with them. Pio was putting a flame under Long-nose's narrow cigar.

Montego considered the man with the deep-lined expression and slightly lifted eyebrows might be Pio's boss, the Mafia don whom Quinn had called "Little Frank DeSimone." The idea of the mob hanging out in this place caused some worry. He recalled Haley's comment about Brunetti and his concern for Lissa. Haley frequented the restaurant because of her. There likely would be many Code 7 meal breaks in the eatery. That posed potential problems. The encounters with Brunetti and Riffelano proved that.

When Lissa set down a schooner of frothy lager beer, Montego asked, "Who's the balding guy smoking the panatela?"

"Sam Giancana. Dante calls him Momo. He flew in from Chicago. That's Phyllis McGuire, the singer, with him—Frank Sinatra and Roselli were here earlier. Johnny Roselli's a movie producer. Hey, with your Latin looks and deep-blue eyes I oughta introduce you."

Distracted by the light freckles visible in the open vee of her blouse he barely heard the words, "oughta introduce you." He quickly looked up at her impish smile.

"Huh—celebrities dine here?" He sensed his face warming.

Lissa appeared not to notice; she had to be used to guys staring at her cleavage. He wondered how she handled the ogling mobsters.

"I've waited on Natalie Wood, Robert Wagner, Gary Cooper and Dean Martin," she said. "Last night, Vic Damone came in with a singer, Anna May. She's performing at the Fogcutter up the street. I think she had her own TV show when she was a teenager. They're not my kind, though."

"Mine either." Movie stars didn't excite him; he'd been around them during and since high school. Anna May was his date at the senior prom. She had sung a song to the delight of the party-goers. *Ancient history.*

Lissa smiled and went to check on other patrons.

He gulped the beer and eyed the goons. Like movie stars, they were easy to spot, thanks to working with Haley. Montego hoped that Haley would show up before the beer lost all of its bubbles.

Why hasn't he been in to see her? She's obviously bothered. Maybe I should talk to her. . . . She might have insight that can help me understand the guy . . . . And I might find out what she knows about Pio and his men.

Montego stopped her when she passed by. "Lissa. Got a moment?"

She paused. "Shoot, Mike—oops." Her hand shot up to her mouth.

"You ever hear what Pio or his guys talk about?"

"Only from Mario—he's a real pest—likes to brag about mob stuff. He pretends he's one of them, but I don't think he is." She looked around. "The braggart's not here now."

"Say, if Neall doesn't show before you get off, would you have a cup of Joe with me—at Big Spike's? I'd like to get a handle on Dante Pio."

"Big Spike's? That's cute." She glanced at the front entry. "I wish Neall would come. I hardly know anything. . . . OK, I'm off at eleven—what are you driving?"

He described his Cameo Carrier truck, and said, "I'll be out front."

Deciding to eat elsewhere, he finished his beer and drove to Ontra's Cafeteria on Vine. After savoring a meat-loaf dinner he went to the station and phoned Julie. He was breaking a ritual when he told her he had some unexpected police business and would be late, but if her lights were still on he'd stop by.

He killed the interim hours scanning divisional crime reports and the Field Interrogation card file jotting the FI data into his field notebook.

Minutes before eleven o'clock, he parked in front of The Palms. When Lissa appeared in the ambient light, she looked a bit down.

She climbed in and closed the truck's door. "Neall didn't show."

Shrugging, he cut across to the drive-in and slipped the truck into a just-vacated space beneath the east-side canopy. A leggy carhop with heavy eye-makeup whom he remembered from his cruising days took their orders.

Lissa tuned the radio to KMPC and was adjusting the volume when a young woman came to the passenger-side window. Lissa introduced her as a day waitress at The Palms. The women chatted until the carhop came and hung the food tray on the driver's side door sill; then the day waitress, eyeing Montego with a knowing look, left.

"Boy, thought we'd never get to talk," he said teasingly. "Seriously, Lissa, I appreciate you giving me this time."

"Why shouldn't I?" She accepted the tall fluted glass he offered, pursed her lips around double pink straws, and drew in the iced tea. Freeing the straws, she added, "You *are* Neall's partner."

"*And* being a nosy cop." He paused to mouth the cherry off the top of the chocolate malt. "Ever since we busted Brunetti, I've wanted to learn more about Dante Pio and his boys."

He set the red plastic basket of French fries between them.

She snatched a small one and popped it into her mouth. Munching, her hand over her mouth, she said, "I hardly know anything about them. They get hush-hush whenever I'm near their tables."

"What about that Mario guy you called the braggart?"

"Humph. He's a muscle-headed pest. Thinks he's in with Dante's group, gang, crowd, whatever—but I don't think he really is."

"A wannabe, huh? And what does this Mario pest brag about?"

"Things like hearing them talking about Marilyn Monroe's death, claiming Dante's men were near her Brentwood home the night before the housekeeper found her. He made it sound so suspicious like."

Montego had heard rumors around the station. If true, they made the mob sound even more dangerous and the braggart's words noteworthy. He tilted the cold metal container and got a dollop of milkshake, more than he'd intended. He quickly wiped off the chocolate mustache. Lissa smiled.

He said, "What can you tell me about Pio, besides him liking your pretty face?"

"Why thank you, Mike. Dante has teased me about my Italian name and not speaking a word of it. I think he considers me a real country hick. He knows I came here straight from an apple orchard in the Wenatchee hills." Her lips puckered around the straws as she drew up more tea.

This woman is darn easy to look at.

Her curves had him recalling the afternoon on the beach when Julie had worn a wet pink swimsuit that clung to her glistening skin—

A honking horn one space over jolted him back to the drive-in. Flushed by his vision, he blurted, "You and Neall a longtime thing?" before realizing he had been asking about Dante Pio.

"We've been dating steady for three months—but lately, I don't know. He's been quiet more than usual—for days." Sighing, she recaptured the straws between her red-gelled lips. "And he's smoking cigarettes now."

"Yep, he sure smokes up a storm. Last night was a bit rough, Lissa, but he'll come around."

Neall's bothered about the shooting, too.

She released the straws, her lips spreading into a sensuous smile. Light freckles rose and fell behind the opening in her blouse.

Stop it, hombre!

"I hope so. I just don't know." She bit into another fry and chewed.

"I can see you've got it for the guy."

She sighed again and swallowed. "I do—really bad." She popped the last of the fry into her mouth.

He fidgeted. This gal had him examining his feelings for Julie.

"Does Neall ever talk to Dante Pio, or any of his goon group?"

"Not that I've seen—oh, he has talked to Leo a couple of times. Don't know what about . . . both times seemed . . . I dunno, intense."

"Hey, it's getting late. Thanks for your time, Lissa. I'd better get you to your car. I'll follow you home—make sure you get there OK."

"You're really kind, Mike, but my place isn't that far from here— it's on Gardner." She pressed the napkin to her moist eyes

"It's on my way, and as your boyfriend's new partner, I insist."

*　　*　　*

Haley, needing the comfort that only Lissa could provide, pocketed the door key to her upstairs apartment. He seldom entered her small home when she wasn't there, but he didn't feel like being around the meatheads at her workplace. He had parked near the two-story building's driveway wanting her Pontiac's headlights to flash on his Porsche when she drove in; and, being a balmy night, he had left the door half open, flipping on the room light to ensure that she would know he was inside. He probably should have called her, but he'd not felt that great when he awoke early that afternoon.

He tossed his bomber jacket on the back of the sofa. Miles Davis' *Kind of Blue* matched his mood. He slipped an LP record from its cover. It featured John Coltrane on tenor sax. He set the platter on the hi-fi turntable, balanced the sound, and lowered the volume.

Shucking his loafers, he fell back onto the sofa, his legs hanging over the padded armrest. Lissa's fragrant presence in the soft gray-blue fabric touched him. He checked at his watch. She should be home by now; the restaurant must've had a late crowd. Were the meatheads there?

He recalled the day he'd spotted Brunetti driving with Riffelano in a yellow Cad convertible. It was around the time of the Wilshire homicides. They had to be the doers.

Thinking of Brunetti's busted nose was somewhat satisfying. Montego had handled himself well. But it had created a problem. If a Chicago jury sent Brunetti to Illinois' death row, the chances of IDing his cousin were slim to none. Haley realized what he should have done was pistol-whip the shit out of the meathead in the prowler, threaten to kill him if he didn't give up his cousin's name . . . but Montego would never have gone for it.

His down-and-dirty fight with the meathead—fast and tough—was impressive . . . and he'd shot straight with Riffelano, drilling the fucker's heart after Haley's round between the eyes . . . and Montego's hog-leg had been holstered. Haley didn't think Montego had seen him slip out the S&W magnum and hold it from view on his left side.

Haley's gut had told him to be Ice Cop so he'd only said, "Gordo," believing Riffelano would react thinking it was a hit by another mobster— and he had—but he'd shot fast—too close, and he got off another round . . . nearly hit Montego.

78

The Purple Hand

All right, maybe I was testing Montego—but damn near a mistake. Coulda been fatal for two cops.

Feeling guilty had kept Haley from talking to Montego afterward at the Brown Derby.

Two weeks of dread and worry had churned Haley's belly sour. Nothing had removed his frantic concern. Brunetti was gone, but there was his damn cousin who had started this bullcrap, and Haley didn't know who that meathead was, or what he even looked like; and, taking the Special last Friday in an effort to identify him hadn't paid off. Even Nancy didn't know the asshole, only that she'd heard Brunetti talking to a Nino on the phone.

There must be a thousand Ninos in L.A. alone. Good luck with that.

Although Brunetti was no longer around, his unknown cousin's unseen presence draped Haley like a garlic-soaked shroud, especially when he was at The Palms and Dante Pio and his gunners were there. The mobsters followed his every move, particularly when he talked to Lissa. They knew he dated her. Had killing Riffelano put her in danger? Haley quivered. He reached for his wallet.

It seemed like the zillionth time that he slipped *The Detroit News* article out and reread it. He shook his head. The subject had turned his life into a cartwheel. Who and what was he becoming now that he'd killed Riffelano? But he knew who Leonardo Brunetti was: The Beak. A funny tag but there was nothing funny about him.

Still, Brunetti's story bothered Haley. He had yet to determine if it was a mob thing or only the meathead and his cousin's bullcrap game? Either way, if it became public, the news that a cop's father had been a mob hit man would destroy the Haley family. Another heart attack could kill Pop.

And if Pop is a Mafia target it will be impossible to protect him.

Haley replaced the clipping. "What to do?" he muttered.

If it was personal with Brunetti, then Riffelano's death might work as a scare tactic on the cousin as hoped. But would it cause the meathead to make a stupid move?

If Brunetti's claim was a mob thing, killing Riffelano had scared no one—just the opposite. Dante Pio's boys would put two Haleys in the morgue. All because of an ex-hit man named Angelo Pinky Sancia who quit the damn mob nearly thirty years ago.

Kneading the wallet, and to hold a positive thought, Haley told himself that it wasn't the Mafia. Pio's meatheads had left him alone, so far.

79

Unless that's how the Italian Mafia operates? It is a secret crime society. Damn it, Ice Cop. Face the suave mob capo, ask him pointblank: Pio, is this your doing, or is it The Beak's personal game?

Haley needed to find out, even though he sensed it was the latter, or was that wishful thinking?

Meanwhile, if it was Brunetti's personal thing, Pop should be safe.

Instinct told Haley that with Beak Brunetti gone, the cousin, Nino or whomever, wouldn't act hastily, regardless whether Gordon Riffelano's death scared him off or not.

Shoving the wallet into a back pocket, Haley buried his face in his hands trying to ease the throbbing behind his eyeballs. It didn't help. He was thinking like a damn hit man.

I've got to identify Brunetti's cousin—then locate and ace his ass.

One thing he realized, until he knew the true score, he had to keep Montego on his side for backup when the lousy cousin was wasted. Haley had used his new partner twice now and he would continue to use him.

Also, he must decide what, if anything, to tell Montego.

Coltrane's smooth tenor sax holding one key for a dozen plus measures was a signal for relaxation. Haley yawned, not liking what he was thinking: *Lissa had to be his eyes and ears.* She was his best hope to learn if Dante Pio was involved. She might overhear something that would provide a clue as to what was going on. Hopefully, she would hear the last name of the finger-pointing cousin.

Haley couldn't explain why he wanted Lissa to tell him what she heard—safer for her to believe it had to do with police work.

Who the hell was he kidding?

Damn it all, he hated conniving; he could be putting the woman he loved in jeopardy.

Hearing motor sounds he got up, padded to the window, bent two slats of Venetian blinds and peeked outside.

What the—? Montego.

Chapter 12

Montego, standing barefoot on the Perch's balcony, gazed out at the choppy sea. A phone call from Kozier had eased his mind. The Brass had deemed the shooting to be within policy and for him to report for duty that night, Friday.

Stepping inside, Montego retrieved his gun-cleaning kit and went to work on his Colt Python.

Strawberry Gal was on his mind. Something was going on with her, she was avoiding him. *Was it her father?*

She hadn't come home last night, and she hadn't called.

Early that morning, coming back from a run, he saw her carrying a large folio of drawings to her sports car. He assumed that she had just come by to get it for her class.

He trotted up as she backed the Austin-Healey from the carport and called out, "Julie—Eagon's having an office-warming party this Sunday, at three—wanna go?"

Turning the wheels and shifting gears, she'd merely glanced at him.

"Pick me up at three—only because of Eagon." She sped off.

"Afterwards we can have dinner at. . . ." he let his voice die out.

What set her on fire?

The question lingered with him throughout the day.

He still thought about her in the station as he sat bent over on the bench before his locker brushing his shoes harder than necessary.

When Haley wordlessly appeared at his locker, it gave Montego pause, but he quickly guessed why the guy was quiet. Upon arrival at Lissa's apartment building, Montego had seen Haley's black Porsche. At the same time, Lissa had pointed up at the light shining through her open apartment door, saying, "Neall's here." She sounded excited.

Obviously, Haley had spotted Montego's Cameo Carrier pickup.

Montego felt a need to explain. "Thought you'd be at The Palms Wednesday night." He kept buffing. "Wanted to rehash the shooting."

Haley yanked open the combination lock. "Yeah, you and Lissa."

"Hey, she hadn't seen you since the shooting. I wanted to ease her mind."

"She told me." Haley swung open the metal door.

"Then you have it all."

Haley slid out a Camel carton. "You talk to her about Riffelano?"

"Nope." Montego's thoughts circled from Lissa to Julie, to the mob, to Haley, and back to Lissa. Tossing the shoe brush into the locker he stood and faced Haley. He could understand why the guy hadn't gone into The Palms. He likely didn't want to talk about the shooting for the same reason Montego wouldn't have said anything to Julie, had she given him the chance. Killing another human, even a mob goon, could eat a guy alive. One never wanted to dwell on it. It was one reason why cops would get chummy over drinks every Friday night at "The Bull Pen." It helped to armor-plate their feelings and to shield their emotions from the insane business they were in. Too often it was a killing business.

But Neall must know it bothered Lissa, his not calling her.

"She did overhear Pio's hoods talking—no telling what she heard."

He studied Haley's profile. It could've been brushed onto canvas and framed as a still life. The portrait didn't change until he pulled a pack out of the carton and peered coldly at Montego.

"I don't want Pio thinking she's talking to cops about things he suspects she overheard. It could be putting her on a hot seat," Haley said. "We're staying out of the damn Palms—for Lissa's sake."

"Probably a good idea—but it sounds like an order. Knock it off. You might be senior man, Haley, but we're partners. We need to think alike—know what to expect from each other—trust each other. Things keep going the way they have, one of us is going to get shot—maybe killed."

Haley quickly stuck the Camel pack into a breast pocket.

Montego slammed his locker door. "And knock off pouncing on the vehicle sign-out log every time we're working together—I'm tired of riding shotgun every night with my ballpoint filling out all the forms." He spun the combo-lock dial as he eyed Haley coldly.

Haley had replaced the carton on the shelf, but glancing briefly at Montego, slid it out, pounded loose a second pack, then tossed the carton back into the locker.

The passing seconds seem like minutes as Montego watched Haley opening the fresh pack.

Finally, Haley said, "You drive tonight. We'll drop by The Palms, but no damn words with Lissa—be cool." Glancing again at Montego, he thumped out a cigarette from the pack.

"Tanto. There you go, Neall, telling me what we're gonna do—knock it off. We're not a one-man L unit, even though it feels that way breathing your—and that's another thing—you smoke too darn much for my liking. You oughta give up those filthy cancer sticks."

Haley's face took on a metallic yellow as he lit up and blew out. The smoke wafted up to the fluorescent lights and swirled.

"Shows to go you, don't it, Montego?"

"How's that?" Montego stepped closer.

Haley shifted, his focus on Montego's hands.

"Chief Parker claims organized crime isn't *operating* in LA."

Montego, noting Haley's stance, accepted the off-the-wall comment as the guy's attempt to ease the tension.

"Yep—and Mister FBI, J. Edgar Hoover, swears there's no Italian Mafia organization *operating* in the US."

"Yeah, they're all hiding at the bottom of the boot—in Sicily." Haley pocketed his Ronson.

"By the way, Neall, while at The Palms, I spotted two *federale* roosters: Peter Santelli and Nedwick Whyte. The agents were eyeballing an older long-nosed goon. Lissa heard Pio call him 'Momo.'"

Haley banged his locker door shut, an eyelid twitched, Montego noted, before he led the way to the roll call room.

He knows more about the mob than he's let on. What about Lissa? Does she know more?

* * *

Leo Brunetti strode through the L.A. International Airport domestic arrivals gate and met with an overweight mobbed-up lawyer. The sun had risen, further brightening his day. It felt good to be breathing free air.

After a brief update, the lawyer, as he handed over the keys to the yellow Cadillac convertible, told Brunetti to call Dante Pio.

Brunetti drove straight to the Roosevelt where he immediately went to a pay phone and dialed the telephone number for the local capo regime.

Following the terse call, Brunetti ambled into the Cinegrill bar and ordered brunch. He finished the meal, guzzled a Compari-and-Soda, then paced out toward the hotel's registration desk. On the way, he stopped at the same pay phone he'd used earlier and called his cousin.

"Nino. Patsy D'Amore's Villa Capri at ten, after I meet with Pio."

Settled in his room, Brunetti phoned the Riviera del Palme Motel and had Room 8 rung.

Following the call for a date, he went through his pre-sex ablutions, then he donned a pair of light blue silk boxers. Flattening himself on the king-sized bed he puffed on a cigar while stroking his aching boner anticipating "Coochie Goochie's" big bazooms bouncing off his chest.

It was close to nine-thirty when, fully sated sexually, he made the walk into The Palms and met with Capo Pio.

Minutes later, Brunetti stubbed out his Roi-tan and drove to the Capri. He joined his cousin in the plush dining area.

"Nino, thanks for doing the fuckin' fix, paesano."

Simeti grinned stupidly, saying nothing as he slurped his Grappa.

Brunetti gave the barmaid his order as he dropped onto a chair.

He slid it closer to the table. "We got us a little job for tomorrow—we'll do it early afternoon. Get us a nice rental, Nino, 'n' meet me at one in the Cinegrill."

He gazed around the dimly lit room. His mind shifting to Blue Eyes and how to get even. He'd heard Haley call him "Tonto" but the jailer called the muhfuck "Montego."

He would jump the damn bull when the chump least expected it—when he was off duty.

Brunetti touched his tender nose remembering how the fast fucker had handled himself in close quarters. The way Blue Eyes had stuffed away his gat to take Brunetti on in the motel room, told him the bull fucker called Tonto Montego was no chump.

Admittedly, the thought gave Brunetti pause.

Maybe I better use Nino.

The Grappa drink was served. Tasting it, he eyed his cousin.

"Nino, I wantcha to get me dupe keys for your pad . . . 'n' for that new red Bird you just got, too. I might need 'em someday."

"No problemo, Leo. Hey, didya hears 'bout Gordo gettin' his fat ass blown away by them two bulls that hangs at The Palms?"

Chapter 13

Montego had to crawl out of the sack too early, but he relished the Sunday morning runs along the beach with Alex Strait. However, yesterday over cold beers at The Clam Digger, Strait had begged off on today's run saying, "I do hate being a sniveler, but I feel the creeping crud getting a mighty grip on Uncle Alex's rather large walnuts—they're starting to feel like filberts."

Not having Strait with them gave Montego a sense of loss—nothing major, more like a subtle void. Strait, although outright cynical, was the goodwill that kept the cop group lighthearted, regardless what they might have experienced on the job.

To Montego, it seemed more of a personal thing. He believed he'd be a better detective if he were Detective Alex Strait's partner.

Big Jim "Wheels" Wheeler, Montego's tall former partner in Accident Investigation Division, and Greg Aurek, an L.A. deputy sheriff, were waiting for him.

Minutes later, the cop trio was running abreast on the hard-pack. Aurek was nearest the surf. His sandy-brown hair topped a broad middle-European forehead and a chiseled chin damp from the crystalline salt spray.

"Becky and I saw you at Tiny Naylor's. Gotta tell ya, Mike, that blonde's a helluva looker."

Montego almost tripped on ropes of stranded seaweed sending tiny flies swarming. He glanced sideways at Wheeler who kept his eyes directed at the El Segundo refinery stacks ahead of them.

The sea air suddenly tasted salty on Montego's tongue.

"It was police stuff."

"Aren't Wednesdays your night off?" Aurek said.

A breaker collapsed with a thunderous clap, seawater rushed onto the sand. Aurek veered in front of Wheeler to avoid the foamy water.

Montego glanced at Wheeler, then Aurek. "She passes on street info." The pointed query reminded him of a time on the witness stand when short and bald lawyer, Harry Weiss, had waggled an accusing finger at him.

"I told Becky it's none of our business. Don't be surprised if Julie hears about it."

Ah ha. Becky Gill wasted no time.

Montego was glad the subject was dropped, but it swirled in his head. He thought about the divisional Christmas party when he'd gone to another table to ask the stripper, Rhonda Reddi, if her TV had been recovered. The top-heavy redhead had drawn major attention parading into the party draped on the arms of a tall burglary detective. Julie had made one teasing comment about the flashy stripper and then had let it go.

"No problema." He sprinted ahead.

Julie was jealous!

Like he'd promised when he'd telephoned her from the station, he had stopped by her studio apartment after seeing Lissa home. Seeing Julie had been sleeping, he'd said, "It's late, and I'm tired—I'll be darn poor company. I'm going to crash in the Perch."

In retrospect, his manner might've been a bit brisk, but at the time he'd felt he couldn't adequately explain how he'd spent the late night.

Another curling breaker crashed, sending sandy slop rushing about his calves. It pushed him sideways into Aurek.

"Sorry," he muttered. Julie's hurt expression flashed in his mind's eye. He must explain about seeing Lissa Renzo. He blew out a deep breath. Explaining that his police job had involved a pretty woman would be tough, especially to a jealous lover.

For sure, don't say that the woman is a looker.

Montego drove with the traffic flow on Olympic Boulevard, his thoughts gloomy. Nothing seemed right. Julie sat away from him listening to radio music. They had exchanged few words.

How to explain? He had to clear the air. "About last Wednesday—"

"Yes, tell me." Her sharp words sliced through the pop music beat.

"I'm innocent." He forced a chuckle and immediately knew he'd sent the wrong signal. He glanced at her with heightened guilt. He'd told her on the telephone it was police stuff. OK, he hadn't been very specific.

After another moment of silence, he said, "I have a new partner and I hoped that Lissa, *his* girl, would—"

"Lissa, *his* girl. Hoped" Julie killed the radio. "What did you hope, Mike?" She twisted on the seat toward him.

"Hey, I plead the Fifth." Again, he'd responded poorly, but she had jumped to a wrong conclusion. OK, he might've had a lustful notion about Lissa, but that wasn't a crime, yet Julie made it seem that way. How could she know what he had briefly thought. . . . Had his guilt shown? Women seemed to be sharp that way, or was it pure jealously?

He cranked the pickup into a small parking lot on South Broadway a block from Eagon Quinn's office and cut the motor.

"Wipe your upper lip, Tonto," Julie spit out. "You're perspiring." She stormed through the lot to the sidewalk.

Swiping at his lip, he snatched the ticket from the attendant who was eyeing her sashaying backside and rushed to catch up. She had never before called him Tonto—at least not making it sound like he was a fool.

Nothing was said during the brisk walk south.

Upon entering the classic Bradbury Building, she stopped, twirled to look about at the woodwork and elegant wrought-iron décor. She gazed at the high glass ceiling as he pulled open the elevator's door.

"Such a quaint lift." She stepped into the black-iron birdcage and took in the surroundings. They rose to the third floor.

Montego grasped her hand. Cold and rigid. She let him hold it as they went to a door with gold-embossed lettering: "Eagon T. Quinn, Esq." Hearing laughter and the hum of voices from within, he led her into a wood-paneled vestibule. In another room people talked, snacked and drank.

At least someone's having a good time.

She tugged her hand free when Quinn rushed over.

"Well, halloo Julie." He leaned and kissed her on the cheek. "You are a breath of freshness, my dear, like an Irish spring morn. But were I twenty years younger, Mike here would be in a wee bit of competition."

Montego grinned as Quinn drew him close in a back-patting hug. Warm tears welled; although blurred, he saw a smile on Julie's flushed face.

"Counselor, you've done a quarter century with the LAPD. The department won't be the same. At least you aren't calling me *little* Mikey as much now."

They knew each other's ultimate goal: Quinn wanted to sit on the Superior Court bench, and Montego wanted to make it downtown to the home of the Detective Bureau and work homicide cases citywide.

Caught by an unexpected emotion, he quickly turned away, saying, "Hey, what a great spread, Eagon—won't last long." He gestured at the other guests while blinking away the blur. Scooping two rye wafers into a bowl of creamy mixture, he turned and offered one to Julie.

"Uh uh, no food—not *if* we're going to dinner later." She flashed a daring look, picked up a cracker, and dabbed it into a different bowl of dip.

Biting into the cracker, she turned to Quinn. "Uhmm—yummy, yummy. Smoked Sturgeon. Delicious."

Montego worked his jaw muscles.

Quinn said, "What do you think of my new abode, young lady?"

"Delightful. The Bradbury is such a unique building."

She slipped a hand over his arm. "Eagon dear, I'd love to see your office suite."

Quinn, smiling, put a freshly lit cigar into his mouth and guided her to the center of activity.

Montego stepped to the buffet table, grabbed a cocktail napkin, speared a bacon-wrapped chicken liver with a toothpick, and followed. "How much are you going to charge me for legal advice?" he asked.

"Double rate, Mikey." Quinn, looking back, winked a hardened eye. "Can't make a living by giving away my services."

He's picked up on the rift.

Quinn stopped the caterer balancing a tray of fluted stemware filled with champagne and handed a glass to Julie.

"Dom Pérignon, my dear."

Montego, snatching a stem-glass, spilled a small amount. He deftly caught the fluid midair in the napkin. Instantly his face warmed.

Julie, making a wry face, waved at a cloud of cigar smoke then took the drink. "Now I know what to give you for an office-warming present."

"A fan. Yes, yes, my dear."

Montego was glad for his mentor, but not for himself. He stepped away, watching Quinn enjoying Julie on his arm. It pleased Montego. He treasured the grand guy, always had.

On occasion, after EOW, when he needed to unload, he'd sit with Quinn in the private room below *El Triste Toro*, The Sorry Bull restaurant, where cops caroused, many till dawn. They referred to the round, Saltillo and Talavera-tiled, basement with its high-vaulted *boveda* brick ceiling as The Bull Pen, and their all-night gatherings as *veladas*. In essence, it was a "Bottle Club" from two until six in the morning to avoid legal hassles.

Montego turned and spotted Roy O'Brody standing in front of Quinn's "hero wall." Several Perma-plaques and a large city proclamation lauded an illustrious police career. Montego went over and put an arm around O'Brody's drooped shoulders.

"When you pull the pin, Roy, your den wall will look the same."

"Not too long from now, I hope." O'Brody sounded blue.

Montego steered the old detective away from the wall. "I once asked Eagon, 'Until you reach the bench, how can you represent defendants you know to be criminals'?"

"And he told you, 'My job is to make certain the DA has done the necessary homework. Lady Justice operates blindly.'"

"Eagon'll dispense justice on the bench—"

"But not blindly," O'Brody finished.

They both laughed.

Montego left O'Brody at the small bar and strolled into the library. He recognized the District Attorney, several deputy DAs, and a handful of judges from the several levels of the judiciary. He had mixed feeling about a few that he'd appeared before. He spoke to those he knew, and when it seemed appropriate, he nudged Quinn to signal his and Julie's departure. Quinn's natural complexion was florid, but more so now; he seemed happy.

"So soon you deprive me of this gorgeous lady." Quinn took Julie's hand as she released his arm.

Montego was relieved that she seemed agreeable to leaving.

"Eagon, you hear about the shooting yesterday morning in the Seventh where one of the Slauson Slaves gang members bought it?"

Quinn grumbled and took several long puffs on the stubby cigar, blowing the smoke high above Julie's head. He eyed the burning end.

"Yes, the gang's leader—and our friend Leonardo Brunetti had a dirty hand in that Wilshire homicide, me thinks."

"The Beak?" Montego caught his breath, his thoughts in a rush.

"Like I told you, Mikey, the gunsel has the knack." Quinn checked the cigar ash. "He beat the rap in Chicago town. I heard the main evidence, the brass casings with his prints, disappeared from their property room."

"That's guano." Brunetti's threat that night weeks ago in the prowl car played back. Montego pinched a toothpick from the passing caterer's tray and speared a Ramaki hors d'oeuvre, cramming it into his mouth and chewed. Recalling Lissa telling him that Haley had talked to Brunetti a couple of times worked on his brain.

Quinn blew a rolling smoke ring that floated over the passing caterer's balding pate and tapped the cigar, loosing the ashes onto the tray gliding by. "Roy has a scared witness who claims he watched Brunetti blasting the Slave bloke gangland style."

"That's good—the big goon probably fired twenty-twos. Great skull-dancers." Montego cared less how his words sounded.

Quinn glanced at Julie, then frowning, said, "Mike, I told you Pio's serious about controlling the black-operated rackets on the southwest side."

"Is it a racial thing, Eagon?" Julie said hesitantly.

"No, my dear. The local mob boss will deal with anyone to obtain control, including outlaw motorcycle gangs like the Hell's Angels. Skin color seldom matters as long as the results are profitable. It just so happens that games of chance seem to be a favorite pastime for many of our poor. I guess it's the promise of the pot of gold that has been denied them. But to the Mafia, it's strictly a cold-cash business."

Quinn took a final puff off his cigar. "Those gunsels can doctor the results of the numbers games, even the penny ante street stuff, and make millions. So they do what they think is necessary, including strong-arming, to raise their profit margin."

Julie's forehead creased. "They're that powerful?" She brought the fluted glass to her lips and drained the sparkling wine.

"Larger and more powerful than most people know, my dear."

Quinn turned to Montego. "Here's a bit of a chuckler. The outfits back east refer to the west coast organization, little Frank DeSimone's group, as the Mickey Mouse Mob. They think the LA don is weak. I can say this now," he exaggerated an eye-sweep around the buzzing room, "because Bill Parker can't snatch my badge when I say the Italian Mafia is running rackets in *his* city." With a grin, he stepped over to a Grecian-style brass floor-stand and stuffed the cigar butt into the white sand.

Returning, he said, "I no longer have to play politics."

Montego wasn't surprised that Quinn disagreed with the chief's public denial. Montego knew first hand that the Mafia operated in L.A.

Quinn grasped Montego's hand firmly, holding it for several beats, his expression conveying a message. *Work things out, son.*

In the parking lot, Montego studied Julie. They hadn't spoken.

"You like Eagon don't you?" He saw that her departing kiss to Quinn's cheek had pleased the ruddy-complexioned man.

She nodded without turning her head. "Please take me home, now."

"Julie, how about giving me a chance to talk to you over a hot meal. I can't let this misunderstanding continue."

"I don't know what you can say that would please me."

"How about I don't want you mad at me anymore?"

"You think plying me with margaritas is the answer?"

"Right now I don't know how to answer you. Come on—give me some time at the dinner table to talk things out. Please."

She climbed into the Cameo Carrier on her own.

"Have it your way."

He sighed and went around to the driver's side.

They drove north toward dark clouds blending into the smog-laden hills of Elysian Park where the Police Academy was nestled among gnarly pines and tall eucalyptuses.

Before arriving at the City of Glendale border, just past a revolving lighted sign, he turned into a parking lot. He had reservations for a booth in the old-world Mexican-styled dining room situated above the Friday night-Saturday early morning gathering place of cops.

This time Julie waited for him to open the door on her side.

"El Triste Toro greets you." He pointed overhead at a black-plastic bovine with massive horns. Its droll expression belied the sparkling stream of teardrops. "The Sorry Bull weeps jealous tears seeing you with me."

Julie's eyes flashed green icicle daggers.

Tanto peor. He'd meant it to flatter her.

*   *   *

It was EOW. The Monday MID-watch had experienced one radio call after another. Montego was glad they had stayed busy. It helped to push his conflicted thoughts about Julie to the back of his mind.

She had jumped on him—and not in the manner he'd wished—upsetting him with her temper, and he'd not responded well, having said things he now regretted.

Arriving home, she'd said, "Just bag my toiletries from your bird perch," and jumped from the pickup while the remote-controlled garage door was still rising. She slammed the truck door and hurrying away, yelled, "Just leave them in my carport."

At least KW was sympathetic when he'd mentioned the tiff. He had his own situation with his fiancée. Yolanda was a social climber, he'd said. Montego suspected KW had similar aspirations, but he downplayed it well.

When they headed outside for their personal vehicles, KW had dropped an arm over Montego shoulder, saying, "Buy her flowers, Tonto. Women love 'em."

Entering the fenced employee parking lot, KW lifted his arm when Montego blurted out, "Tanto peor." He sprinted to his pickup under the sole lamp post. The windshield was cobwebbed.

Flinging the door open, he spotted a bullet hole on the driver's side in the tucked-and-rolled, red-and-white Naugahyde seat covering.

"Some kinda crap—how come nobody heard a damn gunshot?" KW's troubled eyes cast about.

"Maybe it sounded like a backfire." Montego, grinding his molars, surveyed other vehicles. Only his truck had been damaged.

KW offered to drive him home, but Montego begged off. Instead, he returned to the station and filled out a Malicious Mischief Report for insurance purposes. Busting a goon for a misdemeanor was unlikely.

Lying awake in the station's basement "crash" room, his thoughts filled with anger. Brunetti was back in L.A., but Montego's mind wouldn't focus on him as the doer. The act seemed too cowardly for The Beak.

But who knew what the big goon was capable of?

At 0800 hours, Montego phoned Scientific Investigation Division. They sent out a forensics technician. An hour later, a 9mm slug was dug from the seat padding. When the SID man was done, Montego telephoned Hollywood Tow Service and arranged to have the Cameo Carrier hauled to an auto-glass shop on Beverly Boulevard.

Alex Strait commiserated with Montego in the station coffee room while they waited. "A dastardly deed. Any idea as to the culprit's identity?"

"Nope. But Beak Brunetti is back in town."

Strait, obviously surprised, sipped his lightly sugared coffee.

By 1400 hours, the windshield had been replaced and Montego drove to a South Bay upholstery shop he'd phoned earlier and had the seat re-stuffed, patched, and re-stitched. The forensics tech hadn't treated Montego's pride and joy as well as he would've liked.

In the Perch after showering, he checked his pocket watch. Julie's last class at UCLA would be long over. She should be in her apartment. He must clear up things—he hadn't bagged her things like she'd demanded.

Should he tell her how he'd spent last night and most of the day? No, it would only frighten her. She'd told him more than once how nervous she was about his patrol work. Funny, how that suddenly made him feel.

He skipped off the bottom step, rounded the corner, and abruptly stopped. Her Austin-Healey wasn't in the carport. His heart missed a beat.

She probably thinks I spent the night with another woman.

Chapter 14

Neall Haley dropped onto the tan La-Z-Boy and levered it back. Fear had crept through his entire being. He'd just talked to Brad Kozier. Leonardo Brunetti was back. It hit him like a percussive nightmare. Even thinking of seeing Brunetti again rattled him to the core.

With the meathead's return to Hollywood, he realized it was good that Montego had laid into him in the locker room. He had been riding him roughshod, more then he'd meant to. And he was smoking way too much. Blame it on The Beak. Now he needed Montego even more.

The meathead cousins have to go down.

The ringing telephone jarred Haley back to real time. He grabbed the receiver. Lissa's voice sounded urgent.

"Leo's here. He wants to see you *now*—Neall, he looks serious."

Already!

That she was used as a mob go-between sent a sickening spasm through Haley. He had gotten her involved with his mess, even though he'd backed off going into restaurant as often—and he'd also brought danger closer to Montego. A cop's private vehicle being fired on was an audacious act. It had everyone in the division in an uproar. For the past three days cops had been on edge. Last night, he'd joined the routine of circling the entire block to observe the employees' parking area for oddballs before entering the station proper.

The media hadn't gotten wind of it or all of the jerks in Jollywood would be taking pot shots at cops' private vehicles.

He grabbed his bomber jacket and made his way out to the Porsche. He pulled off the tonneau cover, stashed it, and drove to The Palms, his gut cramping in fear for his pop, concern for Lissa, and worry about Montego.

Hell, he still didn't know for certain where Dante Pio stood on this, but the parking lot incident didn't feel like a mob thing. He would have to wait and see how Riffelano's death played with Pio. Haley didn't think this meeting was about that. He also didn't think Brunetti would do anything stupid while inside The Palms, but if he did he'd get a bullet, regardless.

Outside the restaurant, Haley paused to light a Camel. He drew in a deep drag, exhaled, and moved on, noticing his long shadow cast by the mid-afternoon sun. It danced like a specter over the Indian hawthorn bushes along the building wall, over berries turning red on the branches.

Like drops of blood.

Slipping the silver Ronson lighter into a jacket pocket, he passed through The Palms' anteroom to the dining area and worked his way around several empty tables to the corner booth where Brunetti, sitting alone, shoveled in his usual three o'clock lunch.

Haley clamped his jaw and slid onto the seat opposite the mobster.

Brunetti licked a glob of something unrecognizable from the corner of his wide mouth and bit off a chunk of seeded bread.

Haley took another deep drag on the cigarette knowing he had to get rid of the uncouth meathead no matter what.

Brunetti, chomping then swallowing the bread, pushed aside the remains of a Caesar salad, leaned forward, elbows on the tabletop, sneering.

"Surprise. I'm back."

Haley eyed him icily. "Yeah, but this isn't Chicago. You play your so-called 'l'il game' here you just might find your hairy ass up in 'Q.'"

"Yeah, we'll see. I know you wanted to take me out, Haley, but your true-blue partner, Blue Eyes, couldn't pull the trigger. Big mistake. Now I'm gonna have me some real fun 'n' games with you, Neallie Baby."

"Why is it no one else is around when you toss out your bullcrap? It's personal with you, isn't it?" Haley drew on the Camel filling his lungs.

"Think so, huh? Well listen to me good. I'm giving you a contract. Fill it 'n' your pa *might* live. Fuck it up 'n' you can say, 'Ciao, Papa.'"

Smoke exploded from Haley's mouth. Brunetti's words twisted like a lag bolt into his gut. There it was.

Pop is a marked man!

Haley stubbed out the cigarette, pissed that his hand was shaking.

"That a signed contract, Beak?" His constricted throat made the "k" in the meathead's street name feel like a knife had sliced his tongue.

Brunetti snorted, grabbed his Compari-and-Soda, and took a gulp.

"Nothing's ever in writing." He leaned back and took another swig. "You get what I'm saying?" He snatched a cold cigar and snapped fire to it.

Haley wanted another Camel, but felt he'd choke on it. He focused on a large pit snug against Brunetti's now bent nose. Seeing the results of Montego's "knuckle sandwich" appeased him, but he would have preferred Brunetti to be cold morgue meat.

"Neallie Baby, remember, you don't say nothing to your ol' man—not 'til I say so." Brunetti's laugh sounded like an oily gargle. Gray smoke bubbled from his twisted mouth. Downing the remaining Compari, his dark agate-like eyes abruptly seemed to be seeing into the past.

After a moment, he said, "In time you can ask your pa how it was for him in Brooklyn, capering on Taylor 'n' Maxwell in Little Italy. Then you can be asking him about The Patch—'n' the Forty Twos. Hell, your pa was one a that fuckin' gang, too—ran with Willie Potatoes, Fat Leonard, Mad Dog, 'n' Milwaukee Phil."

Brunetti scanned the room then his gaze settled back on Haley. He leaned forward, again planting his elbows on the red-checked tablecloth.

"You're gonna do a nigger name a Ronnie Rondell. He was where he shouldn't've been, 'n' your bull pals snatched him up hoping he'd talk 'n' make their fuckin' case, but they lost the skinny rat—The Rat, that's his calling—now he's running around saying shit the boss 'n' me don't like."

Haley stuck a hand below the table to hold down his shaking knees. With the other, he flicked a stray crumb from the red-checked tablecloth, using the brief moment to wet the cotton in his parched mouth.

"You've got a problem, Beak. Nothing goes down until I have untraceable hardware—with a silencer." His spontaneous words surprised him, but maybe they would buy time to devise a way out of his damn mess.

Brunetti's mouth gaped. Then he straightened up and snorted.

"Chumps like you don't challenge me. Tomorrow—three sharp—here," his tone menacing. "Capisco, amico?"

Haley sank back, still pressing his knees.

One day! Damn. How the hell am I going to get out of this mess? Pop is a dead man—probably me, as well.

Movement by the front entry snagged his peripheral vision.

Crap!

"I'm outta here, Beak." Haley thrust himself from the booth and veered right toward the patio doorway.

Too late.

Montego had to have seen him. Trying to act cool, Haley turned left toward the kitchen door where his partner seemed to be headed.

"Hey, Tonto, looking for someone to have a beer with?"

Montego glanced right across the room, obviously at Brunetti.

"What's going on?"

Haley slowed his breathing, but he couldn't stop his spill of words, "Came in to see Lissa, didn't expect Brunetti to be here. The meathead was alone, so I offered a little advice."

"Oh?"

"Yeah, warned him if he steps over the damn line in Hollywood, the Big Blue Bird would dump a foul load onto his brain case."

"Such *huevos grandes*," Montego said, stony sounding.

Haley eyed his wristwatch thinking he would need large balls to get out of the bucket of bullcrap his sorry ass had plunged into.

"Missy should be home from school," he quickly said. "She's been threatening me with dire consequences if I didn't bring you to the house—and I don't need what Sis can stir up." He forced a grin. "And, today's Mom's baking day—fresh pies every Thursday before she leaves the house to play bridge." His wordy gush rattled him even more.

Calm your pale ass.

He hoped he was wrong as to why Montego had come into the restaurant, but he wasn't up to asking.

"OK," Montego said after a moment. "My class isn't till six."

"Give me a sec. I'll let Lissa know I'm going. Leave your truck here—ride with me—I'll bring you back—want to check the crime reports and FI files before roll call."

Damn it. Shut up—quit talking so much.

*   *   *

Leo Brunetti didn't give a shit that Haley had guessed right about it being personal. His yellow-assed pa was a dead man no matter what. Glaring at the over-confident bull joining Haley near the kitchen, a flame smoldered inside Brunetti. He touched his nose gingerly.

That nose-busting muthafuck Montego bull hasta feel some pain, too. You just wait, Tonto Blue Eyes. Your time is a coming.

Brunetti ambled to the pay-phone near the men's restroom.

"Nino, I want you to get me that pale-assed bull's home phone number—yeah, Neall Haley."

Chapter 15

Montego traced his fingers over the tan leather seat in the '62 Porsche 356, stemming his curiosity as they drove east toward the Los Feliz area. He'd decided the Haleys were affluent, and he now realized that his partner had money as well. He wasn't too surprised. What did surprise him was the guy standing up to Beak Brunetti, but then he *was* Ice Cop. Yet, the close seating allowed Montego to detect a waft of sour body odor.

He's nervous . . . because I saw him sitting with Brunetti? Or my showing up, obviously to see Lissa? Or both?

Whatever, it had to be clarified. "I'm sure glad The Beak knows he can't intimidate us."

Haley worked the gears down smoothly coming to a full stop at the T-intersection of Franklin and Beachwood Drive. He said nothing, waiting on the red phase of the tri-light.

Montego cast the line out farther just as the tri-light turned green. "Guess losing Riffelano must've jerked the goon's chain."

The motor revved, the tachometer needle swung over the red line.

Is Haley trying to act cool—like saying nada about the windshield?

Unable to pinpoint why the guy should, Montego opted not to mention the windshield incident and gazed out the side window.

As they passed Gramercy Place he visualized the houses crammed into the myriad tree-lined hilly streets that crawled like centipedes in and out of the shaded canyons. He recalled atrocities he'd discovered working the hilly beats in uniform and how many might lay hidden somewhere in those leafy shadows at this very moment. He had come upon too many horrifying crime scenes. Would he ever forget them?

Montego shook away the morbid memories and thought about how to explain being at The Palms on his day off.

"Women, I'll never understand them. I'm on the outs with *my* gal, all because I talked to *your* gal."

Haley, glancing left at Western, switched on the radio.

Montego caught himself rubbing a thumbnail.

"Wanted to see Lissa before she got busy—needed a bit of female advice." And to play on Haley's alleged warning to Brunetti, he added, "Like you, I didn't expect the big goon to be there."

He's not buying it. Well, I don't buy his claim either.

Haley dialed to a station playing jazz. He raised the volume and his voice, "Lissa can date *you*—or anyone. I like her a lot. But I've never had a claim . . . it's never gotten that serious."

Again, Montego didn't buy Haley's comment, but sensed a finality, maybe frustration, retreating into his partner's throat. He hadn't missed the accusing "you." Women could do that to a guy.

He's really bugged.

Haley downshifted and squealed onto Berendo Street. Two blocks north he spun right into his parents' driveway.

"Even so, you shouldn't have asked Lissa anything about those lousy meatheads."

Haley willed himself to be calm. Montego seeing him with Brunetti had unnerved him. He had wanted to say in no uncertain terms, "Lissa is my girl, Tonto—keep your damn ass away from her. I love her and she loves me." But he had no right. Not anymore. Because of Beak Brunetti he had nothing permanent to offer the beautiful woman. Haley raised himself out of the car and went with Montego to the front door.

Inside, Haley called out, "Sis."

"The kitchen, Neallie."

Seeing Montego, Missy exclaimed, "Oh," and tossed her dish towel onto the counter, swiped at an errant curl, and smoothed her pleated blue skirt with the other, all in two seconds. "Hi, Mike."

Missy's girlish actions tickled Haley. "Whatever pie Mom baked today—would you please bring us each a big piece? We'll be in the den."

"It's boysenberry." Missy's gaze stayed on Montego.

Haley led the way into the den and to a dark rose-wood bookcase. He pointed at several framed pictures of a uniformed soldier.

"Snapshots of Pop during the war. He fought in the trenches from Sicily, up the Italian boot, and into France."

Missy spun gracefully into the room carrying two big slices of pie served on separate bone-china plates. She placed them on a coffee table.

"Ooh, Mike, I want to show you something."

She dashed across the room to a tall rosewood-and-glass cabinet. On tiptoes, she reached for the top shelf. At its center sat a small burled wood case. She brought it down carefully and raised the hinged lid.

"Daddy's a hero. He snuck up and shot a bunch of awful Nazis—he also saved his buddies and crawled through a muddy minefield to do it."

Haley, standing at the bookcase, toyed with a small glass ashtray with a logo on the lower shelf.

"Sis used to say a muddy miner's field."

Missy frowned at him then she withdrew a small square pad of blue velvet cushioning a ribbon and medal with a silver star in the center of a larger bronzed star. She cradled it against her white uniform blouse, smiling and swaying her shoulders. Turning, she lay the Silver Star back in the case, handed it to Montego, and reached for a small wooden box with a pull knob on the front side. She placed it on the lower shelf of the bookcase.

Haley moved aside the glass ashtray as she slid out the velvet-lined tray containing campaign ribbons, several with oak-leaf clusters.

"Missy is Pop's publicity agent. Everyone gets to see his medals." He went to the sofa and sat, remembering why his dad had always been his hero. He grabbed a fork and cut into his pie. Watching Montego, he ate.

Missy raised the lid on a wooden box containing a medal depicting a bas-relief of George Washington and traded it for the medal and ribbons Montego held.

"Daddy's Purple Heart. He was wounded in the left side," her eyes shaded, "but he shot that awful sniper. The war was almost over when that happened." She lightly touched its surface before she picked up a framed photograph beside the small ashtray.

"This shows Daddy holding baby Neallie. Wasn't he a darling? It was before the air raid sirens started. It had to be really scary." She eyed Montego. "See Big Ben? You knew that's where Neallie was born."

"In the clock tower?" Montego winked slyly at Haley and moved to the sofa.

"No, silly—you know what I meant." She held out the framed snapshot for him to see as she followed.

Haley knew it depicted a young Lonn, gleefully cheek-to-cheek with a laughing towheaded boy. Back then, his pop wore a modishly thin mustache, similar to the one on the gangster in the old Detroit newspaper photo tucked in his wallet. Haley took another bite of boysenberry pie, also knowing it didn't show Pop's left little finger. None of the snapshots did.

Were Montego to see the old news clipping photo would he notice a similarity between Pop and Sancia?

Haley relived the afternoon Brunetti had shoved the clipping inside his jacket, and then Haley racing here to look at that very snapshot. He'd compared it with the old *Detroit News* photograph. The sight had both sickened and angered him. Maybe it was good that Pop hadn't been home that day, because Haley might've unloaded on him: "Pop, tell me—are you Angelo Sancia, AKA Pinky, AKA Ari Sands, a Jewish hit man, infamously repped The Purple Hand who quit the mob and fled to England?" It would have cascaded exactly like that.

Yeah, and with his weak heart, Pop would've dropped dead.

But if he wasn't the ex-hit man, he'd just laugh it off. *Wouldn't he?*

Was it a coincidence his moving to London in the mid-'thirties?

Again, Haley mentally wrangled with the possibility that his pop was the ex-enforcer. He couldn't blame Pop for splitting, if he was. Mobster life was no damn life. Yet, Haley's every fiber resisted believing Brunetti's audacious claim.

But if Pop is Pinky Sancia, he hasn't escaped the damn Mafia.

Haley hated himself for harboring such a thought, but if true, Pop would never be able to hide. The Italian Mafia was like a giant octopus with deadly tentacles that could bring serious harm to the Haley family.

The returning dread burned in Haley's gut, then surged to his throat. He quickly stood, patted Missy's shoulder, excusing himself. Once in the hall, he dizzily sped into the guest bathroom. He sucked in deeply, pissed at his inability to stay calm. Riffelano's jowly face and third eye had erupted in his mind. A haunting image. He had played the role of a hit man.

Is a killer's blood flowing in my veins?

Sinking to his knees, head spinning, eyes blurring, he twisted over the toilet bowl, lifted the lid, and lost the berry pie.

After a moment, he flushed the tank and watched the mess swirling away. *Dammit—tell Pop. Hell, become a pop-son hit team. End all the bullcrap.* But doing so, would mean believing Brunetti's claim.

Haley swiped at his mouth and spit out the sour taste.

No way—Pop isn't Pinky Sancia. My only hero is no damn hit man.

Still, Brunetti had threatened to kill Pop and it sounded personal since it was his lousy cousin who had gotten the huge meathead riled.

If personal, then I need a foolproof plan to take out both cousins, legally if possible—and pull it off without angering Dante Pio . . . I gotta lure Brunetti and his damn cousin to a kill spot where I have the advantage.

Chapter 16

Montego breezed into the detectives' squad room a step ahead of Haley and sauntered to the homicide table where Wayne Nells was tidying his desktop. Seeing the disciplined man there at 1800 hours wasn't surprising.

The brown-suits worked weekdays 0800 to 1700 hours, and by 1600, especially on Fridays, most had a reason to be away from their desks, wanting to get an early start to their weekends, many, by attending the all-night cop party, the veladas, in the belly of The Sorry Bull.

Strait and Nells were exceptions. Strait rarely attended the veladas, and Nells never had.

"Wayne—any word yet about your transfer from Downtown?" Montego had asked it lightly, but quickly realized it had sounded wrong.

"Transfer?" Nells turned to eye Haley who was lighting a cigarette. "Are you going to stand there and let your partner clean out my desk while it still holds my belongings?"

Montego rubbed a thumbnail. Nells sounded darn serious.

Haley blew smoke overhead. "Hells bells, Nells, Tonto might try to fill your oxfords before you get assigned The Counselor's old slot."

"Best keep my laces tied, huh?" Nells adjusted the perfect knot on his narrow-striped tie. Well, the grapevine says I'm on the next one."

"Hey, that's great!" Montego's felt his face warm. "Tanto, you know what I mean." Although he'd jump at the chance to work with Strait, Montego told himself he needed to sew on a five-year hash mark while in the Patrol Bureau before Les Whitaker, the Hollywood detective captain, would even consider him, especially for a seat at the Homicide table.

Nells stood and buttoned his natural-shouldered Brooks Brothers suit coat. Montego had caught a glimpse of the label.

"Our bait tank's empty, men." Nells sly-eyed Montego and nodded toward the doorway leading to the Burglary Squad's room behind him. "Maybe *they* have fresh fish to fry."

Montego started back but stopped when he saw Alex Strait stepping away from Lieutenant Clay Dawson's desk. Montego was glad to see the supervisor working detectives. When Dawson was assigned to Patrol, he had been Montego's watch commander.

Strait moseyed up to the trio.

"You gentlemen just missed the opportunity to straighten out Mister Leonardo Brunetti's busted beak. He looks good for that homicide last Saturday in Wilshire, but Clay says our skipper just got a call from the 'Hats'—the pick up has been canceled."

Haley edged closer to Strait. "Brunetti comes back to LA, makes a hit, and he gets to run loose? That's pure bullcrap." His left fist smashed into his right palm.

Montego was surprised by his blond partner's outburst.

"For sure he has no fear of the Big Blue Bird—might've been fun."

Strait, glancing at Haley, slid out his chair and sat. "Downtown had a witness, but the gent got scared—gave those *pros* the slip." He looked up at Nells while twirling a tip of his baby handlebar. "However, O'Brody wants the witness found and rousted."

Montego suppressed a chuckle. Strait's not-so-subtle term, "pros," was meant to tease his senior partner who would be working with O'Brody. Montego believed Strait was unhappy about losing Nells.

Nells kept silent, not taking the bait.

"Does O'Brody think the wit's in the Sixth?" Haley asked.

"Yes," Strait said. "He avers that he dodged white-gangster lead, and hear this: O'Brody claims the slippery prick might be crawling our neon-lighted streets hunting for Mister Brunetti as we speak."

"How's that, Strait?" Haley stepped even nearer.

"I'll back up. It seems the witness, one Ronald Rondell, was too close when Mister Brunetti shot the Slauson Slaves' main man—"

"A black gang," Nells interrupted.

"Street fighters," Haley added, puffing his cigarette.

"Gang justice—much faster." Montego winked at Strait who looked a bit flustered.

"O'Brody claims the prick's crazy, not that he's lost his aggies— he's simply brash and dangerous." Strait fiddled with his desk blotter.

"Ra—" Haley coughed and blew more smoke. "Rondell isn't very bright to be snooping around mob hangouts."

Montego missed bagging Haley's unfinished word.

Haley turned away and crushed his cigarette butt in a tin ashtray.

"Don't ask me, Haley." Strait leaned back. "On the streets he's known as The Rat—enjoys stabbing people in the back, maybe figuratively, who knows."

"Rat?" Montego thought it sounded much like Haley's cutoff word. He said to Strait, "A crisp Lincoln says R&I has a package on this escaped and nefarious rodent from our downtown *pro's* protective custody."

Strait sat forward, tore off a corner from a notepad and scribbled on it. "Mister Rondell's no cherry—don't have his pedigree or a mug shot, only his LA number."

"We'll pull his sheet." Montego took the paper slip Strait held out. It meant a trip to the large storage room full of criminal files and photos on the second floor in the PAB.

"Montego, let's tell the sarge we're going downtown." Haley started for the doorway. "Unless you wanna stand tall for inspection."

Montego shook his head.

Why the sudden hurry?

"Maybe we can hold the guy for carrying an illegal back-stabber's blade." Grinning at Strait, Montego trailed Haley from the room.

The first half of their shift had turned into a zigzagging chase after a fleeting ghost; rushing around hadn't helped them to find the missing witness even though Haley had taken them to every nook and cranny in the Sixth Division.

"Whoa, mi amigo—I'm darn hungry—let's grab a bite. Rat Rondell is not that important. So what if the guy kills The Beak? Who cares?"

"Good point, Montego. Just thought you'd be curious to see what a meathead-hunting rat looks like in person."

"Not enough to miss a hot meal." Montego patted his belly. "By the way, most guys call me Mike . . . or Tonto—like I recall you once did."

"OK . . . Tonto-Mike." Haley actually half-smirked à la Strait.

At EOW, Haley parked their plain brown prowler near the vehicle service area behind the Juvenile building.

"Frank-One, end of watch." Montego re-racked the radio handset, saying, "Tomorrow, maybe Kay Dub's snitch can help you dig this Rondell character out of his rat hole."

"Surprise me none if a patrol cop in Wilshire or University Division snatches the rat asshole."

The exasperation in Haley's voice was evident.

"That might not please Brunetti. He's gotta be hunting Rondell."

Montego caught Haley throwing him a sly glance.

Chapter 17

"I'm heading over to The Pen—you interested, Neall?" Montego thought a cold beer would relax Haley, maybe oil his tongue and provide a clue to his uptight behavior.

"No velada. If Lissa's awake, I'll be listening to smooth jazz over a nightcap."

Twenty or so minutes later, Montego skipped down the narrow curved stairwell stopping at the oak-and-wrought-iron door. He let the large metal ring drop as he peered through the bars. Ricardo, the barkeep, spied him through the haze and reached under the counter.

The electric lock buzzed and Montego pushed the eight-foot door open triggering recorded voices of *aficionados* shouting, *"Olé,* announcing his arrival in The Bull Pen.

He weaved through the crowd to the circular brass-railed bar and said to the barkeep, "Rico, a Bud, por favor."

Spotting Bobby Diaz standing near the "Bull Chute," the billiards table alcove, he called, "Bad Bobby D—I'd spot you a frosty Bud, but I see you swigging a cold one."

Bobby D came up. "I'm supposed to believe that?" He put on a hurt look, then his brown and bony face expanded into a wide grin. "Hey man, didya find that rat-stabbing *hombre*?"

"Nope. But tomorrow, Kay Dub and Neall will go after him. I'm taking a Special—celebrating my godson's first birthday."

Big Jim Wheeler would tell anyone who'd listen to the lanky man how Montego had saved his life at the end of a hair-raising freeway pursuit. Wheeler had named his first son "Michael Dane" in honor of Montego.

Wheeler, now assigned to West LA AI, liked working accident investigation, especially patrolling the sharp curves of Sunset Boulevard, his traffic beat.

"Hey man, that's *bueno*." Bobby D saluted with the bottle of Bud. "Miguelito's gonna be a *macho* terror now." He slugged down more beer.

"*Mañana*, Trev and me'll help Ice Cop find the stinking rat-fink— *aieee*, did we get swamped tonight, and man, was Brannock sharp. He spied a four-five-nine splitting outta the Taft Building. We lassoed the thieving asshole climbing into his wagon—spent the rest of the watch listing and tagging the Selectric typewriters he'd snatched from the friggin' offices."

Montego grinned. Bobby D was on a roll. "Trev's good people—oh." A familiar jab to his back had Montego spinning about in a bow and swinging an arm as if holding a sombrero while he eyed the petite cocktail waitress in the black toreador pants. The "blue brethren" had a pet name for her: Dottie-with-the-dicey-derrière. Dottie Cortezaro didn't mind as long as they kept their hands off. She had special names for most of them, too.

"Jus' keep those wanderin' blues on a short leash, *hoota*." Dottie's dark brown eyes revealed her amusement. "How come Julie's not with you, Miguel?"

"Things've been a bit rough." He'd brought Julie to several veladas, and they had danced to her favorite tunes played on the bubbly jukebox.

"*Sentimos.* Sorry—maybe Mister Homicide, now The Counselor, can help you." She winked and scooted away. She never got involved with a cop's problems.

Montego eyed the banquette. Quinn looked mellow. A gray fedora angled back on his head exposed a snowy widow's peak.

Bobby D got Montego's attention back by saying, "Hey, Ice Cop ain't here—you wear out his pale Irish ass?"

"Vice versa." Montego stepped to the bar and grabbed the frosty Budweiser from the barkeep's outstretched hand. "*Gracias*, Rico."

He rejoined Bobby D. "Neall's got something going with a gorgeous waitress at The Palms." His comment had him realizing that Lissa must have seen Haley with Brunetti yesterday. Montego filed the thought.

"Hey, Bobby D, you noticing anything unusual about the guy?"

"*Si*, Ice Cop's flatter than piss on a saucer—maybe his *señorita's* having trouble getting him up and fizzin'. Never happen to this hombre." Bobby D chuckled lustily.

"You're a true Don *Juan*." Montego gunned back his cold brew.

Bobby D took several gulps of beer, belched, and said, "You ever find the a-hole who blew out your windshield?"

"Not yet." Montego had no clue. Curiously, Haley still hadn't asked him about it either. Had he expected the goons to make such a warning? The brief picture of Haley sitting with Leonardo Brunetti flashed.

Montego thought of Lissa Renzo, again.

What does she know?

Chapter 18

Haley paused outside The Palms to stuff his cigarette in a butt receptacle. Shooting The Beak and his cousin in a staged confrontation was the only plan he'd come up with and that would be difficult to make happen.

He checked his wristwatch: Three o'clock straight up.

Show time, Ice Cop. Be cool.

He marched across the dining room to the corner booth where Brunetti sat, his thick fingers tapping the red-checked tablecloth. Haley slid onto the seat opposite, noting the Saturday afternoon business was slow. He was glad that Lissa had the day off.

"Gotcha the hardware you wanted—a *pulito*, clean, twenty-two short with a speakeasy." Brunetti leaned sideways and shoved a small canvas bag along the curved red vinyl bench toward Haley. "Beretta Minx—screw-on tube. Y'gotta like it." His thistly black eyebrows meshed. "Now hit that fuckin' Rat Rondell—'n' do it soon, Neallie Baby, or live to regret it."

"How do you know I won't use this piece on your big ass, Beak?" Haley had made his words come out like they'd been sliced in a deli meat cutter. It pleased him.

Brunetti scowled. "'Cause you're smarter than that."

Haley pulled the olive drab-colored sack closer. With elbows on the table, he fisted his hands against his mouth, teeth pressed into his knuckles. He caught a faint whiff of gun oil. The meathead was right. Killing him here would be out-and-out murder, yet Haley wanted to. He lowered his hands.

"You think so?"

Brunetti glared at him. "I know so."

"Yeah? How do you suggest the dumb rat-fuck go down? I'm no pro like you or Riffelano was."

"Bullshit—I heard about the Knick hit. You gotta be some good, Haley—or fuckin' lucky. I seen Gordo's action before."

Brunetti was treating Riffelano's death as no loss, Haley noted. Because they belonged to a different crime families? Different loyalties?

"Neallie baby, this time you're the man. The Rat's gotta go down crying like the sneaky chump he is—four double-deuces in the head—from that Minx. I want you telling me the skinny fuck seen the first one coming too—'n' soon."

"What you *want* is crap, Beak." Haley's hands went to his knees. The upstairs brass would never buy him involved in another shooting.

"Anyway, an APB's been issued," he lied. "Some other cop might pop Rondell's ratty ass."

Brunetti sneered. "You're beautiful."

*   *   *

Haley waited for KW to pull away from the gasoline pumps clearing them from the fumes. When he left the service area, Haley cranked down the side window glass with a grunt. He needed fresh air.

KW steered the green prowler west at Sunset.

"Spoke to my snitch. Rat's been mopin' at the old Sunlight Motel."

Haley, nodding, lowered the visor blocking out the sun's rays. He couldn't let Rondell get the chance to dump Brunetti; that would make finding the unknown cousin tough. On the other hand, Rondell's testimony could send the lousy meathead to Q. With Brunetti in prison, there'd still be a chance to ID and ace his cousin and remove the immediate threat to Pop.

KW parked near the corner of Sycamore facing east on Sunset.

Haley craned his neck. "Most of the rooms face our way—if we go to the manager's office, Rondell could spot us."

"S'pose we sit. Sound right by you?" KW eyed Haley.

"Yeah, Rat'll be the only colored—I mean—"

KW tapped Haley's arm. "It's cool. Hey, just 'cause Downtown claims the Rat's a knife wielder, doesn't mean he's not packing firepower."

"Yeah, like most assholes in Jollywood."

Haley pinched a Camel from his shirt pocket. The last daylight minutes slipped into dusk while he considered the escape routes Rondell could take if the prowler was made. Haley had handled calls at the pre-war motel. The low-life stopover cost a sawbuck and was only a five-minute walk north to The Boulevard. It got him to thinking about how the large plate-glass storefronts along the Sidewalk-of-the-Stars were getting gaudier by the day. Merchants hawked chintzy stuff to fun-seekers and those fans in search of their screen idols.

The gawking tourists, movie star maps in-hand, were joined by scads of young hopefuls seeking their big break, stardom and elusive fame.

Many ending up selling their bodies to get by; and, along with them roamed the sleazy rodent-types, like Rat Rondell, who fed off the hopefuls' ignorance in more ways than one.

It was twilight when KW muttered, "Squat here much longer we might smell some Mary Jane—stinking pot."

"If we do, let's shine it until we have our boy in custody." *Damn— why'd I say shine—and boy?* But KW didn't appear to have taken it wrong. Haley had nothing against KW and in the times they'd worked as partners he'd acted decently. Montego swore by "Kay Dub," and thankfully, both cops were proving to be solid.

KW uncurled a finger from the steering wheel and pointed ahead. "Haley—corner room—his nose poked out the open door."

Haley also had spotted the gaunt figure ducking back inside before the interior lamp went out. Night had fallen but the motel's neon lights illuminated him, making him look almost purple.

"The Rat's moving—let's get his ass."

KW kicked over the engine. "He's going east." With the headlights off, KW shifted the idling prowler into Drive, allowing it to roll forward along the south gutter.

"The Rat's moniker fits," Haley said. Rondell had close-cropped hair on an oblong skull balanced on a skinny neck, hunched shoulders, and he moved in short jerky steps. Haley easily pictured a twitching nose. "He's doing a lot of eyeballing."

KW braked. "He's gonna cross Sunset."

"Can't tell if he's packing." Haley snatched the mic.

"Yo—we're made." KW twisted, checked traffic, and, ignoring the red light, burned rubber as they arced through the intersection. "Rat's cutting through the school grounds."

"Asshole—let's hoof it." Haley quickly radioed, "Six-Frank-One requesting backup. We're in foot pursuit going northeast from Orange Drive through the Hollywood High School campus. Subject is a male-Black, twenty years, five-eight, wearing a tan Nehru jacket and dark trousers—wanted for questioning only, but possibly armed."

Momma Mary's verification seemed to take forever. KW already had disappeared into the campus shadows. *Damn it.* Haley dropped the handset, spun out, slammed the door, and chased after his partner.

The high school grounds had shut down, but well-placed security lights offered moderate visibility. He cut across the lawn at the western end of a building and ran north to a chain-linked fence. It encircled the athletic field where years before he had played shortstop for the Marshall High nine against the Hollywood Sheiks.

He jumped and caught the upper wire webbing and muscled himself over. He landed on a gravel track partly covered by open-planked bleachers, and charged through the tunnel the boards created. He emerged from under the structure and spotted KW across the field to the north by the girls' gym. He had already rolled over the top bar of an eight-foot-tall double-gate.

Damn, he's exposed. If Rondell's on the other side of the—?

Five quick shots blasted the night air.

"Damn!" Haley's heart did the calypso. He pumped his arms and legs furiously but his feet were stuck in deep swamp grass, bogged down in a muddy nightmare.

He hit the locked double-gate and leaped for the top, grasping the uppermost links. Sucking in, he pulled up and tumbled over. A finger tore. He lost his hold and crashed to the gravel, banging his knees. He rose, yanked out his revolver. Blood from his finger made the gun grip slippery. His gut knotting, he lurched forward, half-stumbling to the far corner of the gym. His chest heaved. His heart thumped wildly.

The gun barrel aimed, he peered around the corner.

KW, leaning against the building, his blue-steel in hand, eyed him.

"Yo, Haley. Rat drilled me. Got three into his skanky black ass."

Ronald Rondell, his Nehru jacket bloodstained, lay splayed on the ground scant yards from KW now sinking to a sitting position, still clinging to his service piece.

Haley moved past his downed partner, Haley's S&W still pointed at Rondell's rail-thin body as he released a tight breath. Haley bent over, twisted the snub-nose revolver free of Rondell's hold, and slid it toward KW. Haley felt for a neck pulse. None.

So much for keeping Rat Rondell safe. Brunetti got what he wanted. Would it matter that I wasn't the one to do it?

Holstering his magnum, he swiftly moved to KW's side.

"Rat's no longer a witness against Brunetti." Haley bit his tongue realizing KW might think he was pissed at him for killing Rondell. He tugged out his clean handkerchief. "Let me check you—he got you twice, one feels fleshy—I think it's a graze."

He spotted blood trailing down the rough-textured dark brick wall, so he ran his fingers across KW's back to feel for moisture.

Damn, where's the backup?

"Backup's coming, Dealer. One slug's a through-and-through." He nodded at the Charter Arms .357 near KW's feet as he dropped onto his butt. While supporting KW in a sitting position, Haley pushed the wadded handkerchief against the mushy exit hole.

"The Rat used a three-fifty-seven."

"Feels like a damn forty-four Anaconda." KW groaned and angled his right hip up. "Grab my rag. It's clean, Neall." He grinned lopsidedly and set his revolver beside him.

Haley found the "rag" and balled it into the entry wound. He hadn't missed that his wounded partner had called him "Neall," not Haley, for the first time. Was it because he'd call his muscular partner, "Dealer"?

He smiled inwardly recalling how Montego had referred to him as "Neall" after being called "Tonto."

"Can you hold this, Dealer? Press it hard—"

"We heard shots—sonofabitch," Bobby Diaz whooped as he raced toward them across the schoolyard quad. Trev Brannock was at his heels.

"Yo, Bad Bobby—Trev. What took you so long?" KW's raspy voice sounded forced. He laid his hand on Haley's forearm and winked. The touch felt like a millstone.

Bobby D said, "I'll get an RA unit rolling." He sped away.

Haley unclipped and rolled his necktie. He pressed it against KW's side wound, gnashing molars in anguish for not being at KW's side in time.

*   *   *

Leo Brunetti sat in the Continental Club on Cahuenga. He'd been on the phone with Chicago. Momo had told him, "Take the vig, Leo—play along."

Signaling for another Compari-and-Soda, Brunetti spied his cousin, Nino, jouncing through the doorway, bright sunlight silhouetting him.

"Hey, Leo. Saw your fancy Caddy outside—thought I'd haves me a drink, too." Simeti grabbed a stool next to Brunetti and ordered a Grappa.

When the drink arrived, Simeti smashed his bubble gum wad under the counter, leaving his mouth a slit below deeply sunken cheeks.

"Them cops takin' out that gang rat was some good. Heard it wasn't Blondie—heard it was his fuckin' nigger partner who done it."

"Yeah?" Brunetti, pissed, ripped the cellophane off a fresh cigar.

Time to hurt Neallie Baby 'n' his ol' man bad. 'N' Blue Eyes, too.

Chapter 19

Montego received a phone call from Yolanda three days after the Rondell shooting. To his delight, KW was being released from the hospital. She also said he was anxious to go home, but she was involved in a felony trial, and could Montego please pick up KW at Central Receiving Hospital?

Inside the hospital room Montego beamed at his partner sitting on the bed, dressed in street clothes, obviously ready to go.

"Yolanda called me," Montego said.

KW looked surprised but pleased. "That's four trips in three days. Knew Yola was tied up defending some loser. Thought the dapper little lawyer might show up instead."

"Disappointed?" Montego had gotten a call from Brad Kozier soon after the shooting and had hightailed it to the Police and Fire Ward at CRH, returning each day thereafter to check on KW.

"It shows, huh—wiseacre? Got discharged, had to call the nurse." KW shrugged. "Protocol, you know."

They waited for the nurse. When she came in, Montego went out the rear exit to Loma Drive and up the hill to his pickup. He drove it to the bottom of the ramp where the plump nurse had parked a frowning KW.

A grunting sound escaped him when he rose from the wheelchair. He thanked the nurse, and using Montego's arm for support, climbed onto the truck seat.

"I figured it would take something like a couple of bullets to slow your Jim Brown butt."

"Won't be slowed for long, Tonto—hit nothing vital."

"I might have to tell Strait that you're a candidate for TMA."

"The Toughest Man Alive? Don't be rattling that man's cage."

After a ride to South L.A. filled with idle chatter, they arrived in front of KW's recently painted clapboard house. Montego went around the front of truck to help, but his partner insisted on getting himself out.

Montego grabbed the purple-and-gold-trimmed bag with a bottle of Crown Royal inside. It had been on the floor behind the driver's seat. Seeing a For Sale by Owner sign staked into the dry grass, he nodded to it.

"Leaving the neighborhood?"

"Yola loves a house in Ladera Heights." KW opened the door.

"And whatever Yola wants, Yola gets," Montego sing-sang. "Just kidding. Explains the new paint job—hey," he pointed at the cartons along a wall inside, "moving before you sell?"

"Yola's idea." KW removed a stack of *Sentinel* newspapers, *Ebony* magazines, and what looked like circulars from a worn floral-printed Queen Anne. He motioned for Montego to sit as he eased onto a matching chair.

Montego dropped onto spring-broken chair. "You hurting a bit?"

"Slug missed the vitals. Likes reminding me, s'all."

"I can only imagine. And now, you're moving west, young man?" Montego chuckled.

"Little house on a little hill. Rudy forked over the down payment— a loan. Equity in this pad should help cover it and furnish the new digs."

Montego figured the strain of lifting the magazines had darkened KW's face, but knowing his pal, considered that he might be embarrassed.

After a moment, KW said, "Yola and I are hooking up Sunday."

Montego quickly sat up. "Married? That's in five days!"

"Noon at the new house. Small ceremony. You coming?"

"What do you think?" Montego stretched back. *How Kay Dub's life will change.* KW once had mentioned Yolanda's political aspirations. It reminded Montego of the day KW had told him, "Thought I was Kirtland Wellington till I was seven, when a man named Eddie Deal came around, the day I first heard my true surname. Much rather've been a Wellington— mother's maiden name."

Yolanda probably would prefer it, too.

"You're talking life-time stuff mi amigo, and you *are* still on Injured-On-Duty status."

"Told you, Tonto, I wasn't going be slowed for long. 'Sides, I got the OK from Sergeant Whitehead to be gone two weeks while I'm IOD. Medical Liaison Officer's an understanding man. Saw me twice each day."

"Sergeant Joe's good people." Several years earlier, the gravelly voiced homicide dick had transferred from the Detective Bureau to the Medical Unit in Personnel and Training Bureau explaining to Montego that he wanted to be where he could be of help to his laid-up fellow officers.

Montego also knew Joe Whitehead had taken the new assignment because he had similar misgivings about the unsolved Black Dahlia case. He, too, had sounded like Eagon Quinn.

"And Yolanda doesn't want a fancy wedding?"

"Did." KW chortled. "Not my style."

"There's hope for you yet." Montego handed him the bottle. "This was supposed to help your recovery. Consider it an early wedding present."

"Thanks—appreciate the lift home, too, Mike." KW set the purple-sacked bottle on the floor. Turning slightly toward the front window, he moved the isinglass curtain aside. Sunbeams cleaved the room, spotlighting the peeling wallpaper on the wall behind him. He gazed out the window.

"Ice Cop visited me in the Police and Fire Ward looking kinda blue. Told him it was my fault, should've waited till he finished radioing."

Montego had heard about the Rat Rondell shooting the next day. He realized that meant Haley would be RFD pending review of Nick Karos' OIS report. It didn't matter that Haley's weapon hadn't been fired.

KW still stared out the window.

"Needed more hand speed, might not've gotten drilled."

"Could've been worse." Montego slowly slid his palms over the Queen Anne's tattered arms, grinning. "I reckon the neighbor kids skedaddled when they saw my voodoo wagon rolling down their street."

On his first visit, KW had excused himself and gone outside to speak to several youngsters grouping near the polished Cameo Carrier. When he returned, Montego had asked, "What made the kids split?" KW had answered in a serious voice, "Pointed at the small Apache 31 chrome sign on the side panel and told the rascals that a honky savage already had chopped off thirty-one fingers of every red, yellow, black and white boy who'd ever touched it without his first saying it was 'Yokay.'"

KW then had dipped his head toward Montego, adding, "Told them the blue-eyed devil strung all the fingers together into a voodoo necklace and kept the bloody stubs inside the glove box. Made like I was about to open her up, hoping they'd run, but they were curious. Then I jumped at them like I was the Tasmanian devil—man did they ever skedaddle."

Chuckling, KW let the thin curtain drop back. Bending slowly, he grasped the bourbon bottle and fingered the thin gold cord until it loosened from the gathered velveteen.

"OK, Masked Man." Montego tried to sound like Jay Silver Heels, the Indian actor who played the Lone Ranger's companion. "Powwow with Tonto." That KW might unload something bothering him, pleased Montego.

"Never could fool my sidekick." KW frowned. "Rudy was at the hospital last night. Told me he had something to show you—he's anxious, wants to see you Friday afternoon at our new house. 'Course I'm sitting in—that's *if* you choose to see the little man."

Chapter 20

Montego left KW's home curious. What did the lawyer-turned politician have for him that KW wanted to hear? Wheeling the pickup north toward the station Montego reckoned that the Caribbean cruise honeymoon KW had unintentionally copped to would be good for him.

Neall could use a long break, too.

That morning, Montego had called the DAY watch commander to see when Haley would return to work and learned he was already back on duty but was taking a Special. The guy had accumulated a ton of overtime during the past year. Not that uncommon for hard chargers, especially when the arrests were made at EOW. Montego chided himself. End-of-watch busts weren't that unusual, but the Riffelano take-down? The early hour had been deliberate. Haley had commented there would be no bystanders; did he actually mean there would be no witnesses?

Why did I think that?

Montego cruised north under a canopy of half-century-old elms and sycamores lining the parkways of Rossmore Avenue, past lawns wetted by sprinklers. The lush-green aprons fronted the beaux arts mansions tucked amongst mature and well-maintained shrubbery of myriad varieties.

Hancock Park was mostly in Wilshire Division. He'd gotten called into the Seventh Division's area once during his rookie year. Bobby Diaz, his partner tonight, was his only backup that day. Requests for police in the old-moneyed neighborhood were few. Unseen entry was rare. Too many servants in the daytime made it difficult for even the boldest burglar. In any event, most residents kept their lives private.

A shift with the upbeat Bobby D, the brown sinewy cop with the classic Native American profile, promised to be a hoot. Recently, during roll call, he had let out a loud war whoop and shouted, "I'm a Mexican-Comanche with an eagle totem." Then he'd brushed his sharp-hooked nose with the large feather he kept stowed in his briefcase. He later confided that he'd plucked it from a white turkey at a local poultry store, dyeing the plume to make it appear to have come from a bald eagle.

Their friendship deepened when Bobby D said he was born in Mazatlán. Montego had replied that his father had been born in neighboring Concordia. Montego didn't mention his mother having once made the point:

"Your dad, Jesse Quintero, didn't think of himself as Mexican, but as a Catalan Spaniard with some French blood." Bobby D had spouted, "Aiee, if it weren't for your stony blues, we'd be blood brothers."

In response, Montego had joked, "They're Viking's eyes, Bobby." Who knew their true ancestry anyway?

At the station, he obtained Haley's number but got no answer when he dialed. After roll call inspection, he told Bobby D that he'd like to stop by The Palms and see if Haley was there. "Kay Dub said Ice Cop came by the hospital looking 'kinda blue.' I'd like to ease his mind."

Montego curbed the prowler around the corner from the restaurant as Bobby D radioed, "Code Six."

Strolling toward the restaurant, Montego said, "If any mob goons are inside be cool around the waitress, she's Neall's gal."

When they stepped into the foyer Lissa saw them and came up. Montego looked past her to the empty table by the kitchen entry.

"Neall's not here?"

"No. He called earlier and said he'd be at my place after I got off." Her face briefly lost its glow. "I think seeing his other partner laid up really bothered him."

"Sad, but understandable, Lissa." Montego turned. "Bobby Diaz meet Lissa Renzo." He was amused by Bobby D's reaction. The wiry cop, his hands stiff at his sides, gaped until Lissa grabbed hold of his right hand.

"Hi, Bobby Diaz." She winked at Montego.

He edged ahead and peeked into the sparsely filled dining room. "You expecting Pio or any of his goons?"

She frowned. "Not for awhile."

"In that case, how about a couple of black coffees and slices of warm cherry pie à la mode." He remembered what Bobby D liked.

"You got it." She led them to the table by the kitchen door.

Montego took a seat, but Bobby D remained standing, goggle-eyed.

"Bobby, she's Neall's girl," Montego whispered. "Remember?"

Bobby D glanced down at him and quickly sat.

Montego added, "Kay Dub blames himself for Neall's blues 'cause he ran after Rondell before Momma Mary's Code Six confirmation."

"*Si*, Trev and me got there first. Ice Cop had Dealer wrapped like a *burrito grande*. And Haley looked *muy enfermo*, like he needed a barf bag."

Montego could only imagine the scene. He felt for Haley holding a bleeding KW.

"He's getting hitched on Sunday, Bobby."

"Ice Cop?"

"Nope—Kay Dub."

"Aieee—I met *su mujer bonita* at our division's Christmas party. Dealer's gonna need *mucho mas tiempo,* Bobby D's expression turned serious, "to recover from his wounds . . . and *de su luna de miel,* from his honeymoon, too." He cracked a suggestive smile.

That festive affair also was when Montego had met Yolanda. She had worn a flowing ankle-length, midnight blue, Egyptian-style satin dress looking like a sultry Cleopatra must've appeared to Mark Antony.

"Yep. The woman's smooth looks do hint pleasurable things."

Lissa arrived with their warm pies and a big scoop of French vanilla ice cream on top.

"You boys want anything else?" She smiled warmly.

"Nope." Montego noted that Bobby D seemed fascinated by the large pink blossoms on her button-front blouse. "But this curious cop would like to hear any goon-stuff you hear and think might be of interest."

"I told you, they hush up whenever I'm close, except for that pest, Mario Zippi—he's always bragging about being tight with Dante's crowd."

She paused, smiling. "But I'll try to listen—just for you, Mike."

Chapter 21

Haley stepped into Lissa's kitchenette and withdrew a bottle of Bud from the fridge. Popping off the top, he went into the living area to lounge on the short sofa. His thoughts had been on KW Deal. It had gutted him seeing his second partner in the hospital He supposed it could just as easily have been him, because he would've been slow on drawing down on The Rat. Still, that did nothing to ease the damn pain he felt.

He gulped some beer as his mind centered on Brunetti's cousin who had spied Pop in Brentwood. *Damn bad luck.* Pop must've been out checking on his crews. He had mentioned have job sites from Glendale west to Mandeville Canyon.

Haley had an idea how to snuff Beak Brunetti and his cousin and have Montego be a witness. The plan made him damn nervous: he would tell Brunetti he refused to play his game, that his pop knew he'd been found and was going to turn the tables. He'd say The Purple Hand intended to waste their asses. *Pure bull.* But first he must ID the cousin, and Nancy had yet to come through. She'd said she was leery about getting too nosy.

He'd put his plan to work just as soon as he located that meathead. Snatch his ass and strap him inside the Porsche, make him play the damn "mark" so that Brunetti would kill the meathead believing he was Pop.

Then I'll blow The Beak's hairy ass away.

To pull it off, Haley needed the perfect scenario and a location where Brunetti couldn't get a good look at the Angelo Sancia stand-in. If it went down the way Haley hoped, it would be deemed a legal shooting—although it was a set up. The sole problem was using Montego as a witness.

Lissa, barefoot, came in from the bedroom wearing a sheer pink nightgown. She gave Haley a smile and entered the kitchenette. He watched her pour a half-glass of Chablis and felt a warm surge within him.

"Mike came in tonight—a Bobby Diaz was with him. He's cute," she said. "Mike asked about you."

"That's Monte—Mike for you." The surge subsided. Haley recalled the night she'd mentioned pointing out Momo Giancana to Montego. Why was the Chicago crime boss in L.A.? Was Brunetti's cousin connected with him? He thought of Montego's fancy truck's windshield and swigged more beer, his mind filling with doubts.

If the mob is involved, then the plan is a no go. I gotta find out—

Lissa padded to the sofa, bringing the wine bottle with her glass, and sat close to him. Drawing in the soft, rose-scent of the Joy perfume he'd given her, he slipped his hand under her gown and stroked her smooth thigh. The warm stirring surged within him, again.

"Do me a favor, hon, when Mike, or any cop for that matter, shows up at The Palms, cool it—cut the yakking."

She scooted off the short sofa, snatched the wine glass, and stormed into the kitchen alcove.

"Mike *is* your partner—we're just friends, Neall."

"Hon," *Crap* "don't be sore." His surge subsided. "Look, I don't want any of those mob meatheads agitated. It's not smart, the thick-necks seeing you talking to us cops—I should stay the hell out of there, too."

He chugged the beer, emptying the bottle and feeling the intensity of her brown eyes. Even from where she stood, they burned into him with a mixture of anger and hurt, compassion and passion. *Damn it.* He'd been behaving badly for weeks now: one moment drawing her to him, the next, because of his jealousy, distancing himself—like now. It was obvious she didn't want to be pushed away. He was acting the fool, but her safety meant everything to him.

On their first date, she'd told him how the glittering neon lights had brought her to Hollywood, but the people she'd met were not her type, not until he had walked into her life. She had said he was different. Quiet, but confident. More importantly, caring.

He had come to believe that she would always remain a sweet Washington farm girl, and for a time stay somewhat naïve. He liked feeling the protector, but the jealousy he harbored since the night she'd been with Montego had become another ache.

Haley rose and took the empty beer bottle into the kitchenette. Returning to the sofa, he reached out. She came to him. They embraced.

His hand slipped back under her gown. The surge returned big time.

The telephone clanged.

They broke apart, both sighing deep breaths.

She picked up the receiver and said tentatively, "Hello?"

After a moment she shrugged, frowned, and cradled the receiver.

"Nobody was there. The line went dead."

Chapter 22

Montego held the screen open until KW secured the dead bolt on the front door. Letting the door swing shut, he went with KW down the creaky steps, avoiding the protruding nail-heads.

"Thanks for picking me up, Mike—my Ford's in the shop. Yola will drive me over to get it after this little meet."

Montego had paused to right the For Sale sign on the brown grass, Montego noticed KW out on the sidewalk looking up and down the street.

"The kids skedaddled when they saw my voodoo-wagon pull up."

"Tonto be shuckin'. It's Friday. Kids better be in school. Yo— ready to see the little lawyer?"

"Pretty mysterious—dontcha think?'"

"S'pose the dapper little man will settle your worried mind some." KW eased into the truck and rolled down the side window, grimacing a bit.

Montego climbed behind the wheel. "Yours, too." He revved the V8 causing the twin Glas-pacs to emit a mellow rumble.

The hint of autumn added to his high spirits. The night before, he had aced an evidence exam. He drove west to Ladera Heights where KW directed him onto Vista de Oro and up the grade.

"Whoa, amigo—your new pad? You told me 'little'—my *Perch* wouldn't fill half this house."

"Got a bargain. Told you, Rudy knows people."

"Knows a good *deal*, for sure." Montego, chuckling at his pun, angled the front wheels into the curb and killed the motor.

He scrambled out and around the pickup while scanning the yard and Spanish-style house with an appreciative eye.

Heading for the front door, KW said, "Turned out, the place was being sold mostly furnished, complete with fresh coats of Dutch Boy inside and out—a turnkey, kinda." He casually peeked at Montego. "Owners were the fastidious type."

Rudolph Forrall, his attire was that of a Master's Golf Tournament winner, was waiting for them at the open entry with an arm was around his daughter's belted waist. He smiled widely. Yolanda wore a gold-colored chemise. A pair of tortoise-shell combs held her hair back tightly.

Montego immediately detected her pleasantly sweet fragrance, similar to the small white pikake flower often strung into Hawaiian leis.

Forrall was smiling widely. "It's good to see you again, Mike." He nodded to KW. "It pleases me that you have come." He swung his free hand about him. "What do you think?" His paternal pleasure showed.

"I just told Kay Dub, very impressive."

"Sunday's wedding will be in the rear garden." Forrall led them inside toward a wet bar by the dining room.

"Come with me, Mike." Yolanda gave a tour like an art curator, describing the period furniture pieces, the oil paintings, the porcelain figurines, and the crystal items.

KW followed, both hands in his pockets. At the end of the tour he murmured, "Most of this stuff is on loan from Rudy."

The three went through an arched hallway into the living area where Forrall, in the dining room, was setting down a tumbler filled with an amber-colored liquor.

"We'll sit in here." He waved them to him.

They joined Forrall, who stepped to a side bar and poured a glass of white wine. He returned and handed his daughter a half-full glass.

"Chardonnay, dear." He eyed Montego. "What can I get for you?"

"Coke's fine . . . Rudy."

KW was at the bar, pouring Crown Royal into a crystal snifter.

Forrall slipped out of his cashmere coat, draped it over a chair, and gestured for them to sit. He then picked up a Manila envelope and faced Montego from across the table.

"I'm certain you know that this district, the Eighth, is undergoing a cultural change."

"Yes, you've told me." Montego steeled himself for another boring homily, anticipating it to be political this time.

"Well, change brings new ideas, Mike—ideas that can be profound, but for those ideas to be appreciated fully a bold and progressive leadership will be necessary." Forrall paused to sip from his tumbler. "I believe it's my obligation, my duty, actually, to undertake that challenging role."

Yolanda cast an adoring look. "And so you should, Father."

Montego, imagining Forrall's thin chest swelling with pride under his light-pink polo shirt, glanced at KW whirling the whiskey in the snifter.

"I had Kirtland ask you here, because I have positive proof of wrongdoing by Councilman Preston." Forrall lifted the flap on the large envelope. "I'm not talking about malfeasance in office, I'm talking about poor judgment in his private life. Gross moral errors that, if made public, would subject him to much contempt not only by his colleagues down in City Hall, but also by his constituents as well."

Montego shifted in the chair. *Why me?* He realized he'd drained his glass when Yolanda took it to the wet bar and refilled it.

He believed he knew Eugene Preston's thoughts and for sure knew he'd been approached by "certain people." Something would come of that, and it couldn't be good.

"I've heard that the councilman thinks the proposed ordinance liberalizes liquor licensing." Montego paused, but Forrall stayed silent. Viewing the lawyer as though he were a poker player holding a pat hand Montego continued, "It's common knowledge that Councilman Preston objects to increasing the number of liquor-serving establishments in his district."

"Yes, it's no secret, and I can accept his position. It's his bigotry that's most troubling. That's what had prompted me to go after his council seat." Forrall stepped to the bar and poured another drink from a blue-labeled bottle of Johnny Walker Scotch.

"I'm really not into politics, sir." Montego swallowed some Coke.

"Rudy, please, Mike. Yes, well, we have no reason to dabble in such nonsense, anyway. I simply wanted a moment of your time to show you the positive proof I have." He looked at his daughter. "Sadly, dear, shocking photographic evidence like what I am about to display could well come up in your criminal practice."

Yolanda, smiling, leaned over and kissed her fiance's cheek before doe-eyeing Montego across from her. The scent of pikake wafted.

Forrall fanned a dozen or so 8"x10" black-and-white glossy photographs on the table like they were large playing cards.

Montego, rubbing a thumbnail, listened to Forrall.

"These came into my possession a week ago—quite surreptitiously I must add—and ever since, I have given much thought about what to do with them." Forrall eyed Montego.

"So, let us consider what might be deemed as appropriate action— perhaps better—what action is sorely required."

Montego bore his gaze into Forrall's eyes, not viewing the glossies, knowing they must depict Preston in some kind of compromising situation.

"This is not something I care to be involved in—*sir.*"

121

Rudolph Forrall's focus didn't waver. "I am afraid there is no real choice, Mike. You have a lady friend, I believe—a rather close relative to the councilman."

Montego instantly stiffened. *Ah, that's why he wanted me here.* He caught KW's wide-eyed expression looking at Yolanda who was gazing at the photos.

"Please explain . . . Rudy," Montego said.

Forrall's Chesire grin revealed his small even teeth. "I would think that your connection to the councilman, albeit distant, subjects you to a difficult situation." He paused to down more drink. "Don't you believe that knowing what Preston has done warrants your personal concern?"

Montego eyed KW now finishing his Crown Royal, the raised snifter partially concealing his face.

If I knew the facts perhaps I would be better able to protect Julie from embarrassment.

Viewing the "evidence" had to be. He glanced at the nearest photograph depicting an attractive black woman arm-in-arm with a shorter, well-dressed, white man. The large-bosomed woman wore a shiny dark-colored halter-blouse, a skintight white mini-skirt that accentuated her buttocks, and open-toed, backless shoes with glittery stiletto heels. The pair stood at a numbered door. Eugene Preston's thin face, although shadowed, revealed a silly grin.

Not very innocent looking, councilman.

"A hooker." Forrall took a seat. "I'm told Satin Sheen is her name."

Montego looked at Forrall and took the eight-by-tens, sliding each one to KW after a brief look. Eugene Preston was inside the room on a bed. His pasty face was visible in each picture. Several showed the naked call girl straddling his scrawny body. The contrasting skin colors were striking. In two photos, she held the glans of his penis against her tongue, her fingers concealing the shaft. Preston didn't appear to be actively involved in any of the bed shots. His pinched-face appeared to be lifeless, and his eyes heavy-lidded, not like in the photograph outside the motel room that caught him grinning, obviously alert and willingly accompanying the smiling whore.

His big mistake.

What Montego believed he chose not to say: it was a setup. But it didn't matter, whatever flowed through the councilman's bloodstream during the "posing," had to be given to him after he had entered the room.

The Purple Hand

The narrow-minded politician appeared to have been a teetotaler unless he was a closet drinker. Whatever. He was a complete phony—a hypocrite.

Montego's thoughts circled back to the Sunday in the Preston's vestry library and the prim councilman's bigoted words while he gazed at the large ornately framed Sallman print of Jesus Christ above the mantel.

The Coke had soured on Montego's tongue. He looked at KW glaring at Forrall. Yolanda was slipping the glossies into the envelope. She pushed the packet across to Montego, her large eyes steady on his.

He ignored the envelope and looked coldly at Forrall.

"I take it, Rudy, that you believe it would be prudent of me to approach Preston with these prints and suggest that he consider his civic obligation to the public office he presently holds."

"Kirtland said you were bright, Mike." Forrall downed his Scotch, nodded slightly at his daughter, and rose.

It ended the discussion.

KW's dark eyes stayed fixed on Forrall. Yolanda patted KW's arm.

Perplexed by KW's silence, and not wanting to be accusatory, Montego also stood, and to the three simply said, "*Hasta luego.*"

Forrall seemed to be contemplating his soon to be son-in-law, who remained seated his eyes focused on his future father-in-law.

Meanwhile, Yolanda, smiling pleasantly, got up and accompanied Montego to the front door. She reminded him that the wedding would be Sunday at noon.

He said he'd be wearing a sports outfit.

She seemed hesitant to say anything. Then she thrust the envelope at him, saying, "Semi-formal is fine."

His eyes boring into hers, he said, "Your new home and furnishings are lovely, Yolanda—and your father, Rudy, is *quite* the guy." Reluctantly, he accepted the large envelope.

Once inside the pickup, he squeezed the steering wheel like a boa. "*Tanto!*" Rudolph Forrall Esquire indirectly had involved his daughter and KW—*and me* directly—in whatever he was scheming.

On Crenshaw, Montego pulled over at a public telephone booth, stashed the Manilla envelope behind the driver's seat, and jumped out.

He hurriedly dialed Quinn's office number.

He was surprised when a woman answered, "Eagon Quinn law offices—this is Margie."

"Uh, is Eagon there?"

"Who may I say is calling?"

He gave his name. A moment passed before his mentor came on the line. "Hello Mikey."

"Eagon—you free?"

"Bad timing, son—I'm in the middle of something."

"Can you be at The Bull Pen tonight alone—if Roy won't mind?"

"You buying?—OK, table's ours. Roy's on horseback riding high in the Idaho back country, elk hunting."

"Great—see you there."

Montego left the booth, anger, disappointment, and concern eating at him: anger and disappointment because KW might have conspired with Forrall, and concern because a scandal would embarrass Julie. Her uncle was a blue-nosed prude; still, he had to be told that he'd been set up. Surely he would realize that by not having the photo negatives he was a dead duck. He would have to give up his council seat.

Possession of the sex photos was heavy stuff—it involved the mob. Dante Pio must want Forrall on the council expecting the lawyer to force Preston to give up his seat. But how it was to be done, Pio wouldn't know for sure, unless specific instructions had been given. Perhaps he had given no instructions, expecting human nature to take its course, knowing that Rudolph Forrall sought publicity and power.

Whatever the situation, Rudolph Forrall obviously meant to buffer his soon-to-be son-in-law, his daughter, and himself.

By the time Montego turned into the station parking lot his belly had knotted from a feeling of let down. Betrayal was more like it.

It's a good thing Kay Dub's on IOD status.

Working an eight-hour watch in the prowler with the guy would've been like patrolling for a whole watch in a Crosley mini-coupe. But maybe that would've been better—force the air to be cleared between them.

Tanto—what if Pio knew a cop was engaged to Forrall's daughter? Had he told Rudolph Forrall to use KW's LAPD badge for extra leverage to oust Preston?

But Rudy passed the photographs to me. . . . To use my badge?

Suddenly, a cold snake wriggled up Montego's spine, slithered across his shoulders, splitting into a pair, each snake racing down an arm.

He shivered involuntarily .

Did the mob capo know about Julie?

124

Chapter 23

Montego, using the wood banister, dragged himself up to the second floor where he slogged into the dicks' squad room. The stale cigarette smoke further assaulted his senses. Nervous sweat had him feeling like a wet leaf pasted against a flat rock.

Alex Strait pulled open the top drawer of the file cabinet behind him. "Saw you coming." He slipped out a folder. "Here's a rap sheet, a mug shot, and a felony warrant for a bear cub: Collis Ulysses Blagden—initials C U B." He handed over the small photograph and two papers. Smirking, he twisted a tip of his baby handlebar.

"Cute, Uncle Alex." Montego slid back Wayne's chair.

"We think he's good for the Paoli Salico bombing." Strait patted the case file on his blotter. "Mister Blagden's car got cited. It was parked around the corner on Saint Andrews Place in the Sears Roebuck yellow loading zone—the night of the bombing hullabaloo. A slick-sleeve wrote the parking Greenie. Wasn't that gentlemanly of the fella?"

Montego plopped down. "So Blagden stayed around to watch the fireworks—a good break. You got an address for this bear cub?"

"Twelve-twenty-one Virgil. He also failed to appear on a disorderly conduct charge. We only have a misdemeanor warrant, but its enough for nighttime service." Strait handed the writ over, adding, "If you're up on Greek names, you might know that Ulysses means wrathful. Mister Blagden is six-six and two-eighty. Perhaps, you should wait until your brawny partner, Deal, is available?"

"He's IOD, besides, he'll be honeymooning the next two weeks." Montego jotted down the number into his pocket-sized field notebook. "I'm with Ice Cop tonight." Standing, he shoved the barrel-backed chair against the table. "See you at The Clam Digger tomorrow noon."

"You buying?"

Montego shook his head.

What's with this, "You buying" stuff?

After roll call he joined Haley standing with Sergeant Kozier in the supervisors' room next to the watch commander's office. He told them about "Cubby Bear," the term Strait had given to Collis Blagden.

Later, while maneuvering the prowler eastbound through traffic on Sunset, Montego said, "What do you think, Neall, take a ride to the cub's den, see what it looks like?"

Haley closed his plastic briefcase and tossed it onto the back seat. "Yeah. I'm curious about the asshole. Got a hunch."

"Hunch?"

"Around six weeks ago down on Adams, a store got blown up. Suspect used DuPont Dynagel dynamite similar to what you told me was used at the Saint Andrews blast." Haley cleared their unit, racking the hand-mic on the dash clip. "Blue-suits had a witness claiming a male strange to the neighborhood strolled the street afterward. The dicks never nabbed the suspect's ass, or anyone else's."

Montego recalled Quinn telling him about the south-side bombing. Turning into an area of wood-sided four-flat apartment buildings he coasted the Plymouth to the corner at Fountain Avenue.

"We bust this guy it should be interesting what a search shows."

"Won't it? Looks quiet, let's do a walk-see."

Montego saw Haley flinch and figured he'd realized his faux pas. He'd just decided what they'd be doing. To ease his concern, Montego said, "We'll be the only ones in dressy duds. How about a cruise by first, see what gives?" It was no secret that suspects knowing they had outstanding warrants would be on guard for any cop closing in to bust them.

"Do it."

Passing under a streetlight, Montego noted Haley cracking a slight smile. Montego smiled, too.

Another step closer to being a working team.

Upstairs in the 'twenties-era clapboard structure he saw a light; downstairs the windows were dark. He detected no movement by the upper window and made a U-turn, passing the building again before parking out of sight of the apartments on the next block south.

"You want the front or the back?"

"I'll take the rear corner, Mike—this side. When you buzz, 'Cubby' could head out the back. I'll be waiting."

"Holler, if he does."

Moments later, Montego was on the porch looking at a pair of half-glassed wooden doors. Stamped-metal numbers 1221 and 1221-1/4, with abalone shell doorbell buttons, were screwed to the wall by the entry.

Twice he pressed the button assigned to 1221 and heard the shrill noise in the downstairs unit, but got no reply. He buzzed a third time and waited until convinced there'd be no answer. He jogged around back to where Haley was crouched and said in a low voice, "Nothing gives."

"Give me a minute to check the windows, see if I can spot anything worthwhile," Haley whispered back.

"I'll be on the front porch. I see Cubby, I'll hit the door buzzer." Montego suspected Haley planned to "creep" the pad hoping to find evidence to tie Collis Blagden to the Paoli Salico bombing. Such verbal misdirection between partner officers was one way to cover clandestine actions; also it avoided lying to Chief Parker's headhunters downtown in Internal Affairs Division.

IAD, housed in the PAB, was a necessary but an unforgiving entity. Montego had spent a long tiresome night in a soundproofed closet-sized room on the fifth floor. Once burned, twice learned. He hoped Haley wouldn't do anything stupid that would put his butt up there, again.

Montego eased into the deeper shadows near the 1221 porch entry, and breathed in the late-September evening air, catching the trace of spice left over from home-cooked dinners. He mused. They hadn't talked about Lissa, the Rondell shooting, or about KW, but Haley seemed different—more purposeful, or preoccupied. Whatever it was, Ice Cop wasn't sharing.

What else is new?

Back inside their unit, Haley said, "Picked this up." He held a small card as he switched on the overhead. "The Black Smith's Steel Bar Gym—shows a large solid black figure lifting a barbell—a West Jefferson address. There's a hand-printed phone number on the back."

Montego keyed the starter. "Any Dynagel in sight?"

"No dynamite," Haley murmured.

Chapter 24

A half hour after EOW, Montego took in the recorded sounds of a roaring *"Olé!"* and went to the round bar. He bought a Scotch-rocks for Quinn and a Bud for himself. With the drinks in hand he headed for the banquette.

"Hey, Mikey, I was pulling your leg a bit about you buying." Quinn raised his deep voice over the jabber in the room. "But thanks, son." He slid a coaster under the fresh drink and leaned back on the padded chair.

"You're always pulling somebody's something, Señor Counselor." Montego brought the longneck to his mouth, gunned down a healthy amount, and stared at the red-and-white beer label before worrying its damp edges with his thumbnail. He was unsure where to start.

"Eagon, I just realized where I got the habit of saying 'a bit.'"

Quinn, chuckling, lifted his dark brown fedora enough to scratch his widow's peak. He set the felt hat back at its normal after-hours angle and struck a wooden blue-tipped match to a fresh El Presidente. He rolled the cigar as he puffed. When he seemed satisfied with the burn, he said, "I'm awaiting."

Montego realized it wouldn't matter where he began. "It has to do with Julie's uncle." The hubbub in the room prompted him to speak louder, that or his own agitation. "He's Councilman Preston."

Eagon Quinn's gaze flickered from the flame to Montego while he continued puffing the cigar.

"I didn't know. Are we getting into a bit of politics this early morn?"

After several interruptions from raucous cops, Montego completed the Forrall-sex photo scenario with how KW had ignored him during the display, and having a feeling of being betrayed.

"I couldn't get him to look me in the eyes. First, I thought he didn't know anything, then I see his fiancée, Yolanda, patting his arm, consoling him, like she knew he'd involved me on purpose—if so, why, I wondered?"

Finishing the beer, Montego added, "Kay Dub wanted to sit in—Yolanda sat in, too—maybe as her dad's witness . . . anyway, I got put in the darn middle."

"But you accepted the photographs. Why?" Quinn, using the rim of a glass ashtray, shaped a cone on the smoldering cigar end.

128

"Consciously, I wasn't thinking. Maybe deep down I wanted to hurt Preston—the sanctimonious phony."

"What are you going to do?"

"With Kay Dub, or with what Forrall wants?"

"With those glossies?"

"If I drop them in the mail, Preston just might decide to risk pubic exposure and tell the local feds. I've wiped off my prints, but the *federales*, Santelli and Whyte, could eventually connect me through Julie." Montego thumbed more of the red label until the edges looked like short wings.

"Pete and Ned *are* sharp." Quinn worked his hat back and forth. "And Deal wanting to be there with his lady tells me the two of you had better get some dialogue going if you're going to remain partners—more importantly, if you want to remain close friends. . . . Weigh his baggage, Mikey. If the load is too heavy, shuck it before it takes you down."

"Won't happen." Montego tore a wing off the label.

"Whatever, you boys must talk it out till you're both comfortable." Quinn laid a hand over Montego's and squeezed. "Prowling eight hours together totally depending on each other is like being married."

Like riding in a Crosley mini-coupe.

Montego sighed. "Rudolph Forrall is definitely ambitious. I hope he's not sleeping with the local mob for Kay Dub's sake." He twirled the empty bottle. "Gotta believe in my . . . my friend."

"I hope you're right, for *both* your sakes." Quinn drew in on the cigar. "Say, what brought on the huff between you and Julie last Sunday?"

"A misunderstanding. Stupid in a way, not so stupid in another."

Montego focused on the stripped label and told his version omitting his notion about Lissa—it was only a notion. He hadn't dwelled on it.

Quinn leaned closer. "Don't let the lady slip away. Julie's a gem." He eyed Montego a long moment before replacing the smoldering cigar on the small ashtray and leaning back. "And don't let her uncle's indiscretion affect your feelings for her. She's not part of that."

But to love her while having no respect for her father. . . ?

Montego dropped two Lincolns on the table.

"Thanks, Eagon."

Driving along Vista del Mar he relived the Sunday night when he'd enjoyed fabulous sex on a sandy blanket. He was unable to pinpoint his feelings. He gazed out at the vast Pacific. A large cloud blocked out the moon. The sea was a black void. . . .

Chapter 25

The trill of the doorbell jolted Montego awake. He read the West Clox dial: 8:10. Time to get up anyway. Saturday mornings he often did a workout on the *makiwara* posts down on the deck before biking the mile north to The Clam Digger Bar and Grille. Every Saturday at noon, off-duty cops in the area gathered to swap exaggerations over beers and sloppy chiliburgers. Alex Strait had named the group "The Furry Clam Diggers."

Slipping into volleyball shorts, Montego went to the half-glass door and peered through the lace curtain. He saw a burly figure. Surprised, he swung open the door. "Kay Dub!"

"Woke you, huh? Sorry—"

"No problema. Get your butt inside before my neighbors call the cops on your ebon bod."

KW jumped inside, then frowned, a grin sneaking across his strong clean-shaven face. His hand dropped to his right side.

"Gotcha." Montego, hoping he sounded congenial, shut the door saying, "Welcome to rustic Pelican's Perch."

"Gotta explain yesterday, Mike." A familiar looking V grooved KW's forehead, his hand remained against his side.

"Get comfy." Montego pointed to a stool as he padded barefoot into the kitchen nook, noting KW still was hurting. "I'll start the java brewing."

KW straddled a barstool and spread his hands on the wheat-colored tile. "Those dirty pictures surprised me. Had to be a rigged scene. Don't believe Rudy understood that Preston was a pigeon. Damn well called Daddio on it, too." His words had spouted like rainwater.

Montego, reading a "You believe that?" expression on KW's face, filled a Silex coffee pot from the Sparkletts bottle; then he took an MJB can from the Frigidaire, dumped in three full measures of ground coffee and fired up the gas burner. All the while, KW silently watched.

Montego put the Silex on the stove.

"Go on, amigo."

"Didn't know what Rudy was up to—Yola said she was ignorant too." KW, sighing, pivoted on the stool. "He told me they showed up without his knowing. Claimed his gym manager—found them." KW's tone sharpened. "Rudy's hands are clean—least ways in that regard."

Montego, surprised and curious about Forrall owning a gym, didn't appreciate his nervy method, but KW seemed sincere.

"Little man only saw the hard evidence making Preston look bad," KW said, "and he jumped on it like a bear on a honey pot. I gotta believe that for Yola's sake. . . . For all our sakes." He stopped twisting and rested his elbows on the counter.

Montego pressed the lid sealing the can telling himself that Forrall might have a hidden agenda besides avoiding public conflict with Preston.

KW splayed his fingers. "Know nothing about the man's political doings—like it that way."

"How'd he know about Julie's relationship to Preston?"

"Surprised me, too. Asked Yola about it. Seems she and Julie talked at the Christmas party."

Montego accepted that. "Well, I figure the mob is behind the sex scam. DeSimone's goons pretty much control the pimps and hookers in the Hollywood and Wilshire areas." He placed the coffee can back in the fridge. "My guess is Satin Sheen 'mickeyed' Preston's ginger ale inside the room."

KW looked up. "Satin's a C-note whore. Fills her date book at the Oasis Club down on Western near Adams. Knew about her when I worked Wilshire Vice—never connected Italian thugs to the club, though. Rudy knowing her name surprised me some. Russell must've told him."

"Who?" Montego checked on the perking coffee.

"Russell Smith. Big dude, friendly enough. Manages Rudy's gym down on Jefferson—that's where the dirty pictures first showed."

Montego stopped what he was about to do. "The Steel Bar Gym?"

"Yo, The Black Smith's—know it?" KW, eyes narrowing, gazed at Montego.

Montego unhooked a pair of hanging cups from the cupboard and set them on the counter. "Neall and I had a warrant to serve. It came up."

KW slid his cup closer and ran a finger around the blue-and-gold LAPD logo.

"Warrant suspect tell you about it?"

"He wasn't home."

"Humph." KW, worming about on the bar stool, touched his side.

"Nells connected the Salico bombing to the guy we went to serve, Collis Blagden," Montego said. "The guy had outstanding tickets and a nighttime service warrant for failure to show. The homicide dicks had Rondell's signed statement, but it wasn't sufficient for a felony warrant—"

"Nells thinks this Blagden dude you were serving blew up the hotel room?" KW interrupted. The V reappearing on his forehead.

"Blagden wasn't home, but to answer your question, that's what Nells believes. Say, do you think Rudy's gym manager knows Blagden?"

"Dunno. But he knows how little Daddio got those dirty pictures I'll bet—even if they did show up 'surreptitiously.' Russell rents the suite above the gym. Think he's going to buy the business."

"Sounds like he needs talking to."

"Yo, think you're right. Tonto feel like a drive down to Jefferson?" KW's V-groove relaxed to faint lines. Both of his hands clasped the cup.

"Let me make a call—I'd like to see Rudy's gym, and for sure hear this Russell guy's story." Montego would tell Strait that he'd be missing the Diggers' gathering.

"Mind if we go tandem? Gym's closer to my home," KW said.

"No problema, mi amigo. The java's ready—pour yourself some while it's hot." Montego carried the phone into the hallway.

Following KW through the rear entry of The Black Smith's Steel Bar Gym Montego was thinking Russell Smith had to be an interesting guy, probably a muscle for Rudy Forrall.

They strode down a blue-carpeted hallway into a large weight room with the latest in equipment. The facility made Bert Goodrich's Gym on The Boulevard, where Montego had worked out as a teenager, a sweatbox memory. The summer before his first football season, he'd pumped iron in the gym above the Cinema Lanes. He'd set wooden pins by hand to pay the gym fee and had suffered splinters and more than one swollen ankle from over-zealous bowlers not letting him clear the lane before busting the pins.

"Pretty plush, Kay Dub. You sure they let Scandy-Latins in here?"

"Only with a full-*black* bodyguard." KW glanced back. "Tonto's being a wiseacre, *again*." He pointed across the room to the free-weights area. "Russell's by the squat rack."

Montego gaped. Sliding a hundred-pound plate off the Olympic weight bar was his workout buddy who had never reported to the Academy. Only one man besides Steve Reeves, whom he had worked out with at Goodrich's gym, had such defined arms, and he was staring at him.

A black Hercules.

He wanted to shout "Hey Jordan," but instinctive caution prevailed. Montego shadowed KW as he wove around large pieces of equipment.

132

"Yo, Russell. Got five?" KW called, blocking most of Montego's body from Smith's view as they closed the space.

Smith racked the iron weight. "Always time for the boss' future son-in-law. What gives?"

KW nodded toward the back entry. "Office free?"

"Be my guest—"

Montego saw recognition flash on Smith's face followed by instant alertness. KW hadn't seemed to notice.

Smith spun toward the rear hallway, but stopped when KW said, "Russell Smith, my partner, Mike Montego."

Spinning back, Smith offered an open hand, smiling as though he were seeing Montego for the first time, a warning look apparent in his eyes.

"Hello, Mike Montego."

Montego looked hard at the monster man he knew as Jordan Smith while his own eyes conveyed, *What's going on?*

Jordan, AKA Russell Smith, led them to the office. Matching blue upholstered armchairs occupied the space in front of a double-pedestal desk. An executive-size swivel chair was behind it. On the large desk a dark wood-encased Grundig 960 radio with ivory-toned pushbuttons emitted an instrumental overture. Smith gestured for them to sit. They did.

"We're here about that Manila envelope you gave Rudy last week," KW said. "Mind telling us how it got here?"

Smith slid out the desk's typewriter board and rested both his large black-canvas Converse-shod feet on it. He leaned back in the big chair and channeled his gaze on KW.

"Same as I told the boss, Dealer. Was on the phone sitting here—like I do before the mail arrives. At ten, I went out front to get the daily delivery at the front counter, saw the yellow envelope sticking out of a *Weider* magazine—the boss' name was on it."

Montego felt that Smith was holding something back about the sex photos. Montego decided to let the charade go on, for the moment, anyway.

KW popped a knuckle. "You ever hear of the whore, Satin Sheen?"

Smith repeated the name in a slow questioning tone.

"Assume you saw those dirty pictures—the mama with a cracker." KW, glancing at Montego, leaned forward, his flattened hands spanned an octave's width along each side the brown desktop blotter.

"What makes you assume that, Dealer?" Smith's eyelids lowered. The executive-sized chair's armrests disappeared under his forearms.

"Just trying to understand how they happened to show up in this fancy establishment." KW eased back. "Rudy told me you gave him the mama's name."

Montego concentrated on Smith's intense dark brown eyes locked in a steady gaze with KW's. Neither man blinked. Give them both an Oscar.

"If Rudy told you that, my man, you know what I know."

Montego's curiosity had his backside itching, and no one was about to offer a scratching fork. He wanted to jump in and ask Jordan/Russell if two goons had ever paid either of them a visit?

But caution prevailed. Montego continued to keep his mouth shut. But eventually he would ask Jordan Smith, "What game are you playing?"

Montego also wanted to believe KW about his future father-in-law, but the lawyer-politician was no dummy, and Smith working for the guy was a bit bewildering.

Did DeSimone and/or Pio have something going with Forrall and/or Smith?

Montego replayed the thoughts he'd had after accepting the photos. It made sense that Dante Pio's goons might have contacted one or both of them. The glossies being in Forrall's hands indicated that Dante Pio wanted Preston sitting on the Eighth District council seat. Pio must believe that Forrall would vote for the proposed liberal liquor ordinance, or maybe he had "convinced" him to be for it.

Rudolph Forrall knew that showing the pictures to Eugene Preston would overtly tie him in with the mob; obviously, he had distanced himself from the nasty situation by unloading the sex photos.

KW backed away, stretched out his legs and said matter-of-factly, "Like I said, Russell, just curious s'all. Thanks for giving us five minutes— don't forget noon tomorrow for champagne."

Montego read Jordan Smith's face before leaving: *We've gotta talk.*

Chapter 26

After following KW's powder-blue Ford to Crenshaw and south to Stocker as though heading for Manhattan Beach, Montego took a right. KW continued on to Angeles Vista, the main road into the hilly Ladera Heights community. Turning at La Brea, Montego went north to Jefferson and returned to the gym.

He drew in a lungful of warmish early fall air and entered the air-conditioned building. He sauntered down the corridor to where his former pal conversed with another muscular fellow also wearing a skintight black T-shirt. Seeing Montego, Smith told the other man, "Handle the front, Zeke." He turned to Montego and nodded toward the office.

Smith closed the door, spun about, and reached out, a grin slashing across his obsidian-cut face.

"Mike Montego—you son-of-a-cinnamon. How the hell has Tonto been? I see you still like oxblood huaraches."

Montego, taken aback by the undisguised warmth, took Smith's strong hand. The *spice* reference helped take him in.

Smith pointed to one of the armchairs. "Sit, sit—I know, I know, questions, let me explain." He went around the large desk. The Grundig radio was playing *Ciribiribin* by Harry James' big band. He turned it down and sat in the large swivel armchair. "First, you must swear to the utmost secrecy what I'm about to tell you." He eyed Montego with an open expression, his right hand raised as if to take an oath. "Can you trust me?" His eyes stayed focused, appearing expectant.

Tanto. Can I?

"Sure, Jordan, er, Russell—"

"Call me Smitty. You'll be one of only several cops to know."

Montego sat up. Hearing the word "cops" had an allaying effect, but anxious concerns still prevailed. He smiled. "We were pals preparing for the Academy. Guess I have no reason not to trust you, Jord—Smitty."

"Damn, that makes me want to shout. Dealer said he had a new partner who called their team the 'Salt-and-Pepper Shakers of Hollywood.' Just knew it had to be you, Tonto."

Montego chuckled spontaneously. Moisture had blurred his eyes. "It's true, mi amigo."

"Good man." Smitty's eyes also glistened. He inhaled and the white gym initials BSSB and muscleman logo on his black T-shirt increased impossibly in size. "Here 'tis, Mike—for your ears only." Reaching over, he upped the volume on the Grundig. James' trumpet definitely would cover their words.

"Before you say anything, you've got my promise—long as it's nothing illegal." Montego blinked away the blur.

"Absolutely legal. I'm LAPD—"

"What?" Montego leaped out of the chair.

"Hear me out. The captain of Personnel Division—Lansing—called me at home two weeks before I was to start the Academy. He wanted a meet, and not at the PAB, but on Wilshire, out at the La Brea tar pits."

Montego sat down, studying Smith for any indication of flimflam.

"It blew my mind. The next day, Chief Parker—he's a frosty one—Captains Earle Lansing from Personnel, and Buck Hamilton, head of Intelligence Division, met me. Lansing had given his deputy chief my background file. The DC then gave it to the chief. After questioning, Parker convinced me to work this special assignment. It nixed me from getting any training." Smith swiveled his chair. "Didn't want me exposed to department procedures. 'Fraid it'd make me 'act too much like a cop,' he even secured my badge and ID card. I *was* given a department-issued thirty-eight Colt revolver. It's locked away."

He raised the Grundig's volume even more and leaned forward. "I'm another set of eyes and ears for the LAPD blue. I tape a weekly report describing my activities and to account for my time. Only six officers—now you, know of my true 'sition." He rolled back. "My value to the department depends on me staying incognito. . . . FYI—LA cops work out in here."

Montego, not surprised, delighted in hearing the "'sition" word again, Smith's way of saying "position." Smiling he said, "Your cover's safe with me—but why here, anyway?"

Smith stepped to the hallway, opened the door and peered out, then he closed it. "The super chief told Lansing he wants to keep tabs on the street gangs—actually Parker wants to know everything about Rudy. Who he talks to—what he does. 'Get close to Rudolph Forrall,' he told me. . . ."

Montego shuffled about, trying to fathom what he was hearing.

"That's why I'm working here." Smith retook his seat and swiveled, nonstop. "And here I'll be staying; as long as Parker thinks I'm effective—that's up to Captain Hamilton. He's the man I report to."

Montego stood and paced behind the armchair. He recalled Quinn hinting about secret-type cops working deep cover in strange places.

Does the chief suspect Forrall is involved with the Italian Mafia?

Parker claimed the Mafia didn't operate in L.A., yet he knew they were here—had to be political hay. The mob had set up Eugene Preston and now was involving Forrall with a strong-arm lobbying tactic trying to get a liquor ordinance passed. Or was Forrall voluntarily involved with Pio?

And I've let myself get caught up in all of it.

"If I hadn't known you were testing for the job, I'd be accepting you as the manager of this snazzy gym. That's how it'll stay."

As long as your story holds true—

"Tanto!" Montego cussed and stopped his pacing. "Kay Dub knows about us."

"What're you saying?" Smith ceased his swiveling.

"I told him about you and me working out. It was the day we met. When you didn't show up the first day at the Academy, I asked him if he knew you. He got miffed—no wonder. I handled it darn stupidly."

Smith grinned. "He did mention how you two got together."

Montego slowly exhaled while he stared at the Grundig.

Smith added, "Only a matter of time 'til Dealer hits on the truth and tells his soon-to-be-daddy-in law my 'sition."

"My instincts tell me Kay Dub won't say anything even should he find out." Montego sat back down. "He's never given me any clue he knew you were the no-show recruit. But then you call yourself Russell now."

"Parker came up with that." Smith's grin widened. "He claims it's the Anglo-Saxon name for fox."

"He sure put the fox in the hen house with a banty rooster who's definitely the cock-of-the-walk." Montego laughed.

Smith's lidded eyes suggested his thoughts had gone elsewhere. . . . "Should've changed the Smith part, too, but it's so common."

"If Forrall needs watching, is Kay Dub in trouble?"

The telephone rang. Smith quickly shook his head and picked up the receiver, answering with a pat greeting.

Montego listened for a moment, guessing who it was. When the call ended he immediately asked, "You trust Forrall? Is he clean? Is Kay Dub into something he won't be able to handle?"

"Whoa. Let's walk outside. By the way, I *do* dig your huaraches."

Montego smiled and followed Smith out to the rear parking lot.

Montego strode alongside Smith around the parking lot perimeter.

"I'm buying The Steel Bar and setting up house on the second floor to stay closer to Rudy." Smith paused, waiting as a club member strode by en route to a full-dressed Harley motorcycle. "Dealer must've told you that much, Tonto—besides it's a good investment."

Smith, crossing his arms, paused once more when the big bike's motor rumbled and the soft-capped rider roared out of the lot.

"My take—Chief Parker's a smidgen paranoid. Thinks Rudy's an anarchist. Captain Hamilton plays along because it puts me on top of the street action. Mike, more damn stuff passes through that weight room than you can imagine." He nodded toward the gym building. "I told you, cops, not just LAPD types, work out in there. *All* brothers." Smith's guffaw rolled as he unfolded his meaty arms.

Montego gave Smith a sidelong glance.

IAD would love to hear about the "more damn stuff."

"Actually, that's what brought me here. A guy we're looking for had this gym's business card. His name's Collis Blagden."

"Colly and his big buddies work out in here on an irregular basis. Hard cases—stay to themselves. Overheard them talking about a club in Hollywood—the Sambah . . . I think they hang there."

"I know of it—thanks."

"And Mike, Rudy may be an activist, but he's no damn anarchist." Smith's sincerity came through. "He's good for the community—knows lots of people. Of course there're folks who disagree with his views."

"No doubt—but is the man trustworthy?"

"Count on it. Oh yeah, some people he meets *are* questionable."

Smith headed for the wooden fence at the back of the lot. "I'm convinced that Parker doesn't trust anyone at City Hall—and Rudy having political friends down there doesn't help matters—but the chief's paranoia might've been a put-on for my benefit. But what I've given Buck Hamilton must be reaching the right people downtown 'cause the 'not-so-straight-shooters' have been finding their previous avenues into City Hall cut off."

"Parker's no fool," Montego said. "And Forrall is pretty sharp—just hope he hasn't been compromised by the local mob for Kay Dub's sake." He eyeballed the nearly empty lot.

"Rudy fights like a banty rooster," Smith grinned, "to stay clear of anything looking remotely corrupt . . . with my help."

"You're too much, Jord . . . er, Russell. Tanto, I mean Smitty." He shook his head. "Calling you Smitty will take getting used to—but then it won't matter since I won't be coming back."

"What? 'Fraid of being the only *lighter*-skinned jock pumping iron in *Black* Smitty's gym? Hey, you like the name? Rudy let me use it. He wanted to call it 'Weights For All.'" Smith laughed and slapped Montego's shoulder. His chiseled face took on a familiar look.

"Great name. Glad Kay Dub brought me here—which reminds me. Maybe you can answer a question or three—just don't be laying anything on me that'll get you into—"

"Won't happen, Tonto." Smith stopped and re-crossed his arms.

"OK." Montego, looking around, stepped closer. He related what he had heard about Dante Pio and the Italian mob activities on the southwest side. "I've got the photos. Forrall wants me to show them to Councilman Preston. He knows the guy's my girlfriend's uncle."

Smith's wide-eyed expression caused Montego to hesitate briefly.

"Ah, you didn't know. That's why he's using me. It keeps him clear, he thinks—but it might not work out like he wants." He checked the lot again. "Several weeks ago, I got pissed and told off Preston at my girlfriend's parents' home. There's no telling what the repercussions might be for me personally."

"I'm sorry Rudy's involved you, Mike. It's not right, but he does have his way of getting whatever he wants."

"I'm not that involved . . . yet. My first concern is that Preston, in all fairness, be forewarned."

"Just be smart." Smith stroked his triceps.

"Well, I also wonder about Kay Dub marrying Forrall's daughter." Montego recalled the dark blue, three-ring Police Department Manual, Daily Training Bulletins, and Special Orders in KW's old living room. He was convinced his partner had upward mobility in mind. It was reasonable that KW would want to promote, if only to keep up with his barrister-bride. "I hope he knows what he's doing—for sure, Yolanda's an eye-catcher."

"That she is, and a sharp lady-lawyer with major league aspirations. The future Missus Yolanda Forrall-Deal plans to become the first female Los Angeles county supervisor one day."

"Figures. You can bet that her father won't do anything to hurt her career. . . . Should help Kay Dub's, too."

They resumed their strolling.

"Agree—and you've hit the target with what you've told me about Dante Pio and his expanding into this area's on-going rackets," Smith said. "And here's the skinny on those pictures. The dude you named for Rudy—Brunetti—and another clown—came to the gym last month. They pretended to represent a large corporation that they didn't identify. The ugly bald one played real polite." Smith scowled. "Baldy said their board of directors was impressed with Rudy's open view on the proposed booze bill."

Montego listened while they ambled around the lot and onto the front sidewalk. He was distracted somewhat by the thought that it would've been great to work partners with Smith.

"Rudy was getting interested, until Baldy assured him that their organization had connections that would guarantee a council seat for him." Smith's expression showed his contempt. "I don't think Rudy is that keen about the proposed bill, but he's keeping his thoughts about it to himself."

Montego understood the political issue. Forrall's passion for Blacks did not mean that he wanted to expose their families to more booze outlets. This realization prompted Montego to recall Eugene Preston's spiel at the anniversary dinner. Montego mentally shook his head. It had been after the councilman's tryst with the whore.

The bigoted guy was a total hypocrite.

"Baldy was wrong thinking Forrall automatically would go along. Sounds like the sex photos might've appeared about that same time."

"The morning before you and your blond partner popped Baldy. I heard—it sounded sticky." Smith stopped walking and eyed Montego before continuing. "I spoke to Baldy—Riffelano—when he delivered the Manila envelope. It was just after the mail arrived. While he was here, I looked at the glossie photos. I told him the john looked drugged—that it was a setup. The gonzo clown stared back stupidly. 'Course my undercover cop 'sition kept me from expressing my true opinion." He cracked his large knuckles, grinning. "I did tell Rudy I'd seen Satin Sheen whoring out of the Oasis." Smith's grin widened. "Heard her catchy name mentioned once or twice."

Montego grinned, too. "Gotta go, mi amigo. Need a siesta before work." He turned back. "Thanks for the info—I know it's on the QT."

Smith walked with him to the Cameo Carrier and checked it out.

"Some purty wheels." His look when they cast brief head nods in parting, paralleled Montego's own concerned thought: the Mafia goons weren't through with either Eugene Preston or Rudolph Forrall.

140

Chapter 27

Montego's good feeling changed when he saw that Julie's Austin-Healey wasn't in her carport. His heart rushed a beat. He had been holding positive thoughts, hoping to mend things, invite her to a movie. The sexy French actress, Brigitte Bardot starred in *A Very Private Affair*. It was playing on The Boulevard. Freer attitudes had loosened the rules. Producers now made films like, *And God Created Woman* where Bardot filled the 30-foot screen in living color lying *au soleil*, outdoors, in the opening scene.

Visualizing Julie in the prone Bardot nude pose was all he had as he trudged up to the Perch. The Diggers were sucking up frothy suds at the Clam in El Porto, but he was exhausted and needed to be sharp for what usually was the busiest shift of the week. The night, according to Strait, when "The Boulevard pullulates (teems) with the denizens of the dark and all the lost souls."

Lost souls? Have I lost Julie?

Confronting Eugene Preston with the photographs wouldn't help matters. Before crashing, Montego dialed the Preston's number with the hope that Julie would pick up the receiver.

"Hi, is Julie there?" A click and a dead line. He redialed, but got no answer. He slammed down the receiver and lay back on the couch.

*   *   *

Leo Brunetti met with Dante Pio at the capo's home on Sunset Plaza Drive. They sat on lounge chairs on the travertine-tiled patio overlooking the lights of The Strip, drinking and smoking cigars. Several of Pio's *soldati* walked the grounds out of earshot.

It was only the second time that Brunetti had been called to the Tuscan-style pad. Feeling something was up, he'd called Chicago so that Giancana knew about the meeting; Brunetti had earlier told Momo what Simeti had said about Bonanno's intent to take-over L.A.

Momo's retort had been, "Oh yeah—we'll just see 'bout that."

Dante Pio bullshitted for half an hour until Brunetti got the feeling he was being interrogated about Momo's intentions.

Brunetti played dumb and chewed on his Dutch Master cigar.

Eventually, Pio got down to the main reason for the get-together.

"Forrall hasn't pressed that Preston crumb with those motel room photographs. We've got to put on more heat. We gotta get Forrall on the council—we need his yes vote. I had Armanno on it, but called him off to give the nigger more time. Now it has to be done—the booze bill will be coming up for a vote soon, and I want a guarantee." Pio hard-eyed Brunetti. "Beak, hit that prude, Preston—I don't care how or where, just get it done."

Brunetti had received his order. The capo's tone meant the meeting was over which suited Brunetti. He dropped the soggy cigar butt into a large glass ashtray and split.

None too soon he was coasting the yellow Caddy convertible down the steep hill toward The Sunset Strip. He'd worked out what he would do.

Hurt the Haleys—get fuckin' Neallie Baby dancing to my tune.

His mind set, Brunetti swung the Eldorado into the parking lot at Dino's on The Strip, leaving it running for the bow-tied valet.

Inside the nightclub, he pointed to a dark corner where Nino Simeti sat drinking from a glass and followed the scantily clad cocktail waitress.

She took Brunetti's drink order and left for the bar.

He took a seat.

"Hey, Leo. I gots your dupe keys." Simeti held them out.

Brunetti snatched them. "Thanks—Capo Pio wants another hit."

"When, who—how're we doin' it?" Simeti lifted his tumbler.

"Some city councilfuck—'n' we ain't gonna be doing it, Nino." Brunetti pocketed the keys. "Pinky's cop boy is gonna do it for us—he just don't know it, yet." Brunetti yanked out a handkerchief and honked into it.

"Risky shit, Leo—thinks the bull fuck'll do it?"

"He's got no choice. Look, I want you to get his phone number. When y'do, call it—make sure it's Haley talking. Then gimme the number."

The idea of making Haley into a hitter nearly gave Brunetti a boner.

* * *

The MID-watch troops hit the streets fifteen minutes early. Montego had seen it happen when Brad Kozier was the Acting Watch Commander. The easygoing three-striper often eliminated the training lesson. The sergeant believed it more important to handle Saturday's typical backlog of calls.

Making an effort to not think about Julie, Montego focused on the capture of Collis Blagden and the likely place where he would find him, thanks to Smith's info.

At dusk, Montego and Haley cruised into east Hollywood and down Virgil past Blagden's four-flat building. They determined he was not home.

Smith's additional info that Rat Rondell had been with Blagden in the Salico bombing sounded like the Slaves gang was taking on the mob. Smith said he would try to learn why The Rat had teamed with Blagden. Smith's future input could be valuable.

"Neall, a snitch told me the guy hangs out at the Sambah Room. Want to see what the joint looks like?"

Haley wordlessly sped north toward the club at Five-Points, a spoke-like intersection. He parked on Hillhurst north of the Vista Theater.

"Any cover charge, we'll give Brad the chit. Sarge is good about that—if we make a bust." Haley sounded anxious.

Montego adjusted his gun rig, curious why Haley hadn't parked on the nightclub side of The Boulevard.

"Guess we walk a look-see, get a better feel for the terrain before we leave the unit closer to the nightclub?"

Haley withdrew the ignition key. "We spook Cubby Bear he might rabbit north, try to lose us in all the traffic. Radio's handier here."

Montego accepted that, given the chance, Blagden would split when he saw them. But who knew in what direction? Dodging moving vehicles on main thoroughfares, or running down poorly lit side streets.

Does it matter?

Snatching the radio handset, Montego put them Code 6 at the Sambah Room. "Want me to request Frank-Two for backup?"

Haley, not answering, started across the star-shaped intersection. Montego hurried to follow. On the other sidewalk, Haley yanked out his revolver, opened and wheeled the cylinder.

A double-check never hurt, Montego reasoned, convinced his partner was mentally on the moon. He freed his Colt Python thinking he never wanted to have to rely on the four-inch, but for sure the Riffelano shooting had him appreciating the piece a bit more. The weapon was a necessary tool, but still he depended more on his kenpo skills for close-in situations.

Re-holstering their revolvers they went to the triangular-shaped building. It took up the entire acutely angled southwest corner.

143

Waid Woodruff

Under an overhead street light, Montego looked at Collis Blagden's mug shot once more, then he showed it to Haley.

Haley eyed the small photo. "You or me first inside?"

"I'll go." Montego pocketed the picture, mentally readying himself for any eventuality, and led the way into suffused lighting.

Inside the entry, he paused letting his eyes adjust to the dimness.

No music played in the lounge, only murmuring voices; way early for show time and the indicated $5 cover charge. The room needed airing. A smoke cloud surrounded a man and woman at a table on the near side of a small square dance floor. Next to the couple a bar ran along a mirrored wall where three black men dwarfed chromed-legged stools talking to the bartender. Each man was the size of a professional football lineman. They wore blue-and-gold leather-and-cloth L.A. Ram jackets. Montego figured the middle lineman was Cubby Bear, Collis U. Blagden. His features matched the description Smith had provided.

A bored looking bleached-blonde barmaid showing much cleavage in a spaghetti-strapped bright-red dress leaned against the far end of the bar, by the service counter. She eyed Montego coldly.

At the rear was the fire exit, and right of it, behind the waitress, an alcove with restrooms. A public telephone hung on the wall within earshot of the huddled threesome. That ruled out a discreet call for backup.

Montego gritted his teeth. He should've requested Momma Mary to have Frank-Two meet them on Tac One or Two. The tactical frequencies allowed teams to speak to each other without tying up the division's main frequency. It was a cardinal sin for an available unit to not provide support for a fellow officer. It had happened to him once during his earlier hotshot "John Wayne" period, a time when he was out to prove he could do the job all by himself. He'd almost bought the pine box. He learned what all cops learn: Be a team player or lose timely backup.

Stepping toward the left side of the dim room he took a seat a small table next to the dance floor where he could watch the men at the bar. The middle guy turned and glowered at him, his feral eyes appeared vicious in the low light. It *was* Collis Ulysses Blagden.

Montego must tell Strait that CUB was not a Cubby Bear.

Haley eased onto the chair to his right. "We're made, the middle lineman's our ball carrier—gotta be packing—watch his right mitt."

Montego nodded in sync with the waitress' nod to the linemen as she left the bar. She carried an empty tray to the table where the couple sat in a cloud of smoke and retrieved a "dead soldier." She shimmied back to the bar trio, said something to Blagden, then turned and sashayed across the dance floor toward the cops.

The barmaid's route obstructed Montego's view of their target.

"Ref's making a call." He leaned to see past her just when Blagden made his break. Simultaneously, the other linemen spun off their stools.

Haley jumped up.

The barmaid side-bumped him. "Watch it jerk."

The longneck bounced onto the parquet flooring and rolled toward Montego as Blagden rammed through the rear fire-door crash-bar setting off a ringing alarm.

Montego said, "Get the running back—I'll block the tackles."

Haley shoved the surly barmaid aside, skirted around Montego, and chased after the fleeing ball carrier.

The tackles rushed Montego. "Five hundred pounds to one-ninety, not fair," he muttered, making a hand swipe for the empty bottle at his feet.

The move faked the linemen to their left. A catlike whirl provided a target. Montego, yelling, "Kiai!" kicked the nearest tackle in the chest.

Tackle One sprawled into his teammate and both crashed into the couple's table. The smokers tumbled backward, squawking.

Montego banged through the fire exit and glimpsed Haley running west, well behind Blagden who was crossing Sunset. Montego also crossed but angled through a vacant lot that shortcut the distance between them.

He dashed through an open area behind a large building coming out on Lyman Place.

Footfalls—!

Blagden slammed into Montego, knocking them both off their feet.

Though stunned, Montego rolled into a crouching wide-stance, arms out and ready. Blagden turned toward him, clambering to his knees.

Three shots rang out!

Blagden fell forward about two yards from a crouching Montego.

Haley raced up. His magnum pointed at the downed ball carrier.

Montego rushed to Blagden and checked his neck—a faint pulse. Blood seeped from the man's right rear side near a Colt semiauto pistol. *Tanto!* Had Blagden held it or had it come loose when he fell? Montego's gut flipped like a rock-bound trout as he slid the .45 caliber gun away.

"Get to our car radio, Neall—we need an RA unit!"

Haley eyeballed the wounded suspect, then he looked at Montego.

Both knew Blagden's teammates soon would be thundering to the scene. Even so, they needed the rescue ambulance ASAP.

"No choice, partner—do it! I'm OK here—and get us backup."

"Watch your damn ass—light's lousy." Haley split into the night.

Montego felt wetness only in one spot on Blagden, but he'd heard three shots. Two had missed. He chilled, realizing that three bullets had just flown past his head. He snagged his handkerchief free and pressed it against the bleeding spot in Blagden's torso.

Clomping footfalls sounded. He looked for Blagden's .45 semiauto. *Too late!*

"There's the fuc—sheeit—the man's done kilt Colley."

The single street lamp haloed the tackles' heads. They didn't look like angels.

Montego, about to free the Colt Python, stopped when he spotted four clenched hands—no weapons. "Hold it. Your pal's alive! I've got pressure on his wound. Mess with me and he'll bleed to death."

The tackles wanted to mess. They came with elbows winged out, intending to mow Montego down.

He swiped a leg across the path of Tackle One, tripping him into Two. Uncoiling, Montego kicked the off-balanced Two in the chest, sending him tumbling over his rising teammate.

Both linemen struck the pavement.

Blagden's pistol lay nearer the downed tackles. Montego couldn't reach it before One would have it.

Just as One grasped the gun butt, Montego loosed his revolver.

"Let it go, pal—now, or you're a dead man!"

Tackle Two was on his behind. "The man's got a damn cannon, dude—let it go—man's a muthafuckin' killer!"

"You heard him, hero. Slide the forty-five this way, real easy like." Distant voices behind Montego had him hoping they were "friendlies."

Tackle One's hand stayed on the pistol grip.

Montego cocked the Python's hammer into single action. The click spoke loudly in the night air.

"Hear that? Hot loads—a single round will drill daylight through you both." *A stupid bluff at nighttime.*

He moved out of the line of the .45's barrel, closer to a bug-eyed Two who was waving his hands overhead, yelling, "Muthafuck's gonna kill our black asses—get ridda that thing!"

Montego leaned toward One. "You're about to stare cross-eyed at a hollow-point slug." Another bluff. *Tanto!* He didn't need a second shooting.

Tackle One's fingers stayed curled around the pistol grip.

Montego held the Python a body-length from One's nose and a long arm's length from Two's right ear. A swiping pivot and he could cold-cock Two. He didn't figure the frantic guy for heroics—but One was a cowboy.

"It's 'Murder Big' if Colly dies—it's on you now, pal. Let it go!"

Two wailed again, "Sheeit, man! He's gonna shoot our asses—shuck it fool!"

One growled unintelligibly, hesitated, and then shoved the Colt .45 hard enough that it slid past Two's outstretched legs.

Montego grasped it—cocked and locked as he'd suspected. He stuffed it inside his waistband while keeping the Python trained on One.

Distant voices sounded. Shadowy spectators approaching. Montego told the tackles, "On your butts—side by side." One scooted next to Two.

Gripping his revolver in one hand, Montego pulled out his cuffs. "OK. Hands behind you—thumbs under your belts."

Two complied. One sat motionless.

Not waiting, Montego hooked an open hoop under One's belt—grounded the Python, and grabbed One's right arm, jerking it back and up while pressing his left hand in a C-clamp against the back of One's neck.

One wriggled forward, but using a knee, Montego forced the guy's right elbow higher while pushing his head down. With his free hand, Montego yanked the cuff's open pawl from One's belt and hammered it onto his right wrist. The curved steel swung, and, with a quick press, caught a single tooth, locking it.

Montego snatched his Python from the pavement and holstered it.

The tackles were manacled, right-wrist to right-wrist. Two's right arm behind a scowling Tackle One in a brotherly fashion. One's grumbles, however, were anything but affectionate sounding.

The pat-down search revealed each had an illegal switchblade in an inside jacket pocket. The discovery brought mutterings from the bystanders.

The small chattering crowd separated when a horn sounded and the prowler's high-beams spotlighted the benched ball players.

Haley came out of the sedan, saying, "Tonto's done it again."

Montego fought the urge to yank his partner to the side and ask why he'd shot? But with Blagden's Colt pistol being only inches from his waist, Haley's action was debatable.

147

Bobby Diaz and Trev Brannock, arrived minutes later, followed by a city ambulance. When they asked for witnesses most of the onlookers vanished. A few hangers-on admitted to seeing the handcuffing scenario.

Meanwhile, another patrol unit arrived and transported the tackles, arrested for unlawful interfering, to the Hollywood jail.

Haley, lighting a Camel, eyed Montego. "Wanna roust the referee?"

Montego considered the bleached-out barmaid's role.

"Nope, her time'll come. OIS will be here soon—you got any idea where the two rounds—?"

He paused when the rescue ambulance unit screamed from the scene with Brannock riding shotgun over the unconscious Collis Blagden.

Montego hoped the big guy would survive. He didn't relish another fatal shooting. The OIS detectives might think he was trigger-happy even though he hadn't been the shooter.

Sergeant Kozier parked, and strode up to them. He spoke to Haley, now leaning against the prowler, the side door hanging open.

"Give me the rundown, Neall—all of it."

Haley described his actions ending with, "I was about twenty feet behind Mike when Blagden rolled and came up with that damn pistol." He pointed to the Colt .45 on the prowler's passenger seat. "Mike was down, empty-handed." Haley took a last quick drag from a Camel. "I knew the suspect was packing—we saw him in the club with his hand at his belt."

Brad Kozier fired a look at Montego who nodded in agreement.

Haley said, "I was running—had no time to set. Suspect would've blasted Mike." He shook his head and kicked at a chunk of loose asphalt. "Almost missed the asshole, too."

"All right, Neall, see if you can find where the damn slugs landed." Kozier turned. "Let me hear your view, Montego."

Aware of Kozier's street-smart rep, Montego understood why the sergeant had let him listen in on Haley's rendition. The sarge wanted to be sure their scenarios jived before the OIS team showed up.

When Sergeant Nick Karos arrived, he went straight to Haley while his sergeant-partner, closing on Montego, asked, "What happened here?"

Chapter 28

Haley had overreacted. When he'd seen Blagden moving toward Montego, he'd shot in desperation, as well as in frustration. Two misses made it a bad shooting in his mind. He didn't want to think about how close he'd come to hitting Montego. Thank God, he'd guessed right. Blagden had been armed.

Haley's head was screwed up. The hang-up call had him shook. Who had phoned? Brunetti? If it was that meathead, how the hell did he get Lissa's home number? He must've gotten it from the restaurant manager.

The upcoming interrogation wasn't something Haley needed now.

Nick Karos mouthed a toothpick like he'd done at the Riffelano scene, a habit, Haley decided, taking a deep breath.

"OK, Haley, give it to me from the top."

Haley gave his version, clapping and rolling his hands to indicate the collision when Blagden and Montego had tumbled.

"The suspect's right hand went to his waist . . . I spotted the piece." He clenched his hand in front of him mimicking Blagden's action with the Colt pistol. "I pulled my weapon—fired a burst of three at him." He jerked his left hand three times in a shooting gesture.

"Suspect dropped." Smacking his palms to indicate Blagden going down, Haley realized he was emoting, too many gestures. The toothpick, like a dagger, now aimed at him.

Throughout his telling of the scenario, the toothpick went from pointing at Haley's nose to pointing at the legal pad on Karos' clipboard.

The OIS reports were official. They ended up on the sixth floor atop the final arbiter's desk. Haley wouldn't be surprised if the iron-fisted Chief Parker concluded that he, the repped Ice Cop, was trigger-happy.

Haley bit on a hangnail. Karos had grilled him good. Should Haley's actions be deemed out-of-policy by the Shooting Review Board there could be civil liabilities and megabucks involved, along with stringent discipline: desk duty for starters. Parker might take Haley's badge—destroy his life, what life he had left, thanks to Beak Brunetti.

Haley quaked. His cop career was on the line. All he'd ever wanted was to be an L.A. cop. He'd savored the *True Detective* magazines as a kid and could recount crime stories from them. They were full of excitement. Tonight's police events, however, were less enjoyable. Shitty, in fact.

He lowered his right arm to the unit's headlights to view his watch. Almost 2200 hours. Two hours to answer for two minutes of "exciting" law enforcement activity. He snorted to himself.

Looking up, he spotted the OIS lead sergeant going to Montego while Karos' investigator teammate began drawing a scene diagram.

Haley, staying in the darkest shadows, moved as close as he dared to hear what his partner said.

Montego caught a glimpse of Haley moving toward him, but didn't make it obvious to Karos who had just asked, "What happened, Montego?"

"Can't tell you much, sarge. I was momentarily stunned from the suspect smashing into me." Montego couldn't tell the detective he hadn't seen a weapon in Blagden's hand, or, for that matter, his hand by his waist before Haley's shots sent Blagden into a nose dive.

Montego simply wasn't sure.

"Suspect Blagden was in front of me when I heard three shots. He went down. The Colt was on the pavement near him, it fell from his . . . hand." Montego's statement was based on assumption, but was plausible—besides he had to give Haley the benefit of the doubt. It's what partners did.

Haley held his breath when Karos re-asked Montego, "You're absolutely positive the suspect had the Colt out when you heard the shots, Montego?"

If Montego said he wasn't positive, it would leave a hole for some ladder-climbing inspector or desk-bound deputy chief to crawl through with a magnifying glass. A faint came over Haley.

He braced himself, he was still holding his breath.

Montego, facing Karos, and not wavering, responded a firm, "Yes."

Haley's breath escaped like a whale's spout. He slumped. Why had he doubted Montego? He'd been loyal to the partnership so far.

Damn it to hell—this whole bust had gone down too fast. He shouldn't have fired, but he couldn't risk losing Montego. Maybe that was rationalizing, but Haley knew Blagden hadn't grabbed his piece from his waistband. It had fallen free when he dropped.

Montego likely knew it, too. . . .

I do care about Mike . . . He saved my damn ass . . . I'm an asshole.

Haley blamed it on the crappy situation he was in: Brunetti pushing him to be a lousy hit man.

He eased back to the prowl car. Damn it, not knowing how to deal with Brunetti sent Haley's thoughts tumbling like Bingo balls in a revolving wire basket.

Time was running out for coming up with a viable plan for acing the meathead cousins and ending the threat against Pop. Haley counted on his gut instinct that the mob wasn't involved in Brunetti's nefarious game.

Haley rapped a Camel free of the pack and snapped a Ronson flame to it. He drew in till his throat burned. It had been a pipe dream to think he could have gotten Montego to buy the need to permanently remove Brunetti illegally. Now, Haley must get Montego to understand Brunetti's threat. Maybe Montego would have an idea on how to remove the threat legally— but how could he? He was ignorant to everything that was going on.

I've put Mike in harm's way and I haven't had the balls to tell him.

How would Montego react if he learned of Brunetti's wild claim?

Bust Pop. . . . But without any proof?

What if in my search of criminal records, I missed some obscure warrant for Angelo Pinky Sancia? Mike Montego, a true-blue cop, would have what he needed. Pop might be safer in prison. No—no way in hell!

Deep inside, Haley wasn't up to do any enlightening for Montego. Haley still hoped to devise a foolproof way to finish off both meathead cousins—and do it legally . . . at least make it look that way.

Damn. What if I don't survive because of Brunetti's gun? Would Mike take care of my family? They must be protected at all costs. It was why I got him close to the family—but telling him of The Beak's threat means opening a can of worms—one filled with lousy mob maggots.

Haley took another worrying pull on the Camel, realizing he must get the same loyalty from Montego like he'd shown defending Dealer's reputation.

For what I gotta do, I'm gonna need Mike as backup. But the way I've been acting, how do I get the righteous cop to buy into it?

151

Chapter 29

Montego was proud of KW for taking a stand against Yolanda's wish for a fancy ceremony. The wedding had been a simple affair, even though many people were in attendance. Perhaps their marriage had a chance.

There had been a short article in the *Times Metro* section about the shooting, but it was a two-column item in the *Hollywood Citizen News.* Thankfully, the wedding attendees either had not heard about the shooting, or being polite had chosen not to bring it up.

Upon arrival he exchanged friendly words with Rudy Forrall, and during the ceremony happily sat with the only person he knew, Smith.

After seeing the "new Deal" couple driving off on their way to a Caribbean honeymoon, Montego headed for the Perch and a siesta.

En route, he thought about the shooting and Haley. Neither of them had actually seen Blagden's Colt pistol when they were inside the Sambah.

Haley's judgment was being seriously affected by something. The guy needed help, but could Montego provide it? He parked in the garage, lowered the door and headed for the stairs to the Perch, noting that Julie's carport was empty. He sighed, and climbed to his front door, his mind back on Haley's behavior. Poor tactics could cost one or both of them dearly.

What to do? He needed to better understand the guy, find out what made his tick. But who to talk to? Kozier and Haley were fairly close, that had become apparent, but the sarge wasn't the right person to talk to.

After much thought, Montego, knowing he was risking a jealous Haley's wrath, decided talking to Lissa might provide some insight to the guy. He checked the time: 3:30. Carrying the telephone into the kitchen, Montego called The Palms. When a woman answered, he asked for Lissa.

The woman made it sound like she was doing him a big favor when she said, "I'll see if Renzo's free."

Eventually, Lissa came on the line.

Montego said, "Can I see you after work?" He understood Lissa's hesitation. "Is seeing you alone a problem?"

"Of course not. It's just . . . Neall hadn't been around and—"

"Lissa, he's why I want to talk to you—I'll explain tonight."

She hesitated again. "OK, Mike—but if he shows up, it's off."

Montego cradled the receiver, padded to the bedroom and crashed.

The Purple Hand

Two hours later he awoke, feeling tired. During a bracing cold shower he thought about what he needed to say to Julie if she was home.

Dressed casually, he headed past the kitchen counter, grabbed an apple from the fruit bowl, and munched on it as he descended the stairs. Turning toward her apartment, he stopped when he saw that her carport was still empty. His heart sunk.

He trudged back upstairs, tossed the apple core into the sink drain, and reached for the phone. It felt like he'd been calling the Preston's number *forever*, still, he hoped she'd pick up. The mother answered, again, and like every time before, she hung up—*and she had been so pleasant before my darn blow up.*

He slowly redialed. "Hi, is Julie—?" Another hang up. Pissed and worried, he about threw the phone into the living room. Was it over?

Since he had the night off, thanks to being on RFD status, he decided to call his mother and bum a meal.

Montego spent most of the evening at "Buckingham Palace," his name for his mother's new home; she was a Buckingham now. Steve had promoted to captain on the LAFD and felt they could afford the hillside house.

Putting up with the smug man was always stressful.

After dinner, Montego searched the telephone book until he found the number for Julie's girlfriend, Becky Gill. That petite gal always had something to say to make him feel like a darn heel.

He got her on the line. Surprisingly, she sounded friendly and responded to his query about Julie saying, "Just give her more time, Mike."

At eleven that night, he was parked at the drive-in. He ordered two coffees and waited. Several minutes later, just as the coffee was served to his side, Lissa's bright face appeared at the passenger's open window.

"Hi, Mike."

When she climbed onto the seat her wrap-around coal-black skirt flopped open, exposing a smooth, tanned thigh. He looked away, telling himself that Julie was his lady, even though it seemed otherwise. It'd been too long since he'd been with her. The innocent revealing of a bare leg so close told him as much.

Lissa unclasped her clutch handbag. "You got quick service—must be your good looks." She cast a teasing smile and tugged on the skirt flap.

His face warmed. He handed her the coffee cup and a paper napkin.

Taking the napkin, she shook her head, "Let it cool—thanks."

"How're you doing tonight?" he asked.

"Fine, I guess. Obviously, Neall didn't show and it's bugging me. He's been acting sort of—I don't know—really quiet." She took a gold lipstick tube from her purse, pulled off the cap, and screwed up the red gel.

Watching, Montego realized that his mouth had opened when her lips arched, yielding to the round stick. He licked his own and quickly said, "He's usually quiet." He forced a mental picture of Julie's full lips.

"I know. But it's more than that. He thinks it's not safe for me to be seen talking to him, or to any policeman, while I'm working. I hardly ever see him now." She offered a challenging look and screwed the gel back into the tube. She capped it and dropped it into her purse while working her lips together smoothing out the fresh color. She pressed them into the napkin.

Montego had resisted moving his lips the same way. "I know he doesn't want me talking to you in the restaurant, but here at Big Spike's should be safe enough."

"It upsets me when he says things like that. Dante doesn't frighten me." She put the handbag to the floor, kicked off her flats, and curled onto the seat, her slightly spread knees pointed toward him.

Averting his eyes, he watched a Corvette on his side backing out.

"Neall wants you safe. He knows Pio is dangerous, even if he *is* friendly to you." He turned back and stared past her to a teenaged couple making out in the next car. "He's just protecting you, that's all." Montego sighed and looked out his side window, again, wondering about Haley talking to Brunetti and passing it off as a warning from the "Big Blue Bird."

But had he really? He should have had a partner with him when he spoke to Brunetti—and it should've been done while on duty. And Lissa mentioned that it wasn't the first time Neall has talked to the goon.

"I suppose you're right," Lissa said.

Her voice brought Montego's attention back inside the pickup.

"Dante did ask me for your name, Mike." She lowered her head and looked up at him under fluttering eyelashes. "I told him, too." She pouted. Her knees, a bit wider, still pointed at him. "Did I do wrong?"

"There're beaucoup ways for Pio to get my name, Lissa—forget it."
The Riffelano shooting must have yanked the capo's chain.

Montego realized he was running his fingers up and down a vertical tucked-and rolled Naugahyde strip behind him.

A horn beeped, startling him. He looked at the make-out couple. They were sucking on straws, cooling down with sodas.

"So, how's Officer Mike Montego tonight?" Lissa smiled.

"OK, I guess. My steady is upset with me—ever since some mutual friends saw me in here with you."

Lissa eyed him questioningly, her lips had a purplish-hue from the neon light-rays filtering through the misted windshield.

"I called her before seeing you, but I didn't go into much detail— no need, I'd thought—at least not 'til she heard about it from her galfriend." He took two gulps of water. "What I told her then didn't fly."

Lissa gave him an understanding smile and angled her knees away. "You should've told her everything when you first called. We women are easily hurt—sometimes foolishly so. When our men are away doing their jobs we don't want them forgetting us. When they're home, we want them showing us we were missed."

"It hurts—I mean Neall not being around?" He eyed her.

"Yes, and I'm worried. The last time we were together, he wasn't himself. I think he's seeing somebody else." She reached out and traced a heart with teardrops in the light condensation on the window glass. She still hadn't asked for her coffee.

He studied her facial beauty. "I seriously doubt that, Lissa."

"Then what could it be?" She dragged her moist finger over her knee. "You honestly don't think he has another girlfriend?" She arched an eyebrow, her large eyes glistening.

"For sure it's not another woman—but I'd hoped you could tell me. That's why I wanted to see you. I have no clue to the guy." He had an idea that Haley's behavior had something to do with Beak Brunetti.

"I've met his family and he's actually pretty warm around them, especially to his young sister. You've noticed that, I'm sure?"

"Actually, no . . . I haven't met them . . . yet—but I'd really like to. I haven't pushed it. Neall must have his reasons." She reached down and pulled a hankie from her handbag.

Her answer surprised Montego.

"Do you know how he spends his time when he's not with you?"

"He likes to race his Porsche out on the Paramount Ranch road. He told me they have a fun road course. It's where Cornell Wilde starred in a movie called *Devil's Hairpin* . . . I think. Maybe Neall's seeing another girl there—it's so easy to believe you're being ditched."

"Believe me—he's not seeing any girl." He had to speak to Haley, not that it would do any good. This gorgeous gal deeply cared for the quiet guy. Now who sounded like Becky Gill? Montego finished his coffee.

"Mike, when you believe you're losing the person you really love, it's devastating. If your girlfriend loves you, and you love her, don't let her think she's lost you." Lissa blotted her eyes with the pink hankie.

He hadn't thought of it as devastating, but without Julie his whole being did feel bankrupt—wiped out. Was that true love?

"All I can tell Julie is that you and I are pals." It was the truth, even though he was easily distracted by Lissa's sweet naïveté. Inexplicably her nearness provoked a sense of loneliness.

"Julie." She eased her bare feet to the floorboard. "A pretty name."

She leaned toward him, the vee opening in her blouse to reveal light freckles. She kissed his cheek, dabbed off the lipstick imprint with the paper napkin, and took the cup from the tray behind him. Sitting back, she gazed at him. "You'd better go after her."

Breathing in a faint rose scent, he nodded his head, her presence and the lonely feeling confusing his libido. Was lust the sole basis for his caring about Julie? The question was unshakable.

"Your coffee's gotta be cold, Lissa."

"Suits my mood, I suppose." She held the coffee cup to her lips and sipped before saying, "OK, new pal—how do we get Neall over whatever's bothering him? I do need to stop feeling like he doesn't want me anymore."

"He must work through whatever it is by himself. All I can say is just be there for him . . . like I'm trying to do as his partner and friend."

Lissa smiled behind her coffee cup. "That's nice of you, Mike."

The afternoon he'd caught Haley with Brunetti came back to mind. Surprise had covered Ice Cop's usual deadpanned face that mid-afternoon.

"Maybe Brunetti has something to do with it."

In the ambient light he saw her fingers clenching the cup.

She's seen it, too.

"You said Dante and his boys hush up around you, but anything you hear might help me figure out what's going on with those goons—possibly it could have something to do with whatever's bothering Neall . . . and what that braggart wannabe tells you also might help."

Lissa handed him the lipstick-printed napkin and the cold coffee cup. "Mario—that pest. He did mention a new player they call 'Roger.'"

Chapter 30

During a round of bed-rasslin' with Coochie Goochie, Leo Brunetti was interrupted by a disturbing call from cousin Simeti.

"Don' ask me how, Leo, but I'm tellin' youse—that Mario fuck, Joey A's pal, was who gives me the copper's phone number."

"Wha'—shit. Give me the damn number."

Brunetti had seen the fat Guinea hanging with Joey Armanno in the Cinegrill lounge a week ago and had asked his cousin, "Nino, that fat fuck over there with the Frisco wise guy. Seen him 'round lots. What's with him? —who the fuck is he?"

"Mario Zippi—a big mouth. He's full a shit. Plays like he's fuckin' muscle. He's a nothin'."

"Yeah, well he's a dummy—don't belong. Look at his damn coat—that bulge. He's carrying a fuckin' gat."

"No shit? I sees it. Prob'ly tryin' to impress th' capo."

"Not the way he handles hisself. He better just stay outta my way."

Brunetti scribbled down Haley's phone number. "Thanks, Nino."

Hanging up, he mumbled, "What's that chump, Zippi, up to?"

The fucker must think he's made—or wants to be—fat chance.

Brunetti showered, hurriedly dressed and left the motel room. He drove up Sunset Plaza to the underboss' paver-patterned U-driveway. Brunetti checked his gold Rolex: 10:30. He strode toward the pillared front entry and knocked extra hard on the arched double eight-foot doors.

The door was quickly opened by a soldati nearly Brunetti's size.

"Tell the capo I gotta talk to him," Brunetti said harshly.

After a wait, he was led to a large den off the entry hall where the underboss sat. Dante Pio eyed him a moment then nodded for him to enter.

"What brings you here at this late hour *uninvited*, Beak?"

Brunetti did not like the smooth-ass fucker. "Joey Armanno 'n' his chump pal, Mario Zippi. What's going on with them two?"

"Not that it is any of your concern, Beak, but Joey came down from San Francisco to do a few jobs for me. The fat crumb's his lackey."

"Y'got any plans for the two of us, the Frisco wise guy 'n' me?"

"When the time comes, perhaps."

Brunetti was pissed by Pio's uppity manner. "So, in the meantime I can have me a little face-talk with *Joey*—get to know him some better?"

"So long as it doesn't upset my plans, Beak."

Brunetti left growling to himself. He sped down the hilly roadway to Sunset and east toward the Villa Capri.

What Bananas had told Crazy Nino was right. Slick Pio's fuckin' soft. He needs to know nothing about my fun 'n' games. Time to get serious.

On occasion, he'd seen Armanno and Zippi at Patsy D'Amore's Villa Capri downing bourbons and Parmesan cheese crisps. He would check out Patsy's first. Ever since the wise guy had hit town, the chump, Zippi, shadowed him. Brunetti hoped Armanno would be inside downing drinks.

He was, but so was the "shadow" Zippi.

Brunetti scowled as he crossed the room to their table.

"Say-hey, Beak," Mario Zippi called out, sounding crocked.

Brunetti glared at him. "It's Mister Brunetti to you—'n' only if I want you talking to me." He drew up a chair and sat. With his elbows on the table he looked into Joey Armanno's frog-like eyes. "Tell your fuckin' pal to split."

"Take a powder, Mario," Armanno rasped in a low tone.

"Sure thing, Joey," Zippi slurred, crawling off the chair.

Brunetti watched Zippi wobble to the bar, then he said to Armanno, "He's a fuckin' loser."

"Mario keeps me entertained."

"Listen up, Joey. I got two large if you'll do me a friendly family gesture." Brunetti saw Armanno's questioning look. "Yeah, it's personal."

"I got my ears on."

Brunetti related the essentials after which he laid out ten C-notes.

"Half now, the other half when the job's done. Then I got a little something else for you to do."

Like busting fuckin' Blue Eyes' damn chops.

Upon Armanno's agreeing, Brunetti ambled to the payphone by the men's room, ignoring Zippi leaning at the bar wearing a shit-eating grin.

Haley barely heard the telephone ringing over the whoosh of the shower. Closing the taps, he grabbed a bath towel, nearly slipping rushing to the nightstand, and snatched up the receiver. Before answering, he heard:

"Neallie Baby. I want your fuckin' pale ass at The Palms, tomorrow afternoon, three sharp. Don't be late."

Chapter 31

Haley stood at his kitchen window finishing an egg salad sandwich. He'd stayed home since the shooting, three days now, pitying himself. Because of Brunetti's call, Haley got a new unlisted telephone number. It required him to notify the watch commander and his parents. He had yet to inform Lissa. Fear for her well-being and his worthless feeling had him staying away.

He stared through the window at the tall sycamores teased into shedding by the cooler fall weather. Drying palmate-lobed leaves covered the up-sloping grounds of the Fern Dell Park area. He liked the hilly and grassy terrain of the location, it was convenient to work and roughly a mile from his parents' home, and just a few blocks north of The Boulevard. Because of all the trees and the heavy vegetation, he felt the air smelled cleaner even though the lush plants surely couldn't clear away the smog.

He grasped the telephone and played the long cord around the beige La-Z-Boy. He dialed the station number. While it rang on the other end, he watched a gray squirrel gathering up tiny woody fruit. The animal rolled one in its front paws as it speedily chewed, then, locking the morsel in its jaw, it skittered across the leaf-strewn ground, its fluffy tail flowing weightlessly behind in the still air. Seeing the furry little creature so free struck Haley, reminding him that he was trapped in Brunetti's deadly game.

The DAY watch commander's voice sounded on the line. When Haley asked about his status he was told to be at work the next day, Wednesday. He wasn't that surprised to be cleared by the Review Board.

Thanks to Mike.

He grabbed his bomber jacket, its distressed-leather, comfortable. He needed that feeling because it was time to see Brunetti. The conflate meant nothing good. A new card was about to be dealt from the bottom of The Beak's crooked deck.

Haley drove down Western and turned west onto Franklin, scanning the grass on the elevated grounds of Immaculate Heart High School. He hoped to catch a glimpse of Missy with her girlfriends, but realized it was a little early for classes to be let out.

The stately palms in the narrow parkways gave Franklin Avenue a canyon-like feel, but today they appeared bent and old creating more of a walled corridor, his tortuous road to perdition.

The closest street to The Palms, Lanewood, would be bumper to bumper with customized cars: the lowered, dual-piped, raked, chopped, sectioned and "Frenched" lights of the metallic toys of the more privileged Hollywood High students, so he went south at Franklin Park to Hawthorn and parked. The short walk to La Brea would allow him to get set.

He approached Lanewood, thinking of his first watch working with Montego, when his new partner had busted The Beak's beak. Haley's amusement was short-lived, however, as he recalled his own stupid mistake. It nearly had landed him on a cold stainless steel drawer in the morgue.

Pressing the Ronson's lever, he put a wavering flame to a Camel.

Beak Brunetti calling him "paesano," along with Montego's ribbing comment, though innocent, had unhinged Haley. He feared the meathead might be right, maybe his veins did carry Italian blood. That Pop might not be the man Haley thought he was had undone him. He didn't have the balls to alert Pop, but then Haley felt confident that he still had time.

He'd love to get Brunetti so pissed in front of Montego that he would do something foolish, like pulling a piece. Haley recalled when they'd busted The Beak's ass. He had dipped his head toward Montego with a look that seemed to say, "Just you wait." Brunetti had to be wanting to get even. Maybe he would try something stupid and Haley could waste his ass, and with Montego, a righteous and respected cop, as a solid witness.

The dangerous idea intrigued Haley, but the shooting must be legal, or at least justifiable-looking. Montego had a conscience. Hell, Haley wanted to believe he had a conscience, too. Still, he couldn't risk another shooting, or put his partner in danger, again. . . . Damn, he just didn't know what to do. He wanted to tell Montego about Brunetti's hairy-assed claim, but Haley's thinking was too scrambled. One thing he did know, he had to identify and locate The Beak's cousin.

Taking a quick drag Haley flicked the cigarette into the gutter and turned onto the path leading into the motel's courtyard. He marched to the dining room's patio entry. He was early because he wanted to get this meet over before Lissa's shift started. The fewer times she saw him with Brunetti the better.

Through the paned-glass door Haley spotted Brunetti sitting alone in the corner booth. Two meatheads, their backs to Haley, sat at a nearby table. He eased inside. Walking lightly, he deftly slid into the booth and was facing his slouching tormentor before the paired thick-necks feeding their faces became aware of him. Their pissed-off looks pleased Haley.

Brunetti's head jerked up, but he covered his surprise by tossing back his clear drink, and then saying, "Neallie Baby—y'wanna Grappa?" He raised his empty tumbler and waved it at the day-shift waitress.

"I'm not here to party, Beak—get on with your damn bullcrap."

"Tough guy, huh? But not so tough with that spook. I thought you was a better shot." Brunetti pulled a Dutch Master from an inside pocket and slipped off the label ringing it.

Coolness spread through Haley. It felt good. "I'm not here to discuss marksmanship." Knocking a cigarette loose from a fresh pack, he fired up, drawing in while sizing up the munching mob muscles shooting eye-bullets at him.

"Y'know shit. Listen up real good, Neallie Baby, here's how it is." Brunetti raised the empty tumbler and waved it at the dayshift waitress. "Hitting Gordo at the Knick was wrong. Riffelano was my right arm. I ain't said nothing about it, thinking he fucked up, but the boss is pissed, 'n' when he's pissed I'm pissed."

Brunetti sat back, snapped fire to a golden lighter, and puffed while eyeing Haley apparently waiting for the waitress to bring his fresh drink.

Why is Pio just now getting pissed at losing the Florida gunner?

Holding onto his thread of confidence, Haley waited as the waitress set down Brunetti's drink and left.

"Tough shit, Beak."

"We'll see whose fuckin' tough, Neallie Baby." Brunetti pocketed the lighter. "You're gonna make things right by doing a handshake hit on a pantywaist politician name a Eugene Preston. 'N' cut his ass down soon. Y'know what I'm saying?"

Haley's insides flip-flopped, his resolve to defy the lousy meathead obliterated. He took a longer draw making the cigarette red hot and almost choked on the acrid smoke. His mind reeled. Was the underboss getting even for Riffelano's death by ordering a high profile hit? Did Dante Pio honestly believe he could take out a civic leader without Parker's LAPD coming down on his suave ass?

Hell, plugging Brunetti *and* Pio while they conspired in this booth would be easier than killing a city councilman. A sick feeling hit him.

Did Pio sick Brunetti onto me? I gotta find out?

The thought that Pio was behind Brunetti's threat made the ingested egg salad sandwich churn into a sour fluid. Haley wanted to vomit.

He jammed his bony knees together, not wanting the thick-necked meatheads to see his legs bouncing.

Was my gut feeling wrong? To get out of this mess, will I have to take out the whole mob? Impossible.

Haley's knotted belly told him something about the high-profile hit was wrong. Why would the underboss have waited until now to exact his revenge for Riffelano?

There had to be another reason.

Haley's mind raced through various scenarios as he dared to lift his hand to take another drag. He simply refused to believe that the capo regime was part of Brunetti's damn game—

Haley's spinning thoughts were interrupted by Brunetti's snarling, "Hey, what'd I tell you, Neallie Baby? Use that twenty-two Minx I gave you. The little gat's clean—make it happen like yesterday, *capisco amico?* Y'fuckin' know what I'm saying?" He raised the tumbler and nailed the fresh Grappa in two gulps, then he crunched on an ice cube.

Haley now understood why wild quarry in the field got the shakes.

Wordlessly, he crushed the spent Camel into the ashtray and pushed his weak-kneed tense body from the booth, ignoring the twin thick-necks.

Haley headed for the men's pisser.

DeSimone and/or Capo Pio might want the stupid councilman dead, but it wasn't a smart move.

And killing Councilman Preston won't save Pop.

Chapter 32

Montego watched his blond partner's fingers playing a silent keyboard on the steering wheel as their Plymouth rolled east along The Boulevard. Maybe it was the various colored neon lights that eerily washed Haley's face, but the guy was ghostly looking. If Ice Cop looked like this on Halloween and wore a Count Dracula costume he'd fit right in. That was the evening when The Boulevard would teem with masked goblins of all sizes and ages scurrying about like the elfin creatures of folklore dispensing evil mischief now called trick-or-treating.

Today, however, the goblin was Brunetti, and the trick and the treat were stewing in a nasty pot: The trick was the Eugene Preston setup with Satin Sheen—the treat was giving the sex photographs to Rudolph Forrall.

Preston would not see it the same way. To him, the treat had been the whore and the trick, the photos he had yet to lay his eyes on.

Montego wondered if he'd accepted the black-and-white glossies because he wanted to shove them in Eugene Preston's pious face?

Whatever, he now held a long wooden ladle in a witch's black pot. But how to stir the boiling brew? The councilman should be warned. It was only fair. *Fair.* Was that the criterion? Had Rudolph Forrall been fair to his new son-in-law when he'd used him to bring his partner into the potentially dangerous scenario?

KW had suggested that Montego keep clear of it, still the guy had involved him, maybe unwittingly. For sure, Montego wanted to stay clear of dirty politics, but showing Preston the photos involved more than politics. It involved criminal extortion by the local Italian mob.

Yet, the Manila envelope remained secreted behind the driver's seat in the Cameo Carrier because Montego wasn't sure what to do.

He didn't like mobsters or bullies, but he was loath to coercing any person, even a bigoted politician like Preston whom Montego had no respect for, into resigning their public office. It meant flirting with danger.

If I give them to Preston, I risk losing my badge—besides that I would become an expendable pawn in Dante Pio's criminal hand.

The stewing pot brewed wickedly.

Inadvertently Montego grumbled aloud, "How to stir the pot?"

"What?"

Haley's sharp-toned query startled Montego.

"Just thinking about DeSimone's so-called Mickey Mouse mob."

"That's a good one," Haley said in a gritty voice. "DeSimone can blame Mickey Cohen for that."

They pulled behind a lowered, customized black '51 Merc convert with its top down. Five cigarette-smoking teenaged boys were pointing their index fingers and mouthing "Ka-pow" shots at the unmarked Plymouth's headlights.

Montego, grinning, raised his hands palms forward in submission. "We know the mob goons are causing problems on the southwest side."

Haley wordlessly followed the jeering teenagers from Cahuenga east to Cosmo where he left them to turn south.

While harboring clouded thoughts, Montego pictured his partner with Brunetti. The image looped in his mind's eye, reminding him that Haley seemed pretty much up on the mob. He decided to check the water.

"It's the murders—the hits that need stopping."

Haley paused at the crosswalk and scanned Selma Avenue in both directions. "The mob killings will never stop."

Montego treaded water, hoping not to splash too much. "Maybe, but you know the mob better than me—couldn't we do something to cramp their style?" The swift current swirled around his legs.

Haley didn't budge; neither did the Plymouth.

Montego waded in deeper.

"Intelligence Division, Captain Hamilton's men, eyeball the goons in plain sight and give the chief feedback, but it goes no further. Not many on the department seem to know about the Mafia." Montego's white pickup with a bullet-smashed windshield supposedly secure in a police parking lot came to mind.

The unit idled. "Mob families fight each other, waste their own— call it business." Haley made a snorting sound. "They don't give a rat's ass about a person's life."

Montego viewed the outside mirror; several vehicles had lined up behind them. He glanced at Haley sensing a troubled man.

It has to have something to do with Brunetti.

When car horns blared, Haley jerked, his foot hitting the gas pedal. The four-door "brodied" west onto Selma Avenue, the tires whining in a spinning protest to the side-sliding maneuver. He eased off the pedal.

"Sometimes the meatheads bait rival gangs into warring. When the sides get weak they snatch both turfs."

"Plant seeds of conflict and see what sprouts—I like that." The turf comment caused Montego to think of Rudolph Forrall's bid for Preston's seat. Haley's abrupt mood change also had Montego doubting he should mention the photos. Still, he chose to move in that direction. "Has Kay Dub ever mentioned that his father-in-law wants to unseat Eugene Preston?"

"Dealer is married?"

"Last Sunday—Kay Dub's father-in-law is Rudolph Forrall."

"*Now* you're bulling me, aren't you?" Haley side-glanced at him. "Forrall's a radical lawyer—a militant racist. Dealer's gotta know that?"

Montego reiterated what Smith had told him, and assumed that KW would agree. "Kay Dub swears the guy is neither a racist nor as extreme as some people claim."

Haley canted his head, his eyes squinted to avoid an oncoming car's high beams. "You believe Dealer?"

"I've heard Forrall's spiel—I know James Baldwin, the writer, impresses him. Forrall *is* passionate about his beliefs. Claims he's standing up for the rights of his people."

Montego rubbed his thumbnail. Were the sex photos showing up at the gym simply a subterfuge on Forrall's part? Was he mob-connected and purposely setting Preston up? But Smith should know. Yet, it might be one of those things that he couldn't talk about.

As they approached Selma, Montego pondered his next words. The photographs weren't a secret, KW knew of them. Why not tell Haley?

Maybe he can help me decide what to do.

"Speaking of Forrall—I'm involved in a sticky matter I don't quite know how to handle."

Haley eyed Montego off and on while he explained the arranged meeting with Rudolph Forrall and receiving the glossies. He ended with, "They were left at The Steel Bar Gym. Forrall owns the place."

Haley blurted, "Like on the card from Blagden's?"

"Interesting, huh? Not that I care if Forrall gets a council seat."

After reflecting on Julie, Montego added, "There's something else making things a bit messy. Eugene Preston is my girlfriend's uncle."

Haley looked over at him. "No? Again, you're bulling me?"

"Nope, and he's a genuine Puritan. . . . Apparently, Dante Pio is pushing Preston to vote for the proposed liquor-licensing ordinance. Preston

165

claims to be adamantly opposed to it. Explains the set up, the blackmail, and the photos." Montego watched various gaudily dressed transvestites, several arm-in-arm, doing what cops called the "Selma Avenue Troll."

"How did Preston screw up?" Haley asked.

"Being horny—picked up a whore. Probably arranged by Pio—"

"Attention all units, and Six-A-Five—motor officer requesting assistance." A frantic sounding Momma Mary broadcast a location not far from F-1's present spot.

"Frank One responding, Code Two," Montego radioed back.

Within seconds they were on the scene. He recognized the black Mercury convertible and the rowdy teenagers giving Ruggles a what-for. Seeing that they could handle the situation, and to ease Momma Mary's concern, Montego immediately radioed, "Codes Four and Six."

The five boys had encircled the motor cop. Haley shoved his way to Barry Ruggles' armed side, protecting his revolver. At the same time, Montego tapped the noisiest loudmouth hard on one shoulder from behind. The young tough, inches taller than Montego spun about, grunting, "Yeah?"

Smiling, Montego stepped sharply on the teen's arch without the others being aware and got the breakaway push he expected. A quick maneuver dropped the kid flat. His buddies shut up and stepped away while he handcuffed the loudmouth.

Hubba Bear completed penning the Greenie while Montego and Haley scratched out "shake" cards IDing the teenagers and describing the circumstances. The FIs would end up in the Field Interrogation Card file for officers to review; the same file Montego had gone through on the first night he had talked to Lissa at the drive-in.

He warned the boys about acting stupid then kicked them loose to foot their way to their homes in the Fairfax district. They looked unhappy, grousing to each other as their transportation was hooked up to a tow-truck.

Hubba Bear "ooga-ooga'd" a good-bye as Unit F-1 left with the scowling "Not-so-loudmouth" slumped in the back seat beside Montego.

The boy was treated for a scuffed elbow at the receiving hospital and then booked for assault on a police officer.

Receiving the PM lieutenant's approval for his completed report, Montego glanced at the front desk and saw the tall teen's jewelry-bedecked "Queen Bee" mother taking her son in hand.

Driving from the breezeway, Haley gave Montego a sidelong look.

"Are you thinking of a face-off with the councilman?"

"I haven't decided, yet. For sure, Rudolph Forrall wants to stay a long arm's length from the situation." Montego scanned the area. "Without the negatives, Preston is one dead duck. . . . And in time, he'll likely figure out who's behind the whole thing. Then Julie's father will hear about it and that I was the messenger. . . . The brothers will soon tie me to the goons."

"Hell, tell him that some snitch dropped the photographs on you—only fair to warn him."

Montego scrunched his mouth.

True. And if I do, Julie and I are history, for sure.

Chapter 33

A block from Lissa's apartment Haley parked the Porsche. He contemplated what Montego had told him. It might be the key that could get him out of the mess regarding Preston. If the councilman were forced to leave his seat, maybe Pio wouldn't need to take him out. Laying out the facts to the politician didn't bother Haley, and he didn't care whether Forrall knew he had done it, or not.

That's Mike's problem.

Because it was, he should be happy to let someone else show the photos to Preston. Haley flicked the cigarette into the dark street, his mind shifting to his main problem and how to do the impossible: Find Brunetti's cousin then ace both meatheads. Nancy still hadn't come through with a last name for Nino, or identified Brunetti's cousin, so now it was time to do what Haley had never wanted to do: involve Lissa.

He prayed he wasn't putting the woman he loved at risk.

What an asshole I am, but it's Pop's life.

He keyed the ignition and drove to Gardner Street.

Lissa saw him through the window and opened the door. She was still wearing her work outfit.

"I'd about given up seeing you here." She sounded upset.

He gave her a peck, and fought the urge to hold her close. He had to remain focused on his primary reason for being there. With what lay ahead of him, there was no future for them. The thought shredded his very being.

"Am I interrupting you?"

"Only my peace of mind—what do you think, Neall?"

"Damn," he spit out. Thinking about Brunetti's unknown cousin had him coming across gruff. Not what he'd wanted. "Sorry, hon."

"Would you like a beer?" Lissa's tone quickly softened.

"Thanks." He sank back on the small sofa sighing, unable to deny his desire to make love to the delicious woman he longed for.

She popped open a Budweiser, handed it to him, then poured *Soava* white wine into a crystal-stemmed glass, placed it on the coffee table and sat close, her leg touching his.

"I care about you, you know?"

"I know." He gazed about the apartment. Lissa's tender touch was everywhere. "The job must be getting to me."

"Has it got anything to do with Dante or Leo?"

He eyed her. "Why're you asking that?"

She bent forward, grasped the wineglass, swirled the Italian wine a moment, then turned her head toward him, her eyes intent on his.

"I had coffee with Mike. He said you want to protect me from them, but I'm not afraid. They treat me just fine."

Mike again!

"I do." Haley, crossing his right ankle over his left knee, rubbed it.

"I think it bothered him when I said Dante wanted his name."

"Huh?" Haley's right foot dropped to the floor. "See, I've told you Pio is not one to fool with. Hasn't Mike told you that? You know he's set on cramping Pio's action—and Brunetti's, too."

Damn. I shouldn't've said that.

Without any conscious design he realized he was preparing her for whatever might happen to him in his dealings with the Mafiosi.

"I'm sorry, Neall—but you hadn't been around, and I was worried."

She reached for the wine and sipped. Setting the glass back on the table, she said, "Isn't Mike asking for trouble? I mean it sounds dangerous."

"It is." Haley's free hand covered hers.

"Want me to tell you what I heard." She inched closer. "Yes, no?"

"I guess." He gripped the bottle.

"The pest and Joey Armanno, his blimpy friend from the Bay area, overheard Dante, who was sitting with Johnny Roselli, a movie producer, talking about pictures and a big hit." Lissa snuggled closer.

Haley stiffened, and not in the way he desired.

Armanno must be Riffelano's replacement.

"The pest told me they have a new player called Roger. Probably an actor, or maybe he's a movie mogul."

Haley clenched the bottle harder. Could Roger be Brunetti's cousin, the meathead who had seen Pop in Brentwood?

She reached for her wine glass. "I never know what to believe, but later, the pest said that 'Joey had a meeting with The Beak,'" she drank her wine, "and afterwards, Joey told him about a 'friendly family gesture' that Joey would be making. The pest thought it had something to do with Roger if he wasn't a hit, or didn't make a hit—I don't remember his exact words."

"Your friend mention where Roger's from?"

"The pest is no friend." She abruptly pushed away.

"Hon, I was kidding."

Neall, you ass—don't blow it!

"You better be."

Haley feared that Roger was no actor or a movie mogul, and the friendly gesture sounded ominous, even the way Lissa had mimicked it.

"Sounds like they expect the new picture to be a success." Her hand fingered the short hairs on Haley's neck. "That's why I think Roger's a movie actor. But afterwards, Mario laughed real wicked like—Neall, I don't like that pest." She sipped more wine.

"Hon, I know I've told you before to be cool around the meatheads . . . but, well I do need a favor."

Yeah, I'm a genuine asshole.

He set down the bottle and touched her smooth arm, hating himself.

"Brunetti's got a cousin, possibly his first name is Nino. Would you see if you can learn his full name or if he is Brunetti's cousin—find out who the cousin is and what kind of car he drives . . . maybe where the meathead hangs out . . . anything—but be damn careful."

Lissa, finishing the Soava, set the stemmed glass on the small table. Her breasts crushed against Haley's arm. Her lips brushed his ear. She blew lightly.

"What's in it for me?"

Damn, she had her ways—even how she'd cupped the wineglass was a turn on. Accepting her love while two lousy mobsters controlled his future was wrong, but he had to have this woman—always would. He gazed into her chocolate-colored eyes and saw his gloomy reflection swimming, then drowning.

Haley touched her chin, her lips rose to his. They kissed hungrily.

She loosened his belt as he twisted toward her and worked her skirt up to her hips. They tugged at each other's clothing, shifting awkwardly, ending up on the floor, bumping into the coffee table, knocking the empty wineglass and beer bottle to the floor.

He didn't deserve Lissa's love, but there was nothing he could do about his desire for her. It consumed him.

After a long, pleasant carpet dance, his release was exquisite, more than passion. These tender moments sharing intimacy, apart from the sex, not only brought a physical calm, but also the warm feeling of security—not unlike when he was a boy and had enjoyed being with his family on

Christmas Eves when Mom read aloud to the children cozily arranged around Pop on the floor by the lighted fir tree; and Neall Haley starved for that closeness now.

His security had been shattered because of Leonardo Brunetti.

Lissa gazed into Haley's eyes and whispered, "I love you beautiful Neall," and kissed him again with fervor.

When they parted, he straightened the small oval table knowing the words she wanted to hear. Loving the woman and not telling her because of his bleak situation, wrenched his soul. It brought unshed tears. He should tell her, regardless what might happen to him.

But the tender words, *I love you, too*, stayed locked inside him.

His future looked bleak.

A quiver of fear sneaked through his body.

Lissa picked up the wineglass and bottle and sat back against the sofa, her knees up, her ankles crossed.

He sat beside her, silent for a long moment, taking in her essence.

Finally, "Hon, just be damn careful around Pio and his meatheads."

Craven images swarmed like locusts in his head, mocking him.

"Neall Haley is just like us—an asshole."

Chapter 34

Montego swung open the large oak-and-iron door setting off the recording that announced his entry into The Bull Pen. Cops exchanging ribald banter occupied the swivel stools around the bar. The early AM mood was upbeat, the air overused. A "45" disc spinning in the bubbly Wurlitzer played "Sherry" by the Four Seasons. On the postage-sized dance floor a couple, seemingly oblivious to the din, leaned into each other, eyes shut.

Winding his way through the throng of off-duty cops he came up behind Dottie moving con brio ahead of him balancing a bar tray with "dead soldiers." He gently poked her side. She spun about, the three bottles steady, her dark eyes flashed. Before she could respond, he went through a familiar routine, bowing and saying, "*Con permisso, señorita*, but Beano, my tired leetle burro, is thirsty for a taste of your sweet cactus water."

"Señor Miguel, your tired leetle beano burro almost got some sweet agave *pulque* over his long ears." Her ruby lips formed a bright smile that endeared the pretty lady to the cop brethren. "Shoulda known it was you. The Counselor said you were coming." She peered up at his table. "Backups for Eagon and Roy?"

"*Si*, but only a Bud for me, no shooter." Seeing O'Brody was a surprise. "You've sure got a noisy bunch here this early morn."

"Tate's transferring to Metro—jus' bought the house a round."

Montego spotted the blond crew-cut cop squeezed between gleeful gals at the mahogany-and-brass bar. Tommy Tate's dream had been to work with the Patrol Bureau's "troubleshooters," his term for the Metropolitan Division—a resource that augmented various department entities, primarily at labor strikes. Plans to expand its functions were in the works.

Abruptly, a rousing cheer sounded: "Hooray for him—hooray at last—hooray for Tate—*he's a horse's ass.*" A loud "Oohrah" followed.

Montego went over and saluted the brawny ex-Marine, telling him, "Looking good, Semper-Fi."

Leaving a tipsy but happy Tate, Montego shouldered past several women who bumped into him, each casting a flirty look, each saying, "Oops."

Clearing the three steps up to the banquette level, he swung a leg over a chair beside the table where Eagon Quinn and Roy O'Brody sat.

"Since Tate bought you gents a round I'm not about to be bringing you another one."

Quinn shoved up his brown fedora and patted O'Brody's shoulder. "Why not? Roy bagged himself a Boone-and-Crockett-sized bull elk—on his second day out no less—it's why he's back home so soon. We're celebrating." He shoved his empty tumbler aside and jostled O'Brody.

"It's your lovable pink face, that's the real reason."

Montego guessed that O'Brody had been at the table eating his dinner, if any, downing Seagram's Seven Crown-on-the rocks, while he waited for his buddy to arrive. Loneliness was the real reason he was there.

The reflective thought had Montego sensing the same feeling.

Julie . . . quit avoiding me—I miss you.

Dottie breezed up, set down their drinks, and whisked away.

"Ah yes, most kind, m'lad," O'Brody slowly raised the tumbler like it was a jewel. "Most kind. Yes indeedie." His thick speech a contrast to his effusive exuberance.

Quinn grinned. "You still hitting the text books, Mikey? A college degree's important these days, you know."

"Yep—say, you got anything on a goon called Roger?"

"No—but he could be another Pio import." Quinn uncapped a gray tube-container and released an El Presidente cigar. "Airport Detail notifies Bucky whenever mob gunsels fly into Angel Town—I'll ask."

Montego had no doubt if he wanted to, Eagon Quinn could find out anything the Intelligence captain knew regarding the local Mafia, unlike Montego trying to find out things about Quinn's career. Over the years he'd to realize that his mentor held things inside that might never be unlocked. Quinn's time in the Homicide Bureau in the '40s when the department, and the city government for that matter, were being purged of corruption had apparently scarred him. What secrets Quinn had came from that period.

The man had never married. He lived frugally aboard his big boat, a '56 Chris-Craft. He had gone back east following the death of O'Brody's son and purchased the 54-foot Constellation model cruiser. He then had it shipped west. It was an escape for O'Brody, Quinn had said. It might be the same for him, Montego thought, having never seen his senior friend serious about any woman.

Except one perhaps, long ago.

Letting out a deep breath, Montego glanced at a nodding O'Brody who often spent most of his off-duty time tinkering, along with Quinn, on the sleek craft.

In early July, Roy O'Brody had lost his wife of twenty-five years to breast cancer. Montego and Quinn were pallbearers along with Captains Hamilton and Whitaker, two lieutenants, and Detective-Sergeants Nells and Strait. Montego still felt the weight of that casket.

To hear O'Brody say it, Quinn was his only true pal, even though in attendance at the funeral were more than a hundred officers of all ranks, including Chief of Detectives, Thad Brown. Also, plainclothesmen from nearby agencies the O'Brody-Quinn team had worked with on cases had filled the Rose Hills chapel. The homicide cases they had solved had made them law enforcement icons throughout southern California.

Detective-Sergeant O'Brody enjoyed more genuine friends than he'd ever cop-out to. The first day Quinn's law-practice ledger showed profitable figures, O'Brody would get the word to clean out his desk drawer and join the Quinn and Associates law firm, and he'd be "damn proud" to be doing investigative legwork for his "only true" pal, too.

Warmth flooded Montego.

O'Brody unexpectedly straightened up, shoved back his dark gray fedora and brought the tumbler to his lips. He slurped the watery bourbon.

Quinn, who never tried to keep pace, thumb-lit a Blue Diamond stick-match. When the flame quieted, he put it to the long cigar he rolled between moist lips. "Forgot to tell you, Mikey," he took a puff, "Bucky was not unhappy about that gunsel, Riffelano, going down."

The memory of gunfire ricocheted. Montego raised the longneck and took a lengthy pull. Shaking away the violent picture, he studied Quinn's lined face, understanding why he had waited till now to mention Hamilton's approval of the shooting. Montego's mentor had been there, more than once he could well imagine, and would know that he had needed the emotion-settling time.

Quinn let the match burn nearly to his fingers before he spoke. "Bucky mentioned that the Miami homicide boys were most appreciative." He dropped the burnt skeleton-like stick into the ashtray. "They invited him to ride shotgun on the hearse. He got to enjoy three days on their links swinging his Ping persimmons." Winking, Quinn puffed on the cigar.

Montego, knowing the ruddy-skinned ex-detective didn't unwind to just anyone, glanced at O'Brody who appeared to be lost in a memory.

The Purple Hand

"Got anything more on Brunetti?" Montego knocked back his beer.

"After Chicago PD cut him loose, he went to a mob hangout in the Nineteenth Ward—the Little Italy section—and met a 'buttonman'—his cousin." Quinn blew a billowing smoke ring overhead. "The same gunsel that Bucky's boys overheard yakking at the Continental Club not long after the two arrived in LA. They talked about an old time mob enforcer out of New York who's living in Hollywood." Quinn leaned closer. "That's when the eye-boys picked up another name: Angelo Sancia. What's interesting, when they checked their files they discovered that Angelo Sancia ran with Sammy Purples' Jewish gang, the Purples, in Detroit during Prohibition."

"Sancia's a Dago," O'Brody spouted, coming out of his reverie.

Montego, confused, looked at O'Brody, then Quinn, while rocking the Bud on its base. "An Italian in a purple Jewish gang?"

"In the early 'thirties there was a violent turf war between two Jewish gangs in Detroit. Sammy Purples, head of the Purples gang, needed extra protection for his bootlegging operation. He went to his Mafia friends. That's when Sancia came in from the Big Apple. Soon after, the Licavoli brothers from Saint Louis arrived."

Quinn sat back. "While muscling for Sammy Purples, Sancia took the Semitic name, Ari Sands."

O'Brody raised his left pinky. "Called 'im Pinky. Los' a li'l finger."

Quinn winked at Montego. "Bucky says Sancia had a rep for being mighty fierce. The Detroit booze war ended primarily because of his gun. Angelo Pinky Sancia, aka Ari Sands, became infamous. He got himself repped The Purple Hand."

Lifting his hat, Quinn scratched his scalp. "But in 'thirty-five the infamous hitter upped and disappeared. There were different stories about that. One version claimed that Sancia wasn't happy—got sick of the blood. Another was that the feds were hot on his tail." Quinn blew on the cigar's burning end. "But once in, no one quits the mob. The last anyone saw of Angelo Sancia was on Christmas Eve—at a Times Square jazz joint. . . . That night was when Bruno Brunetti tried to take out—"

"Brunetti!" Montego stopped rocking the warm Budweiser bottle.

"Yes. The gunsel's old man tried to kill Sancia—but it was bye-bye time for 'Poppa' Brunetti—and now his son, Leonardo, carries a vendetta."

"Brunetti, Simeti, spaghetti—nothin' but damn noodles." O'Brody belched. "Killin' Poppa don' figger." O'Brody's nodding head wobbled, the brim of his hat hiding his eyes. "Same Dago family," he mumbled.

Quinn shifted his rump about, grinning at his inebriated partner.

Montego had no sympathy for Brunetti, but losing a father was darn tough. "I suppose Brunetti has settled up with Sancia here in LA?"

"Bucky doesn't think so, but his eyeboys haven't stuck to his tail. They're concentrating on DeSimone—who sticks close to his home for the most part—and Pio's movements." Quinn twirled the cigar tip in the ashtray until the ashes on the burning end formed a short cone.

O'Brody's head lifted jerkily, his eyes bleary. "Bucky's suits got no clue." He noisily sucked up the rest of his watery drink. "Pinky's prob'ly dead by now, anyhows."

"So, Angelo Pinky Sancia might still be alive," Montego fingered the bottle. "And Brunetti has to be looking for him. If Hamilton's eye-boys are focusing on Pio they might miss out on Brunetti's personal retribution."

Quinn blew a large smoke ring, then shrugged. "That's the breaks." He downed the last of his Scotch.

"Does Sacramento have Sancia's prints on file?" Montego asked.

"No, and NYPD's file vanished along with him. Even with a DMV ID card and a thumb-print, there's zilch to compare it with even if he were nabbed." Quinn blew another smoke ring chased by a smaller, thinner one.

Montego was tempted to stab one. "Must've had an inside contact." Killing the remaining Bud in one gulp, he quickly poked at the thinner ring. "Maybe this Roger guy was brought in to help Brunetti find Sancia?"

"It's possible," Quinn said. "But chances are, the gunsel's here for something bigger."

"Interesting—well it's past my bedtime, gents."

Montego got up, patted O'Brody's slumped shoulder, and tugged lightly on Quinn's brown hat brim, knowing that his mentor would see that O'Brody got home safely.

Climbing the stairs leading from The Bull Pen, Montego thought about Councilman Preston. His being set up with the Wilshire whore might be part of that "something bigger."

Chapter 35

Montego heard the click and the telephone line go dead. He redialed. Same thing. Obviously, his voice was being recognized. He swore he would keep calling until the Prestons changed their darn number. After the fifth attempt, he threw the telephone onto the sofa.

Treading slowly downstairs and into the garage he grabbed his old Schwinn ten-speed and pedaled north to the beach community of El Porto and the home of The Clam Digger Bar and Grille.

The Furry Clam Diggers, a self-described beer-drinking society of cops residing locally, were gathered in the sandy outdoor patio. Even on foul-weather days, the men deigned to sit inside the wood-sided building, a shack, where local salt-crusted tars enveloped themselves with used tobacco smoke and hacked into several brass spittoons.

The Furry Diggers seldom talked about their jobs, if one did, the "culprit," Alex Strait's term, forfeited a pitcher of beer, but only for those sitting at that specific table.

After washing down sloppy chiliburgers with suds, Strait stood and fished out a tiny wad from his bike shorts. "Gentlemen, I fear I must break The Diggers' cardinal rule this fine midday in honor of Tonto's recent bust." Strait undid the damp bills and waved a crumpled Abe Lincoln, saying in a sober British accent, "I regret to say that the oversized bear cub, one Mister Collis U. Blagden, was strangled quite dead last night."

"At County General?" Montego exclaimed, almost spilling his beer.

"Face-up on the clean white linens—a hemp-rope double-looped around his mighty neck. He had been strapped to the bed, made it easy." Strait added, "Typical mob stuff."

While Strait pranced into the shack, Montego swigged his beer. He remembered what Quinn had once said; it made sense that Dante Pio had one of his goons kill Blagden in retribution for Salico.

Strait returned to the patio and made a big show of setting down the penalty pitcher. Froth overflowed onto the weatherworn tabletop.

Montego and Aurek sounded, "Hoopla's," and held out their empty steins as cops at the nearby table hissed and booed. Soon, salty mob-related jokes filled the balmy ocean air.

Montego finished his chiliburger, glanced at Strait's wristwatch, and realized if he wanted an hour-long siesta before Missy's birthday party he had better bid good-bye.

At 29th he coasted down to his home knowing he wouldn't be able to sleep until he understood a few more things. Moments later, upstairs in the Perch, he dialed the number to The Black Smith's Steel Bar Gym.

Montego arrived at the Haley's Spanish-style residence and parked in the driveway per his partner's earlier instructions. Before he stepped onto the porch the front door opened. The cute teenager with the long black curls stood there, all smiles, and all dressed up, party like.

He thrust out a big box wrapped in white tissue with a pink ribbon and a large fancy bow. "Happy birthday, Missy. Seventeen years and quite the charmer."

"How sweet." She eyed the package. "You shouldn't've, Mike." Sweeping it from his grasp, she shook it before hooking her finger under the ribbon and grabbing his arm with her free hand. She pulled him inside, saying loudly to the group, "Here he is, everyone. Mike Montego."

The chatter in the front room went silent.

Missy paraded him around to each of her girlfriends, bypassing the boys, until Lonn rescued him. Except for isolated giggles and a whispered, "Did you see his eyes?" the noise dropped to a hum of voices as Montego trailed Lonn into the den. The murmurs behind them erupted into muffled chatter.

"That was some gift you gave my daughter." Lonn, smiling, placed a strong hand on Montego's shoulder.

"But inexpensive." Montego felt the man's viselike squeeze. "I had no idea what to give your daughter—wait till she sees how dorky it is."

"Doubtful. You're her current crush," Neall Haley said, coming in.

Montego winked at Lonn. "Hey, I saw how all the girls ogled Neall. Anyway, it's just a stuffed pelican in a sailor's outfit—it'll get tossed into a corner."

"Don't be so sure, Mike." Irene, grinning, had followed her son into the leather-and-wood den. She set down a silver tray full of lemon cookies.

"Not you, too." Montego cast a beseeching look at the blonde woman, her steady, light-gray eyes twinkling.

"Don't let my boys pick on you. Now listen—twenty minutes, and we do the candle lighting. It will be in the dining room."

The Purple Hand

"If you gentlemen will excuse me a moment, I need to wash up." Lonn, an arm around his wife, said, "Make yourself at home, Mike."

The parents left the room.

Neall Haley sat on a burgundy-colored wing chair across from the rosewood cabinet containing Lonn's war medals, his back to the doorway.

Montego sat opposite him on a matching chair.

"Seventeen—hard to believe," Haley said. "Seems like yesterday Mom was changing Missy's diapers . . . when I rocked her in my arms."

Montego had yearned for a sister when he was a boy. One day, he would father two children. He thought of Julie and sighed.

"I've been thinking about those sex photos of Preston," Haley said.

Montego's eyes widened. The topic was unexpected.

Haley raised an ankle to his knee and massaged it. "When Preston sees them he'll know it's over for him politically. Why should you risk making matters worse with your girl by showing them to her uncle?"

Montego picked up a cookie. "He's gotta be told—it's only fair."

"Let me do it, Mike. I've got nothing to lose—not like you."

"You? Uh-uh. I can't let you get involved in this." A burst of laughter in the living room gave Montego a moment to think. . . . In his mind's eye he pictured Haley and Brunetti together. "Forrall expects me to be a buffer—he doesn't want Dante Pio able to pull his strings." Montego saw Lonn stepping into the room unnoticed by his son.

Haley pinched a cookie. "Forrall's best chance of *not* becoming Pio's puppet is for me to do it. He shouldn't hear about it, and if he did he probably wouldn't give a damn. With me doing the delivery, you'd be clear—it would be a double-blind."

"Maybe, but you'd be doing mob stuff." Montego noticed that Lonn had paused near the doorway as if not to disturb them. "I'll think about it— let you know." With no proof that Haley and Brunetti were up to no-good— only guilt by association—Montego had to admit the offer was appealing.

"Also, Mike. I'm taking a Special tonight—to party with Sis."

"Have fun—hey, did you hear that Blagden's dead—last night?"

"Cubby Bear? You're bulling me?"

"At the hospital—strangled. What you told me about him strolling around after the Ralph's store-bombing site didn't fly with Intelligence." Montego glanced at another lemon cookie. "The eye-boys believe Salico, under orders from Dante Pio, was responsible. His mistake was bombing a

179

white-owned store that killed a black kid. Collis Blagden retaliated by blowing up Salico at the Saint Andrews hotel. The homicide dicks agree."

"Interesting." Haley knuckled a crumb from his lip.

"What's interesting is Rat Rondell telling O'Brody and Nells that Blagden was responsible—claimed he'd seen Blagden do it."

"What?" Haley shook his head. "That puts Rondell in the middle."

"It goes back to the Slauson Slaves shooting. Rondell was upset, blamed Blagden for the gang leader's death. According to Roy O'Brody, Blagden was able to convince the leader that the mob would take over their local rackets if he didn't stop Beak Brunetti. Blagden hated white people—he wanted the Italian mobsters out of the neighborhood, as well—he'd been harassing white landowners, trying to scare them into moving." Montego had learned this as a result of his phone call to Smith.

Montego eyed another cookie. "The irony is that's what Pio wants, too. Anyway, O'Brody thinks Rondell played Blagden—got the guy to let Rondell act as a lookout at the hotel so he could finger Blagden to the mob afterwards. But saying he'd seen Blagden put dynamite in Salico's room put Rat Rondell's butt on the hot seat. When questioned, he changed the 'seen Blagden do it' to 'hearing Blagden brag about doing it.'"

Lonn moved toward the sofa.

"We knew Rat wasn't too swift—his hot head got him killed—running from Dealer and me—" Haley, now aware of his dad, stopped talking and eye-cued Montego to be still.

"Yep. Rat wanted to continue his personal hunt for Brunetti—couldn't wait for Lady Justice. . . ." Montego noted the scowl on his partner's face. "For sure he thought you guys were going to bust his ass."

Lonn was lowering himself onto the sofa when Irene called out.

The three made their way into the festively decorated dining room.

Irene brought in a candlelit cake.

Everyone sang, ". . . Happy Birthday Dear Missy."

Taking in an exaggerated breath, the teen blew hard. The eighteenth "to grow on candle" flickered but went out—to her obvious relief.

A chubby, freckle-faced girl excitedly asked, "What'd you wish for, Missy?"

Missy beamed. She looked at Montego standing across the room, her dark brown eyes sparkling.

"Now Shirley, you know that's supposed to be my secret."

Chapter 36

The sun was low and orange-red in the haze-laden western sky when the Cameo Carrier crossed Normandie heading for the station. Montego looked up at the Observatory poised high atop Mount Hollywood in Griffith Park. Its curved white face wore a slight blush as if embarrassed, reminding him of his reaction to Missy's cute mischievous look.

The cute kid will be a handful for some lucky guy one day.

Smiling, he reflected on the talk in the den. Haley had seemed upset when he'd realized his dad was in the room and had heard some of their discussion. Lonn hadn't heard about the sex photos involving Preston— probably a good thing.

Was Neall upset because I mentioned Brunetti?

Again, picturing Haley with Brunetti bugged Montego. Something was going on there, and it was affecting his partner—his judgment as well.

Haley's proposal to show the photos was surprising. He seemed to want to be of help. Admittedly, it was a relief knowing the offer was there.

While finding a spot in the police lot Montego decided that Monday morning he would phone Quinn and ask him for advice. Quinn had said, "Use your noggin about those photographs, Mikey, but please do keep Julie out of it."

Out of it?

Montego hadn't been able to talk to her for what seemed like ages. With all of his calls getting hang ups, he'd about driven to the Preston's home, but had thought better of it. Confronting the parents asking to see Julie would only exacerbate things.

He strode up to the assembly room and slid onto the bench beside Trev Brannock in the back row. He and Bobby Diaz were rotating between Units F-1 and F-2 while KW was honeymooning.

After a guns-and-ammo inspection, Montego and Brannock paced out to their plain sedan parked across the street in the vehicle service area.

"Frank-One, clear." Brannock re-hooked the handset and filled out the top portion of the DFAR while bringing up KW's wedding. "I could never handle being married to a lawyer, especially a defense—"

Three quick and loud beeps sounded on the radio speaker followed by Momma Mary's voice, "All units and Six-Frank-One—two-eleven in progress—Rancho Liquors—Santa Monica at Westmoreland—Code Three. No other units available."

Brannock quickly grabbed the hand-mic. "Frank-One, that's a roger. Proceeding Code Two east on Santa Monica from Normandie."

Montego pulled the headlight knob on to make their prowler more visible while en route to the robbery scene. Their one-colored unit wasn't equipped with a "growler," a siren, or rooftop reds cops called "Antlers."

Momma Mary added, "Two-eleven suspect was last seen on foot, going north on Westmoreland. Described as male, black, over six-feet, wearing a blue-and-gold jacket. He displayed a handgun."

The description triggered memories of the Collis Blagden shooting. Montego scanned the next intersection and accelerated through on the yellow light, streaking past a slow-moving gray Nash Ambassador.

"Twice this month for that store." Brannock's tone sounded sour.

"Owner refuses to put his cash register by the front window so cops can see it cruising by—punks know it too," Montego said.

Crossing Vermont Avenue just when the tri-light turned green they were forced to veer around an oblivious jaywalker busily tonguing a vanilla cone as he walked south from a Foster's Freeze.

At Madison Avenue, a big Harley-Davidson, reds burning, whipped a fishtailing left in front of them.

It was Hubba Bear Ruggles.

"Stick with him, Tonto."

Montego fell in close behind.

"Gotta hunch, Trev—let's go nightclubbing."

Taking a chance, Montego passed Ruggles, who was braking at the liquor store, reds lit, siren dying, and continued speeding east. At Virgil Montego mashed the brake pedal and cranked a hard left, peeling off rubber and power-drifting northbound. He raced to Sunset where he stopped for a red light, not wanting to.

When he had the green he turned left and quickly parked behind a blue Dodge pickup parked near the Sambah Room's rear fire exit. He killed the motor as Brannock put them Code 6.

They jumped out. Montego signaled Brannock to join him in a crouch at the rear of the pickup.

"I bet it's the ornery suspect Neall and I took down for interfering a while back. If I'm right, he'll be coming to join his teammate on the other side of that fire door." Montego figured the ringer alarm had been disabled.

"The jerks always make bail—hey." Brannock nodded to the west. "Tonto called it."

Montego simultaneously heard the heavy footfalls getting louder.

"Let's take the guy before he knucks the door, Trev—don't need his big-ass teammate coming out here."

"You got it."

The robbery suspect hurried by the pickup's front bumper and was angling toward the fire door when both cops sprang out behind him.

"Freeze or die, Jerk," Brannock said loudly.

Tackle One whirled, stumbled, and barely caught his balance before he went rigid. His eyes danced between two four-inch steel gun barrels.

"Sheeit—muhfuck." He raised his large hands, a dirty cloth sack with the words "Security First National Bank" dangled from his right hand.

"This time, pal, you're staying behind bars." Montego pulled a Ruger semiautomatic from Tackle One's belted waistband as Brannock snatched the night-deposit bag from One's grip.

A series of "oogas" sounded. Officer Barry Ruggles revved the chromed Harley as he motored up, grinning. "Heard your unit going Six. Somebody must've known a *bit* of something." He winked at Montego.

"A bit, Hubba Bear." Montego grinned back. "Suspect's buddy might be inside, but we have nothing to hold the guy for."

"Like I've heard you say, Tonto—his turn'll come." Ruggles waved while he tooled away on the heavily chromed hog.

At the station jail, Brannock stood by during the booking process while Montego, across the lobby in the Records Section, completed the Robbery and Evidence Reports. He felt upbeat as he dictated the scenario. Harlene Settles, the long-haired blonde, and senior stenographer, was the softique sweetheart of the Sixth Division. She typed his words as fast as he spoke them. It was as if she knew what he'd say before he did—but then, pat statements were a part of most police reports.

After Sergeant Kozier approved their paperwork, Montego and Brannock returned to the breezeway where their four-door was parked.

"At least we beat the bastard back to the streets, Trev."

Brannock grumphed. "Jerk should still've been behind bars for messing with you and Ice Cop the other night."

Montego understood the frustration. All street cops shared it. The bad guys bailing out and making a joke of the system that law officers were sworn to uphold. He hoped his comment to Tackle One would hold true.

Brannock cleared their unit as Montego headed for the poorly lit residential streets. While patrolling, they searched for anything unusual.

One of Montego's first arrests had been catching a dark-clad man on Fuller Avenue with his right leg over a ground floor apartment window sill. Whether the suspect, a USC assistant physics professor, was a cat burglar or a rapist, Montego never learned. What he did learn was that felons came in all types.

Leaving the dark side streets, they cruised the lighted main ones checking for hot rollers, stolen cars. At Highland and Sunset, Montego abruptly swerved their unit into the side lot next to Stan's drive-in.

Brannock's hands flattened on the dash. "Whoa—what'd I miss?"

Montego looked in the rear-view mirror. "Nada—radio is jammed with calls—you want to call in and request Seven at The Palms?"

"That's it—what I want?" Brannock chuckled. "Has nothing to do with a sexy blonde waitress I heard about?" He spun out of the prowler and shadowboxed his way to the Gamewell phone.

Montego had kept an eye on a black Chevrolet sedan passing through the intersection, the same direction they'd been traveling. He'd been unable to see the driver's face, but in the wash of streetlights he made out a dark-haired man with almost no neck. He was sure the squat driver had been following them for blocks. Coincidence or not, Montego wanted to check out The Palms, see what goons were dining there, and check the area for the black Chevy sedan.

The Gamewell box's iron door-slamming noise pulled Montego's attention to Brannock who was removing the brass skeleton key. Grinning widely, he mock-trundled back to the idling prowler.

"Chow time, or should I say party time, Romeo?"

Montego shook his head. The tingling on his arms subsiding. He figured Bobby Diaz must've told Brannock about Lissa.

"Lissa is Neall's gal, Trev. . . . She *is* mighty easy on a guy's eyes, but I have a girlfriend."

Do I?

"I gotta tell you, Neall doesn't want us talking to her when Pio, a mobster boss, and/or his goons are there." Montego didn't mention that Haley didn't even want them inside the restaurant.

Brannock looked questioningly. "Ice Cop's jealous, huh?"

Montego accepted that. But was he putting Lissa in harm's way by going there? His foot eased off the pedal momentarily, still he kept driving.

184

In the foyer, he cautioned Brannock as he paused and peered inside the dining room. Dante Pio and Miss Long-Gloves occupied the corner booth. Brunetti wasn't there, but at a nearby table sat a pair of dark-suited wrestlers. One was a new face.

Lissa danced up. "Hi pal." She winked and then she eyed Brannock.

Montego introduced Brannock. She shook his hand. Her breasts jiggled and Brannock's eyes joggled.

She led them to the small table by the kitchen door, Brannock right behind her. Montego ignored the corner booth even after they sat.

Lissa gave them menus. "You want something to drink?"

"Coffee for me." Brannock turned up his cup. Montego followed suit, taking the menu she handed him.

When Lissa returned with the full pot, he asked her in a low voice, "Who's the guy with the braggart pest?"

"Joey Armanno." Not looking around she added. "He's Mario's friend, came from San Francisco a while back." Lissa left for another table.

Montego surreptitiously eyed the heavy-set goon. He matched the driver's profile in the black Chevrolet, but so did Mario Zippi, the wannabe, whom Montego actually had suspected of being the follower.

"Armanno?" Brannock whispered.

"Apparently another mob gunner."

Montego discreetly studied the squat man. Number Two appeared to be in his mid-forties. His black hair, slicked-back, was silvered at the temples, like it had been sprayed on by a professional hairdresser. A ring on his left little finger had a stone that trapped a distant light and sparkled. The underboss had a confident bearing and black-marble-like eyes. His look seemed to dare other men, but softened on women's curves, like now with the tall brunette wearing elbow-length gloves close beside him.

Dante Pio dipped his head and caught Lissa's attention. She moved behind a nearby partition. When she came out, she held a silver champagne bucket. She went to the dimly lit corner booth, lifted out a dark-green bottle of Dom Pérignon, and deftly wrapped it in white linen. She popped the cork expertly. After pouring the bubbly into the couple's cut-glass flutes she twisted the bottle into the bucket of ice and placed it within reach of the mob underboss.

The capo regime has it all.

As if sensing an intruding energy, the suave underboss looked over at Montego. His head seemed to nod imperceptibly saying, "I know it."

Chapter 37

Montego skipped down the stairs from the Perch, his mind on Dante Pio and his brute enforcer, Leonardo The Beak Brunetti. On the street Montego joined Strait and several Diggers for their weekly long run.

This early morning they jogged the hilly Palos Verdes peninsula. Montego intended to go to his mother's for a swim and lunch afterwards. On their return run, however, he decided to surprise Smith with a visit.

Montego, hearing Bessie Smith's bluesy voice, strode into the gym office, his oxblood huaraches squeaking.

Smith was flipping through a *Weider* magazine.

"Hey, Smitty—what's the tariff for a guest workout?"

"On the house," Smith put down the magazine, "unless you decide to be a regular." He reached to the Grundig and lowered the volume. "That happens, I can't call it a promo to hook your wallet." He grinned and shoved the muscle magazine aside.

"A good inducement to stay out of here. Got a minute?"

"Always." Smith padded to the hall, peered into the gym proper, closed the door, and returned to his desk. "A quiet Sunday morning."

Montego sat in one of the armchairs in front of Smith's desk.

"I'm glad that besides telling me you also told Hamilton about the Blagden-Rondell connection—it opened the door so I could talk about it to Neall Haley, my other partner."

"Keeping the skipper informed is my job." Smith sat back in his executive-sized chair sly-eyeing Montego.

"Thanks," Montego said. "I came by to ask if you've ever heard of a mobster-goon called Roger?"

"Hell, I thought you wanted to play with the iron plates."

"Later, maybe."

"Never heard of any Roger."

"How about a Joey Armanno—a squat guy with wiry black hair?"

"Could be the clown I told you delivered the envelope. Hamilton told me he's from the Bay Area—I believe he did the camera work on the Sheen shindy." Smith swiveled his chair. He's one of those gonzos thinks I've bought into his boss' scheming."

"But Rudy's clean—right?"

"Bet on it, Mike."

Montego pressed a thumbnail. "Did he drive a black Chevrolet?"

"A black Ford—a rental. Why?"

"Curious—by the way, I told Haley about the sex photos."

"Your other partner, right?"

Montego nodded. "He's offered a show-and-tell with Preston—because of Julie, my girl."

My girl? Hopefully, she still is.

"The dude must like you. A steady, huh—and she matters how?"

"She's Eugene Preston's niece."

Smith stopped swiveling.

"Yep." Montego stood and stretched. "OK—bring out the two-foot railroad tracks. Your twenty-twos look a mite puny. Must be this cushy job—not the guns I saw during our fitness testing days."

"Hah. No track rails, here. How about a Smitty-sized steel bar?"

Following a one-hour workout and a hot shower, Montego slipped on a pair of Vaurnets and drove the Cameo north toward Laurel Canyon. He removed the sunglasses when he approached the Preston's manor. Julie's British green sports car wasn't in the driveway as he'd hoped. Had it been, he would have gone to the door, regardless of the consequences, having told himself he would not argue with her parents if they refused his entry, which he expected. He simply needed Julie to know that he'd been there.

He cruised over the brushy mountain crest and coasted into the driveway leading to a California Ranch-style house on Mulholland Terrace. Birch leaves whirled over the pavers when he parked. The large place spoke of Steve Buckingham's materialistic values. It overlooked Studio City to the north. The house was a far cry from the thirty-dollars-a-month duplex on Lockwood Avenue, Montego's weekend home during the 'forties.

He looked forward to a hot soak in the *Jacuzzi* spa and then a warm meal while responding to the never-ending prying questions coming from the "Commander-in-chief" of Buckingham Palace. Montego was prepared to bite his tongue if the guy started his usual prying stuff.

Montego's mother spied him through the kitchen's garden-boxed window and waved. He waved back, smiling.

In the kitchen he breathed in her familiar powdery fragrance and the aromas she created with her cooking. The savory smells carried him back to the Sunday midday meals . . . so long ago . . . his "last suppers." He squeezed out the lonely feeling it brought by giving her a bear hug.

"You are sweet." Her lightly powdered face held a pleased look. "And how is Julie?"

"She's avoiding me, Mother. It has to do with my job—the hours." He couldn't tell her the truth.

His mother grasped a flowery potholder. "It has been quite a while since Julie and I talked," she stepped to the gleaming white O'Keefe and Merritt range, "but I know she worries about you on patrol." She lowered the oven door and peeked inside. "She's never said you shouldn't be a police officer, and she knows you want to be a detective."

Julie deliberately staying away had him doubting her love for him. He questioned his ardor for as well. That perturbed him. One-sided affairs were painful, but not as hurtful as having no dad around. If she criticized his work hours, there could be problems. He didn't want another divorce. His children would have both parents to love; marriage included a promise to the progeny and a commitment to their proper upbringing.

The fleeting image of his Latino father, Jesse, a *bailador*, a dancer, had him fingering the silver Bulova, the only gift from the man. Montego's entire life had been a longing for his dad's closeness, even though Mother said his proclivity when drinking was to fight. But having a belligerent sot around would've been better than having no dad, Montego believed.

The last time he'd seen his father was after the Pearl Harbor attack, before Uncle Sam's army shipped him overseas. He'd dropped by the duplex on a Saturday night with a boxful of wire-haired terrier puppies. Montego had ached for a puppy to love, but the foster people in the Valley wouldn't allow it and his mother had no time for one. So, bringing puppies over for him to see, although wonderful, was a hurtful tease. But his dad's parting promise that he would write hurt the most. No letter ever came.

Montego fumbled with the short leather fob on the pocket watch.

A dozen years later, after eight years of *dating*, his mother married Steve, now a fire captain. Montego remembered how that had come about. It had been an early Saturday evening when he'd spied her sitting on the side of her bed in the dim light, weeping. She'd told him that Steve had just called. Pressing her, Montego heard how the guy had stalked her, how he would phone her whenever she returned from a night out, regardless if she had been with a woman or a man.

She'd then said Steve was coming over. Montego was so upset that when the big man arrived at the front door, Montego had confronted him with an ultimatum: *either marry my mother or leave her alone.*

The Purple Hand

The heavy-boned guy appeared to want to challenge the whip-thin thirteen-year-old kid blocking his entry but backed off, perhaps because he knew of the kenpo training, but more likely because of the negative affect it would have on Montego's mother was the real reason.

Whatever, Steve Buckingham promised to marry her.

And I've regretted it ever since.

Montego fumbled with the watch fob. Mother gave him the watch on the day of the simple wedding ceremony. It was held in the apse of the Congregational Church on Wilshire Boulevard.

The watch was a double reminder: a lost dad, and a pretender dad.

Over the years, Montego became convinced that his mother, Helen Montego-Buckingham, was an unhappy woman, but she never complained, at least not overtly.

And it's been my cross to bear.

He sighed. "I'm glad Julie wants me to promote to detective, Mother, but she'll have to cope with my odd job hours and the call-outs—and understand that there will be cases I won't be able to discuss."

"Unless you two talk, how will you ever know?"

She eased the oven door closed, set the pot-holder on the counter, and wrung her hands in the pink apron folds.

"Say, if you're going to soak in the hot pool you'd better go do it. In forty minutes that leg of lamb with the mint jelly you like will be on the dinner table." She smiled and patted his arm.

Montego sensed something deep inside that made him realize he would be fortunate to find a woman like his mother. He chided himself for the thought; he'd heard that men had a tendency to marry women reminding them of their mothers.

For sure, Julie wasn't like his mother. But with Julie refusing to see him, it didn't really matter.

I should stake out on the Preston's pad until Julie shows, then force her to hear my feelings. But if I can't tell her the "love" word, what good would it do? Besides, her father probably would call the cops and accuse me of trespassing, and likely assault for accosting his daughter.

Montego left Buckingham Palace and drove down Laurel Canyon toward the Preston manor.

189

Chapter 38

Neall Haley pulled his Porsche to the curb on Gardner and stared across at Lissa's apartment. Afternoon sun rays shot through the trees. His mind was on what he'd said in the den yesterday that Pop might have overheard. He'd gotten pissed, but not at Montego as much as for his own blabbering mouth.

How much had Pop heard? He assumed that when his pop read the *Hollywood Citizen News* he'd know that Collis U. Blagden had been arrested for the deadly St. Andrews hotel explosion that killed an alleged mobster, Paoli Salico. What pleased him was Pop not displaying any signs of recognition when Brunetti's name was mentioned, but that by itself shouldn't cause Pop to think the Italian mob had found him, assuming Pop was the ex-hit man.

Pop is not Sancia—but if he is, he doesn't know Brunetti's after him. Pop was cool—so if he is Sancia, his heart obviously is handling it.

Still, Haley would never forget five years earlier, the afternoon he had graduated from the Police Academy when his pop had keeled over. Mom's panicked expression had whammed Haley, and the memory was indelible. That vivid image of Pop lying on the grass field was what kept Haley from telling his pop about Brunetti's bold claim that Pop was Sancia, or about Brunetti's implied threat to kill Pop if Haley warned him.

Haley knew his sour mood had shown when Montego drove off, because Pop had probed him, casually asking if he was having problems at work. He'd been prepared for more questions, but none came.

At last night's dinner table, he had attempted to sound convincing to explain his mood, saying it wasn't the job but his love life that was bothering him. His parents had yet to meet Lissa, so he'd described her, and his feelings for her. Then, using the line Montego had once mentioned, he'd explained how Lissa would worry because he patrolled the dangerous streets. He had added that he was afraid his cop job could wreck a marriage.

Missy had played into it by saying, "Neallie, you're being silly— your job won't spoil anything. Lissa worrying, means she loves you." Missy had then dropped to her knees, hands clasped flat in front and implored dramatically, "Just tell her every morning, noon and night, 'Oh my darling, I love you—madly, madly, madly.'"

Mom and Pop had laughed, nodding in agreement. Haley did love Lissa, so painfully, but he couldn't guarantee a life for her—not while being under The Beak's threatening hand. To even think of being a mob hit man was out of the question. Still, Haley had to ace the meathead cousins, and do it with or without Montego.

Haley thought long about that.

He'd brought Montego, a proven fighter, in as backup, But if he knew about Brunetti's crazy claim, would that scare him off—not from intimidation, but because of the legal issues if he thought Pop was Sancia?

What if Montego were told that it was pure bullcrap except it was something Brunetti believed to be true? But what could be done to convince Montego of that?

Maybe he would go along with a hit on the cousins if he thought he was protecting Pop, an innocent man? *No.* Haley simply couldn't mention the threat. Montego had to be convinced that confronting Brunetti about his murderous activities was necessary. The meet would be a trap . . . and it must include Brunetti's finger-pointing cousin or the threat wouldn't end.

Haley's top priority, however, was getting Preston to resign. That meant getting hold of the motel photographs and showing them to the stupid councilman. Doing that should eliminate the need for a damn hit.

A passing automobile's backfire jerked Haley alert. Letting out a tremulous breath, he removed his driving gloves.

Thinking straight any more is impossible.

He eyed Lissa's Pontiac in the carport. On his last night with her, she'd held him like a woman fiercely in love, filling him with more guilt.

He lifted himself from the Porsche, crossed Gardner, and slowly climbed the stairs to her small home. She opened the door wearing a silky slip with a pink rose-petal pattern. The bodice gathered under her breasts wrapped in white floral-patterned lace. Smooth jazz music sounded softly. Johnny Hodges was blowing an Ellington melody on a sweet tenor sax.

"Wanna go out or stay in?" Her presence always aroused Haley. "Nothing going on—typical Sunday afternoon."

Lissa smiled wickedly. "Stay in."

Hodges' saxophone hit a high note.

Haley followed her into the kitchenette, stopping at the fridge to get a Budweiser. He popped off the cap while watching her backside as she tidied the countertop and moved to the sink to rinse her hands.

She folded a dishtowel and bent to hang it on a door bar. The silky fabric clung to her curves. When she stood on her tiptoes to open an upper cupboard, the slip crept higher. She brought out a bottle of sparkling white wine. Reaching up again she grasped two goblets, more of her legs showing. She opened a flatware drawer, took out a corkscrew and twisted it into the bottle's top. Below the lace her bountiful breasts were enticing.

"You wanted to know if I heard anything, Neallie," she peered at him. "Well, the pest told me something that made absolutely no sense."

Haley tensed, his arousal beginning to wane.

"Something about a bull that ran with Roger who had a beach mailbox and lived above a pol-tic's niece . . ." Her words chilled Haley. He quickly reached into the refrigerator and grabbed a bottle of orange juice.

Mike has to be the bull—I'm Roger!

". . . And he also said 'it made The Beak happy as—' you know." She turned slightly and poured the bubbly wine half filling the two goblets. "I told you, crazy stuff."

He tried to control his trembling hand as he topped the wine with the orange juice. "You're right, hon, crazy stuff."

One of the capo's damn gunners must have followed Mike home. Brunetti? He still had to be pissed about the busted nose. Whatever, now the lousy meathead knows that Mike is dating the councilman's niece!

Haley sank onto the short sofa, blew out to relieve the slight pain in his chest, and gulped most of the Mimosa. He watched Lissa come to him. She sat close. He sighed, sensing his growing tumescence.

"Enough of this talk, hon. Got any games we can play?"

Lissa lightly dragged her fingernails across his knotted shoulders. "Oh, I know a game or two we can play." She eased her body over his, straddling him. A showering fragrance of rose petals enveloped him.

*   *   *

Montego neared the Preston's home mentally prepared to do what he had decided while driving down the canyon. His shift started in thirty minutes, leaving no time to stake out on the house, still he had enough time to at least knock on the door, make his presence known.

He slowed and signaled a left turn, but seeing several dark-colored sedans parked besides Julie's sports car, he hesitated turning.

They've got company—not good.

192

Slamming the steering wheel, he continued on to the station.

After roll call, while heading out to the breezeway, Haley abruptly said, "Mike, I was a cold-ass at the party—sorry. My damn fault—I started the shop-talk. I don't like my family hearing the crappy side of our job—that's all." He glanced sideways at Montego.

"No problema, mi amigo. Most parents can handle it pretty well." Montego laid a hand on Haley's shoulder. "It's better that they know."

Haley stopped at the passenger side of the prowler. "You happen to bring those Wilshire whore photos?" his voice sounded tight.

Montego unlocked the driver's door, peeked at Haley, then tossed the keys over the green prowler. "You sure you want 'em?"

Haley snagged the keys in flight, opened his side door, climbed in and inserted the ignition key. "Offer stands."

Montego felt a wave of pleasant lightness. "They're in my pickup." He drove into the police parking lot. "I told Kay Dub about your offer."

"No big Deal." Haley snickered.

Montego looked at Haley's profile for a moment before speaking.

"Been thinking I wouldn't show them to Preston."

Haley jerked his head about. "Like you said. Warning him is only fair. My doing the deed will keep *your* girl from getting more upset with you—and it'll keep you away from *my* girl." Haley snickered, again.

Montego was caught off guard. This was not the way the guy had sounded a week ago. Parking the prowler by the Cameo Carrier and before getting out, Montego said, "You saw Lissa today—didn't you?"

"Being damn weird, huh?" Haley popped open the passenger door. "Incidentally," his tone serious, "she told me that Mario Zippi made a crazy comment to her about a bull having a beach mailbox and living above 'a pol-tic's niece.' You've been pinned, Mike—it could be why Pio wanted your name."

"We've yanked his chain, for sure. What can the capo regime do—put out a contract on me?"

"That's not funny, Tonto."

Chapter 39

A fall breeze flowed into Montego's face from the driver's side window as he stopped the prowler behind his pickup. He climbed out to retrieve the Manila envelope noticing Haley taking his car key from his briefcase before joining him.

Accepting the envelope in both hands as though it were a treasure, Haley strode to his Porsche. Montego watched as he keyed open the front hood, placed the photo packet next to a small canvas bag with a drawstring and relocked the lid.

Haley rejoined him and they returned to their unit.

"Time to go bowling," Haley said.

On Friday, Strait had left a warrant for them to serve along with a mug shot of a robbery suspect and a note: "Bank-211 suspect's a Sunday night league bowler—check out the Hollywood Legion Lanes."

Ties removed and collars opened they entered the bowling facility. The sounds of rolling balls, clacking wooden pins, and the clanging, banging of pin-cages created its own excitement for Montego. It fit with his high feeling before any imminent bust.

They mounted black, vinyl-padded, chromed stools at the neon-lit mirrored bar and ordered Budweiser drafts. Nursing the tall blond lagers, they surveyed the active scene.

Montego saw Haley eyeing an alley that had opened. "You thinking of bowling a few lines?"

"If I had a chartreuse shirt and my name embroidered in red on it." Haley tugged at his sleeve. "The punk spots me bowling in this white shirt, he'd split down a lane—I'd end up sliding in a gutter—miss my strike."

"Yep—for sure Ice Cop *is* weird tonight—"

Montego nudged Haley and nodded toward an approaching man. "Our heister."

Simultaneously, the felon saw them and ran.

Montego sprinted in pursuit.

Haley, on his tail, called, "The shirt color's right."

They collared the bank robber, who'd been slowed by a coupe screeching to a stop on El Centro. "Not so fast." Montego grabbed and wrenched Charlie Blary's right arm back to his left wrist and Haley snapped on the Peerless cuffs.

Haley flipped up the tail of Blary's shirt and lifted out a snub-nose revolver. "Hey, Charlie, were you gonna shoot down the head pin?"

Montego glanced at his partner and shook his head as they headed to their unit. They drove to the station and escorted their prisoner into the watch commander's office where Montego showed the arrest warrant, Blary's driver's license, and the snub-nose.

"Strait will call the Bank Squad in the morning. They'll want to talk to bowler boy before the federales get to him."

"Yeah, to hear about Chartreuse Charlie's gutter balls," Haley said.

Montego swore that Haley had half-smirked, just like Alex Strait.

"Good work, men," Lieutenant Cowland said. "Montego, a call came in a short while ago from a West Hollywood deputy."

"Aurek?"

"That's him. I had Rosy radio you on Tac One—you must've been chasing Blary. Here's the call-back number. The deputy said it was urgent."

"Go ahead, Mike. I'll book Charlie." Haley pulled Blary's arm.

Montego, pressing a thumbnail, went into the supervisors' glassed-in room. He glanced at the wall clock while the phone buzzed on the other end of the line.

What could Greg want? He should be EOW.

A man's voice sounded at the same time Montego saw his tan uniformed deputy friend heading toward the front desk. Cradling the receiver, Montego rushed through the narrow corridor and into the lobby.

"Greg—what's up?"

Aurek spun about, saw him, and came over, his sun-reddened face drawn and anxious looking.

"Gotta apologize about Becky—told her to mind her own business. She's an independent little spitfire—"

"It's cool, Greg, she cares about—is Julie OK?"

"Sorry, thought you were pissed—it's not about Julie. It's about the blonde we saw you with at the drive-in."

"Lissa?"

*　　*　　*

Haley, standing at the booking counter, heard a sharp rapping on the small square of safety glass inset in the steel jail entry door. He turned and saw Montego's intense eyes peering in. Haley went over and unlocked the door.

Montego, securing his Python in a gun cubicle, eyeballed Haley. "Lissa's been assaulted, she's at Kaiser—unconscious."

"No!" Haley grasped the heavy door to steady himself.

Montego stepped into the jail. "Go, I'll handle things here."

Haley, jolted, spun toward the wall cubicles, retrieved his revolver, and sped outside.

He ran the Porsche's rpms past redline, heel-and-toeing the brake and clutch pedals, working the gears. He dodged cars and peds during the two-and-a-half mile race east to the hospital. He blew between clamped teeth and milked the leather-wrapped wheel to drain off the adrenaline his heart pounded through his system.

Brunetti's damn doing!

Hurting Lissa was because Eugene Preston hadn't been aced. Her words echoed in his ears: "—a friendly family gesture that he would be making. Mario thought it had something to do with Roger if he wasn't a hit, or didn't make a hit—" The "he" was Joey Armanno.

And I'm Roger!

Should've gotten the photographs sooner, forced Preston to resign. Haley hadn't considered his woman to be a target. It was supposed to be Pop and him.

Not chancing that he'd find a parking space in the hospital lot, Haley turned right at New Hampshire and immediately pulled to the curb. He locked the car and rushed to the admittance desk where he was met with deference. The nurse refused him information. He shoved his badge at her. A gray-haired nurse was called to the counter.

He showed her his red-and-gold identification card. She studied it. Finally, she told him the room number, hurriedly saying, "She's in a coma," as he hurried toward an elevator.

Upstairs, he raced down the glaring hallway to the designated room. Skidding to a stop, he peeked in to a dark and deathly silent room. Lissa lay supine under a lightweight blue-gray blanket. Her head, slightly raised, was wrapped in white gauze. Her face, what he could see of it, was bruised red and swollen. She looked to be on the brink of death.

"No-no." He sank to his knees at her bedside, sobbing.

Oh, how I love this woman—God save her . . . please!

196

He was still on his knees when Montego arrived, slid up a chair, and helped Haley into it.

Standing by him, Montego asked, "Have they told you anything?"

"Only that she's in a coma." Haley's voice lacked its usual tone.

After a moment, Montego knelt. He dropped an arm around Haley's shoulders. "Neall, this is going to be darn rough to hear, but you've got to know. The sick bastard had his way with her."

Both broke down holding onto each other, their bodies trembling.

The hours passed in worried silence, interrupted only by a nurse on her rounds. At daylight, Montego squeezed Haley's arm and slipped away.

Haley remained on vigil watching Lissa's unmoving body; all he could see was her left eye, now purple and ballooned shut. It was early afternoon, fourteen hours since the attack. He rose to his feet slowly, driven by hunger; his low back sore and stiff, his legs cold and heavy feeling. He needed to get outside, to go to a familiar place, one where he and Lissa had spent time together.

Careful not to disturb the IV tube feeding her arm, he lowered his face to hers, listening. Her breathing was too shallow. He kissed her colorless lips, their iciness frightened him. At the doorway he looked back hoping to see her stir. She didn't.

Outdoors in the fresh air, he realized how suffocating the acrid medicinal smells inside had been. He took deep breaths and long strides to his sports car, not realizing he'd parked in a red zone. He caught the flapping end of a parking ticket stuck under a wiper blade, stuffed it in a jacket pocket, and unlocked the door. At least Hollywood Tow Service hadn't flat-bedded his wheels to their impound lot.

He sank into the hard bucket-seat and drew in a deep breath, wanting to capture a whiff of Lissa's soft rose presence. He pulled on his driving gloves, kneaded the steering wheel, and when the motor was humming, shifted and popped the clutch. The right-front tire screeched along the red curb as a murderous picture reeled past his mind's eye. A gnawing ache in his empty stomach pressed down on his corded guts.

At Pink's food stand on North La Brea, he ravenously gobbled down a pair of cheeseburgers and guzzled a tall Coke. He and Lissa often came to the eatery. He pictured her beside him . . . he shuddered.

Dropping back into the Porsche, he drove north to The Palms and made his way to the business office. He told the manager that Lissa wouldn't be able to work for a few weeks. He fabricated a story as to why she was hospitalized. Then he stepped around several occupied tables to Pio's favorite spot, anticipating Brunetti's arrival for his 3 o'clock lunch.

He slouched in the corner booth, smoking and waiting. Before him, an empty place-setting, and a tall glass of lemon water he hadn't touched. The room felt empty without Lissa's cheerful face and smooth movements. He imagined her flowery blouse and wraparound skirt; again he shuddered.

One wrong word, Beak, and you're history.

When the swarthy mobster swaggered through the foyer and spied Haley, his pock-marked expression contorted, but changed quickly to one of confidence as he ambled up to the booth.

"Neallie Baby—y'got me some good news, huh?" Brunetti glared at Haley's crossed arms and hidden hands, obviously not appreciating what he saw. He slid onto the seat opposite Haley.

Keeping his left hand gripping the S&W's hard-rubber grip, Haley focused on Brunetti's bent nose busting it again, mentally.

"Siccing Joey Armanno on Lissa was your fucking mistake, Beak. That sick fireplug is about to be hosed."

Brunetti's puzzled look was unexpected. "Whatcha talking about—what the fuck's happened?" He scanned the room. "Where's Lissa?"

"Good acting, but knock off the bullcrap."

"Tell me Haley—what's this here shit about Lissa?"

Haley studied Brunetti's deep-set eyes, embedded beads under a single row of black bristles. "You really don't know?"

"What'd I tell you?" Brunetti's mouth twisted ugly. "Hear what I'm saying—I don't fuckin' know."

Molten lava flowed in Haley's gelid veins. "That fucking asshole, Armanno, raped her—hurt her bad."

Brunetti straightened his broad shoulders. His dark eyes widened, then narrowed. "No fuckin' way. When did this go down, anyways?"

"Last night."

"Uh-uh—no way was it Armanno. He's in Vegas." Brunetti turned, snapped his fingers. When the waitress came over he ordered the daily lunch special. "But first a Compari-and-Soda." He looked back at Haley. "Armanno ain't got nothing to do with nothing."

Ice water sizzled as it mixed with the fiery lava now oozing in Haley's veins. He pictured a hole above the ugly meathead's bent beak—.38 caliber-sized.

Haley hated believing Brunetti. It meant an unknown asshole had hurt Lissa.

"Twenty-four hours to come up with a name, Beak." He uncrossed his arms and thumbed his right side over the magnum revolver while glaring at Brunetti. "Or the sonofabitch, Armanno will be feeling six slugs."

Beak Brunetti pulled a Dutch Master from an inside pocket, his face turning dark, menacing. "Now who's fuckin' acting, Neallie Baby?" Sneering, he fingered off the wrapping and ran the cigar under his nose.

"Armanno hurting Lissa better *not* be part of your fun and games." Haley re-crossed his arms. "And don't even think about me being a player."

Brunetti's elbows banged the tabletop. He growled, "You're gonna play, all right. Lemme tell you something. Whenever skinny-ass punks like you come along, I squeeze their damn balls till they're fuckin' raisins. That's pressure." His words spit out like pig grease on a hot grill.

Haley fought to maintain his bravado.

Brunetti smugly gazed around the room before his beady eyes locked onto Haley's.

"Gotta pearl for you, paesano—'n' hear me good. I'm fuckin' sorry about Lissa getting hurt, but it ain't Joey Armanno who done it. Capisco?"

Haley gripped a knee. "Twenty four hours—a damn name, Beak."

"Forget it, Haley." Brunetti leaned closer. "Here's something else y'gotta know. Time's running out on you doing that stupid councilfuck."

Garlic vapors assaulted Haley's nostrils. "Uh-uh. Preston's going to give up his seat. No need to hit him—and you damn well know that, too." The lava was cooling in Haley's veins.

"Huh? Why's he gonna do that?"

"Because I'm holding the fuck-photos your thick-neck bud took. So, no damn hit. My priority is Lissa." Ice Cop was back.

Beak Brunetti sat up, licked the cigar, bit off the tip, and shoved the long dog turd into his mouth.

"Like I told you, Haley. I'm sorry about Lissa, but you're doing the fuckin' hit—'n' get it done *now*. To hell with them nigger whore pictures."

Leo Brunetti rolled the end of his Dutch Master cigar over the lighter's flame and puffed as he watched the ghost-faced cop storm out of the restaurant. His mind was no longer on Haley, but on the damn fucker who'd raped Lissa Renzo. He'd always liked the broad's hick ways, specially her body, but now she was spoiled. He hadn't hit on her, partly because of the bull, but mainly because it would screw up things with the capo. Besides, Brunetti liked keeping the mystery of Lissa's sexy body for his wet dreams. Anyhow, he had all the pussy he needed with Goochie, but he would miss Renzo's slit-skirt action around the dining room.

He yelled at the passing waitress, "Where's my damn Compari?" He shouldn't have spoke so rough, but he was fucking pissed. He drew long on the cigar asking himself who in the hell had fucked the waitress doll?

When his iced drink was set before him Brunetti laid down a crisp Hamilton.

"Keep it, darlin'," he said, the cigar sticking out from his mouth.

He watched the waitress sashaying away, her long brown hair swinging. He grumbled. Her action didn't come close to Renzo's.

Tasting the drink, he thought about the fucker who had violated Renzo and what he'd do to the miserable chump if he found him. Five years back he'd heard how Jimmy Squillante, the New York garbage collection boss, had handled bad punks. The thought had him smirking. Squillante had invited Joe Scalise to a party at his house and when the Guinea got inside the doors Jimmy's boys fell on him with butcher knives. Sliced his ass to pieces and hauled the meaty parts outside to a waiting garbage truck.

Brunetti grunted with morbid satisfaction. He tasted more of his Compari, then mouthed the Dutch Master, drew in smoke and gazed about.

He spied his flashy dressed cousin strutting through the front entry. It was only his second time in The Palms. Simeti preferred the Villa Capri.

Nino Simeti scooted into the booth, sitting where Haley had been.

"Oh fuck me—can tells somethin's not so good. Spills it, Leo."

"Renzo, the waitress, got beat up 'n' fuckin' spoilt."

"That th' gorgeous blonde? What th' fuck—when—who?"

"Dunno, dunno. . . . But we're damn sure gonna find out."

"An' axe his fuckin' ass likes I did that big nigger, Blag-shit?"

"Yeah, something like that, Nino."

Only the muthafuck is gonna taste it—know he's buying some turf.

Chapter 40

Montego reached in front of Haley, pushed the "L" button, and watched the elevator door slide shut. He'd been to see Lissa each day before, during, and after work, always leaving with a pang in his heart. Her comatose condition remained unchanged.

Crossing the marbled lobby, Haley said, "Five damn days," his words barely audible. "Doc's told me nothing good."

Montego rested a hand on Haley's shoulder. "Be thankful the doc's said nothing worse." He wanted to sound upbeat, but felt his guilt for what had happened to Lissa came through in his tone, betraying him.

In the parking lot, Haley sidestepped between vehicles to slip into the brown Plymouth. When the unit cleared the space, Montego climbed in.

"In the elevator, you said you confronted Brunetti and he told you Joey Armanno was in Vegas. Do you believe the goon, Neall?"

"Have to—for now."

Haley eased the sedan onto Sunset.

"I'll try and verify it." Montego, unable to ease the pain in his heart, noted Haley's appreciative look. "Mind dropping by the station?"

They drove west, neither speaking. The four-door coasted into the station's breezeway.

"You still want the photos, Neall?"

"Yeah—yeah. Tomorrow I'll snag Preston's damn ass coming off the eighteenth green."

Montego had explained Preston's Saturday AM ritual when he'd given the envelope to Haley. It brought back the Sunday night blowup. . . . And Julie avoiding Montego added to his hurt. He did care for the gal.

When Haley braked, Montego popped open the door and said, "Hang loose—shouldn't take me long."

Leaving the station, they cruised by the police employee parking lot. Montego gave it a glimpse, but his mind had centered on Aurek's information. During their morning hard-pack run along the shoreline, he'd learned that the county lab people had detected semen stains on the carpet in Lissa's apartment, and blood residue under her broken fingernails—her attacker was a secretor, and scratch marks would be somewhere on his body, hopefully on his ugly puss.

"Suspect can be blood typed," Aurek had said, adding, "They also lifted a print from the entry doorknob, but the Sex Crimes dicks found no match in file. They need a suspect."

Montego pressed his legs into the floorboard trying to ease an anxious feeling. If Brunetti's claim about Armanno was true, it was time for a bit of nervy action. Montego owed it to Lissa.

"Don't suppose you've been by Lissa's pad? Might need cleaning."

"Don't wanna see it." Haley flicked a Camel butt out the window.

"Understand. Just thinking—the lab boys must've left a big mess." Montego choked back a stirring emotion. "She'll be coming home soon, Neall. I'm sure of it." He winced. "You wanna find her a new apartment?"

"Good idea—yeah, she can't go back there." Haley sounded bitter. Seconds later, he pounded the steering wheel. "I know a place."

"Great . . . I'll help you with the move—think she'd mind."

Haley side-eyed Montego. "I'll handle her personals, Tonto."

Montego drove under The Sorry Bull revolving sign and parked beneath the canopy of several aged Italian stone pines. Haley had gone directly to the hospital, it didn't matter that it was after 0300 hours. Montego had told Haley he'd drop by later. He didn't mention that he was going to see Quinn, although Haley likely surmised that Montego was heading to the velada.

Olé. The aficionado shouts clashed with Elvis' 45-disc rocking out *Heartbreak Hotel* on the bubbly Wurlitzer. A soft jab to Montego's back— and a "*Hola*, Miguel, where's your tired leetle burro?"—had him spinning about, amused.

"Tell Rico, your sinewy Sonoran *amante*, refills for The Counselor and Roy, and *un doble Don Julio añejo y una cerveza fría.*"

"Long night, huh?" Dottie, smiling, scooted to the service bar.

Bobby Diaz came up and asked him about Lissa. He told Bobby D what Haley had done on the spur of the moment.

"No kidding?" Bobby D rubbed his fairly pointed chin. "Ice Cop's gonna lease her new digs? What a Don *Ju*an." He grinned as he fanned a passing cloud of cigarette smoke.

"Good busts you and Ice Cop made—I heard." Bobby D cuffed Montego's arm.

Bobby D was referring to unit F-1's capture of a cat burglar, just inside the city line. Montego had had to pull a raging Haley off the bleeding felon. Montego was sure the 459 would think hard before sneaking into another private residence.

"You guys did all right, too, Bobby."

After the booking, Montego had jawboned with the desk officer, his landlord, Rosy Rosenbloom. Rosy had told him about the Brannock and Diaz busts: While chomping on a soggy Roi-Tan, he'd spouted, "Oy, I'm not kidding, Bad Bobby D's got some chutzpah. Half a yard shorter than them schmucks they nabbed, but he still kicked the crapola outta the biggest one. He jumped up and pounded the dipshit in the schnoz. Knocked the putz colder than a cross-eyed mackerel on a block of ice." Rosy's fists flew about when he explained.

"Was Brannock refereeing?" Montego had asked.

"Trev gave them other two schmucks each a Joe Louis uppercut and a Jack Dempsey short right." Rosy shifted the stogie in his mouth. "Decked 'em both. Bam-bam—fast." He simulated the action.

Chuckling at the colorful recollection, Montego saluted Bobby D with a clanking of longnecks and then followed Dottie to the banquette where O'Brody was saying, "I was 'bout to shred that burr-head's fan belt."

Montego grabbed a chair and gunned half his shooter. He chomped on the lime wedge, finger-tapping the table's edge, while he listened to O'Brody complaining about Nedwick Whyte, a federal agent.

Eagon Quinn, noticing Montego's restlessness, quickly jumped in when O'Brody paused to taste his fresh drink.

"Look what Bucky gave me." Quinn flattened out what looked like a newspaper clipping. "A photocopy of an old article with a picture of two gunsels in Detroit." He pointed at one of the men. "Angelo Sancia—thought to be the doer of Bruno Brunetti."

"Called 'im Pinky," O'Brody said thickly.

Montego glanced at the photo, but his mind was on Joey Armanno. "Did Hamilton confirm whether the goon was in Vegas or not?"

Quinn laid his dying cigar in the glass ashtray and slid it aside.

"The goon actually was in Vegas?"

"Afraid that be the case, Mikey—Bucky's contact, a Bob Mahieu, verified it. Joey Armanno was seen at the Desert Inn the same Sunday night that Miss Renzo was assaulted."

Montego stared at the discarded cigar butt. He felt cold and stale, too. "We need to ID the bastard who did it. Sheriffs got one print, and some stains—the goon bastard's a secretor—but they need a darn body for a comparison test. Otherwise—"

"Think positive," Quinn said, "and Mikey, the day Lissa regains consciousness, she will likely know what happened, but she won't want to talk about it."

Eagon Quinn paused and softly put his hand on Montego's forearm.

"Being violated like the poor woman was is extremely traumatic. The lady will need a lot of time and a ton of tender love."

The words, though given tenderly, jarred Montego. He rose slowly.

"I'm going to Kaiser. Thanks, Eagon." Leaving his beer and the remaining tequila untouched. Tears welling, he patted Quinn's shoulder and said, "Goodnight Roy."

The oak-and-iron door thudded behind Montego, melding with his heavy heartbeat. The vicious attack, his fault. He should never have talked to Lissa the night before at The Palms. He visualized the several goons he'd seen at Patsy d'Amore's Villa Capri, and also at The Palms. None of the bastards could be ruled out.

One of them was Mario Zippi, the mobster wannabe—a pest, Lissa had said. Montego had paid little attention to the braggart. He would now.

Chapter 41

The alarm bell jangled Montego awake. Blurry-eyed, he glanced at the West Clox before smothering the bell knob with a hand, cutting off the irritating ringing, but more irritated that he'd overslept. He prided himself on being able to wake up whenever he chose by thinking a specific time when crawling into the sack. Blame it on the kaleidoscopic dreams. The distorted visions of Lissa, then Julie, both swirling about him, their frightened faces accusing him, making him feel guilty—Lissa's condition sickened him. He was guilty.

When he had stepped into the hospital room, he had experienced a shocking moment: instead of Lissa, it was Julie he'd seen lying helpless on the narrow bed. The flashing sight had struck an emotional circuit streaking from his head to his heart. He'd lost his balance. Haley hadn't noticed. Montego could accept it if the guy had blamed the rape on him, though it deeply hurt, yet Haley had never showed any anger toward him.

He had stayed with Haley at Lissa's bedside until nearly dawn.

Montego resisted the temptation to lie back and drowse, he wanted to talk to Strait and Aurek. The Diggers met in less than half an hour. Tumbling from the sack, he plucked the top-sheet from his damp body.

Dressed in white-twill Canterbury volleyball shorts and a dark blue sweatshirt, its sleeves whacked mid-forearm, he headed to the lower deck and retrieved the morning *Times*. Hearing the purr of Julie's Austin-Healey, he tossed the rubber band-wrapped newspaper up to his porch and sped to the rose-covered railing in time to see her entering her apartment.

The Diggers could wait. He took a deep breath, warning himself not to confuse things by allowing his guilt for Lissa's condition to show. He skipped down the stairs, around the corner to her door and knocked.

She opened it halfway.

Julie's expectant face unexpectedly became Lissa's battered face. Dismayed, he blurted, "I care about Lissa, but not in the way you think."

"You think?" Julie slammed the door, her dark expression giving him a painful pause.

Why hadn't he simply said his partner's girlfriend had been raped and he was worried? She had misread his words. Blame it on his guilt about Lissa's condition.

He retreated up to the Perch and retrieved the remote control for the garage. Putting the paper inside, he murmured "I'm really screwing up."

Back downstairs, he wheeled his salt-pitted ten-speed out onto the roadway, pressed the remote, lowering the door, and jumped on the narrow seat mashing his privates. *Tanto peor!*

He pedaled as hard as his pounding heart—and aching balls—would allow, along Ocean Drive to The Clam Digger.

Racking his red Schwinn next to Strait's new silver Motobecane, he eased into the enclosed patio, pulled up an old rusty chair, and sat beside Wheeler who was claiming to Strait and Aurek that Don Drysdale, the Dodger's ace pitcher, was a lock-on to win the Cy Young Award.

When Wheeler paused to suck up some suds, Montego rose to his feet and knuckle-rapped the table to get their attention. "Excuse me Wheels, but I'm about to be a culprit—my fellow diggers, I gotta buy a pitcher."

A cheer went up. Wheeler wiped beer froth from his nose, having quickly finished off his lager, and held out his empty stein, saying loudly, "You're forgiven—I'm ready."

Aurek was telling the others about the $3500 price tag for the new Chevrolet Impala advertised in the latest *Car and Driver* magazine when Montego returned from The Clam Digger bar.

When he set down the penalty pitcher, foam cascaded over the rim. Hoorahs came from the recipient trio. Typically, boos sounded from cops at the other tables.

"Greg what have you heard from your crime lab boys?"

The deputy's face sobered. "Outside Renzo's apartment they found a corkscrew stuck into a red wine-stained cork—and inside, a drawer was on the kitchen floor—flatware all over the place—and no cork-remover." Aurek gulped some beer. "They think she was struck with one of those wine bottles wrapped in raffia—or is it straw? The forensics tech found a fiber snagged in her hair."

"Straw." Wheeler belched shamelessly.

"Chianti." Montego, thinking Italian goons, immediately ruled out Brunetti figuring his nightly routine with the chesty redhead had to satisfy his libido. But then Montego recalled Quinn telling him that violent rapists were sickos and the act of sex wasn't necessarily the primary reason they attacked women. He knew his mentor was referring to the "unsolveds" during the late 'forties. Such killers often were acting out in rage, he'd said, seeking revenge for some perceived wrong in their earlier lives, or for something big or small currently affecting them adversely.

Wheeler said, "I've seen those bottles-in-a-basket hanging—"

"At Sorrento's in Playa del Rey," Strait interrupted.

"Even if the wine bottle was hers it proves nothing," Aurek said. "Our dicks think the rapist got invited in—no signs of forced entry."

Montego's hands clenched. "Lissa wouldn't've invited just any guy into her apartment." He suddenly visualized "the pest" on her doorstep.

"I heard that her blood analysis showed no alcohol in her system." Aurek gulped more beer. "The assault went down before she had any wine."

"Because the bastard surprised her. He brought it thinking he was going to party." Montego took a long swig of beer. "She serves all sorts at The Palms."

Aurek nodded his head vigorously. "She's a real looker too."

"Well," Strait eyed Montego, "it's quite apparent the prick knew where she resided. And I believe you are right, Tonto. The evil doer showed up with the Chianti with ill intent."

"And uncorked the bottle afterwards," Wheeler said. "To cool off."

"More than likely, Wheels," Strait said.

"The miss might've fought hard, but a wine bottle is much harder." Wheeler dipped his head as if agreeing with both Strait and himself.

Strait emptied the pitcher into his stein. "The prick must've thought he was Casanova, got rebuffed, and being pissed, bonked the poor miss."

Montego, irked by Strait's "bonked" comment, attributed it to the beer his older pal had consumed.

"Uncle Alex—have you got a file on a Mario Zippi—a wannabe mobster? The guy pestered Lissa at the restaurant where she worked."

"I am unfamiliar with the Italian name." Strait tongued the froth off his baby handlebar.

Montego's gaze went from Strait to Aurek to Big Jim Wheeler. Nothing they'd said had changed his mind about what he intended to do. The next thing was to convince KW, his partner that night.

Downing the last of his brew, Montego got to his feet.

"Color me gone, gents."

Alex Strait called out, "Super Weave at dawn's early light, Tonto.

Chapter 42

It was near noon when Neall Haley left Kaiser Hospital and drove his Porsche toward the Wilshire Country Club. He enjoyed taking in air that wasn't antiseptic, but his mind and heart held onto Lissa's frail image. She hadn't moved on the bed, but she didn't appear worse either. The swelling was down and the bruise on her face had darkened to a deep magenta color. All but one bandage along her hairline where the bottle had struck had been removed, yet she still lay in a coma.

The moments he was not thinking about her, his mind reverted to his predicament and the bleak afternoon he'd gone to The Palms in response to Brunetti's veiled threat about the future. Haley thought about the news clipping and the old photo of two men in double-breasted suits and fedoras low over their eyes. The image was indelible in his mind, as was Brunetti's claim that Ari Sands—Angelo Pinky Sancia—was his "ol' man."

Haley heard jazz coming out of the Blaupunkt radio but mentally he was replaying Brunetti's words, trying to recall if he'd said the cousin's name. The one clue had been a "Nino," and Nancy had yet to come up with anything useful. She'd said she was leery about asking Brunetti directly. Haley only remembered Brunetti saying, "'Dago luck' . . . he damn near ran into the van."

And then Brunetti had laid out the yellowed news clipping and tapped a finger on the photograph, saying, "See this?"

Haley had closed his mind to the picture. He'd needed space to breathe, and time to think. None of it had made sense then. It still didn't.

He braked the Porsche for the red light at Vine Street, signaling a turn, his thoughts swimming in the morass of Beak Brunetti's bullcrap story: a Little Jewish Navy gang fighting the Purples, another Jewish gang, over booze in south Detroit three damn decades ago. Italian mobsters from New York and St. Louis helping Jew mobsters fight each other. Pop wasn't even Italian; he was Irish with Moorish blood. That's why his skin was olive-complexioned.

But compounding Haley's fear about his pop's past were vague family comments about a cousin once in trouble with the police somewhere back east; yet, whenever he'd moved close to the conversing adults the talking always had stopped. Haley had come to expect it from grownups.

No—no way! Pop is not Pinky Sancia.

But damn it to hell, Brunetti and his meathead cousin believed it. That mattered.

Making the turn, Haley sped down Vine, double-clutching into third gear, but quickly downshifting when he caught another red. When the light was green, he raced ahead. For certain, when this Preston crap was over he'd find out if Dante Pio was a part of Brunetti's threat. But first, get Preston to quit the city council. Make the stupid hit unnecessary.

Haley checked his watch: 12:15. Preston should complete the back nine within the half-hour. Parking the sports car near the golf course on Arden Boulevard, Haley braced himself, fighting the lack of sleep that had him feeling unsteady.

After "badging" his way onto the elegant grounds, he clipped the leather-cased shield to his belt, and headed toward the clubhouse. He knew what the wispy-haired man looked like from the sex photographs. He chuckled. Definitely, it was different than the picture of the pompous prude awarding a thirty-year diamond service pin to a graying police stenographer in *The Beat,* the LAPD magazine.

Several chain-smokes later, a pair of white-canopied golf carts approached—a male foursome riding in tandem on the narrow path from the eighteenth green. The skinniest golfer, Eugene Preston, wore blue-plaid knee socks, white-and-black saddle shoes with flared tassels, and a blue snap-brim cap. A silly looking pretender.

Preston and the other players stopped in front of the clubhouse. The politician, being a teetotaler according to Montego, would not stick around. The other players had the portly shape of golfers who enjoyed making quadruple bogeys at the "19th hole."

Haley watched the councilman and the other two losers removing greenbacks from their billfolds. The most rotund of them accepted the money saying magnanimously, "Great round, gentlemen—I'm buying."

The three drinkers left their paraphernalia in an alcove, waved at Preston, and went into the lounge.

Preston head-shook off the golf attendant, *probably to save a tip*, and drove to the far side of the parking lot, stopping at the rear of a late-model Lincoln Continental four-door. He unlocked the trunk, raised the lid, and sat on the trunk's rim to change shoes; then he stood and struggled to free the golf bag from the cart. It displayed his name in bold white letters. He stooped under its weight as he wrestled the clubs into the trunk.

Haley waited until the golf equipment was stored before coming up behind the man. Eugene Preston's hand was still on the raised trunk lid.

"Sir, Councilman Preston." Haley displayed his leather-backed badge. "Officer Haley, LAPD. It's important that you see this." He thrust out the Manila envelope. "Take a good look, sir."

The man, obviously startled, gawked at the badge, then his focus shifted to what Haley held. Preston's twitching fingers slid off the trunk. Hesitantly, he accepted the large envelope.

"What is this? Why is a police officer doing messenger service?"

"Look inside—you'll get the picture." Haley had to smirk, slightly.

Preston's eyelids lowered to mere slits. He unclasped and opened the flap, and peeked. Instantly, his face took on a cadaverous pallor.

Haley feared the rigid politician might drop dead. Instead, the slight man threw back his narrow shoulders, canted his head up, peering at Haley.

"Who are you really?" Preston's tone was sharp, but weak, his Adam's apple bobbed. "Bill Parker's spy?"

"I'm not the chief's courier. I happen to have a snitch who jacks off on shots of bigots getting their privates peeled by naked black whores with big tits." Haley stepped closer, re-clipping his badge to his belt. Preston faltered and would have fallen into the open trunk had Haley not grabbed Preston by his upper arms. The snap-brim cap fell from Preston's head.

"D-don't hurt me!" he whimpered, clutching the envelope to his chest. "What do you want?" His eyes white-ringed under flitting lids.

A sour smell reached Haley's nostrils. He released the trembling man. The scrawny sap was scared *pissless*. Damn, if Haley couldn't relate.

"Councilman Preston, sir, you *shall* resign your elected position effective early Monday morning."

Eugene Preston sank into a sitting slouch on the trunk rim and was wordless for what seemed an eternity to Haley. Then, to his amazement, the wimpy councilman rose like a hooded cobra in a swami's reed basket. A "pointy" tongue snaked out between his thin lips. He moistened them before his words spewed forth.

"Well, young man, . . ." he drew in a ragged breath, his flat chest barely expanding, ". . . you can just march back to your hooligan associates and tell them I adamantly refuse."

Haley yanked the packet from Preston's tight grasp, saying evenly, "Time to publicly advertise your political demise, Councilman." Holding the envelope open side down, the large glossies slipped free, fluttering out, most landing picture side up on the asphalt; vivid images in the midday sunlight.

Eugene Preston's balding head ratcheted down, the earlier bravado draining from his sallow face; but surprisingly, the man stood his ground.

Haley had expected the frail politician to sink to his hands and knees, and plead for his career. Instead of succumbing, he remained erect, lifted his head high, and gazed at Haley narrow-eyed, not looking at the scattered photographs.

Feeling sickly warm from lack of sleep, Haley drilled an icy glare into Preston's defiant eyes until the councilman finally blinked and his lips began quivering.

Haley chose his next words: "Sir, you will resign your seat on the LA city council *this afternoon*, not Monday morning, or you will have swung your last six iron."

Chapter 43

Montego, sluggish after his three-hour nap, made his way to the bathroom and stepped into a cold shower. After two cups of reheated MJB, black, he got a phone call from KW who told him he had flown in from his Nassau honeymoon the afternoon before.

KW apprised Montego that as soon as he got in he had contacted Joe Whitehead in the Medical Unit and was told to report for full duty.

When Montego told KW about Lissa's assault and her condition KW sounded upset. Montego understood, and explained that it meant KW and he would be partners that night as Haley had informed Montego that he couldn't keep working while Lissa was lying unconscious on a hospital bed.

They agreed that no doubt Haley would be a permanent resident at Lissa's bedside until she was out of danger, or until Haley's overtime and vacation days ran out, hopefully the first. They also agreed to find the time to drop by the hospital to check on Lissa and to console Haley that night.

Montego then advised KW that Haley was going to show the sex photos to Eugene Preston at the golf course that day. KW simply grunted.

Montego felt lucky to find a parking spot in the employees' small lot on a Saturday. He hoped to have time to drop by the hospital during the watch, believing that KW wouldn't mind, but he was a bit uneasy about how the newly married guy would react to his planned little stunt.

Driving into the police employee lot he spotted KW climbing out of his powder blue '50 Ford convertible. If Yolanda had her way, KW would be driving a Cadillac. Montego honked twice to get KW's attention.

Montego joined KW at the gate. "So tell me, what's it like being a worn out married man?"

KW scowled at him. "What's that s'posed to mean?"

"Did you ever see the outdoors—the sunshine—during that island-hopping, or should I say *humping*, honeymoon of yours? You're a mite pale looking. Yola wear you out?"

"Tonto's a wiseacre." KW spun and feigned a punch.

They bantered their way through the breezeway and upstairs to the detective squad room. The night-duty detective, a cigarette between his lips, checked his files. "Nothing for you tonight."

After patrolling for an hour backing up the uniforms, Montego said, "How about we do a walk-through at the Villa Capri?"

KW, shrugging, headed for Yucca Street and the Italian restaurant.

Montego explained what he intended to do and got the surprised look from KW that he'd expected.

"There're two ways I can do this, Kay Dub. The easiest requires the barmaid's help—but she might not do it and warn the goons. The tricky way is a bit audacious—it means sticking it in their pusses."

KW shook his head, his expression now appearing distressed, his lips squinching. "Bit audacious, huh? What you mean is it be donnybrook time."

Montego might've laughed, but recalling Lissa's bruised face, he remained staid, convinced he had to follow through with his plan. "I guess that could happen, but I want to make a bold statement that'll alert the bastard who hurt Lissa—in my book, I'm targeting the prime suspect."

"You'll kinda be drawing a line in the sand with the thugs."

"I *kinda* don't care. Besides, the goon I want is only a wannabe."

"We'll be on thug-turf."

"I'm not challenging the doggone Mafia—I'm flushing out a rapist, maybe a Pio grunt—I'm not sure. All you've got to do is cover my backside in case a goon tries to shoot me." Montego faked a chuckle.

KW whipped the Plymouth to the curb on Wilcox, opened the door, rolled off the seat, slammed the door and stomped to the sidewalk.

Montego stayed seated and watched, a bit uncertain.

On the walkway, KW paced like a cadet on a parade field, back and forth, first north, then south, lips moving, obviously letting out a verbal stream.

Replaying KW's comment, Montego briefly considered whether he was being foolish or not.

It wasn't five minutes—but seemed that long—when KW climbed back into the prowler and growled something unintelligible, followed by, "Yo. Maybe you're right, Tonto Montego. The thugs might let it go now, but what about later? You'll forever have to be watching out for your cinnamon-spiced ass." He kicked over the V8 motor.

"It's worth the risk. Like I said, the target is not one of Pio's goons. Besides, the underboss knows Lissa's brutal rape accomplished nothing but unnecessary trouble for him . . . possibly from a mobster wannabe."

Montego wasn't as confident about Brunetti staying out of his way, but maybe the goon wouldn't be there. If he was, so be it. Montego no longer cared. Hearing Haley telling him about a "pol-tic's niece" he now feared for Julie's safety, especially since she had returned to her studio apartment. The vision of Lissa lying on the hospital bed because of him, meant he had to find her attacker, no matter what.

Glancing at KW he couldn't deny that what he was about to do was risky, but he enjoyed heady thrills. It was just one reason why he was a cop.

He radioed Code 6, and gave the restaurant's location.

KW parked their unit in the nearest available spot, a red zone, and on foot, they closed in on the Villa Capri. Outside the entry, Montego handed KW two brown-paper lunch bags.

"Keep these handy—best you wait here, amigo."

Montego, once inside, scanned the dimly lit dining room. Most tables were occupied. He spotted Joey Armanno and Mario Zippi, no Brunetti. He glanced back at KW in the entryway and nodded it was a go.

More at ease, Montego went to the bar exhibiting an Alex Strait half-smirk. Through the smoke-tinted wall mirror, he kept close watch on Mario Zippi as a swarthy young bartender whisked up, ran a cloth over the counter and said, "What can I get you?"

"A round for the two men at that table." Montego nodded toward his targets in the middle of the room. He laid down a sawbuck, then slipped on a pair of thin deerskin gloves. When the fresh pours were set down, he wiped the glasses clean of the barkeep's prints, and worked his way around several candlelit tables. A quick turn at the end of his circuitous route put Montego next to his conferring targets.

The goons shut up and glowered at him, their dark eyes like augers.

Montego quickly set down the tumblers. "Barkeep broke a bottle— some chips flew into your drinks." He nabbed their glasses, glared at Zippi, and spun away, briefly eyeing Armanno. Behind him he heard a whiskey-toned voice grumbling, "What the fuck?" followed by a deep growling, "Let it go, Mario—this ain't the time."

Zippi kept on rasping, "The nerve a that sonofabitch."

KW held the entry door open for Montego, then trailed him to the curb where the watery liquor contents were dumped.

"*Por favor,* Kay Dub—pop open those bags."

KW snapped them open and Montego placed a glass into each.

"Tonto's too smooth. Those thugs're looking kinda unhappy."

214

"I kinda expected that." Montego had hoped to see scratch marks on Zippi's face and felt a twinge of disappointment not spotting any.

With the tumblers secured, Montego strode to the police car and notified the dispatcher to show them out to SID.

At the fourth-floor counter of the Scientific Investigation Division, he penned an Evidence Report and submitted a request-for-fingerprint run against all LAPD and LASO files, hoping it matched the print the sheriff's lab boys had found. The chance of saliva traces on the glasses was good, but Montego chose not to pursue the lengthy analyses involved.

He handed the tumblers to a latent-prints specialist who happened to be their classmate: Officer Leroy Howe. The blond cop had weekend duty. Howe did them a favor and dusted both while they stood by. He lifted several prints saying he had enough points to make a worthwhile run. Since it would take too much time to get the results, the felony cops returned to Hollywood.

After assisting radio units on a rash of hot calls, KW pulled their Plymouth into Tiny Naylor's for Code 7; it was an hour before the rummy bars kicked out their drunken patrons.

Montego didn't believe that it was his earlier stunt, but his partner seemed bugged by something. KW acted down in the mouth, suggesting it could be personal. Perhaps he was finding his new son-in-law role to the high-profile Rudolph Forrall tough—tougher than KW wanted to let on.

While they ate, Montego tried to draw KW out, but he kept chomping his double cheeseburger as ketchup oozed from between the sesame-seeded buns and over his fingers. Content to wait, Montego raised the metal milk-shake container and shook it until the last dollop of ice cream slid into his mouth.

KW licked the oozing ketchup streams from his fingers, dabbed them on a napkin, then said, "Tell you something, Tonto. Ever since dapper Daddio laid out those dirty pictures, he and I have developed a much better understanding." KW took another bite and chewed with a satisfying look.

"There's hope for you, yet." Montego swiped away a thin chocolate mustache, pleased that KW was holding his own with Rudolph Forrall. "Remember me telling you on the phone, that Neall was seeing Preston at the golf course today."

KW blotted a napkin to his mouth, then gulped down some cola.

"What do you think Ice Cop told the honorable bigot?"

"That paying a lady-of-the-night for a blow job will get his name in the *Times Metro* section. I can picture the byline now, written in reporter Jack Smith's inimitable tongue-in-cheek style."

KW, putting down the Coke, displayed a toothy grin and snatched his cheeseburger.

"S'pose threat of public exposure'll work—don't really matter. Either way, Rudy will go after the council seat." KW tongued escaping ketchup, then stuffed the cheeseburger into his mouth. He looked sated.

"Preston is self-righteous—he might rationalize—claim his ginger ale had been 'mickeyed' and that the satiny whore took advantage of him."

"But he *was* with the hooker? Paying for a sex act *is* against the law, and he kinda did that before the hooker drugged his skinny ass."

"Yep, he kinda did go into the Oasis Club, and one photo showed he wasn't dragged into that motel room—still, Wilshire Vice would have to convince Satin Sheen to testify in open court. What's the likelihood—especially if she did spike his ginger ale?"

KW grumphed, balled his soiled napkin, dropped it on the tray, and finished off his cherry Coke. "What do you s'pose Pio will do if Preston is still seated when the booze bill hits the council floor for a vote?"

"For sure he wants the bill passed—whatever he does will be soon."

Montego tugged a couple times on the headlights knob to signal the carhop. Then he slipped a Lincoln from his wallet and weighted it with the moisture beaded water glass while he scanned the area for a black Chevy.

Placing three Washingtons on the tray, then anchoring the bills with a stack of quarters, KW eyeballed Montego.

"Preston'll be roughed up."

"Yep. Or worse."

Chapter 44

Montego, wanting to check out the new Santa Monica Freeway, drove south on Highland to Edgewood Place, then cut over to La Brea and south to the on ramp. Taking it to the San Diego Freeway and south to Rosecrans he found that he'd saved a few minutes. All the while, however, his mind had been on Mario Zippi's glass tumbler. He had no choice but to wait for the results of Leroy's print-comparison search. His academy classmate had said it'd be Monday before he would have anything.

He triggered the garage door open by remote when he neared the Perch; he saw that Julie's carport was empty. Sliding out from the pickup, he left the garage with a throbbing ache. He punched the button, lowering the garage door.

The moonless night, dark, like his concern about Strawberry Gal. Hopefully, she would be home by the time he finished the morning run. He'd go to her door and ask to hear her side—maybe it would help him to understand how she truly felt about him. It might assuage his own doubts.

He pulled himself up the stairs, looking forward to three hours of sleep before taking on Strait's challenge to the Furry Diggers to run the "Super Weave at dawn's early light." The TMA might have sneaked in extra training, Montego guessed, preparing to out-leg "the hopeful TMA" on the long two-way course, a double length of the Weave.

Stripping nude, he crashed, mentally setting his internal alarm.

Awake at seven, he donned a pair of blue Columbia volleyball shorts and trod down the flight of dewy steps to the wooden deck to retrieve the Sunday *Times*. He gratefully breathed in the scent of roses that clung to the deck railing. A fine day, and he meant to use every minute to relax and forget every thought of Haley, police work, and even Julie.

Returning to the Perch he let the bulky paper unfold.

The banner headline read: *Councilman Preston Slain.*

Stunned to a standstill, he skimmed the article.

"Hey, up there, Taygo Tonto. Drag your brown buns down here," Big Jim Wheeler called from the street below.

"Hold your horses, Wheels," Montego yelled back, going inside. He deposited the thick newspaper on the kitchen counter, not taking the time to read the lead article. He had to see Julie.

After guzzling a glass of cold tap water he went downstairs.

The Diggers were stretching against his garage door. He would've told them to go on without him but saw that Julie's carport was still vacant. *She must know.* It was too early, but when he got back he would call her parents and hoped they would understand and let him talk to her.

He joined the group. "Hey, you guys hear about the councilman?"

"Yessir—run off the road near Fifth Street," Wheeler said.

"His head was filled with lead, too—mob style," Strait added.

Montego's thoughts whirled, his gut abruptly twisted. He visualized Haley confronting Preston. If it had occurred after the councilman left the eighteenth green it would've been a little after noon—close to the reported time the killing . . . and not that far from the golf course.

Hearing "fink" caught his attention. "What was that, Uncle Alex?"

Strait replied, "I said, the two-eleven prick that you and Ice Cop booked—Mister Charlie 'Bowler' Blary—turned fink."

"And?" Montego pressed his bent right leg over his left knee.

"*And*, the prick *said* he could ID the gunman who pulled the bank heist on North Broadway—if the Bank Squad went easy on his cherry ass. Claimed it was his first bag job. Mister Blary is looking to get probation."

"Turkey'll get it too." Aurek finished retying is shoelaces and rose.

"Thought Tonto would like to hear who the prick ID'd," Strait said.

Montego continued to press on his knee, thinking about the evening "Chartreuse Charlie" was busted followed by the terrible news about Lissa.

Strait bent into a wide-legged stretch, saying, "Mister Mario Z."

"Who?" Montego, unbending his leg, let his foot drop.

"You heard right—Mario Zippi, the prick you mentioned yesterday at The Clam." Strait, righting himself, wore a full-fledged smirk.

Montego questioned the risk he'd taken getting Zippi's fingerprints, but what was done was done. One way or the other, the wannabe mobster would soon be in custody.

"When you see Wayne, tell him I think Zippi also looks good for Lissa Renzo's assault."

Aurek, twisted about. "Great—our sex crimes dicks will love that."

"Gents—time's a wastin', the streets are awaitin'." Strait pointed. "Onward, my hirsute Diggers, to the double super up-and-down challenge."

"Lead on, oh mighty TMA." Wheeler gently shoved Strait ahead.

At the start they chatted about sports and beachside gossip, but as the miles passed and the sun rose they grew quiet. Montego appreciated the silence. His mind had been whirling about all the violent contacts he'd had with Brunetti, Riffelano, Blagden; and KW's fatal one with Rat Rondell.

Three of the four men now dead.

The run ended in a sprint to Strait's house at the base of the pier. Montego cajoled Strait into jogging along with him to the Perch for snacks and a game of chess, but he also wanted his buddy's thoughts in reasoning out his own confused ones about Haley, and he had to be careful what he said to Strait.

Montego trudged up the stairs while peeling off his sweat-soaked T-shirt and entered the Perch ahead of Strait.

"Does the TMA want a jolt of my famous concoction?"

"Aargh." Strait clasped his throat then snatched a Budweiser bottle from the refrigerator. He sat by a small table with black and white wooden chess pieces strewn about and set up the game board.

Montego blended his liquid breakfast, gulped it down, and grabbed a box of Keebler crackers from a shelf. Taking a plate of Jack cheese slices out of the fridge, he slid up a chair opposite Strait who had guzzled half of his beer.

"How're you and Mister Ice Cop getting along?" Strait asked.

"I'm that easy to read, huh? We're making it OK, but the Rondell shooting is bothering the guy—and not because of Kay Dub getting shot—yet, he did seem to take that hard. Bobby D told me he had Kay Dub burrito-wrapped in his arms comforting him. Then, at the hospital, Kay Dub said that Neall had stopped by acting 'kinda blue.'"

"To be expected," Strait took a long swallow of beer, then burped. "I did hear that he missed being at Dealer's side when the gunfire erupted."

"Yep, but something else is bugging the guy. It could be Brunetti skating on the Slauson Slaves hit and losing Rat Rondell as an eye witness."

"That bugs me, too." Strait started the game with a flank English opening: White pawn to c4.

"Mister Rondell's death takes the prick off the proverbial hook."

Haley's rush the night before the shooting to find Rondell still bothered Montego. And Haley's claim that he'd warned Brunetti that if he stepped off the line the "Big Blue Bird would dump a foul load onto his hairy brain case" had sounded brash for Ice Cop.

Strait's restive expression caused Montego to make a countermove without much thought: Black pawn to e6. "Rondell blamed the Cubby Bear, Blagden, for the gang leader's death."

"Interesting. How so?" Strait asked.

"Collis Blagden's cousin was the clerk killed in the store bombing on the southwest side. Blagden, his hackles already up over the mob's incursion, blew his cool when it happened. He tried to stir up the Slaves' gang leader by urging him to take on the white encroachers; however, Cubby Bear was unaware of the mob's main intention."

"So I heard." Strait glanced up from the chessboard. "The gangsters hope to scare the white-owned businesses into vacating the area."

"Yep, the underboss, Pio, intends to push his penny ante gambling business. Thinks it'll be more profitable with non-whites. Bombing the store was a scare tactic. Cubby Bear's cousin getting killed was a mistake. It apparently rankled Dante Pio."

"Where do you hear this stuff?" Strait moved his Knight to c3.

"Rumor." Montego couldn't mention Jordan AKA Russell Smith.

"If Mister Rondell was that sore at Mister Blagden, why didn't he do something about it?"

"He did—fingered Blagden for the Salico bombing to a Pio goon."

Strait cast a fish-eye at Montego. "And, pray tell TMA hopeful, how did Mister Ronald Rondell make that dubious connection?"

"He set up Collis Blagden—convinced the guy he needed a spotter so Rondell could be a part of the bombing caper. Got the Cubby Bear strangled, too."

Strait shrugged his eyebrows and studied the game board.

Montego, realizing he hadn't gained any insight regarding Haley, chose to drop the subject.

Five or so moves later, his mind still worked on the mob's activities and Haley's possible connection.

Montego was check-mated, but then he rarely beat Strait, still, he chalked the loss off to his mind being in a turmoil.

Minutes after Strait left, the telephone rang.

"Tonto, what the heck's with Ice Cop?" KW sounded agitated.

"You've seen the *Times*?"

"Yo—you told me Haley was giving the dirty pictures to Preston at the golf course—did he do it?"

"He was supposed to, but I've got no idea if he even saw the guy."

"His timing was lousy if he did. Called 'cause I was curious. There was no mention of the dirty pictures in any of the papers."

Montego, feeling a chill, said, "Don't know what to say, mi amigo. See you at roll call."

Cradling the receiver, Montego picked up the *Times* and perused the lead story. He shivered, not because cool air was blowing through the open balcony door, but because KW was right, there had been no mention of the incriminating photographs.

If Haley had in fact confronted Eugene Preston, then likely he was the last person to have seen the councilman alive.

A wave of dizziness sent Montego onto the balcony and grasping the railing. He needed to hold onto something solid, to feel the ocean breeze against his face.

Again, the memory of Haley in the booth with Brunetti flashed, and a worrisome thought arose: *Is Neall somehow mixed up with the mob?*

Chapter 45

Montego was glad that he and KW had gotten tied up doing reports. It had helped keep his mind off Haley. At home, lying in bed, Montego pondered. He was convinced that Neall Haley needed his help, possibly more than he would be able to give—or be willing to give.

He awoke well after sunrise, his throbbing skull wrapped around a distressing thought: Had Haley gone off the deep end because of Lissa's assault? Montego considered facing the guy directly with his deep concern. Working with a partner he couldn't trust was unacceptable.

As things now stood, their partnership was headed for "Sour City." What hurt most, Haley had grown on him. Although it seemed like it was one-sided, Montego liked Ice Cop. But he couldn't figure the guy out. And he had to, how else could he help him?

Climbing from the sack he began seriously considering talking to Lonn Haley. Wouldn't a dad want to know if his son was in serious trouble? It was an assumption, but having had no father to talk to had provided no basis by which to make a judgment. On occasion, when talking was needed, Eagon Quinn had been there. He always listened, and each time had offered sound advice.

Montego realized that if he followed through with this and word got out, he'd be viewed as having violated an unwritten loyalty code among cops. But in his gut he knew that helping his partner was more important than worrying about keeping his plainclothes assignment, or for that matter, making detective.

If his partner had crossed over with Eugene Preston—gone rogue—what else was there to do?

No—I can't buy that! But still, I have to know I can trust Neall.

Montego dropped an Alka-Seltzer tablet into a glass of water and watched the fizzing, accepting the gamble that Lonn could misunderstand, the man was savvy. Montego told himself that in the very least the father might provide a clue to figuring out his son.

I just hope it's not too late.

His mind finally made up, Montego dialed the PPSI phone number and was a bit surprised when Lonn's raspy voice sounded over the line.

The Purple Hand

"Mike Montego here—I apologize for calling at your business, sir, but I didn't want to concern Missus—er, Irene or Missy by phoning your home when you'd likely be there."

"Is Neall OK?" Lonn's low tone sounded friendly, but anxious.

Montego sensed the father's concern, his gut churned. "He's fine, sir—if you don't mind, could we meet privately?" He held his breath.

"Without my boy?"

"Yes sir—it has to do with him." Montego bit down on his lip.

Lonn did not hesitate. "I'll be at a job site high up on Coldwater. How about one o'clock at the corner of Franklin Canyon?"

Montego, letting out a long breath, scribbled down the location.

At the appointed hour, he approached Lonn as he climbed from a light-gray van displaying *Professional Plumbing Systems, Inc.* on the side. Without preamble he said, "Sir, I'm sure Neall doesn't talk about our job—most of us don't when we're at home."

"No, he doesn't." Lonn reached back for a clipboard on the seat.

"I'm sure you overheard us talking in the den about the Rondell shooting—that was one of three Neall's been involved in since we've been partners. I was with him on the other two." Montego rubbed his thumbnail.

Lonn stayed quiet, his dark eyes had leveled on him.

"The Brass is watching us. One team with that many shootings, two fatal, and in only a few weeks, is almost unheard of. I can't say they were unavoidable, but in my mind the two with me were close to the edge."

Montego described the Riffelano shooting without mentioning a name, although the incident had made the newspapers.

Lonn's focus never wavered. He remained silent.

"The third shooting was the closest call. We thought we might be chasing an armed suspect—turned out to be true. He possessed a semiauto."

Montego, his eyes still fixed on Lonn's, swallowed a forming lump.

"Neall shot him. . . . After the suspect was down, I saw the pistol on the pavement near his waist. I recovered it. If the suspect was holding it like Neall had claimed, I'd missed it—for sure, the poor lighting didn't help—just an overhead streetlamp."

Lonn, still wordless, looked down at Montego pressing a thumbnail.

"I didn't lay my concern out to the reviewing investigators, yet there was no way Neall could've known the piece was cocked and locked—that wasn't an issue. But he shot fast—three times—from behind me. . . . Only one round hit the suspect."

Lonn's heavy eyebrows lifted. His deeply lined face hardened.

Montego released his thumb. "Sir, I—"

"It's Lonn, Mike. Makes me feel younger." Lonn smiled slightly, but his concern showed.

Montego couldn't help but like the man. He had to be a terrific father, one who must have shared all kinds of experiences with his children while they were growing up; and, he had to possess a parent's keen insight.

If I don't believe that, then this meeting is a big mistake.

"I'm telling you this because Neall is troubled by something I think is darn serious, and I want to be there for him . . . and his girlfriend getting brutally attacked hasn't helped—"

"Lissa? What's happened?" Lonn swiped the clipboard knocking off a yellow leaf that had fallen on it.

He doesn't know!

Montego was rubbing his thumbnail, again. "She's in a coma—hasn't stirred for days."

"What hospital?"

"Kaiser. Neall's at her bedside. Your son loves her."

"I know. I must tell Irene. She'll want to go to her." Lonn appeared to study Montego. "Neall will know we talked when his mother shows up at the hospital—guess you knew that."

"It's your call. You probably know that Lissa is—was a waitress at The Palms. Neall and I have been going in there and into the Villa Capri—mob hangouts—to bug the goons." Montego didn't know why he'd said that, as he had never thought about it in that manner before, but that's what it came down to.

Eyeing another leaf falling onto Lonn's clipboard, Montego noticed something he hadn't seen before. Without thinking, he pointed at his own left little finger.

"Plumbing accident?"

Lonn briefly touched his pinky, then flicked the leaf. "War injury."

Montego's thumbnail began to itch. He folded his fingers over it and squeezed.

"We must sound like an unfeeling family, Mike—Neall not telling us about Lissa—"

"I don't believe that for a second, sir—he just didn't want to worry you. Lissa's gotta be his main concern. . . . But, there is something more." Montego was still squeezing his thumb. "I think it may involve an Italian mobster named Leonardo The Beak Brunetti." He watched Lonn's dark eyes. They stayed steady, not a trace of fear or even concern, and then the lines on his leathery face softened.

He closed the van's door. "I can only imagine how difficult this has been for you, too, Mike, being Neall's partner . . . his friend. You've had dinner with us—you've been to Missy's birthday party—you've seen the love our family shares."

Lonn glanced at one of his workers up the hill and waved him off, then he turned to Montego, smiling.

"Irene and I think of you as another son—although, Missy might not see you as another older brother." Lonn winked, a twinkle in his eyes.

Montego shrugged, a warm rush suffused him. The man couldn't know how he'd longed for a family with siblings.

"I've been honored, sir." He was reminded of the Okinawan adage Yoshi had told him so long ago: "*Ichariba chode.* Once we have met, you are as family."

Lonn placed a hand on Montego's shoulder. "It's not easy raising children, Mike. One day you will learn that they have their little secrets." He smiled. "Many they never tell their parents. Perhaps, the same could be said of their parents."

Chapter 46

Neall Haley spent Monday with Lissa. His Sleeping Beauty lying so still sent a desolate feeling sweeping through him. He couldn't lose her. To offset his panic, he hugged himself and rocked side-to-side, trying to capture the feeling of her arms holding him while infusing his mind with her warmth, her rose petal fragrance.

While in a dreamlike state, he relived the times they'd laughed, the places they'd visited, and their lovemaking pleasures. Then his memories were shattered by screams and thick grunting sounds. He quickly rose, shaking off the horror that had barged into his head. He must do something.

But do what?

Pounding a fist into his palm he sensed the need to hurt someone, but who? He had no idea as to the identity of the attacker. His gut said it was mob related even though Beak Brunetti claimed to not know about it. But the meathead asshole *was* screwing with him.

Haley feared the meathead might do something drastic. Pop's time was running out. Haley glanced at Lissa. His guilt about her condition crashed over him like a tsunami. He shuddered, then a snapshot of Pop's body supine on the grass, flashed. *Damn it.* His pop could end up even worse. Haley bent over, kissed Lissa's cool cheek, watched her another moment, then left the room.

Passing by the gift shop, he saw the *Times* banner headline.

It shook him. Suddenly feeling the need of a family's warmth he went to a pay phone, dropped a dime and dialed, his hand unsteady.

"Mom, what's for dinner?"

Fifteen minutes or so later, he was in his parents' den reading the newspaper article about Eugene Preston while taking in the savory aromas escaping the kitchen. The aroma calmed him somewhat, but not the article.

At the dinner table, he teased Missy about having a crush on Montego. After the family finished their chocolate cream pies, Missy and his mom left the dining room and he and his pop remained seated.

"Pop, I have to talk to you." Haley rose and started for the den.

"Let me pour a Pinot, first." His pop got up. "Want a glass?"

Haley nodded. When Pop joined him, Haley closed the den door.

"Must be a private talk—you look haggard, son."

"It is, and I *am* tired." Haley made an effort to slow his thoughts, not wanting to shock Pop and risk his heart failing. "How're you feeling?"

"Don't worry about me—so talk." His pop appeared deadly serious.

Haley drank some wine, then, focusing on the stemmed glass, broached the subject chronologically.

"About seven weeks ago I was accosted by a man who claimed his cousin had nearly run into your van." Haley glanced up, expecting his pop's show of surprise. Refocusing on the glass, Haley continued.

"The cousins are Italian Mafiosi from back east." Haley glanced up again but saw no change in his pop's expression. Relieved, Haley held his gaze and continued, "The mobster, Leonardo Brunetti, is tagged The Beak."

His pop's dark eyes revealed amusement.

"I recall hearing the name the day of Missy's birthday party." His pop twirled the wine glass, then sniffed the pinot noir. "Later, I asked you if you were having job problems. Being your usual self, you said nothing."

"He's convinced that you are Angelo Sancia, a Mafia hit man who quit the mob in the mid-'thirties. I guess once in always in." Haley had trouble looking into his pop's hardened eyes. "I know it's bullcrap, Pop—but the lousy thing is, Brunetti believes it."

His pop laughed abruptly and looked at his hands. "Such nonsense. Don't buy it—I've never been a mobster or a hit man." He laughed more. "And, son, I *can* take care of myself . . . I've had to on occasion down at the union hall." He tasted his wine and smiled.

His pop's confident words surprised and pleased Haley. "But still, Brunetti believes his crap" he repeated. "And what about your bad heart?"

"My ticker's fine. Don't worry, I'm shipshape. You know I grew up in Brooklyn—the Irish section. I've had my run-ins with gangster punks—Irish *and* Italian—I handled them whenever I needed to, and I'll handle this so-called 'lousy meathead'. . . if I have to."

Haley, tickled by his pop having copied his term, sensed a heavy weight lighten, but he still felt a pang with each heartbeat, and his pop's brow had furrowed.

"I see there's more bothering you. Get it off your chest, Neall."

Realizing he had kept his private life from his parents for too long, Haley decided that it was time. He described what had happened to Lissa and that she was in a coma at Kaiser, and how he spent most of his time at her bedside. Expectedly, his pop's brow furrowed deeper.

His pop put his strong hand on Haley's knee. It was comforting.

"Lissa has to be a wonderful woman—especially for loving you. Your mother and I will be checking on her tomorrow—what hospital is she in?"

"Kaiser—I love her, Pop. It's my fault she's hurt—I can't let what has been happening with Brunetti go on. I know you can handle yourself, but dammit you *are* in serious danger—you gotta stay alert around those lousy meatheads."

"Don't worry about me, Neall. Be with Lissa, and know this— women *are* forgiving. Let the lady you love feel *your* love. Believe me, she *will* sense your energy . . . it might well bring her back to you . . . and when Lissa wakes up, hold her closely and tell her how much you love her."

"You make it sound so easy."

"It is, son."

Chapter 47

Montego relaxed outside a Superior Courtroom waiting for his case to be called; it was the second day he'd been standing by. He found his mind wouldn't let go of Neall Haley. He'd been unable to touch base with him at the hospital on Sunday because that night he and KW had gotten tied up assisting a patrol team. They filled out crime reports until daybreak.

And the past two nights when he and KW visited Lissa's bedside, Mildred, the head night nurse, on both occasions had told them, "You just missed Officer Haley. He goes out for an hour or so to get fresh air and a bite to eat—not always at the same time."

Last night, after leaving the hospital, Montego had spotted the black Chevrolet shadowing their unit and was about to stop it, but couldn't when they'd received an "Officer needs help" call.

He now believed that what'd happened to Lissa was an independent act by a sicko, perhaps Mario Zippi, and not an attack ordered by Dante Pio. The latter didn't equate. But the idea of a connection between Haley and Brunetti still nagged Montego, especially since the hit on Preston.

For the Haley family's sake, and for his peace of mind, he had to believe that Haley wasn't involved with the mob and that he knew nothing about Preston's murder except for what he might've read in the papers.

Montego had chosen not to bring up his concern about it to Lonn after being surprised by his not knowing of Lissa's assault.

It was mid-afternoon, when Montego's testimony ended. He drove to Kaiser hospital and spotted Haley's Porsche pulling out of the parking lot but was unable to get clear of traffic to hail him. He sorely wanted to talk to the guy about his meeting with Preston; again, it was not to be this day.

Montego stayed with an unmoving Lissa for nearly an hour pacing, rubbing a thumbnail. Maybe it was wishful thinking, but she looked better.

After leaving her room, he cruised by the known mob hangouts. In the small parking lot at Frank Zappa's Continental Club on Cahuenga he believed he'd found the black Chevy sedan. He jotted down the license plate number and drove to the station. His telephonic inquiry with DMV revealed it to be a Hertz rental. After a few authoritarian-voiced demands, the reticent rental clerk finally identified the driver as Mario Zippiletto.

Montego cradled the telephone receiver with information that caused Lissa's complaints about the braggart pest to become a shrill alarm. Believing that Zippiletto, AKA Zippi, also might be the sneak shooter of the Cameo Carrier's windshield, Montego raced upstairs and apprised Strait.

"Mario Zippi's gotta be the no-necked bastard who followed me. His true name is Zippiletto. Probably shot out my windshield too."

Alex Strait focused on Montego sharply.

"No-necked? Followed? Zippiletto? Shot? What are you saying?"

Montego explained, ending with, "Lissa called the guy a pest who liked to brag about his mobster pals." More convinced than ever, he added, "I'll bet Zippi's the sick animal who attacked her." Saying it aloud brought a slithery feeling across his shoulders. He pounded the desktop jarring a cup full of pencils wishing it was Zippi's head.

Strait, eyebrows arched, quickly pushed back, his chair's legs scraping the floor.

"Easy does it, officer." Eyeing Montego, he leaned forward and retrieved a folded legal paper from his desk drawer. "You might call this timely. It just came through intra-departmental mail from the Bank Squad downtown—an arrest warrant for the prick you're so all fired up about. Apparently, the deputy DA bought Mister Charles Blary's finger-pointing testimony."

"I love it—you've made my day, Alex." Montego grabbed Strait.

"Hey, Tonto—stop trying to buss me!"

*　　*　　*

Montego sat on the *tatami* facing Yoshi, also cross-legged. The elder had asked Montego to stay following an intense sparring session. He knew why. Venomous thoughts had affected his reactions and Yoshi had seen it.

They sat quietly for several minutes; it was Yoshi's way of finding one's center.

Finally, Yoshi said, "Michael-san had much passion this evening."

"True, *shihan*, master. Serenity refused to flow through my body." Montego's hostile thoughts still circled. Myriad visions floated behind his mind's eye: a bandaged head, lovely doe-brown eyes swollen shut, now purplish, and a mobster wannabe who might be responsible. And added to the swirling in the window of Montego's mind, the *L.A. Times* banner headline: *Councilman Preston Slain.*

Also, eerily overriding Montego's mental milieu, an ominous gravelly laughter from an aphotic pock-marked face: *Leonardo Brunetti.*

"Michael-san, in close combat you must always be focused, and be tranquil. Measure your power when you release it. Use only that force necessary to disable your enemy." Yoshi rose gracefully and bowed low.

Montego, over the years, had become very familiar with the elder's advice, but thinking of Lissa lying on the hospital bed bruised and swollen had made any restraint seem impossible.

"Please take a moment for *haragei*, to meditate, before you depart." Yoshi bowed again and quietly left the dojo.

By the time Montego arrived back at the Perch, Yoshi's words had drifted to the back of Montego's mind. His thoughts had gone to the warrant and Friday night's service. Maybe he should have left the writ for the other team, but he wanted to serve the pest-braggart-wannabe the *Montego* way.

Should Mario Zippi AKA Zippiletto be Lissa's attacker, Montego would know. There were no scratches on Zippi's puss, but there would be on his fat torso. And when the bastard was booked he'd be strip-searched.

It's a good thing Haley wouldn't be working, or likely he would have to be pulled off of Zippi to prevent a homicide, even if justified.

Montego saw that Julie's sports car was gone. He sighed, figuring she must be commiserating with her parents because of Eugene Preston's murder.

Upstairs, in the hot shower, he watched the steam escaping into the night through the small bathroom window.

Have Julie's feelings for me drifted away?

Toweling off, he entered the bedroom. The radio announcer was talking about Councilman Preston's murder. Turning it off, Montego lay back on the bed thinking about Haley confronting Preston. Why had there been no mention of the photos was in the newspapers? After reading the *L.A. Times*, Montego had bought the *Examiner*, the *Herald-Express*, and also the *Mirror-News* and perused them re-confirming what KW had said.

Montego couldn't ask Nells or O'Brody without revealing that Neall Haley had the photographs. Maybe the dicks had placed them into evidence, keeping it hush-hush, perhaps to protect Eugene Preston's good name. Or maybe Chief Parker had ordered the "Sixth Floor Brass" to deny to the press that it was an organized mob hit.

The hit had to have pleased Dante Pio. Would Forrall be his pawn?

A terrible thought the Montego had refused to consider flew back into his head: Neall Haley could've made the hit.

No, no way—the photographs would trap him.

What if Haley hadn't confronted the councilman at the golf course? Maybe Preston hadn't even seen the glossies. But Haley had said he'd be seeing Preston.

Montego wanted to believe that his partner had nothing to do with Preston's death, but he'd sure like Haley to tell him that face-to-face.

Lonn's comment about little secrets, then his smile and saying, "Many they never tell their parents. Perhaps, the same could be said of their parents," came to mind. Montego wondered about that. He realized that Lonn had said nothing about his son that suggested he would talk to him or even be able to help him. But at least he knew what Neall was dealing with, and that it might involve and Italian mobster, Brunetti. Lonn had been cool when that was mentioned.

An earlier wild notion, had Montego sitting up and swinging his legs over the edge of the bed. Was it possible that Lonn could be Sancia? Montego reached into the nightstand drawer and slipped out the dated *Detroit News* article Eagon Quinn had given him. Montego had never looked at it closely. Unfolding it, he read the caption below the photograph:

Harold Keywell and Ari Sands, alleged members of the notorious Purple Gang, leaving police headquarters.

One goon did resemble what a young Lonn might've looked like.

Neall, a mobster's son? Come on.

But the recurring idea brought a shiver to Montego's heart.

The memory of Lonn's vise-like grip teased Montego's mind, but imagining the man as a Mafia enforcer killing people wouldn't play. Montego would never have gone to the plumber's job site if he believed that. Lonn simply did not come across like a mob goon. Besides, the Army never would have accepted him with a missing fingertip.

For that matter, why would Brunetti sit with the son of his dad's killer? It didn't make any sense, unless Brunetti either didn't know or didn't believe Lonn was Sancia.

What if Brunetti did believe? Then what was his reason for sitting with Haley? Did Haley know about the Brunetti vendetta? If Haley did, why would he meet with the goon? And what is Dante Pio's involvement? He must be aware of the vendetta.

Too many questions and no answers . . . yet.

Placing the article onto the nightstand, worry sank into Montego's gut. Suspicion filled his head. Lissa had seen her boyfriend with Brunetti more than once. Did she know or suspect something? A woman in love probably wouldn't say anything that might hurt her lover, not even to his partner, her "pal." Even if she thought Haley somehow was involved with mobsters, she likely wouldn't divulge it.

And Haley's "Big Blue Bird" claim. Montego wanted to believe that, but couldn't shake the idea that what Haley had said was not true. Montego hated thinking that his blond partner had anything going with the oversized goon, but, again, why would he be talking to Brunetti in private, and what about?

Montego thought about Haley and what the guy was going through with Lissa's condition. His long hours at the hospital had turned Haley's pale face into a grim mask. He practically lived at Lissa's bedside . . . the man truly loved the gal.

Montego felt a palpable ache. He took a deep breath and lay back.

Would he, could he, ever capture that wonderful emotion with Julie? Or had his feeling of abandonment as a child scarred his emotions permanently? It was easy to place blame, but it wouldn't be right. Still, he remembered as a child, believing he could take care of himself after school in the Lockwood duplex. After all it was only a matter of a few hours until his mother would be home from work.

But now as an adult, he could better appreciate the worrisome issues that a mother might have felt, and he loved her more for it.

He also had blamed his lonely feelings on the divorce. It seemed like it was his dad's fault . . . Mother had never actually said it, but maybe his dad had been a gigolo. It wasn't hard to picture a Latin dancer playing such a role.

Stretching his arms and legs, he yawned, his mind going to Lissa and seeing her comatose body lying so still. He wanted the sick bastard who had hurt her. His deep anger at whoever had done it had had him grasping at straws.

Straws.

Bottles in straw baskets—Chianti—Italian wine. Italian gangsters.

Tanto!

Montego sighed, his mind back on Julie. It was way past time to for them to talk. His numerous calls to the Preston's phone number had gotten mostly busy signals, and hang ups whenever calls got through.

He had sent a condolence card regarding Eugene Preston's death, but didn't expect a reply; the intent was for Julie to see the gesture and know he was thinking of her.

He missed how they'd reveled in fierce lovemaking—he a rutting ram, she a bucking ewe until sharing breathtaking climaxes, when their movements slowed to a lilting rhythm and they took pleasure in being intertwined until sated. The vivid thought of her bare body aroused him—

The rumble of Julie's Austin-Healey had him quickly sitting up and ready to race down and catch her before she got inside, but he didn't want another misunderstanding and rushing down there without thinking clearly was asking for it.

Somehow, he must make sure there would be no misunderstanding.

OK, if she refused to see him, he would stay outside and plead his case through her closed door. She would have to relent eventually or Rosy, the landlord, might have something to say about it.

Montego slipped into a faded pair of Levi's and pulled on a dark gray sweatshirt with the sleeves cut off at mid-forearm. Stepping into his huaraches, he went out the door telling himself: *Just listen, hombre.*

Arriving at the bottom step he heard a sharp rapping.

He paused.

A man's guttural voice sounded loudly, "Speshal deliv'ry."

Chapter 48

Montego peeped around the corner. A short heavyset male stood outside Julie's door holding something. Montego quickly checked Ocean Drive for a delivery van. None. The door opened. What he saw in the escaping light, electrified him: The no-necked mob wannabe wearing white Bermuda shorts, sandals, and a flowery Hawaiian shirt.

"Surprise!" Mario Zippi bulldozed his way inside.

"What're—get out!" Julie shrieked.

Montego catapulted from the bottom step, sprinted to the closing door, and rammed his way into the studio apartment.

Zippi, a round wine bottle-in-a-basket in hand, had thrown a beefy arm across her chest, yanking her toward a small sofa.

Screaming, Julie clawed his arm and face.

Seeing Montego, he tossed her aside like a rag doll and grabbed for the pistol butt protruding above his waist-belt.

The gun was freed when Montego, in midair, kicked out with both feet. One foot knocked the weapon from Zippi's grip; the other caught his chin reeling him backward over the sofa. His flailing arm sent the wine bottle bouncing unbroken off the wall as he twisted, landing on his knees.

He tried for the 9mm semiautomatic on the carpet behind the sofa.

Skirting the sofa, Montego shoved a foot hard into Zippi's buttocks, smashing him headfirst into the wall.

Zippi clambered to his feet slobbering a loud grunt and swung a wild backhand.

Montego blocked it and followed through with knifing fingers deep into the fat below Zippi's ribs simultaneously shouting, *"Kiai!"*

Bloody spittle sprayed. Another lash. Another block. A knee into Zippi's groin and an elbow to his chin sent him crashing onto the coffee table, splintering it. He rolled, his momentum carrying him through the doorway and into the street.

"You OK?" Montego asked an ashen Julie.

She nodded rapidly.

Montego hurtled the flattened table in pursuit, but stopped just outside the door when Zippi, his belt pulled free, spun the black leather about him. The silver metal buckle whistle-sliced the night air.

Moving quickly side-to-side, Montego "deked" in-and-out, high-and-low, knowing his actions were hard to follow due to his dark clothing.

Zippi's white walking shorts and the light patterns on his Hawaiian shirt made him a visible target in the light spilling from the open doorway.

Montego slipped off his huaraches, moved closer, and threw them into the goon's ugly puss. Leaping, he trapped the wannabe's fat neck in a scissors-grip, and twirled downward. Zippi's nose smashed onto the asphalt a split second after the leg hold released him.

Zippi lay still a moment—then, spitting out gobs of bloody mucus and broken teeth—he gained his knees only to be kicked flat followed by Montego's knees dropping on Zippi's supine torso—an expulsion of bloody air spattering Montego's sweatshirt and face.

Astride Zippi, Montego pounded fiercely, unloading pent-up anger. His fists drove harder and harder. It felt like slow-motion, but he didn't stop. He struck the ugliness beneath him relentlessly.

Kill the sick animal. Hit him hard. Hurt the bastard! Hit him—!

"Stop—stop it, Mike—stop you're killing him!"

Montego heard Julie, but refused to stop. He wanted to maim. . . . yet a silence overspread his mind, and the white fury he'd been unable to control responded to a greater force: a dozen years of disciplined training. The calming voice of the elder, Yoshi Kono, echoed in the darkness: *"Nuchidu takara, life is a most precious thing."*

Montego stopped his assault.

With a grunt, he pushed off the inert and bloody hulk, stood and sucked in the cool fall air, his eyes catching Julie in the diffused light clutching herself; horror on her stricken face.

Montego blew out. "You OK—?"

"What in Sam Hill's going on out here? Rosy Rosenbloom's bright flashlight beam bounced off the pavement. "What the hell's going on?" his voice rising as he entered the edge of light spilling from the apartment.

Julie pointed down at the splayed body mass of her wannabe rapist. "That—that monster forced his way into my home."

The cop landlord threw a circle of light onto Zippi's head, revealing a pulpy dark glob for his face. The Hawaiian shirt was one color: blood red.

Grabbing a deep breath, Montego said, "Our Bank Squad has a felony warrant for him, too, Rosy—name's Zippi AKA Zippiletto." He nodded toward the studio doorway. "You'll find his nine-millimeter on the floor inside."

Rosy squeezed Montego's forearm. "The schlemiel left his calling card, huh? Be interesting to see what it matches."

"West Hollywood Sheriff's should look at him for rape."

"Guess we'd better cuff his fat ass, quick. Sonia!" Rosy yelled over his shoulder to his wife visible at an open window. "Call out the gestapo. We got us some garbage needs hauling away—and dear, toss me my spare handcuffs, please."

"Rosy, can you stay with him?" Montego reached for his huaraches. "Gotta wash up before the local badges arrive."

Julie called from the doorway, "Mike—are you all right?"

He stood still, hesitant to go to her. He was a bloody mess and still high from the near-death fight. "I'm OK," he rasped turning to Rosy.

"If the beach troops arrive before I get back, tell them to look for a black Chevrolet sedan—a Hertz rental registered to a Mario Zippiletto."

After telling Rosy the plate number he'd memorized he faced Julie. "We need to talk, but first I gotta calm down—clean up and then make a statement to the boys in blue."

Montego headed for the stairs leading up to The Pelican's Perch.

"Sonia will be with Julie, Mike," Rosy said.

At barely past midnight, Montego was back home. The interview at the Manhattan Beach police station had been lengthy.

To give himself a moment to unwind, he remained in his pickup. During his earlier madness he'd wanted to kill Mario Zippi, and now was glad he hadn't, silently thanking Yoshi . . . and Julie.

Montego hoped Nells and O'Brody would get worthwhile info from the braggart, but didn't think the bastard knew much about the L.A. Mafia, or how the Italian mob truly operated.

Tonight's attempt on Julie just about proved that Zippi was Lissa's rapist. Brunetti likely wasn't behind it simply because of a broken nose or because his big butt had gotten busted. If The Beak wanted to get even, Montego assumed the goon would do it more directly.

It made sense that Mario Zippi had acted alone, perhaps thinking that by attacking the girlfriends of the two cops who had busted Brunetti, it would please the huge mob enforcer; maybe Zippi even thought Brunetti would vouch for him to Dante Pio, or to the local don, Frank DeSimone.

But then, the attack could've been payback for the glass-switching maneuver at the Capri. Montego shuddered. That had been a darn mistake: getting the sick bastard's prints had turned out to be unnecessary.

Shaking away the mob thoughts, Montego climbed from the truck, closed the garage, and strode to Julie's studio.

Sonia opened the door. He saw Julie rise from the sofa behind her.

"It's pretty late, I can come back tomorrow," he said.

Julie hurried up. "I want to talk, Mike."

Sonia stepped outside, smiling. "Take care of her."

"Sonia made a pot of green tea," Julie said, "and I have fresh gingersnap cookies." She pointed at the card table. The splintered remains of the coffee table were piled in the corner.

"Sounds good." Unzipping his leather jacket, Montego slumped onto one end of the sofa, and eased out a breath. "How're you doing?"

"I'm fine." Julie brought an ornate tea service with her and joined him. "Sonia is a dear. We talked some . . . Mike, I've been such a brat."

"Hey, I mishandled it. I should've been more clear about seeing Lissa." He smiled slightly. "For sure, you had me going."

"Mike, I heard you tell Rosy that Zippi was a rapist—"

"I'm sure he's the sick goon who hurt Lissa—she's my partner's girlfriend. . . . She's still in a coma."

Julie's emerald-like eyes intensified and wetted. "God, I'm sorry."

He thought he saw a flash of guilt, but it didn't come close to the guilt he felt for having talked to Lissa before her assault.

"Lissa is why I was messed up when I came to see you."

"Mike, I don't ever again want to be so jealous that I won't listen to you." She dabbed her eyes. "My feelings for you are too strong."

Although he had talked around the subject with her before, it had never been in any meaningful depth. Now seemed to be the right time.

"I was beginning to think otherwise. I believe you do care for me, and I care for you . . . Julie, my problem goes back to my childhood."

She sipped her tea, her green eyes steady on his.

He tasted his tea then continued. "It was the Sunday afternoons as a three- and four-year-old, being taken from my mother's arms; and when I was six, being sent to home in the Valley. Mother had told me to love my weekday guardians like they were her. I dreaded those days . . . I refused to love anyone else."

Biting into a gingersnap he recalled the feelings of those long ago days. It still brought a chill. He drank more tea.

"I'd seen my father only a few times—I loved him—hurtfully so." Montego paused in reflection.

Julie remained silent.

"Love became a vague feeling, except my love for Mother. Later, as a GI in Germany, I pursued a girl—was attracted to her looks. We married eight months later in Idar-Oberstein, near the Luxembourg border. Cherli's maternal family lived there. The wedding took place in a unique church overlooking the town. It was built into the side of a mountain, the Felsen Kirche. It was a happy day. . . ." He crunched on another gingersnap.

"When I was discharged and back in LA, I joined the LAPD. It was only a short time later that I learned that I merely had been her ticket to Hollywood—to what she thought would be the good life. Anyway, she claimed she couldn't handle my being a policeman—the odd hours. To compensate, she'd found a job at a Bob's Big Boy diner in Van Nuys. Later, without telling me, she worked at a nearby bar—Drysdale's Dugout." He sighed and drank more tea, trying to relax.

"When I found out, I was concerned, but I wanted her to be happy. Well, a buddy, Big Jim Wheeler, discovered that she was seeing an LAPD sergeant—she was cheating on me. Jim came to the house on my night off when Cherli was working. He wanted me to know what he'd witnessed. Jim convinced me to ride with him to the bar and see for myself. We arrived when the bar closed, and after the usual cleaning time. When she came out, instead of getting into our family Chevrolet, she got into another car. A man was behind the wheel—it wasn't even the sergeant. Jim kept me from doing something bad." He eased out a long breath, again reliving the night.

"Cherli kissed the driver, then get out and climbed into our Chevy. She followed the guy to an apartment building. We tailed them while discussing what to do. It was tough. I wanted to bust in on them, but Jim convinced me to go home saying it wasn't worth losing my badge over.

When Cherli finally got home that early morning, she was surprised that I was awake. She immediately pushed up her long hair. It was down on her shoulders—she always wore it pinned up when she was working."

He put the cup down. "She made a feeble excuse. . . . I made an effort to forgive her, having fallen back on my Christian upbringing, but it was difficult living with the memory of her cheating. I also thought it was my fault, that I'd not made her happy, even though we often made love, sometimes more than once a day. Cherli enjoyed having sex." He bit into another gingersnap cookie, noticing a flicker in Julie's moist eyes. He knew her lost-love story but had never revealed his. Again, now was the time.

"Several months later, I came home early—I'd caught the flu bug. When I walked into the bathroom," he shuddered, "I caught her in the tub with a wire coat hanger—she was self-aborting."

Julie's pained look had him reflecting on her own confession; it had nearly destroyed their relationship, the vivid memory indelible in his mind.

"Seeing the bloody glob—a male fetus. I felt ill, wanted to puke.

Cherli screamed that it was my fault. I couldn't help wondering if the fetus truly was my child or . . . anyway, I couldn't handle it—our life together was over at that moment."

"I realized I had confused love with lust. I was too darn young . . . being a GI eight thousand miles from home didn't help."

Julie drew her legs beneath her. "Lust *did* attract me to you."

"Yep, me too. . . . And I—"

"And now you're uncertain about us. . .?" Her eyes had reddened.

"I've had my doubts trusting my feelings. I tell myself I love you, but I don't know what that kind of love is supposed to feel like—for a wife, I mean." Her look distressed him.

She put down her teacup. "Are you happy when you're with me? Do you miss me when I'm away?" She spoke rapidly, swiping away a tear. "Do I please you—when I'm not being a brat?" A quick, sad-looking smile. "Do you want to please me? You must feel yes is the only answer to be truly in love." She swiped at another tear. "Love can be a bubbly feeling that overflows when you're with a person you deeply care about. It's being bouncy like a balloon on a string—and it can be quite overwhelming at the same time. . . . For me, the feeling is like being wrapped in a warm comforter. It's different for each of us." Her moist eyes were intense on his.

Julie's words and look brought him as close to her as he'd ever felt.

"Mike, I'm sorry. Loving you so much really messed me up—"

She moved into his arms. "I love you and I think you love me, too." She stroked his chin, her glistening eyes pierced his emotional armor.

"I need to feel we're in love even when we aren't being intimate."

"Sex is only one form of love—thrilling—and oh so wonderful."

Her body pressing into him brought an arousal that thickened his voice. "I'm feeling a bit of—"

"Me too."

Chapter 49

Haley's head swung up and banged the plaster wall behind him. He'd been praying for Lissa to wake up and had nodded off. Again, as he'd done for days, he studied her face, what he could see of it not covered by the white gauze head wrap . . . it was the same ashen color.

He picked up the paper coffee cup from the bed-stand and tasted the dregs. Cold and bitter like he felt.

Yawning, he slowly stood. His feet prickled. He gripped the chair for balance, grinding his molars until the tingling subsided.

Steadying himself, he shuffled to the hallway.

En route to the cafeteria for a coffee refill he approached the nurses' station, smiling when he recognized the onion-bun hairdo worn by Mildred. The head graveyard nurse looked to have a fresh blue hair rinse. The second night of his vigil, she had draped a light-weight blanket over his legs. By the week's end, the doctors, the nurses, and the orderlies on all the shifts knew that he was an LA cop. Now, they regarded him as a hallway regular.

While getting his coffee he realized it had been fifteen days since Brunetti had told him to cut down the pantywaist politician. Now that the hypocrite was dead, Dante Pio should be pleased.

A sickening anxiousness suddenly filled Haley. Was it Brunetti's and/or Pio's original intent to rat him out? He felt a flicker of panic.

Back at Lissa's room, he paused in the doorway to sip the steaming coffee, his gaze resting on her sleeping face. Something looked different. After a hard look he took a rapid breath. Her head seemed turned more his way. The attending nurse must have come in while he was out and adjusted her pillow. He glanced at his watch. His breathing rushed when he realized it wasn't time for the nurse's routine rounds.

He scooted to the bed, careful not to spill his hot coffee. He swore that an eyelid had twitched. He studied Lissa.

"Lissa, hon, it's me, Neall. You awake?" He held his breath to not miss any sound she might make. He waited. Nothing. He whispered, his lips near her ear, "Lissa, you hear me?" He listened closely, but no sound came. "Damn it, woman, I need you. Wake up—please."

Sinking to the chair, he put down his coffee and reached out to hold her hand, but stopped when he saw her fingers quiver. When they moved again he grasped them, mentally forcing love and energy through his fingers into hers, willing his strength into her frail body.

"Lissa, it's Neall—wake up, I'm here—wake up, hon." He shook her hand gently and repeated his plea.

Her eyelids fluttered, then opened. She looked toward the ceiling without expression. Yet, squeezing her cool hand, he saw her eyes take on life.

Her fingers gripped his. "Neallie . . . Nea. . . ."

He bent closer to hear better, but her eyelids closed and her fingers relaxed, yet a trace of a smile now softened her bruised face. He kissed her cool hand, his eyes streaming tears.

A long moment later, he brushed her lips with his. His fallen tear on her pallid skin, a message of hope and deep love.

He grasped the coffee cup, slipped out of the room and strode down the bright hallway to inform Mildred. She gave him a warm look and a peck on the cheek, then she rang for the doctor while asking more questions about the councilman's murder, still a main topic of the staff.

He pled ignorance.

She also mentioned that the evening-shift nurse had mentioned that Officer Montego and stopped by, each time just missing him. Montego apparently had not told the dicks about the sex photo-delivery meeting with the hypocritical Preston, Haley realized, or they would have come to the hospital to question his ass. They hadn't and it had been four days.

Early the next afternoon, Lissa's eyes fluttered open. He instantly pressed the bedside button signaling the floor nurse. Before she arrived, Lissa looked at him and suddenly let out panicky words. One sent white-hot rage through him. He knew who had hurt her!

She fell back to sleep seconds later while he, trembling, clasped her cool hand. He rubbed it softly, repeating, "I love you, hon. I love you, hon."

Noiselessly he padded out, nodding at the arriving nurse. He went downstairs to the florist shop and bought a dozen long-stemmed red roses with directions to deposit them beside Lissa Renzo's bed, along with his scribbled note.

He paced briskly through parked cars in the lot trying to walk off his anger-induced shakes.

Mario Zippi, you are a dead, lousy, meathead wannabe.

He unlocked the Porsche and eased onto the seat. Lissa's words days before she was hurt fired through his mind. Joey Armanno would be making a "friendly family gesture." Haley's inner being felt gutted. He'd jumped on Armanno as the rapist, but it had been Zippi. Haley's worry about Lissa had his mind in a fog. It had been that way for days since the hit on Preston.

The family gesture had to mean a mob hit. In the Mafia's eyes, Lissa was not his true family. Family meant the Haleys, his parents, his siblings. Who, then, would Joey Armanno hit? Had Zippi joined Armanno?

The intimidating thoughts raked Haley's mind, like a hawk's talons.

He peeled rubber out of the lot and accelerated down Sunset toward La Brea and The Palms. He parked at the curb by the restaurant but remained seated, sorting out his mixed thoughts. He tried to apply logic before he went inside to wait for and confront Brunetti. The shaking had subsided, but the placidity that gave Haley confidence was missing. He'd been away from the streets too long, out of the loop so to speak. He had been ever since the night he'd told Montego he would see Eugene Preston.

Haley's off-duty time had been spent mostly inside the hospital, and the weariness of it all had dragged him into the pits. He pulled off his driving gloves and rapped the nearly empty cigarette pack against his knuckles. He lipped a protruding Camel, hoping that with Preston dead, Brunetti would call off Armanno. Haley suspected he was kidding himself. If the meathead thought he hadn't made the hit, the friendly family gesture threat might still be on. Whether to buy into Brunetti saying his boss was getting itchy, or not was an unknown. But, the lousy meathead believed that Pop was Angelo Sancia—Brunetti would keep playing his "fun 'n' games" with "Neallie Baby."

Did that include ordering Lissa's assault?

Lighting the Camel, Haley recalled the night he'd peered into the dining area from the restaurant's kitchen and had observed Joey Armanno and his thick-necked buddy, Zippi, the mobster wannabe. Haley couldn't discount the possibility that they operated as a team. He took in a long and tasteless drag, blew out a jagged billow of smoke, and watched the breeze whip it away.

Damn it, he had to find Armanno and especially Zippi before they made their so-called friendly family gesture. It could be anytime. He took another deep drag trying to avoid panic, trying to think clearly. It was the not doing anything that had his damn gut flip-flopping like a fly-hooked trout over a fast-running stream, warning him the time was now. Work the damn line, Haley, get the fish on the stony riverbank, or risk losing it.

His mind raced as did his heart.

Think. Think.

One sister and his younger brother resided out of state. It seemed doubtful that the meatheads would travel that far if they didn't have to. Mom, Pop, and Missy, however, were in danger. Mom and Missy being the most vulnerable. Killing Pop would end The Beak's fun, but not killing Mom or Missy—and Brunetti knew their home address. He's getting his rocks off making "Neallie Baby" worry.

Am I too late? No, I would've heard if something had happened.

A blurred ugliness spun like a dust-devil coming at Haley down a crooked and dirty path. Panic surged, about to become overwhelming.

What is today? Thursday.

Mom's card day—home in the morning baking a pie, then off to a lady friend's house to play bridge, usually a different home each week. She should be safe. But Missy?

He looked at his watch, needing to grip his wrist to read the dial. She would be getting out of school shortly.

Damn!

He pitched the cigarette, slipped on his gloves, fired up the Porsche, and laid arcing tire trails north on La Brea. He hard-turned east at Franklin, tires squealing and nearly broadsided a green Buick. Caught by a red light at Highland, he moaned. Traffic was too heavy to break through. His heart pounded out the seconds waiting for the go light.

Dear God—make me wrong about this!

When the light changed, he snaked through a cluster of vehicles on Highland and power-slid right at the continuation of Franklin cutting off a white Olds. A horn blatted.

He jammed the gas pedal to the floor, redlining east over the steep Franklin hill. He crossed Cahuenga and hummed over the freeway. Only one patrol unit worked this area and the cop should recognize him and his black sports car.

Haley busted through on the red at the Beachwood T-intersection. Less than a mile and he'd be at the Catholic high school. He knew where Missy likely would exit the main building where her locker was.

Did Armanno or Zippi know?

Chapter 50

Haley considered where the meatheads best tactical position might be. He quickly downshifted and burned more rubber. The school's two parking lots would be crowded. He turned north up St. Andrews Place one block short of the campus and angled the Porsche into a tight spot.

He cramped the front Michelin against the curb and dashed down to the corner where he whirled eastward.

At the elevated school grounds, parents were driving up in various makes of automobiles, a world of moms picking up their teen daughters. Girls with matching pleated blue skirts, white blouses and navy blue sweaters strolled everywhere.

He sprinted across the parking lot, around a building and along a path toward the upper lot by the athletic field, all the while searching every car moving or parked.

Were the meatheads together or separated? Was there only one?

He tried to imagine how professional killers would do it knowing they would have a moving target. The thought brought bile into his throat. He spit out the sour taste and surveyed the areas where the killers could be until his eyes burned.

Missy's habit, he knew, was to bounce around and gab with friends. He had to believe she was still hanging out inside the main building at its north end. He slowed to a walk until he sighted the exit where he expected her to emerge, if she hadn't already.

Please, Sis, still be inside.

The warm Santa Ana's blew smoggy gusts, sweat streamed down his chest beneath his shirt. The sports coat hid the magnum. Missy must not see him. She'd tell Pop, and no telling what he would do. He might think his heart was shipshape, but it could fail.

Haley prayed that his gnawing gut instinct was wrong, that Missy was safe. He slipped among the autos filing from the parking area. He'd decided if the hitters were on campus, they had to be on the south side of the lot where moving cars couldn't block their view. Continuously craning his neck, Haley examined every non-moving automobile in sight.

"There—a black Ford," he mouthed fearfully.

Side-skipping between the creeping procession of cars, his focus sharpened, his heart revved, his chest heaved.

He quickly approached the sedan, the revolver slapping against his soaked shirt. The driver's side windows were up. Hoping to look casual, he moved behind the Ford and immediately recognized Joey Armanno.

Haley inched along the rear side until he could see the door-locking buttons. The one nearest him protruded above the sill.

He looked around. No Mario Zippi, only small groups of uniformed schoolgirls talking, giggling, and waving to each other.

Harried mothers were calling, "Hurry up—let's go."

No one seemed to notice him, even though he was in plain sight.

Armanno sat low in the right front bench seat, hunched by the open window. He was watching the main building—the north exit.

Haley spotted the silencer. He inhaled sharply and scanned the immediate area. Still no Zippi. In the distance, long black curls caught his straining eyes.

Missy!

His kid-sister strolled toward the passenger side of the Ford talking animatedly to her girlfriend, Shirley.

Armanno knew exactly the path she would take.

The meathead had been stalking her!

He'd shoot Missy when she was far enough away so that Shirley wouldn't know from where the fatal bullet had been fired.

Haley eased the nickel-plated revolver from its rig, opened the rear door, and quickly slipped inside.

"Freeze, fireplug!"

He struck the steel barrel against the twisting Armanno's skull.

"The rod asshole. Pass it back—now—with your left hand."

Armanno mumbled, staying rigid until the metallic cocking of the Magnum, then he slowly raised his Browning 9mm to his left shoulder.

Haley shifted his magnum to his right hand, then clasped the pistol grip over Armanno's fingers with his left, jerking the gun-wielding arm up, hearing a growling, "Fuck."

"Listen good, Joey, and live," Haley spoke tightly. "Right hand— roll up the window." He clamped Armanno's fingers still wrapped around the semiauto's grip. There were grunts and a grumble but the right shoulder moved in a motion indicating compliance.

Haley held his breath, but the glass seated into the upper door frame just as the girls passed by the car. Wrenching the silenced pistol back, he wrested it free of Armanno's grasp, hearing another, "Fuck," but it sounded more like a yelp.

The two girls hadn't noticed, Haley noted.

Clenching the firearm, he pressed the barrel hard below Armanno's left ear while simultaneously lifting his right elbow hiding the magnum and the 9mm pistol from any onlookers. Glancing about, he saw none.

Using a coat sleeve, he blotted the stinging sweat from his eyes.

"Where's Zippi?"

"Huh? Mario ain't here—where th' fuck ya been?"

What Haley heard confused him. Maybe Armanno was acting solo.

"Slide your fat ass behind the wheel easy like. Now!"

Armanno didn't budge.

Haley cracked both steel barrels against Armanno's ears.

The meathead, grumbling, edged across the gray vinyl bench seat.

Screwing the gun-sights into the soft hollows behind Armanno's earlobes, where an oily mixture of sweat oozed with blood onto the collar, Haley said, "Start her up. We're taking a short drive to a quiet talking spot."

Clearing the lot, he directed the hit man to St. Andrews Place.

"Turn right." His throat was constricting, his body cramping. He quickly looked behind him, sensing another presence, like someone was following them. Armanno had confused him about Mario Zippi. Maybe the mobster wannabe was lurking—but Haley had seen nothing untoward.

Fiery blood rushed through his veins until he spotted the protected spot he'd hoped for. It was farther up the hill beyond the black Porsche.

"Pull over there—by the bushes."

Armanno maneuvered the Ford into the afternoon shadows.

"Kill the motor, Joey. It's time for our little talk."

Chapter 51

Montego peeked into the quiet hospital room. The gauze wrapping had been replaced by a gauze pad taped on. The purplish tattoo on the side of her face had lightened to a pasty yellow. Her cheery expression and husky words, "Hi pal," made the sickening color all but disappear.

He smiled, pleased by a wonderful feeling, his guilt temporarily abated, and went to her bedside, eyes misting.

"Where's Neall?"

"I haven't seen him, but when I woke up a man was standing by that window—the sun blinded me. I was scared—I yelled, 'Get away you pest.' I thought it was. . . . What happened next, I don't know. I must've blacked out." She shifted her body. "I suppose it could've been Neall."

That's why Haley isn't here. But he won't find Mario Zippi.

"I'm sure you're not aware of this, Lissa, but he's been here at your bedside continuously since you were hurt. . . . I've come by, too—I'm darn happy to see you awake and as beautiful as ever."

"Thanks, pal. I'm just happy to be alive." She smiled as she pointed to a glass vase with tall red roses.

He looked and saw a card ribbon-tied to it. He fingered the card. "May I?" She nodded. He read the note: *Lissa, hon. Your life will get better, soon. I promise. Neall xoxoxo*

When she reached out her hand to Montego, he took it, his heart racing, each beat a reminder that he was responsible for her being there. He had plenty of time until roll call. He wanted to apologize but he didn't want to risk upsetting her.

Instead, he slid up a chair and got her to talking about traipsing through the Wenatchee hills when she was a kid. He was surprised when she said her parents had yet to meet "her beau." Likely, they didn't know what had happened. It prompted him to ask, "Would you like me to contact your folks?"

"No—but thanks, Mike." Her eyes lidded. "I might tell Momma . . . not Poppa. Don't misunderstand—I really do want them to meet Neall."

Her eyelids were dropping even more.

"I understand, Lissa."

Do I?

"I'm going to let you sleep, now, pal—I'll be back."

He patted her hand lightly, she gave him a sleepy smile.

He left.

At his pickup, he flicked a crusted bird dropping off the driver's door, grabbed a rag from inside, and wiped the spot clean. Nothing could ruin his high spirits.

He turned on the radio catching The Four Preps' lilting hit about Santa Catalina Island 26 miles across the sea. He smiled, they had been his high school classmates.

Waiting for the light at Western Avenue, his mind pictured Lonn and Irene. Good people; and coy Missy, so outgoing. Not like her oldest brother. The Haleys treated him like a son. . . . And Neall was good people, too, but screwed up. Lissa's brutal assault hadn't helped.

The ugly thought brought a familiar ill feeling to Montego's gut.

He crossed Gower, his mind drifting to the sex photos. Preston had paid too high a price for his indiscretion. The killing didn't make real sense, the bigoted prude surely would've resigned to save his public image.

Montego pulled the Cameo Carrier into the police lot and circled the center row of autos. A full roster was working the PM and MID watches. He angled into a space paralleling the chain link fence. The popular Lancers quartet were ending their harmonizing of the radio station's identification: *"K M P C, Los Angeles."*

Spotting KW's blue Ford convertible reminded him of yesterday's morning *Examiner* article, a follow-up to Eugene Preston's funeral: *Today, Mayor Sam Yorty will appoint Rudolph Forrall, a prominent local attorney, to fill the vacant Eighth District seat until the upcoming election.*

KW might be teamed with Bobby Diaz tonight, if Haley chose to work, still Montego would rag KW a bit about his future promotions being greased by a bigwig father-in-law.

Montego made his way inside and up the stairs, wanting to hear Strait's opinion about the Preston homicide. He stopped at the squad room doorway when KW called to him from the stairwell's mid-landing.

"Yo, Tonto—s'pose you heard?" KW came up.

"About Rudy? Yep—guess I'd better start being nice to you if I ever want to get my stripes, huh?" Montego's chuckle was stifled when KW grabbed his arm, and moved him to the nearby window.

"Forget Daddio—think we've got us a miscommunication here. You hear about the mob thug getting dumped this afternoon?"

Montego shook his head, now fully attentive.

"A Day Watch L-car got a citizen's call on Saint Andrews Place just above Franklin. The cop found a bloody corpse behind the wheel of a black Ford rental. Thug's brain-case was popped mob style."

"Who's handling it?"

"Rosy said Strait's back from the scene. Was going in to see him."

Haley, climbing the stairs, spotted Montego and KW entering the dick's squad room. He paused, inhaled deeply and told himself to be icy cool. The "mob hit" had the station buzzing. He'd decided to come back to work thinking it might help him to find out what Armanno had meant about Zippi when he'd said, "Huh? Mario ain't here—where th' fuck ya been?"

Rosenbloom had stopped Haley at the front desk and told him about the "gorilla" who had bought a plot on a hilly side road. It was all Haley could do to listen and remain casual, even though Rosy wouldn't be looking for anything odd. But when he'd said that Montego had dumped and pummeled Zippi for busting into his girlfriend's apartment, Haley had bit on his lip. He'd never doubted that Montego could be a target—*but not his woman!*

Thank God, Montego had been there. Rosy's words had settled Haley for a moment, but he would've liked hearing that Mario Zippi was history, like Joey Armanno.

Damn.

Sickened and near panic, Haley had to go on, until Beak Brunetti and his cousin were dead.

Then what? Prison? Suicide? Haley gripped the wooden railing.

Be tough, Ice Cop. There's much to do.

He visualized Lissa's bruised face and tried to share her pain. It electrified a tortuous path to his tormented heart. There also was Montego. Haley did care about keeping his partner's respect. Respect for himself seemed impossible.

Worry had prompted Haley to pen a statement to be opened in the event of his death, telling Montego about Brunetti's hold over him. About Haley's fear that Angelo Pinky Sancia, the hit man from the '30s, might actually be his pop; and about Joey Armanno's attempted hit on Missy. Haley wrote that his intent had been to motivate Montego; maybe together they could come up with a way to protect the Haley family from Brunetti and his finger-pointing cousin.

Several neat single malt Scotches mixed with deliberation while inebriated had Haley tearing up the confession. He'd felt muddle-headed. What could Tonto do that Ice Cop couldn't do? That's when he'd called Brad at his home to see if he could come to work. By doing so, Haley had deprived some blue-suit the desired exposure of working a felony car.

Whatever.

He flicked a flame to a cigarette, plodded up to the second floor, and blew out a harsh wisp of smoke. Tonight would be hell. He'd soon find out how cool Ice Cop truly could be; his slight booze buzz might help.

It was time to face his partner's cobalt-blue intensity. He feared that ultimately he would have to convince the cop called Tonto to believe a lie.

Mike Montego's eyes penetrated to a man's very core.

Montego hurried along with KW straight to the Homicide desk.

"Alex, what's the skinny on the mob hit up on Saint Andrews?"

Alex Strait, shuffling through papers, hesitated, then said, "A mob prick bought the proverbial mahogany box—a single nine-millimeter slug—but I'm certain that the downtown *pros* can easily sort out the sordid mess." He tweaked a tip of his baby-sized handlebar, half-smirking.

"Bad guy, huh? I guess Wayne and Roy have it?" Montego glanced at KW.

"They believe it's tied to the Preston case." Strait tweaked the other mustache tip. "You know how it is. The *big* cases are too sophisticated for us lowly divisional grunts to handle." He stood and lifted his dark brown sports coat off the back of his chair and slipped into it.

"It figures. The councilman made the headlines." Montego lightly slapped Strait's shoulder. "I'm sure *Sir* Wayne Nells will keep you up to date, Mister TMA." He sensed his pal was holding something back.

"You should call Ray Pinker in SID—get a ballistics check against the nine-mil slug they removed from your pickup's seat." Strait buttoned his coat. "I found a Browning Hi-Power with a suppressor on the floorboard behind the driver's seat. It was recently fired . . . it also fit into the empty shoulder rig that Mister Armanno wore—the only firearm in the vehicle."

"Armanno—Joey Armanno?"

The goon Mario Zippi hung with!

Chapter 52

Montego, glancing at Haley entering the dicks' squad room, said to Strait, "Kay Dub told me a citizen made the original call on Armanno—who made the discovery?"

"Two bubble-gummers walking home from school." Strait adjusted his tie. "Immaculate Heart High's a long block away."

Tanto. Montego hadn't linked the killing site's proximity to the girls parochial school. He quickly looked at Haley who was eyeing no one in particular. Apparently, he hadn't heard Strait's comment.

"Yo, Neall," KW said. "How's your pretty lady doing?"

With the excitement about Joey Armanno, Montego realized he'd not told KW the good news.

"Lissa woke up this afternoon," Haley's voice was low and even. "Was touch and go, but Doc found no signs of permanent nerve damage—he's keeping her a few more days as a precaution."

Strait gave Haley a kindly look. "Glad to hear it, Haley."

"We're all glad," Montego added, trying to read Haley's expression through the cigarette haze. His icy-gray eyes had a strained, faraway focus.

"The burglary team gave me this warrant." Strait held out a folded paper to Haley. "You heard about Mister Armanno's recent demise?"

"Ah, he's who it was—Rosy told me that some 'shmuck' bought a hilly plot." Haley took the writ. "What've you got on it?"

KW said, "Downtown has it—probably a mob hit. Nine-millimeter was used, same caliber that killed Preston—happened near Missy's school."

Montego again tried to watch Haley's face, but the guy spun away and stubbed out his cigarette in an ashtray.

"Damn—don't like hearing that crap." Haley moved toward the doorway. "Mike, let's tell Brad we've got us a burglar to bag." He left the squad room. KW tagged along.

Not able to read Haley's facial reaction, Montego figured the guy was preoccupied with Lissa.

Montego's mind switched to Brunetti's vendetta and Pinky Sancia.

"Alex, Beak Brunetti might be considering another hit."

Strait, stepping to the stairwell, shrugged. "That's no big surprise." Two steps below, he paused to look back. "What has Tonto heard?"

Montego told him what he knew about The Purple Hand.

"They say no one quits the mob," Strait brushed off his sleeves, "but if the hoodlum is still around, you can bet he has a new face and name. The Purple Hand." He scoffed. "The mobster pricks do like their fancy monikers, don't they, Mister *Tonto?*" He finger-smoothed his mustache tips, and an eyebrow arched.

"It seems that way, now *don't* it *Uncle* Alex."

Skipping down the steps past the front desk Montego waved to Rosy before entering the supervisors' room.

Haley was answering Brad Kozier's query about Lissa's condition.

Prior to the small group breaking for their units, the plainclothes supervisor warned them to step lightly around the mob, strongly suggesting that they leave them to Intelligence and Homicide Divisions.

"Captains Hamilton and Whitaker want the local Mafiosi to think the heat's off." Kozier seemed focused on Montego.

What heat, and why is he staring at me?

"Maybe we ought to bring in an Italian cop to make the goons feel more at ease." Montego's comment brought a chuckle. "The eye-boys and the local federales are nothing more than mob babysitters." That brought a circumspect look from the sergeant.

Montego, recalling Smith saying he'd informed Captain Hamilton about Rudolph Forrall being accosted by two Mafiosi, said, "Sounds like a bit of politics to me."

Kozier gave Montego another look, then he offered "atta boys" to Diaz and Brannock for their "hot prowler" bust. Releasing the two teams he said, "Remember, men, cool it with the damn dark-suits."

Heading for their prowler, Montego, fighting an inner tension, told Haley about KW calling him and talking about Eugene Preston's murder.

"Kay Dub wanted me to know that Forrall didn't have anything to do with it—not that I'd've thought that anyway. We both thought it was a stupid hit." Montego side-glanced at Haley who was expressionless.

They arrived at their sedan behind the Juvenile Unit.

"I suppose you saw Preston at the golf course?" Montego asked.

Haley swung the car door open. "In the parking lot—laid it on the line." He tossed the keys over the top.

Montego caught them and opened his side, anxious to hear more.

Haley, already behind the wheel, took the keys. "It shook him—then the twerp stood up to me."

Montego studied Haley. He remained his impassive self.

After a long and wordless moment, Haley added, "I left him staring down at the photographs. I'd dumped them at his feet. Last I saw of the silly hypocrite—here, you hold this—I see a note attached to it." He laid the writ on the seat between them.

Montego, adjusting his shoulder holster, merely glanced at it.

"I'm curious—there was no mention of the compromising pictures in the newspapers."

Haley over-revved the motor. "Strange, isn't it?" He eased the gearshift into Drive. The Plymouth lurched north on Wilcox.

Montego, assuming Haley's reaction was due to his being tired, chose not to bring up that Armanno had been killed near Missy's school.

While waiting for a red light at The Boulevard he did say, "Rosy tell you about Zippi?"

"Yeah." Haley, on the green, wheeled left, spinning the rear tires. "That the wannabe attacked your woman—I'm damn sorry about that, too, Mike. I'm glad you dumped his ass. Wish it had been me . . . he'd be dead."

"He almost was." Montego opened his notebook and penciled in pertinent data on the DFAR. "Anyway, the incident helped me clear the air with Julie—we're now copacetic, as Louis Armstrong likes to say."

"Great." Haley, slowing the sedan, fired up a Camel. "I mean that." He blew out. "And smashing Zippi's fat mug saved me the trouble. Brad told me that Lissa had done a number on him—besides what you did. Gouges on his torso and bruises on his legs and crotch. The asshole was way too much for her to handle. . . . But she put up a helluva fight."

"I'm sure she did." Montego pocketed his Scripto ballpoint, closed the binder and tossed it onto the back seat.

Haley took a deep drag and through the escaping smoke stream said, "Let's stop by the Villa Capri."

"What's on your mind?"

"Since Armanno's bought it, I wanna see what meatheads show up under the neons tonight."

Montego realized that Kozier hadn't given them a direct order, but they would be flying in the face of the three-striper and two captains' strong suggestions by going into a known mob hangout.

Hair-brained cops have no place in Deputy Chief Thad Brown's detective bailiwick.

"Remember, amigo, we have a little task to take care of." He picked up the warrant and read the attached note aloud, "'Suspect's a he/she—check Pergola's, Hollywood and Bronson.'"

Haley looked straight ahead. "We can do that when it's darker—better chance *she/he* will be at the popular fruit stand."

Montego shoved the warrant into a coat pocket.

"Wonder how Dante Pio's handling the rising body-count—three of his goons now dead?"

"I hope the kill-count skyrockets—lousy maggots."

"But maggots don't kill their own, and that seems to be the Mafia's way of life." Montego had read how Albert Anastasia had bought it five years earlier in New York City. His body had been riddled with mob bullets while he reclined in the Park-Sheraton Hotel barbershop.

"Killers, all of them." Haley flipped the cigarette butt away and turned north on Las Palmas.

"They don't forget the hits on their family." Montego grabbed the handset and requested a time check. "They have a blood thing. The Beak was a kid when his dad was killed by another goon. Brunetti still has a vendetta—thinks the old hitter's here in LA—hasn't found him, yet—"

Haley swerved to a stop yards short of the corner at Yucca, a tire screeching. "Sorry about that."

"About Papa Beak or your parallel parking?" Montego verified Momma Mary's response with the time showing on his pocket watch. He lowered the volume, not going Code 6. Kozier monitored the frequencies and would recognize the address as being the Villa Capri.

"What d'you think?" Haley freed the key, climbed out and stood in the crosswalk blocking traffic waiting while he lit another cigarette. A horn beeped. Haley didn't move, paying no heed to the driver.

Montego glanced at the motorist, her fingers danced on the wheel.

Haley said, "What's this crap about Beak's old man being aced?"

Montego, not mentioning his source, told him about Angelo Sancia quitting the mob, The Purple Hand tag, and the death of Leo Brunetti's dad.

"Don't know whether or not Sancia is alive—no local record, but FBI Microfiche shows him with another moniker, too: Pinky. The goon's missing a little fingertip."

Haley, grinding the weed underfoot, opened the door to the Capri.

"Stroll time, Tonto."

"This is the eye-boys job, not for us patrol cops," he muttered, but Haley had gone through the doorway, a man on a mission.

Montego did not like parading for no reason in front of Mafiosi only hours after Joey Armanno's murder. All it would take is for one of the goons to make an awkward move and Haley might shoot him. Like it or not, Ice Cop had to act fearless, let them know their reputation didn't daunt him.

The casual walk-through ended inside the men's room where Haley checked the commode stall before using a urinal.

Montego lathered up his hands. "Guess The Beak's someplace else mourning—that's if he gives a darn."

Haley ripped off a towel and peered at Montego in the mirror. "How'd you hear about his old man?"

"I learned about it when I checked on Armanno's whereabouts. Vegas Intelligence cops overheard Brunetti's cousin talking to an older goon, a Moe Dalitz." Montego tossed the paper towel wad into the waste container. "Dalitz used to run with the Purples gang." At the door, Montego added, "The old goon probably knew about The Purple Hand too."

Outside, on the sidewalk, Haley said, "Beak's cousin gotta handle?"

"Nino Simeti."

Haley coughed. "What's that meathead's game?"

Montego stopped at their prowler. "He's here for something big. Maybe he killed Preston." He'd mentioned the hit hoping Haley would say more. When no words came, Montego continued, "Suppose Lissa told you about the new player named Roger?"

He had to reach fast to snag the keys flying over the sedan at him. "I guess she didn't."

Inside the car, Haley slowly rolled down the side window.

"Yeah, she told me. . . . Maybe Simeti is Riffelano's replacement. He could be Roger, I suppose."

Montego didn't buy it. Quinn had said that Simeti arrived in L.A. before Gordon Riffelano showed up in Tinseltown.

"Hey, mi amigo—you ready to brave Pergola's den of iniquity?"

"If you promise not to kick the damn crap outta the fancy queens hoping to net your salty codfish."

Montego shook his head. His partner's behavior mystified him.

Neall Haley removed the handcuffs from the lanky prisoner they had nabbed at Pergolas. "Gerry-*deen*. Time to remove that fancy faux-do."

The Purple Hand

The tall transvestite gazed down at him, but raised his hands and fumbled with the curly red wig. Haley quickly grasped Gerry's fingers and carefully removed a beaded hatpin.

"Naughty, naughty." Haley gave the broad-headed straight-pin to the jailer, George "Bull" Cybulski, and flung the hairpiece onto the booking counter.

"Bull, tonight you have the honor of incarcerating Hollywood's notorious jewel thief: Gerry-deen the fairy queen."

"Make sure she-he's hanging genuine jewels under that fancy-ass gown, Haley," Cybulski dropped the pin into a small envelope.

During the processing, Haley reasoned out his situation. He realized that Mike Montego knew a hell of a lot more than he'd give him credit for. Lissa might have told him a few things, but somebody else, maybe O'Brody or Nells in Homicide, had fed him some damn good info—stuff that could help Haley squash Brunetti. The meathead's vengeance hunt meant it was personal. That didn't mean that Dante Pio would stay clear. After all, it *was* a mob thing . . . in a way.

Fate—and Montego—finally brought Haley the name he'd sought. Now to find cousin Nino Simeti and turn his damn ass into a clay pigeon.

Two birds—one blast. Haley unexpectedly laughed out loud.

"And what do you find *sooo* hilarious Officer Haley, my dear?"

"Nothing, Gerry. Slip outta that slinky shift. Show us where you stash your jewels—and anything else you've got hidden in odd spots."

"Well, dear boy, you'll just have to come and undo my back side." The twiggy-legged arrestee shimmied about.

Haley wide-eyed Cybulski. "I need a damn raise."

*   *   *

Leo Brunetti would never admit that he could get shook, but he was. He got on the phone and called his cousin, who'd returned from Vegas. "Nino—gotta see you—now. Get your skinny ass over to Patsy's."

Within the hour, Brunetti was two Grappas into his commiseration with Simeti inside the dimly lit Villa Capri bar.

"Who in th' fuck coulda rubbed out Joey A, Leo?" Simeti gulped his Grappa. "Whoever he was, hadda be damn good."

"Dunno-fuckin' dunno." Brunetti wasn't sorry about Armanno, but he felt queasy, his gut growled uncomfortably. The way that Armanno had

257

got his ass fucking rubbed out—and not even at the school—had sounded professional. Getting snatched before he could do the job. . . .

Brunetti's balls were dancing on twisted cords. Had Pale-face or his fucking old man done it? Must be one of them. If it was Pinky Sancia, then Brunetti knew he was in trouble. It was possible the cop had told his old man. Should never have expected the blond bull to keep his trap shut.

'N' none of the boys knew nothing . . . fuck me.

Nino Simeti slid his empty tumbler across the counter signaling for a third drink. He looked at Brunetti.

"So, tell me, what was Frisco Joey A up to, anyways?"

"Was doing a job for me—was pressuring the pasty-assed bull— hitting his kid sister."

"Leo—Leo—fuckin' stupido! Messin' wit' them bulls—bad shit."

"Hey, I wouldn'ta, except I wanted his ol' man to feel the pain like I did—'n' I ain't finished with Blue-Eyes, not yet."

Brunetti knew he'd fucked up. His shriveled nuts and loose bowels told him that much. He'd seen the teenaged girl the Sunday he'd checked out the Haley pad.

"Y'er right—shoulda just gone after Pinky 'n' been done with it."

"For damn sures, Leo. Heat's gonna be on our asses now . . . fuck."

Brunetti took some comfort in his cousin saying "our asses."

"I know, Nino, but nothing's tying us to the damn hit—no one knows about the contract, unless Joey said something to that fuckin' Mario, and that chump opened his big trap."

Brunetti downed his Grappa and nodded at the waitress for a refill.

If Pinky Sancia was the damn hitter who did Joey Armanno. . . ? Don't let Nino hear this shit. Scare off his crazy ass 'n' I'll be on my own.

"Let's order lunch, Nino. Soon as we finish eating, we gotta see that nigger lawyer—get fuckin' Pio off a my damn back—'n' I want us to use separate wheels—I got me something to do afterwards."

Coochie Goochie would help get him over the fucking shakes.

The Guinea's fuckin' fierce Purple Hand rep's gotta be shit.

But Brunetti's aching balls told him something different.

Chapter 53

The jangle of the telephone roused Montego. The clock-radio dial: 6:10 AM, twenty minutes from when he'd intended to get up. He'd left the TV playing on mute; the screen showed Generals Power and LeMay arguing for the bombing of Cuba. Dan Rather was asking, "Should the USA go to war with the Soviet Union over the missiles stored in Cuban silos? "

Nope, Kennedy will control the headstrong military Brass—he'll also face down Krushchev.

Missiles or no missiles, the annoying ringing couldn't be ignored. Friends knew not to call before ten.

Montego reached over and lifted the receiver, but before he said anything, he heard, "Tonto? Rousted you, sorry. Smitty here . . ." The tension in his voice spurred Montego alert. ". . . need to see you. I'll be parked at El Segundo in a Bel-Aire across from Hawthorne High."

"Give me ten." Montego killed the connection and dialed Strait.

"Figured you'd be up—can't make this morning's run. Take it easy on the Diggers—gotta go." He disconnected before Strait could respond, not that he'd ask questions, but why chance it?

Spotting the aqua-and-cream '57 Chevy Montego pulled his pickup in behind it, noting the chromed dual exhaust pipes.

"You rode hard, Tonto. Thanks buddy." Smith's dark face showed strain, the whites of his eyes were yellowish. Perspiration glistened on his lined brow. "Mind riding around while we talk?"

Montego dropped onto the tucked-and-rolled leatherette. "Go." He wound down the side window. A small cardboard box with a business card taped to it was on the seat by him. It read: "Russell Smith, owner/trainer." He glanced at Smith. "I see that The Steel Bar is your gym now—congrats."

Smith, appearing preoccupied, keyed the V8 sending a rumble through the twin mufflers. Lowering the radio volume, he motored east.

"Yesterday afternoon, I was standing at the back door of the gym when Rudy drove up." Smith turned north onto Inglewood Avenue and continued speaking, "Next thing I knew, Brunetti and another gonzo clown came around the building and grabbed him. Before I could help, a skinny dude with wiry hair and sunken cheeks shoved a cannon in my face, but Brunetti put the kibosh on him, yelling, 'Cool it, Nino.'"

"Nino Simeti and Beak Brunetti, they're cousins," Montego said.

Smith spit out the window and glanced at him. "I felt like a helpless fool. The Brunetti clown had lifted Rudy by his shirt-front, threatening him about getting the liquor bill onto the council floor for a yes vote by Thursday or he could kiss his daughter *'Ciao.'*" His fingers tightened on the wheel, bulging his triceps.

"And?" Montego had no problem picturing what his monster-sized pal would've done had he not been staring at a steel hog-leg.

"That was it—clowns took off in separate cars, a yellow Caddy and a red T-Bird. Rudy was petrified." Smith's fingers still worked the steering wheel. "I told him I'd never let the gonzos hurt Yolanda."

"And Forrall doesn't want the rough stuff known, either—right?"

"He doesn't, but I've got to report it to my captain. It's Hamilton's call, not mine." Smith turned at Century Boulevard and headed east passing the Hollywood Park racetrack.

Montego, guessing the route, lowered the sun visor. They'd started out in the city of Hawthorne. Next, they'd driven through the Lennox sheriff's area, and now they were cruising in Inglewood. Smith was staying out of LAPD territory. The next turn likely would be south on Crenshaw.

"What're we doing about this, mi amigo?" Planting his feet on the floorboard, Montego flexed his toes inside the huaraches, waiting. His guess was correct, Smith turned south.

"Mike, I've gotten close to Rudy—I like what the man stands for." He took a deep breath and blew out. "I'm not about to let mobster clowns screw him over. But I walk a damn tightrope."

Montego nodded. "Understand."

Smith eyeballed him. "I can't allow them to touch Rudy's family."

They rolled into the City of Gardena where playing poker was legal. Several blocks went by.

"Hows about a Gambler's Special, Mike?" Not waiting for a reply, Smith coasted the Bel-Aire into the Normandie Club parking lot.

Montego scanned the parked cars, questioning if the nearest church had its lot as full? Inside the fluorescent-lit gambling establishment, the large fluorescent-lighted card room was where the main action occurred. The poker playing crowd occupied numerous smoke-hazed tables.

He followed Smith into the coffee shop where they ordered a couple of Joes. A moment later a bottom-heavy waitress topped their cups with hot coffee. Montego figured she hadn't passed the requisite physical

260

requirements warranting the lucrative nighttime tips. She waddled away with their breakfast orders.

"Dealer told Rudy you were a straight-up cop. "Course I knew that." He winked. "Here's what it is, Mike. Dealer's pissed—wants to ream Brunetti's sphincter with a creosoted telephone pole."

Montego could only imagine. Grinning, he slid his cup to him.

"Rudy and I calmed him down." Smith also moved his coffee cup closer. "He's cool now, and he'll stay clear of this 'cause I took him aside, let him think it was going to be handled extra-legally and to keep his badge he didn't need to be involved."

Montego, nodding, realized no matter what KW might think of his father-in-law, Smith had provided an easy out. His burly partner wouldn't want his upward mobility hindered, especially this way.

"I'll help, but also I intend to keep my badge." He gripped his cup.

Smith blew into his coffee before saying, "I'd like you to be handy, s'all. When I call, bring two sets of cuffs. Mine aren't handy." He winked.

Montego eased back. The extra bracelets made it sound like the cousins would be alive.

"When can I expect the dime to drop?" He sipped his coffee.

"Thursday night—if the ordinance isn't on the council floor by then I expect the clowns to make another visit." Smith rubbed his forehead. "Dealer's working, and Yolanda will be at her aunt's, out of the area." He carefully tasted his hot coffee. "Rudy will be tucked away, safe and sound, and I'll be ready."

To be available for the phone call, Montego would skip his class and arrange for a Special, or maybe he could work a trade with Brannock or Bobby Diaz.

Should a new councilman's personal employee take down a couple of Mafiosi, the repercussions could be explosive.

Montego could only guess how Chief Parker would deal with that.

Chapter 54

Neall Haley lightly touched the relief nurse's crisp white uniform sleeve. "Tell Mildred I'll be back during graveyard to give her my thanks."

The cheery day-shift nurse wheeled Lissa to the main entrance.

"I'm quite certain she will be happy to hear that Officer Haley."

Holding Lissa's hand he helped ease her out of the wheelchair. Arm-in-arm they made their way to the close-by Porsche. He continued to hold her hand as she eased onto the bucket seat. He rushed around, got behind the wheel. Before he started the motor, he gazed into her doe-brown eyes. Hints of discoloration remained on her forehead, but her natural beauty drew in his breath.

"You're beautiful, Lissa."

She brought her face closer, smiled and placed a finger on his chin. "You truly are a romantic." She kissed his lips softly.

He wanted to feel truly romantic, but he was unable to remove the dagger jabbing his heart. As they neared Gardner, the street she had resided on, he noticed her hands clenching, her knuckles turning yellowish white. He hadn't told her about the new apartment, wanting it to be a surprise.

"We're not going to your old place." His feelings became acute. He glanced at her. Relief and loving warmth filled her liquid eyes, touching him deeply. "I've moved your Pontiac and belongings to a new complex— its over on Crescent Heights." He quickly added, "Mike helped me."

She touched his leg; he wanted to touch hers. His throat constricted.

"Hope you like it. Your future home, hon." The pang in his chest shot down to his tight gut. He surmised her thoughts: she was damaged or some such thing, and he didn't want her.

Not true Lissa—not true!

"*Our* home," she cooed, patting his knee.

He grasped the gearshift knob tighter. An aching cry lodged in his throat, a silent groan. As much as he wanted to put the ring on her finger at that moment, it was impossible. Yet he loved her. He wanted to take her hand and propose, but still he saw no future for them. Even if Brunetti and Simeti were dead and the Haley family safe, could he—would he—still be the man Lissa thought him to be?

She put her hand over his and whispered words that touched his ears like lips brush kissing, "Mister Haley, I want you in my home."

The roadway blurred. He refused to blink. He breathed in slowly, her familiar rose-petal presence, as always, enveloping his entire worthless being. Tears tumbled. "I know, hon."

Such a strong and beautiful woman.

He parked in front of the complex and pointed to her blue Pontiac. "There's your—"

"Ooh, it looks brand new."

"I polished it."

"Not my car, silly—the apartment house—can I really afford it?" She needed no help lifting herself up from the Porsche.

Her reaction had him jumping out while blotting his damp cheeks with his sleeves.

He took her hand and they went up a flight of stairs to her home.

After she checked out the new pad, he busied himself by arranging the furniture the way she wanted. The queen bed was the hardest for him to position. Not because of its location, but because he wanted to place her upon it and make love. He refused. Even thinking of it this soon sickened him. Satisfying his physical need could devastate her. Sex had to be abhorrent to her now.

He fumbled with the small blue-flocked jewelry box in his pocket. The diamond ring had been in his pocket since the attack. Again, he wanted to propose this instant, go down on one knee like he'd done in the hospital at her bedside, unknown to her, but his gut reminded him that he didn't deserve her. He stopped his fumbling.

Roll call time was nearing, he had to get going. Holding her close, he gave her a tender and lingering kiss. Her warmth began to melt his resolve. He did not want to leave the security of her arms.

The ache stayed with him while driving to the station. He worked at unraveling the turmoil within him. It was a milieu of mind and body. Her presence filled him with immense joy. Touching her thrilled him beyond expression, but committing to her would be selfish. It agonized him that she could be no part of what was coming. It damn well frightened him too.

The Beak had poked a broadsword into his back, forcing him onto a gangplank. Riffelano had pushed him to the damn edge. Eugene Preston's departure should've pulled Brunetti's murdering-blade away, but it hadn't.

Now he'd jumped off the plank with Joey Armanno, defying the lousy mob. He swam in an angry sea with two killer sharks.

That his pop had played off Beak Brunetti like he was no big deal concerned Neall. Pop might be able to handle himself, but did he truly understand the danger he was in? He must.

But I've gotta save my ass first. Pop might not survive without me.

He blew out a sour jagged breath and wheeled the sports car onto Wilcox Avenue. Uncontrolled fury had caused him to kidnap Armanno. Why hadn't he shot the lousy meathead in the damn school parking lot and simply claimed self-defense?

Because Missy would have witnessed it.

What he had experienced afterward shocked him past all reality. Not only had it panicked him, it had gutted him.

Damn, damn, damn.

He parked in the city employees' lot with the hopeful thought that Armanno's death would pass for a gangland hit. . . .

Was that possible?

Luckily, he had spied no one else on the street when he'd raced down the hill to his Porsche. He'd never shake the frenzied event from his mind. Nausea and fear had his belly still roiling, he could puke, again.

To ease the unremitting torment, he would always have to focus on Missy's sweet face, on her long black curls. She was the sole justification for what had happened. He was no better than Pinky Sancia. There was no other way, now. He must protect Pop. He must harpoon the killer sharks, and he must do it soon.

Convinced that Brunetti was behind the attempted hit on Missy, he asked himself, who else was on the meathead's hit team—on his payroll? Obviously Nino Simeti.

Haley made his way up to the locker room and refocused on the night ahead. Montego sat on the bench at one end of the aisle silently putting blank report forms into a three-ringed notebook. Haley, sensing that he was intentionally ignoring him, opened his end locker and grabbed a rag. He oiled it with Hoppe's, and began wiping down his S&W magnum.

"Looks like Tonto's planning to be log man tonight?"

"If that's what you want, Neall." Montego snapped the binder rings closed, not looking up.

Is he upset?

Haley forced a pained chuckle. "Lissa loves her new apartment." His words sounded hollow.

Montego dropped the binder into his plastic briefcase. "Expected she would. You found her a darn nice apartment." He stood, grabbed the case, and moved toward the hallway. "I'll check with the night-desk dick—see if there're any warrants to serve."

Haley snapped a flame to the silver Ronson, lit a cigarette, and went into the roll call room. He took his usual back row seat, feeling spent.

Several minutes later, Montego slid onto the bench next to him. "No warrants tonight." He sounded uptight.

Uneasiness rippled through Haley. He stubbed out the Camel as the watch commander began calling out the assignments.

Haley answered, "Here" when his name was called.

Montego leaned closer. "On the QT—Brunetti and Simeti have put some heat on Rudy Forrall—threatened him." He replied, "Here" to the lieutenant's call of his name. "I also learned that Simeti's middle name is Rogelio—could be the new player they call Roger."

Haley continued to stare toward the front dais. How does Montego find this crap out? Must be his "in" downtown. Haley knocked out another Camel. How much more does Montego know?

Nino Simeti was back. No matter what, tomorrow Haley would execute his plan: snatch the lousy meathead's ass, set him up; make it look like a double gangland hit. This time, however, he would be carrying the untraceable and suppressed .22 Minx.

Haley lit the cigarette and inhaled the smoke. Unwanted icy ripples returned. Rings of frost surrounded his rapidly thudding heart. Like a damn Mafioso, he was filling the role of a ruthless killer.

Weapons inspection was completed and while Montego headed downstairs, Haley went to the locker room latrine. He splashed cold water onto his face, thinking: Dante Pio likely believed that he had made the hit on Armanno, that's if the capo knew Missy was the target; Pio wasn't stupid. Maybe how Armanno was dumped would cause Pio to think Ice Cop was dangerous. But not if the intended hit on Missy was Brunetti's personal doing. If so, would Pio have known? Would he even have approved?

The worrisome question persisted: Why was the capo's gunner, an import from Frisco, sicked onto Missy? This was Leonardo Brunetti's vendetta. Haley had thought the capo regime was not involved; everything was dollars-and-cents to the underboss. Now Haley wasn't so certain.

On Sundays, Dante Pio and the tall brunette Montego had called Miss Long-Gloves liked to plant themselves in The Palms' corner booth for dinner. Haley hoped Montego would disregard the Brass' direction to lay off the local mob one more time. Confronting Pio guarded by his thicknecks was damn risky, especially in a public place, but time was running out.

If the meet went badly, more banner headlines would be made.

* * *

Leo Brunetti sat in his convertible, the top was up. The Catholic Church parking lot was emptying. He'd attended High Mass, praying for his life.

He fingered the rosary beads, feeling a time crunch.

"Gotta get things done, 'n' soon. Killing Angelo Sancia is *primero*, before the yellow fuck hits my ass," Brunetti muttered. "Shoulda done him that Sunday at his house when his bull-son was there. But no, I hadda play my game with boy Haley first so Sancia would feel the kind of pain I felt as a kid."

Still, Brunetti wanted to settle the score with Montego. "Don't want the bull interfering when I do the Haleys," he muttered. Simeti would have to be cover on that one—Blue Eyes was too good. Brunetti touched his bent nose—fuck, it just dawned. His cousin had never seen the blue-eyed bull.

Switching on the ignition, he drove to the Hillview Apartments where Simeti had a suite. Brunetti used his dupe key to enter, even though he knew Simeti was inside. An open bottle of Grappa was on a table. He found a glass and poured the Italian version of "white lightning" halfway to its top. He swirled the clear liquid with his finger, then took a big gulp.

"Hey, what gives, Leo?" Simeti had come in from the other room, toweling his kinky hair dry. He took the half-empty Grappa bottle and poured two fingers worth into a tumbler.

"Y'need to know what the blue-eyed bull I told you about looks like, Nino, 'cause I got me a personal score to settle with his fucking ass."

"Not smart, Leo. Gettin' inta it wit' the fuzz is bad news. 'Sides, why d'youse needs me?" Simeti swigged his drink.

"Nino, all you gotta do is eyeball the fucker—see his pretty mug."

"What th' fuck does that mean?" Simeti took another swig.

"It means you gotta know what the damn copper looks like should he come outta the shadows when we're doing a job. Just being smart, s'all."

"Awright, Leo—longs youse don' do somethin' stupid."

Chapter 55

Haley drove north on Wilcox from the station as Montego, waiting for their frequency to clear, perused the Daily Crime and Arrest Sheet. Commercial burglars had hit several businesses for Selectric typewriters, but he found his mind on the Preston and Armanno killings.

He had brought up the threat against Forrall to get Haley's reaction, and he'd gotten one. Ice Cop had reverted to his expressionless way, but his icy gray eyes had taken on unusual intensity. Impossibly, he smoked more, filling the tin ashtray with cigarette butts during roll call.

Because of Preston, or Brunetti . . . or both—are they connected?

Montego, consciously rubbing his thumbnail, reproached himself for his unshakable suspicion. If Smith had surmised correctly, the answer would come Thursday evening. Sergeant Kozier had let Montego trade days with Bobby Diaz. Working with Haley that night would be the telling moment. The guy would be having a face-to-face with Brunetti, again.

"Frequency One clear," Momma Mary broadcast sweetly.

Montego snatched the microphone. "Six-Frank-One clear." Racking the handset, he took in their surroundings as Haley steered them west onto Selma then turned south at the next corner to avoid the setting sun.

Cassil Place. Montego mentally filed the street name: A patrol cop knew his precise location at all times, like he knew the six chambers in his service revolver were always fully loaded, even though his thoughts might be on other things. For the moment, Brunetti's vendetta and where his lifelong target, Angelo Sancia, might be, occupied Montego's mind.

Haley was butt-lighting another Camel while crumpling the empty packet against the steering wheel.

Montego said, "I'm curious about Brunetti looking for the old-time hit man who killed his dad."

Haley flipped the butt out the window, tossed the crushed cigarette packet onto the back seat, and turned west at Sunset, lowering the sun visor.

What seemed like minutes later, the fresh cigarette still burning in his mouth, he said, "Yeah, old what's his name?"

Montego heard the delayed reply as a question. Feeling a bit tense, he wiggled his toes while he continued to watch Haley's stony profile, and said, "Angelo Pinky Sancia infamously known as The Purple Hand."

Haley nodded slightly, the dangling Camel lost its ash.

"If what you said is true, The Beak will be looking to ace Sancia. I've been thinking, Mike—what if we used a stooge? Tell Beak that we have Pinky Sancia, and then set a trap. Maybe he'd pounce on him and we could bust his hairy ass."

"A stooge? What if he's already found Sancia? I can see us telling him that we've ID'd Armanno's killer, then set a so-called stooge trap. If he goes for it, bust him before he can silence the guy." A brash remark, but Montego's own impromptu word: *silence*, had caught his attention. Strait had said that Joey Armanno had been cut down with a suppressed Browning semiautomatic. A silencer made sense: the kill-spot was in a residential neighborhood.

Haley stopped for a red tri-light at Highland. He took a long drag on his cigarette. "Hell of an idea, Tonto." His voice was flat and parched sounding.

Montego thought more about Joey Armanno. The goon had been a pal to Mario Zippi, and yet the mobster wannabe had acted alone against Lissa and Julie. Had the assaults upset Dante Pio? Quinn had been surprised that Brunetti resisted arrest. He'd said that the Mafiosi "gunsels" usually left the police alone. That should apply to their women, too.

"Do you think the mob capo ordered this Roger player to take out Armanno because he'd chummed with the wannabe?"

Haley looked over. "Another hot idea." He flipped the Camel out the window. On the green light he gunned the prowler. Moments later, he pounded the steering wheel.

"You game for a quick run through The Palms? I want to pull a hairy bluff on capo Pio—it's his usual dinner time."

"Explain yourself."

"Your idea about Pio ordering Armanno's hit is hot, but we have no proof. I have another idea. I'll tell Pio we know who aced his trigger-boy. Tell him it was revenge—and that we're taking care of it. Also, if Brunetti or any other of his gunners go after the shooter, we'll have no choice but to bust them all for interfering."

"I gotta say, Eliot, Ice Cop, Ness is sure full of *hairy* ideas tonight. Tell me, Señor Gangbuster, who're you naming as the vengeful hitter?"

"Cubby Bear's teammate, the big tackle you mentioned was inside the Sambah when you nabbed his bruiser bud for the Rancho Two-Eleven."

"Tackle Two—revenge for Blagden? You think that explains why Joey Armanno's Browning was used—that Number Two tackled him unarmed?" Curiosity corralled Montego's thoughts. "You're reaching pretty darn wide to rope in Blagden's bud as the hitter. Dante Pio won't buy it—not if he ordered the hit."

Haley's logic had Montego thinking the guy was up to something. Maybe facing Pio would be revealing, assuming he'd even talk to them.

"You're right, Mike. But if the capo did order the hit, hearing us pointing the finger at Blagden's bruiser crony would amuse him. He'd think we were on the wrong trail." Haley brought out a fresh pack of cigarettes. "Hell, Blagden did team with Rondell to blow up Salico—that's our story."

Haley eyed Montego. "Who's to say Joey Armanno didn't face off the tackle bruiser?" He fingered off the red cellophane pull-strip away and turned north on La Brea heading for The Palms. "Blagden's teammate simply was better—took Armanno's sniping ass out."

"You're thinking Pio might reveal something . . . ? I suppose it's more probable than one of his soldiers shooting Armanno with his own gun." Montego thought about it, then decided to go along if only to watch the showdown. "OK, let's do it."

Dante Pio waved off his twin bodyguards when he spied Montego and Haley approaching. The attractive long-gloved brunette sitting beside Pio gazed at them with a fascinated look.

Staying close behind Haley, Montego stood prepared for anything while he scanned the players, their gun hands were inside their suit coats.

"Capo, we both know who took out Joey Armanno last Thursday," Haley said.

Montego studied the underboss taking his time sipping his red wine slowly before setting it down. Pio gazed from Haley to Montego and back with dark eyes that revealed little.

"Yeah, a crony of the bruiser we busted for bombing Salico," Haley added, "Guess Joey thought he was getting even, but Blagden's buddy was faster. Got the drop on him." He stepped closer. The thicknecks fidgeted. Pio's cold-eyed look kept his broad-shouldered pin-striped muscles at bay.

Haley said, "And The Beak had best stay away or get his big ass busted." He turned toward the foyer, paused, and looked back. "Also, Capo, leave that lousy sicko, Mario Zippi, alone. He belongs to us, now."

Dante Pio finally spoke, his low tone harsh. "That crumb thought he was making his damn bones. Whatever falls on the idiot he deserves."

Outside the premises, Montego mentally shook his head. All they had learned was that Mario Zippi was a chump who had acted solo.

"No way did Pio buy your line, Haley—and why did you bring up Brunetti?"

"I want the meathead hearing about this—get his hairy ass riled. Maybe he'll make a damn mistake and *you* can bust his beak, again."

The picture of Haley with Brunetti flashed in Montego's mind. If the two were involved in something, what had severed the relationship? He pondered each and every event he'd witnessed that involved Haley with the mob, and when he thought he had it figured out, he lost his mental grasp.

The key to Haley's odd behavior continued to bother Montego, but he still believed it had to do with Leonardo Brunetti. Placing the blue binder into his briefcase, Montego reflected on tonight's confrontation with the capo. It puzzled him.

They locked their unit in the lot behind the Juvenile Unit building and headed across Wilcox toward the station.

Montego, on Haley's left side, noticed a coupe idling at the curb a few yards away. He paid it scant attention assuming that a date was waiting for her blue-suited boyfriend; still, an uneasiness had Montego wary.

As he stepped into the street, the dark-colored two-door suddenly sped toward the two plainclothesmen, tires squealing, high beams popping on, burning into Montego's eyes.

Turning his head away to avoid being blinded, he pushed Haley forward, hard, and jumped out of the car's path. In the streetlight's glow, he spied a skinny-necked driver and recognized Brunetti sitting on the passenger side. Montego heard a loud cackling as the coupe flew past.

He watched the car, a Mercury, speeding south on Wilcox, before retrieving his briefcase from the far gutter where he'd flung it. Turning back to Haley, he said, "Sorry about the shove."

Haley was snatching the keys he'd dropped, then, fumbling out a bent cigarette and his lighter, he said, "I'm not . . . thanks, Mike."

Montego said, "I think Brunetti's pal was only trying to scare us— the driver's laugh sounded a bit crazy, like he thought it was a big joke."

"Brunetti?" Haley fired up the Ronson and lit the crooked Camel.

"The underboss must not've been amused and told the meathead about *our* fun 'n' games tonight." Haley spit out a tiny piece of tobacco.

"Maybe. My guess, Brunetti wanted his cousin to get a look at us."

Chapter 56

Montego's comment had chilled Haley. He didn't know how right he was.

Seven weeks dealing with Brunetti had frazzled Haley's judgment. He drove the Porsche west on Sunset. He didn't think he'd gone overboard confronting Pio, especially since the capo had listened. The bluff had been a risk, but Brunetti should hear about it. Tonight's crap, however, seemed too soon. It had to be more of The Beak's "fun 'n' games."

It could mean that Brunetti wanted Haley to worry about how long his pop had; or, maybe he was letting "Neallie Baby" know that he'd be the first one wasted because of Joey Armanno. *Not good.*

Time had run out to snatch the cousin and lure Brunetti into a setup. Forget using Montego for backup. Haley would have to take out both damn cousins solo, and soon.

When the cousins were corpses, he would tell Pio that Brunetti had been behind the attempted hit on Missy—Armanno had copped to that— besides, the underboss had the smarts to reason out the Armanno hit once he learned the truth. If he already had known, he had given no hint. Either way, Dante Pio would realize that Brunetti was a loose cannon in his outfit. Maybe the capo had been truthful and would forget making a damn pay back for Armanno.

Haley turned south onto Crescent Heights Boulevard and several blocks later slipped into a parking space. Though late, Lissa expected him.

"Beak—you've made a big *fuckin'* mistake," he muttered.

In the streetlight glow outside the station, he'd seen Simeti's face. It was now indelible. Before watch tomorrow Haley would end Brunetti's fun and games. Two hits, what did it matter? Once gassed, forever gassed.

Lighting up a Camel, Haley was struck by a flash of fright for both Pop and himself. He sucked in the cigarette smoke till his lungs could hold no more, allowing the harsh nicotine to blast his brain cage.

The nicotine hit made him lightheaded; either that, or visualizing a cold, dense fog settling over the San Francisco Bay, shrouding San Quentin. He had never been privy to the "Green Room" but he'd heard about the heavy wooden armchair, the buckled restraint straps, and the bucket beneath that caught the large cyanide tablets, but he damn well could smell it.

Is that where my pale ass will end up?

A convulsive shiver overcame his body, imagining the leather straps sweat-stained with fear binding his clammy flesh, hearing the large tablets plop, feeling the acrid fluid oozing from his dying pores. His gorge rose. He stuck his head out the window, needing fresh air.

Sitting back, he remembered when he was a kid, and visualized his mom's face. He felt her warmth. It helped. He recalled fooling around in Pop's back-yard shop and pinching a finger on the oily pipe-threading tool. Mom had heard Haley's crying. She'd rushed in and scooped him into her arms, so strong, so warm. She had laid a kiss on the reddish spot saying, "There, all better now sweet Neallie."

And it was.

If Mom knew Pop was an ex-hit man, she had never let it affect her love for her family. Haley loved her so much more for it, and he loved Pop.

The man had given his children plenty of love, yet he'd always used a firm hand with Haley, the oldest, probably setting the example for the other siblings. It had strengthened his love for Pop, his only hero.

Locking the sports car, he hurried across the street through sparse traffic. His shoulders drooped as he plodded up to Lissa's door while gazing at the stillness of the lighted swimming pool. She seemed happy in her new more spacious home. It pleased him; but her pleasure increased his dread. He had been living too long with sickening fear. He feared he would never be able to share the apartment with the beautiful woman who had captured his heart. Trembling, he felt the unseen evil closing in.

Whenever he embraced Lissa, he tried to infuse both tenderness and strength while wishing to soak up her deeply hidden pain. In her gentle brown eyes and in her unspoken words, she hurt, and he hurt for her. He wanted to make love to her, but would give her whatever time she needed. No one but he had put the beautiful love of his life in harm's way, and it was he who'd failed to protect her. He would not fail again. . . .

*　　*　　*

Montego rolled along Ocean Drive still pissed by the goon-cousins' cute trick with the Mercury. He was pretty sure it was Simeti behind the wheel. At first he'd thought it had happened because they had accosted Pio. The underboss had concealed his thoughts well, but it didn't fit the capo's style. Pio had stayed impassive during Haley's bruiser-crony comment, likely believing the stupid in-your-face style was something Brunetti would do.

The Purple Hand

Once inside the Perch, Montego kicked off his huaraches, stepped to the hall closet and stripped to his BVDs. In the kitchen he took a "church key" and popped the cap off a Budweiser, his mind on the 9mm Browning that Strait had said was found with Joey Armanno's body. It made no sense. A killer without a weapon? In an earlier discussion with Quinn, he was told that the mob didn't play "whodunnit" games by using the victim's weapon.

Montego dropped the bottle opener into a drawer, thinking about the coming Thursday night and what questions might be answered. How would Haley handle confronting a handcuffed Brunetti? Montego knew if his partner had his way, the cousins would either end up in cold storage drawers down at the morgue or strapped to narrow beds on the thirteenth floor Jail Ward at County General.

When *Russell* Smith had said he'd telephoned Captain Hamilton at his home, it had impressed Montego. The Intelligence Division skipper now knew that the mob had threatened Rudolph Forrall.

Toeing the sandals aside, Montego flopped onto the sofa to ponder. His thoughts got no further.

"Not coming to bed?" Julie's filmy pink outline was enhanced by moonbeams streaming through crystals of ocean salt on a window pane.

"Kicking back, is all, kiddo. Clearing cobwebs from my head."

Julie kneeled before him, her hands on his bare knees. "Can I do something to help your head." Her wide eyes belied her words.

He grinned, set down the bottle, and took her hands in his. Women were intuitive in more ways than he wanted to imagine. He preferred not to bring the job home, and swore he wouldn't when he carried a detective's flat badge, but talking now might help him sort things out about his partner.

Releasing her warm hands, he grasped the frosty bottle, and said, "Neall and I have worked together for nearly two months now. In that time I've gotten closer to him and to his family—they're good people."

Julie drew her fingers softly down his leg, watching him closely.

"I can't get a read on the guy." He relaxed, her fragrance a therapy. "He's darn moody, mostly quiet, then abruptly talkative. Tonight he was both. Lissa's seen it, too—I mean before. . . ."

Montego took a big gulp of beer. Julie's focus remained steady, her expression sympathetic. He realized that she'd never met his two partners.

While her fingers continued to tease him, his mind drifted to the three shootings, then to Lissa and his nagging guilt. He gulped more beer, thinking: Mario Zippi dead . . . Armanno dead—so close to Missy's school.

Had it been Mario Zippi instead of Joey Armanno, Montego would have to look at Neall Haley seriously as a suspect.

Why was Armanno's weapon used?

Julie's smile had a wicked glint. She continued her soft stroking. Goosebumps sprouted up Montego's arms and legs.

"Enough of this—I'll figure Neall out, in time."

Montego set down the near empty bottle and held Julie's hands.

She eased onto the sofa. "I would like to meet Neall, and Lissa."

He thought about that, but not for long as she was leaning into him, her erect nipples lightly brushing his chest, exciting her, exciting him.

Julie shrugged out of the sheer nightgown, quickly pulled down his shorts, straddled him, and deftly guided him into her moist warmth.

Overcome by a physical desire within surging and wanting to bust loose, Neall Haley's behavior was the furthest thing from Montego's mind.

*   *   *

Leo Brunetti, back in his fourth floor room at The Roosevelt, gulped a healthy amount of Grappa, questioning himself why he had let his crazy cousin talk him into being the one to drive the rental.

He was damned pissed at Nino Simeti.

Should've controlled things.

He'd had Simeti rent the Mercury so they could stay incognito. Brunetti had meant for them to wait outside the police house till Blue-Eyes and Haley showed. Then Simeti was supposed to go inside, take himself a look—that was all. Fuck no, the bulls had to drive into the lot near where Simeti had parked. Then the fuckers walked right in front of the Merc.

Nino hadda do his stupid shit—'N' that crazy-ass laughing a his.

All Brunetti had wanted was for his damn cousin to know what that fucking Montego looked like, not try and run their bull asses over.

If Haley's old man, Pinky Sancia, got wind of it. . . . Brunetti poured another shaky two finger's worth of Grappa and jerkily downed it.

Suddenly, he needed to take a dump.

Grabbing the string of 55 beads off the table, he went into the john.

Gotta take care of business tomorrow. What time is it?

Leo Brunetti looked at his golden Rolex watch, while nervously running the rosary through his fingers.

Fuck, tomorrow is today already.

Chapter 57

Later that morning, after a long so-long kiss, Montego watched the forest-green Austin-Healey rumbling north carrying Julie to her Monday graduate school class. He remained emotionally confused about his feelings: was it true love and great sex, or simply great sex that felt like true love?

He trotted south briefly visualizing Ted Preston thrumming the worn cover on his Bible, probably wondering how to get his only daughter to stop seeing the Scandy-Mex cop. The vision was bothersome. Montego feared it might be affecting his feelings about Julie. He was unwilling to believe he couldn't love a woman with a bigoted father . . . but her dad's haughty manner did bug him.

Seeing Strawberry Gal driving away *had* brought a brief pang—but this time she would be coming back.

Approaching Marine Avenue he spied Greg Aurek stretching.

"Hey deputy dawg. Wanna race?"

Aurek straightened and adjusted his running shorts. "No way, José. What gives?" His sand-colored hair flipped in a sudden gust of wind.

"Julie and I are back together, finally."

"That's cool. Becky and me are tip-top, too. We worked out the little problem of her blabbing about you being with that snazzy blonde—Say, how's Renzo doing?"

Montego could only imagine how the well-stacked, petite lady and Aurek had worked it out. "Lissa's home and doing great."

They jogged down to The Strand and weaved their way around the slower joggers, the dog-walkers, and the mothers pushing baby-strollers.

"Hey, Wheels is running down on the hard-pack—let's catch him."

"Man, I knew I shouldn't've come outside to stretch."

Montego sprinted over the warm sand and the broken seashells, cutting toward the ragged-edged surf.

"Hey," Aurek yelled, "Wait for me. Ten-four?"

"Roger," Montego called back. His blithe reply had him recalling Broderick Crawford's "Ten-Four" on the hit TV show: *Highway Patrol*.

Montego abruptly stopped running, a longtime eddying worry had settled into place. *Tanto—so simple.*

Aurek had run past, but circled back. "Tonto quitting on me?"

"Yep, caught a side-ache. Gonna walk for a bit. Go catch Wheels. He urged Aurek with a light push to the shoulder.

Aurek, shrugging, sped off skirting an incoming sweep of sea foam.

The ill thought Montego had harbored for too long had begun to take shape. He could no longer deny it. An urgency compelled him to move. He kicked up the swash around his ankles and legged it back home, his toes splaying over the depressions of burrowing sand crabs until he hit the dry sand. He had to get to the station, see Strait, find out what was new with the Armanno case. But first, he had to unload his concerns with another cop, his emotions demanded it. And it couldn't be a cop involved with the homicide.

On the Perch's small balcony, telephone in hand, he watched a young girl being pulled along The Strand by two Boston terriers straining against their leashes until a woman's voice sounded on the line.

"Eagon Quinn, please—this is Mike."

Margie said pleasantly, "Hi Mike—Eagon's in Superior Court this morning."

She's probably gorgeous. Leave it to Eagon.

Not reaching his mentor stymied Montego. Who could he talk to that would understand? He trusted KW, but chose not to involve him. Glancing down at the dumbbells by the makiwara posts on the deck he knew whom to call.

He dialed. After several rings Smith answered.

"Smitty, I'd like to see you as soon as possible."

"Give me thirty to drive to our breakfast club."

Apparently, Smith wasn't able to converse freely.

About a half-hour later, as Montego downed the last of his coffee, Smith materialized at the entrance inside the Normandie Club's cafe. His black T-shirt, like a second skin, accentuated his imposing shape. He drew the attention of other patrons.

Spotting his meet, he strode over. The bottom-heavy waitress who had served them on Sunday, menus in hand, followed on his heels.

"The Gambler's Special." Smith told her, sliding onto the red vinyl seat across from Montego. "You eating, Mike?"

"Just coffee." Faking a smile at the dour-faced waitress, Montego said, "I'll take the check, please." She didn't acknowledge him.

Smith waited while Montego gathered his thoughts. Meanwhile, Pear-bottom returned and filled Smith's cup, giving Montego the dregs.

Must be my rotten view of things.

"You buying some info for a fast brunch or is Thursday eve a no-go?" Smith, grinning, raised the steaming cup to his lips and blew into the rising vapors.

"Opposite's more like it—and Thursday's cool." Montego rubbed a thumbnail, cops did not gripe about partners to other cops. But Smith, although a cop, had no cop companions except for him. The true "'sition" of "Officer" Jordan AKA Russell Smith was an unknown among police officers, except to a handful, and the guy had yet to work with a partner. That's why Montego had taken the gamble to spill his guts.

"Gotta tale for your ears only—the consequences could be severe—not for you, but for me . . . and several other people." He got Smith's nod before starting the story.

Montego told about Neall Haley's changing moods, and about his girlfriend's brutal assault, and about the Riffelano and Blagden shootings. He didn't reveal his dark thought about the Armanno homicide. He finished with Blagden's death just as the dumpy waitress brought Smith's meal and sloshed more coffee into their cups.

Smith waited for her to leave. "Tie another tag to that knotty string. Hamilton told me that clown, Mario Zippi, cashed in this morn—poisoned."

Montego nearly sucked hot coffee down his windpipe. He tabled the cup and sat back, a pale expressionless face in his mind's eye. Haley's hard words to the capo echoed: "Zippi belongs to us now," followed by the underboss absolving himself of "that crumb."

Gazing around the busy room, Montego knew it was time to say the words he'd been refusing to voice out loud. He leaned forward, elbows on the table, and spoke barely over a whisper, "Smitty, I think Neall might be involved with the local mob."

A wordless moment passed, their eyes locked. Finally, Smith said, "What makes you think that?"

The coffee on Montego's palate had soured. He explained seeing Haley with Brunetti, and his behavior when spotted, ending with, "I don't want to believe he's mobbed-up, but it's possible he's gotten too close—maybe to take some of them out. He wanted to kill Brunetti the night we busted the goon, which baffles me since I've seen them together." Montego glanced about. "Then Riffelano went down by our hands, a close call; next, Neall shot Blagden—OK, he wasn't a mob goon, but the shooting stunk. Now Haley's talking about taking out Brunetti and his cousin, Simeti."

"Brazenly shooting gonzos and calling it justice isn't what our job's about." Smith's eyes hardened. "You really think Haley's crossed over?"

"Let's say he hasn't—but for the life of me, I can't get a handle on why he's talking to the goon."

"I heard they do find weaknesses in the people they want to use or to manipulate." Smith drank his coffee. "Preston's proclivity for illicit sex is one example. Maybe they found your partner's."

"Smitty, let's say Haley's being pressured by Brunetti—but for what reason, I can't figure," Montego said.

Smith sat back and rested his arms over the top of the booth-seat.

"I guess there could be circumstances where committing a criminal act might seem like the only way out."

Montego shoved his cup away, the sour caffeinated taste burned his stomach. He remembered how close he had come to crossing over with Mario Zippi.

"Under enough pressure anybody could fold, I suppose."

The dour waitress came back and left the bill near Smith's saucer.

Montego, swallowing water, slid the tab to his side.

Smith sat forward, arms on the table. "I've been tested a few times, but I always think of Dad when life gets too tough."

"I know," Montego said. The undercover cop had told him years earlier how he gave credit to his father for surviving the raw streets of south central L.A. The senior Smith had passed away of heart failure while his son was overseas serving Uncle Sam.

Montego pictured Lonn Haley, a decent man, a loving patriarch. The family obviously cared for one another. Haley's display of tenderness with his younger sister had touched Montego. How would Ice Cop react if told that his partner had developed a warm feeling for him, not just his family? Was it too late to tell him? And how would the father respond to learning that his oldest boy was involved with the Italian Mafia—?

An ugly thought jolted Montego: *If Lonn is Angelo Pinky Sancia, likely Brunetti has found him, and learned his son is a cop . . . and Neall, aware of the Brunetti's claim and the vendetta, could've been telling the big goon to back off when I spotted them. No—no way. I can't buy Lonn being The Purple Hand. Still, something is going on between Neall and Brunetti, and it very well might have something to do with Sancia. Whatever it is, it could be the reason Neall seems so stressed out.*

"I can't say that Neall has done anything criminal—but here's what bothers me, Smitty. He was going to confront Preston when he came off the eighteenth green—it was last Saturday, the day the councilman was killed."

Smith put down his cup and fingered the handle back and forth, gazing at Montego, a question in his steady brown eyes.

"I know, mi amigo. I've got to confront the guy with my concerns." Montego's gut rebelled like a cornered cougar to his own words.

Smith began running a finger around a glass pepper shaker.

Montego's thumb was itching from all the rubbing.

He visualized Lonn, Irene, and the insouciant Missy at her party. *What would such bad news do to them?*

". . . Don't be forgetting this coming Thursday eve, Tonto."

Montego hadn't been listening, but he heard enough to get the gist.

"I might show up with Neall." He covered the tab and checked his pocket watch. "Say, has Captain Hamilton told you about Beak Brunetti's lifelong vendetta?"

"No," Smith said, edging the pepper shaker next to the salt shaker. "Whose the gonzo's feud with?"

"Some old time Mafiosi called Angelo Pinky Sancia. The hit man killed Brunetti's father back in the 'thirties."

"That's a long time to hold a grudge." Smith toyed with the shakers while giving Montego a curious look. "Is this Sancia gonzo in LA?"

"Apparently. If he is, Hamilton might know where . . . and maybe what he's calling himself these days." It seemed plausible to Montego that the head of Intelligence would know, if anyone on the Department knew.

"Gotta hit the road, mi amigo." He stood. Smith rose with him.

They strode outside and parted for their respective vehicles.

Montego sitting in the idling Cameo Carrier, turned up the radio volume to match his loud brainwaves while he tried to think things through.

After a long moment, he decided that swimming 75 lengths in the Buckingham pool would loosen the knots between his shoulder blades and maybe clear his head. But first, he needed to hear his mentor's thoughts.

Montego returned to the coffee shop and went to a public phone.

"Officer Montego—I'm glad you called. Counselor Quinn phoned moments ago. He said if you should call back, to let you know that he would be taking his lunch at The Pantry should you wish to join him."

"Thanks, Margie."

Chapter 58

Montego strode into the popular café at Ninth and South Figueroa Streets, spotted a gray fedora, and headed for it.

Quinn saw him approaching. "I ordered mine already, Mikey."

"That's fine. The huge platters here hold way too much food for my trim bod." Montego's smile felt more like a grimace.

Just then, Quinn's lunch arrived. When the waiter left, Quinn said, "What's on your mind, son?"

"My partner, Neall Haley, was going to show Eugene Preston the sex photos at the Wilshire Country Club when he came off the eighteenth green. I don't know if Neall did, but it was last Saturday, close to the time the hit went down, and it wasn't that far from the golf course."

Quinn seemed to be concentrating on eating his food, but Montego could tell he was listening closely. Montego reiterated everything he'd told Smith earlier except divulging his suspicion that Haley's father might be Angelo Sancia.

Montego's mentor put down his flatware and studied him awhile.

"Before you were born, Mikey, I was a naïve rookie walking a foot-beat on East Fifth Street. Saw things I'll never forget." Quinn tasted his coffee, then continued with unexpected words that Montego realized his mentor had silently carried for years: "In the 'thirties and early 'forties, Frank Shaw, the mayor, along with our chief, James Davis, watched graft and corruption going rife within City Hall. Sadly, many cops had their greedy hands out—crime was rampant."

"Had to be tough." Montego thought back to when he was a toddler and had crawled the green carpet in his mother's eleventh floor office suite.

"There were times." Quinn drank some water. "I stayed clear of the bad stuff, although I did accept gratuities—cigars and such. I think getting the *Habanos* cigars for free is what got me to smoking the damn things. Anyway, the war came along and I was pulled from the beat and transferred to Homicide. That's when I met Roy. He'd been working the Main Jail."

Quinn paused. "Apparently we were considered too valuable to fight for Uncle Sam. We would much rather've been sailors, but we soon learned there was plenty of important work to be done on the home shores. 'War emergencies' we were called."

280

The Purple Hand

He studied the ceiling as if in reflection, then took a bite of beef. "That's when an old timer told me, 'Eagon, lad, you've gotta put yourself into the dead vic's shoes because you're the only person who's gonna catch their killer. Only you, young man, only you can do it,' he'd said. So, Mikey, I became a hard-charging gumshoe—until the war ended in 'forty-five . . . when my gung ho feeling ebbed."

He sat back. "In the late 'forties, there was a string of murders and female bodies being dumped around town. The victims were dark-haired, terribly violated, bludgeoned to death, and cut up." Eagon tugged a white handkerchief free, shook it loose and dabbed his nose.

Montego believed the gesture hid an immense bit of emotion.

Quinn refolded and pocketed the handkerchief.

"Boss detective, Thad Brown, put his brother, Finis, on as the lead detective on the gawd-awful slaying of Elizabeth Short—the Black Dahlia, the more notorious murder." Eagon pulled out a tube-contained cigar.

Montego would never forget the Saturday thirteen years ago when he'd overheard Quinn and Joe Whitehead talking about the heinous crime.

Quinn uncapped the long tube, tipped it and let the El Presidente slip into his hand.

"Harry Hansen was Finis' partner, but it was Thad who was solely responsible for what went into the murder casebook. It was Hansen's case now, but it was a futile hunt."

"I remember you mentioning a disappointment when you turned in your badge?"

Quinn eyed Montego. "Less than four weeks after the Beth Short killing another nude female was found on Grandview in West LA. Huddleston caught that case—the Jeanne French murder. Hud was the old timer who got me charged up when I was a junior dick. Anyway, by 'forty-nine, women city-wide were on the verge of real panic, convinced that a sex maniac was running loose. I had to agree—but I didn't buy into the idea of a dozen sadistic madmen raping and beating one woman to death and then dumping her severed remains in a public place . . . like some did."

Lifting his fedora slightly, Quinn scratched his widow's peak.

"So, on the QT, I voiced my opinion to my skipper, Jack Donahoe. He revealed nothing, yet I felt he agreed. Then, trying to develop leads, he went to the press and connected the Dahlia kill to the Jeanne French homicide. Well, that got Jack transferred to Robbery where he works today. That told me: keep my mouth shut."

Eagon settled his hat. "Suffice it to say, out of the 'forties came the birth of Internal Affairs, along with the promotion of 'Whiskey' Bill Parker to deputy chief in charge—yes, he had a bad drinking problem back then."

Montego nodded, he had heard that from others.

"In 'fifty, Bill made super chief, and instituted the 'new breed' of LA cop." Quinn chuckled. "Had the lady commissioner favoring Thad not died before the final vote, he would've been Chief of Police. The troops supported Brown—he'd always backed them." He paused while the waiter cleared their table.

"Norman Chandler, owner of the *Times*, wanted Thad Brown, too— called him 'the master detective.'" Quinn put a flame to the long cigar.

"The point of my somewhat lengthy diatribe is that our lives are full of choices. Thad made his, and I made mine—we both have had to live with them." He blew a smoke ring overhead out of Montego's reach.

"Perhaps, one day the cold cases will be solved, but for now, what I've told you is strictly confidential. Sit on it, Mikey, like I've had to do . . . or you can forget ever working Homicide—especially downtown."

His eyes bored into Montego's.

"We must do the best we can with what we know at the time. You'll do the same with your partner . . . I know."

Montego realized that Quinn wasn't going to respond to what he'd been told about Haley, but he definitely understood the lesson just taught. He must reconcile his concern about his blond partner judiciously.

If the result isn't favorable . . . what should I do?

282

Chapter 59

Montego stroked the 75 laps at a leisurely pace while filled with racing thoughts and gnarly questions: Joey Armanno a hit man? *Yes.* Lonn Haley an ex-hit man? *Maybe.* Neall Haley a hit man? *Also maybe.* Could Lissa know the truth? *Another maybe.*

After showering off the residual chlorine, he dug out the phone number Lissa had given to him at the drive-in. He hoped it was still active. He'd asked for it saying he might need to reach Haley one day through her; he didn't wish to rethink his reason. Guilt hung like a dark misty cloud over Montego's heart as he spun the dial.

Now that she was home, he would make the apology for putting her in jeopardy, but not over the telephone. He couldn't dismiss the fear that he'd screwed up badly by asking about the new goon seated with Brunetti the night before she was attacked. Montego needed to see her.

He was elated when she picked up the line.

"Lissa, it's Mike—can I drop by for a few minutes?" He heard recorded jazz playing faintly in the background.

"Yes, come on over, pal. Neall's here—we're listening to music."

He would be uncomfortable with Haley present and was about to beg off, when she said, "I've got beer and beef-on-rye sandwiches made."

Realizing that Haley would know he had called, Montego gave in.

"OK—on my way." *What will he think? Did it matter? Besides, he* wanted to draw the guy out. It was time to rattle his partner's cage.

See what happens.

He drove to West Hollywood unclear how and what to say, exactly.

Lissa, wearing a flowery sarong, gave him a warm hug. It helped to ease his pain. She was thinner, but her face had lost most of its hospital pallor. She moved fairly sprightly showing him out to the small balcony where Haley sat on a two-person swing-chair.

Haley grunted "Hello," while watching several tenants cavorting in the large rectangular pool in the courtyard below.

Montego eased onto a canvas lounge chair. Lissa was right there with a cold Bud for him and sandwiches for the both of them.

She sat beside Haley.

Montego spoke about her new abode and how well she looked. He gunned back his beer hesitant to make his apology, and hoping that bringing up a bad night wouldn't be upsetting to her. But that was why he was there.

"Lissa, I came by to apologize for asking you about Armanno when you were working—I'm truly sorry." His guilty heart banged against his breastbone.

Haley casually draped an arm over her bare shoulder, while eyeing Montego.

"Armanno had nothing to do with it—you damn well dumped the lousy meathead who was responsible."

Lissa squeezed his hand. "Neall's right, Mike—but thank you for your thoughtful concern. . . . I knew the risk." She kissed Neall's cheek, leaving a blush-tint from her lips. "Thank God, Julie wasn't hurt. Neall told me what happened. I'm so thankful that you're safe, too."

Montego smiled, going no further with an apology, relieved that it was finally done.

"Please, let me know if I can help you with anything."

Haley drew her closer. "You've already helped plenty." His gaze now held hers. "Don't worry, hon. That sick meathead won't ever see you again—I promise."

Rattle time.

Montego scrutinized Haley's face: no expression. "You're right, Neall. Mario Zippi was poisoned early this morning. He's dead."

Lissa's fingers jumped from Haley's hand to her throat, her focus shot to Montego. Nodding, he looked back at Haley: only hardened eyes and a furrowed brow. Montego surmised that Haley felt foiled.

Appropriate.

A silent moment passed. Haley knocked out a fresh Camel and put his Ronson lighter's flame to it.

"Good," he finally said, smoke flowing from his mouth toward the railing. He leaned and kissed Lissa on the cheek. Her hand slipped from her neck down to his arm. In a low voice he added, "Forgot to tell you, hon, Tonto is on top of most happenings in the LAPD."

"Tonto?"

Montego smiled. "That's what some people call me." Strangely, he felt a prickle raising the short hairs on the back of his neck.

"By the way, Trev wanted off tonight—I traded for Thursday." Haley glanced down at the pool. "I'm working. You can drive if you want."

Montego, taken aback, saw Haley's slight smirk. Quickly finishing his beer, Montego said, "Time to head out, guys." He got to his feet. "I want to see what Strait's learned about the Joey Armanno homicide."

Lissa's eyes showed surprise. Haley's face paled impossibly more.

"Later, I'll be telling a pair of goons that speeding through dark crosswalks is a dangerous game—hope you're up for it," Montego said.

He left, wondering if Haley's facial reaction was to the comment about facing the goons, or to the mention of Joey Armanno. Whatever. Tonight, Montego would be confronting Brunetti about the little car stunt—hopefully Nino Simeti would be with him. With Haley present, maybe it would clarify things—remove the awful suspicion that nagged.

Going by the front desk, Rosy called, "Tonto—hold your horses." He snatched a pink slip off a clipboard. "Gotta message for you."

Montego pulled out his Bulova: 4:55 PM. He didn't want to miss Strait. He accepted the note.

"Do you know if Uncle Alex is in?"

"Haven't seen him leave." Rosy stuffed a cigar into his mouth.

"Speaking of seen, I haven't *seen* your hiney around our pads since the sicko hit. How're Sonia and your two rambunctious teenagers doing?"

"You're the one who's never around—oops, shouldn't say that, you do tend to get your scanty rent in on time, usually. Hey, I'm kidding." Rosy bounced the stubby Roi-Tan cigar with his teeth. "We're fine. I'm putting some hours in at the family liquor store. Papa's damn anxious to sell out. The south end of town ain't the same anymore." He pinched out the cigar. "The kids miss you, especially Davy. He wants to learn how to do your snazzy kick-pow tough-stuff."

"Been riding a merry-go-round, Rosy. Tell your kids I miss seeing them, too—have Davy come up to the deck-dojo around ten any Saturday."

Noting the phone message was a pre-lunch return call from Quinn, Montego tossed it. He paced to the stairs and bounded up.

Strait spied him. "What brings the hopeful TMA in so early?"

"Looking for an update on the Armanno homicide—and the story on Mario Zippi." Not feeling close to being the toughest man alive, Montego wondered if his pal would hold anything back.

"Who told you . . .?" Strait half-smirked. "Thought Quinn was retired. Well, I did happen to call Wayne. Our lab found a light-blond hair on the rear floorboard of Armanno's rental."

Montego dropped hard onto Wayne Nell's yet-to-be-filled chair—the merry-go-round whirled faster. After a moment to regain his composure, he said, "Congrats TMA on making senior homicide dick. You'll be filling the next open slot downtown, for sure."

"Perhaps, one day." Strait brushed eraser debris from his trousers. "I must tell you that the Zippi case is a zippo. You probably already know that his baculiformed body was found by the nurse on his four AM rounds."

"Yep." Montego tilted on the chair. "OK, explain the fancy word."

"What, a new adjective for Tonto? Well Mister Hopeful, Zippi was stiff as a rod when found." Strait's delighted expression turned smug.

"The corpse reeked of wine, later confirmed. His stomach contents included the red grape. Mister Zippi expired from merc poisoning. For your information, serving up a Mercury Cocktail is an old mob-style killing method. Apparently the mob underboss, Pio, wasn't happy with him."

Montego's stomach suddenly felt like a slimy bag full of leaping frogs. He hoped that Strait was correct about Dante Pio. The "crumb" *had been* a pest.

The desk dick called out, "Strait, line two."

Strait snatched the black receiver.

Montego willed himself to a calm, again, and waited, listening to Strait's side of the conversation.

"Thanks, Ray." Strait hung up and caressed his mustache.

"Ray Pinker from the crime lab?" Montego asked.

"It seems like Mister TMA Hopeful has gone and bagged himself a high-profile Mafioso hit man."

"No way?" Montego had called Pinker earlier, but the criminologist had yet to complete the ballistics comparisons. "The sicko guy was only supposed to be a wannabe mobster."

"That well may be, but a slug from his pistol matched the one dug out of your fancy truck's pretty pleated seat. They also matched the bullets cut from Mister Eugene Preston's corpse."

Montego stopped tilting, and hard-dropped the wood chair forward. The prior spinning thoughts abruptly shifted to doubts. Should he have said anything to Smith or to Quinn about his awful suspicion about Haley? The light-blond hair found in Joey Armanno's rental car, however, overrode any doubts.

"It's probably why Mister Zippi was given the cocktail. Mister Pio apparently didn't appreciate the prick's showboating," Strait said.

Montego nodded. Shooting his pickup was a bit of grandstanding.

Strait tore off the last sheet from a yellow legal tablet.

"Don't let it go to your head, Mike. Wayne told me Downtown wants you gents to back off of DeSimone's mob. Obviously, you've been ignoring their wishes. Wayne also apprised me an Intelligence team saw you and Ice Cop at The Palms last night."

Montego tilted the wooden chair back again, nodding. He'd spied the eye-boys while approaching Dante Pio, but too late to stop Haley.

"Mike, Parker formed Intelligence Division to watch the gangsters come and go at the airport and to baby-sit them when they go wining and dining. He wants Hamilton's boys trailing their puny pecker tracks. Think about that if you ever hope to work on this floor—not to mention sitting your behind on that chair you're trying to break."

It was the first time that Strait had even hinted that he had a chance for a spot in Hollywood detectives, much less a seat at the homicide table. He touched the spotless green blotter in front of him with a fanciful thought, but the notion was short-lived knowing he would soon be facing down Brunetti and his cousin. The goons had made it personal.

"By the bye, hotshot—Roy O'Brody pulled the pin today." Strait eyed Montego and half-smirked. "Next transfer does have my name on it."

The frogs were leaping again. "That's great—you and Wayne back as partners. Guess you're gonna be a *pro* now?" Montego forced a slight chuckle and eased forward on the chair. He would never work with Strait.

Strait, still steadily eyeing him, removed a yellow sheet of paper from his desk drawer. "No warrants tonight, but here's a list of suspects wanted for questioning—that's if you should see them during your non–Mafia patrolling."

Montego offered a poker player's face while he scanned the names and descriptions. Obviously, word had spread that he and Neall Haley were messing with the local mob.

If the troops only knew.

Chapter 60

Neall Haley, unbuttoning his brown sports coat, followed Montego into the Villa Capri. Montego's damn idea. The low-lit restaurant had a moderate dinner business. They stepped around tables heading to where Brunetti sat drinking with another lousy meathead who only could be described as ugly. Haley wasn't about to forget that face—it had to be Nino Simeti.

But for the moment, Haley worried about what Brunetti might say.

Brunetti saw them and scowled. He leaned to the man next to him. "Don't say nothing, Nino. I'll do the talking to these fuckin' bulls."

Haley's gut tightened. He'd read Brunetti's lips. *It is his cousin!*

Brunetti seized a half-burned cigar from an ashtray and shoved the soggy end into his mouth.

Haley wished it had been a pistol so he could dump them both. He glared at Nino Simeti's vacuous face and imagined choking his scrawny turkey-neck, feeling the crunch of the meathead's protruding Adam's apple.

Montego stopped beside their table, his foot set back, balanced, and ready. Haley stayed to his rear side, listening. The urge to piss hit him.

"That cute act last night didn't amuse me Beak. Either one of you guys feel the need to try me, do it man-to-man. *Comprende*, amigos?"

"What—Blue Eyes don't like us having some fun?" Brunetti's twisted mouth waggled the stogie. He side-glanced at his sniggering cousin.

Haley's intestines made every step in the Veloz and Yolanda dance folio while under crossed arms, his right hand rested on the nickel-plated S&W's rubber butt. He liked the angle he had on the goggling Simeti.

"We played your game once, Beak," Montego said. "We play it again you best consider the final score."

Brunetti clamped down on the short cigar, a line of brown juice seeped from the corner of his mouth. Obvious malefic hatred emanated from his glowering eyes, mixed with another look that Haley couldn't define. He realized at that moment, he no longer existed to Leo Brunetti.

Montego snap-pointed his trigger finger at Simeti. "And you— you're a crazy bastard *primo carnal*, my friend."

The sudden movement nearly had Haley pulling out his piece.

Haley was let down that they'd remained still for Montego's bold stand. Actually, Brunetti had his skinny cousin's arm clamped to the table.

Too damn bad.

Montego hard-eyed Simeti and spun toward the front entry.

Haley followed, still clenching his magnum's butt.

Simeti yelled, *"Va fa in culo,* fuck youse assholes."

Glancing back, Haley was ready to blow both meatheads away, but Brunetti hadn't moved and Simeti's arm was still pinned to the table-top.

Upon reaching the street, Haley took in a ragged breath, coming down from an emotional mixture. He'd feared what the cousins might say, then was frustrated because they had done nothing physically threatening, thwarting his chance to plug them on the spot. He no longer had to piss.

Turning from Montego to hide his quavering hand, he lit a Camel.

In the prowler, feeling calmer, he cranked down his side window.

"Dealer told me Tonto was ballsy."

"No more than Ice Cop. I got the idea seeing how well Pio accepted your Sunday *sermon.*"

Montego had picked up on the subtle message to the capo. Haley, blowing smoke out the window, snatched the hand-mic and asked Momma Mary if their unit had received any calls? He used the time to gather his thoughts. His protective wall was cracking.

"No calls, Frank-One, I show you clear," the RTO radioed back.

After a moment, Haley said, "Pio's too busy running his rackets to control the meathead cousins. Brunetti's gotta be running his own show." He took that as a bonus from this meet. Brunetti's threat was personal. "Don't be surprised if the lousy meatheads pop up unexpectedly and want to play street rough."

"I'm counting on it." Montego drove west on Yucca.

Haley's trigger finger itched. He hoped his partner was correct.

Brunetti's hand stayed on Simeti's bony forearm while he watched the bulls leaving. The blue-eyed fuck's way of looking had sent electric shock waves into Brunetti. He couldn't let Simeti see how Montego had unnerved him.

"Nino, Nino, cool your damn ass—we can take care of 'em later. This ain't the fuckin' time or the place." He swallowed hard, tasting sour tobacco juice. He hated not having the damn edge.

"Cocksuckers. Talkin' that tough shit." Simeti tried to yank away.

"Like I said, Nino, we'll get even later."

Good—he's pissed at the fuckin' bulls.

"Fuck later, Leo. I wants 'em now."

289

Nino really is crazy.

It explained the Section 8 dishonorable discharge from the Army during Simeti's first week in boot camp. Brunetti had missed the draft and still felt lucky. The war had ended before he'd turned eighteen.

Brunetti kept a hold of Simeti until certain he would remain seated. The tremors waving down from his narrow shoulders helped camouflage Brunetti's own shakes.

"Hey, Nino, you was the one who told me it wasn't smart to take out the bull's kid sister—now you wanna take out two bulls—that's worse."

"Worse, smurse. They fuckin' threatened our asses."

"So we figger out a way to do 'em in *silencio* . . . but no talking to no body about what we're gonna do. *Omèrta.*"

"Omèrta's a lotta shit, Leo. Th' damn bosses thinks nothin'—*pentito*—a rattin' to th' bulls to gets ridda competition. We *soldatis* are stupid if we thinks we're protected—we's jus' bones thrown to th' bulls to keeps 'em off th' bosses' asses. Omèrta be damned. 'Sides, I knows how to keeps my trap shut."

"Tell me, Nino. What'll make you feel better?"

This was damn good.

Montego had confronted Brunetti to see what, if anything, would happen between the huge goon and Haley, but The Beak had controlled himself, and Ice Cop had played it cool, too, standing off to the side where he couldn't be observed.

Not knowing what the heck was going on between the two couldn't continue. Time to deal with the issue—toss the dice—win or lose. A wiggly tickle teased the back of Montego's neck as he steered the prowler east, away from the diminishing sunlight.

"Neall, what the heck is going on between you and Beak Brunetti?"

He side-eyed Haley who stared ahead; his face looked glacial. There was no melting in his frosty reply, either.

"Let's take Seven at Musso's."

Haley took a last drag then shot his cigarette butt out the window with one hand while yanking the microphone off the dash clip with the other. He put their unit out at Cherokee and Hollywood near the restaurant, neither giving the address nor requesting Code 7.

Montego massaged the steering wheel.

A public place—why not?

Chapter 61

In Musso and Frank's, Montego would be able to study Haley's face and icy gray eyes, watch for any telltale sign. But would he spot it?

On Cherokee just north of The Boulevard, he worked the sedan into a tight space at the curb, thinking just lay it out straight. Hit Ice Cop point blank with his suspicions. He no longer saw the need to tread cautiously. His FCU assignment didn't seem that important since Alex Strait was transferring downtown. Overriding everything now was whether Haley had crossed to the other side, or not.

Montego slowed his breathing, measuring his thoughts. Pocketing his clip-on tie, and loosening his collar, he followed his partner to the corner and across Cherokee to the restaurant where local politicians had been drinking their lunches for nearly forty years. A red-jacketed waiter took them to a booth and handed out menus. The old guy could have started working in the historic place the day it was established.

George Putnam, the popular Channel 5 newscaster, sat with several men at the sought-after round booth. What the *KTLA* Anchor wouldn't give to eavesdrop on their conversation, assuming Haley was going to talk.

Montego imagined Putnam's opening line: "Hollywood cop—Mafia hit man."

Haley lit up a Camel, then stared blankly toward the front entry.

When the wordless period became uncomfortable, Montego said, "Neall answer me. What's going on between you and Beak Brunetti?"

While waiting for a reply Montego steeled himself. Meanwhile, their tossed salads were served.

Haley continued to stare blankly, silently lighting a fresh cigarette from the one he'd been puffing on.

Montego rubbed a thumbnail. "When we first partnered I accepted your quiet way and the wall you'd built around you." A lump formed in his throat. "I can see why you got the Ice Cop tag. But since meeting your family, I've been able to see over your wall . . . you're not the same guy—your moods are all over the place now." He paused, waiting for their prime rib cuts to be set before them.

Haley crushed the barely smoked Camel in the ashtray and grasped a serrated knife and a fork. He soaked a slice of beef in the dark au jus.

Montego ran fingers along the table rim, feeling the scarred edge. "Lissa's seen it, too."

He studied his partner's white granite-like face while he munched. The expression matched Haley's pale visage on their first night as a team when he'd said, "Numero Dos is about to lose one of his main men."

Haley shoved the juice-dripping meat into his mouth and chewed, still appearing unfocused.

Picking up a knife, Montego sliced off a piece of prime rib.

"You've either been careless or you've been operating by design from our first night together. Something is going on between you and Brunetti—and probably Simeti. I don't think Pio is involved—at least not directly. Beak's surly words: 'Don't you like us having some fun?' reeked of personal vengeance, Neall."

Pausing and glancing over Haley's shoulder at the newscaster talking animatedly, Montego sipped some water, then, putting it down, he said, "You intended to shoot Brunetti at the motel, but he surprised you— the same at the Knick. You purposely startled Riffelano to get him to draw. Why? Both times we could've been shot—maybe killed."

Haley, wincing slightly, laid his knife and fork on the plate with trembling hands, his face taking on a bit of color, his light eyes stared at the water glass.

Still, he spoke no words.

"Beak Brunetti is up to no good—and you're involved, somehow. The stress shows all over you." Montego leaned forward.

Haley's jaw muscles rippled, and he wasn't chewing.

"Time to let it out—I need to hear the truth. What is going on?"

Haley still focused on the water glass. He made no answer.

"When Lissa suggested that Roger was Dante Pio's new player, I figured another mob-goon import. This morning it suddenly gelled. It's our radio lingo. We use 'Roger' for message confirmation, and I think the mob goons were using it to mean 'cop.'" Montego glanced at his roast beef then up at Haley: a study of blank text.

Haley wordlessly lifted a shaky water glass.

"The newbie is you, Neall—not that goon Nino Rogelio Simeti. He's been in LA too long."

The water still vibrated in the glass Haley held.

Montego sat back, unable to eat, the lump in his chest had risen to his throat. He flexed his legs and sighed, waiting, still no words came forth.

"Preston getting hit zonked me—the thought that you might've done it—I was sick." Montego realized he was rubbing a thumbnail, again.

"Nothing about the sex photos was in the newspapers. I figured if you'd actually made the hit—God forbid—that you'd kept them knowing I would make a connection. I didn't find out until later that Downtown was keeping the photographs hush-hush."

He gulped some water. Another silent minute or so passed.

"I wanted to trust you—but I worried that you might've tied in with the mob, become a hit man. The ugly thought gut-wrenched me too."

Haley set the glass down with both hands, his left going to his lap.

Montego, alert, placed his water glass on the table.

"When Strait told me the slugs cut out of Preston came from Zippi's Beretta, it was a darn big relief." He tried another bite of beef. It had cooled. Swiping the napkin over his mouth, he chewed.

Haley, still wordless, now stared at his coffee cup.

Montego laid the napkin on his lap. "Zippi was the wild card. Pio told us the 'crumb thought he was making his bones'—I guess the fat guy wanted to impress the capo." Montego waited as two couples passed by. It gave him a moment to sort out his many thoughts.

"Zippi's brutal acts put heat on Pio. Explains why the wannabe was poisoned." Montego moved his unfinished meal aside. "Armanno's murder, being a mob hit doesn't wash. Killed with his own gun—uh uh." He paused, allowing the bent-backed waiter to remove their nearly full plates.

"Another thing, Strait found a light-blond hair in Armanno's car."

Haley's eyelids fluttered briefly.

Montego caught his breath in a sudden realization. "The Catholic school's proximity was no coincidence—but Armanno at Missy's school?"

He saw a fiery intensity rise in Haley's eyes.

"You knew! Somehow you got wind of the hit and stopped the bastard. Incredible."

How horrible it must've been for him, the older brother. . . . And he would've used Armanno's pistol knowing, should he ever be suspected, that his service revolver would be tested for a ballistics match.

"Thank God Missy is safe."

Joey Armanno hitting Missy—Dante Pio would never have ordered that. It had to have been a personal contract hit. But how did Beak Brunetti play into it? Montego groped for an understanding.

"Neall, talk to me—" *or you'll be answering to Downtown.*

293

*   *   *

Haley lipped a fresh Camel, needing both hands to steady his Ronson. Lighting the cigarette, he sucked, then whooshed the smoke through tight lips toward the aisle. He couldn't look at Montego, his damn piercing stare was too daunting.

What to say? Haley's protective wall had completely crumbled. He must not go down before acing the meathead cousins. He had to save Pop.

Can I make Mike understand my side? Buy me enough time?

He mashed the empty Camel pack and dropped it onto the table, but held onto the silver lighter to have something to occupy his hands.

"You're right, Mike. Brunetti has me under his gun. I did want to take him out—still do. Riffelano was a screw up—I suppose I drew him out to make an impression—have had to live with my gunplay, too. I'd hoped Brunetti would back off. I was a fool. The Blagden and Zippi snuffs weren't my doing—I did want to waste Zippi, even after you thumped his sick ass."

Haley took a deep drag, sweat dripped. The smoky haze helped to hide his face. "When Brunetti beat the Chicago rap and came back to LA, he started his damn 'fun 'n' games' with me. The lousy meathead told me to take out Rat Rondell, and later, Preston—"

"He wanted you to be a hit man? How was he pressuring you?"

"You tell me, Tonto."

"It's got to be something to do with an infamous hit man who killed The Beak's father years ago—the so-called Purple Hand. That hit started a darn blood feud—the vendetta I told you about."

"Yeah, against Pinky Sancia AKA Ari Sands, a phony Jew."

"So, you did know! I've got an old article with a photo—"

"Got one here," Haley sniped, opening his billfold to finger out a yellowed newspaper clipping. He pointed at the faded half-tone picture. "The Beak laid it on me. He thinks—he believes that my pop is Sancia."

"So it *was* your pop?"

"No! It's some *other* meathead—my pop is *not* Angelo Sancia."

Mike—don't buy Brunetti's crap. Pop's my only hero. He needs you if I don't survive this damn mess.

Haley, the Camel now hot on his lips, was afraid he was correctly reading Montego's disturbed expression.

Mike's conflicted, but he still gonna bust me for the Armanno hit!

294

The Purple Hand

Montego glanced at the dull and faded news photo, then at his partner. His contorted expression wrenching. *What terrible anguish Neall must feel.*

"He does look like your dad might've years ago, I suppose. Both men have similar features . . . and they are missing their left pinkies." Montego paused, the stabbing beat of his heart painful. "Do you know that your dad is *not* Sancia?" He paused again. "Neall, I can understand if you haven't asked him. It's hard to imagine your dad copping out to you . . . unless you know for sure."

Haley glanced up, and Montego realized he'd just drilled him with a magazine full of machine-gunned bullets straight to the heart, targeting where the distraught cop likely had been afraid to venture since Brunetti's coercion started.

"He does know about this—doesn't he?" Montego asked.

The bent-over waiter stepped up and placed the money tray with the tab on the table between them, then he hobbled off.

Haley seemed to be working at steadying his breathing as he pulled a tattered ten from his billfold.

"He doesn't know about the vendetta . . . his bad heart—I couldn't risk telling him. Like I said, Pop is not a mob hitter—The Purple Hand— that's pure bullcrap. And if Dante Pio knows about The Beak's wild claim, I doubt he cares. Pio's given me no indication that he gives a damn about some old fart ditching an eastern Italian outfit in the 'thirties—but that won't keep Pop alive. The Beak and his damn cousin believe he's Sancia."

Haley's moist eyes bored into Montego, sizzling like red-hot pokers in water. Haley's malevolence appeared feverish. His chest heaved visibly.

"Mike, the meatheads need to be dead!"

The words, like a stiletto, pierced Montego's soul. This was not the end of Ice Cop's intentions. Keeping his eyes on Haley, he freed his wallet and loosed two Abe's. He dropped them on the small tray.

The red-jacketed waiter reappeared, snatched it and scooted away.

"So, the goon cousins hate your butt because in their narrow minds you're Angelo Pinky Sancia's son, a cop no less," Montego said.

"Yeah." Haley gripped the coffee cup and watched the waiter return with the change.

"OK, Neall. Now tell me about Joey Armanno's death."

Chapter 62

Haley, noting Montego's intensity, hoped that he could plead successfully for understanding. He set down the cup with a sigh.

"When Lissa woke, her first words were—I knew Mario Zippi was the one." Haley noticed Montego nodding, agreeing, as if he had known. "Yeah, I wanted to kill him. . . . Something she'd said before the—anyway, she'd overheard the meatheads talking and had said enough for me to realize that my family was in danger."

Haley pushed the coffee cup away.

"Missy was the most vulnerable. Maybe Irish luck got me to her school in time." He quickly crossed himself. "When I got there, Armanno had her in his gun sight—he was about to shoot her." He swiped at his eyes, puke burning his throat. "The meathead was gonna shoot my kid sister."

Haley dared to look up. His blood rushed. What Montego was about to hear would damn well sound like a murder confession.

"Thank God you got there in time." Montego pocketed his wallet. "So, you believe killing Missy is part of The Beak's 'fun 'n' games'?"

Haley, feeling a damn chill, shrugged, then he braced himself.

"Mike, I've screwed up—bad." His blurred eyes stung. "I'm damn sorry, too." He blinked, clearing his vision, and watched as Montego tasted his coffee. Kidnapping Armanno was a felony. Montego would think it was a premeditated hit since the body was found blocks away from the school.

But it had seemed so justified.

Why hasn't Mike asked if I killed Armanno? Maybe he understands. Like me, wouldn't he risk going to prison—even the gas chamber—to save his family?

Montego studied Haley. The guy had admitted to kidnapping Armanno, but he didn't actually confess to doing the hit.

And I haven't asked him directly. Why?

Montego realized that he was not up to pointing an accusing finger. He wanted Neall Haley, his partner, to make it easy and say, "Montego— Bust me—I killed Joey Armanno."

Maybe I should just drive to the station without a word, park in the breezeway outside the jail, and say, "Partner, how do you want to do this?"

The Purple Hand

*   *   *

Haley looked toward the entryway, still hoping beyond hope to reason with Montego—stall him from busting his pale ass.

"Mike, tonight, when you challenged the meatheads, it had to've set them off. Every fiber in me says it won't just be against you, but against the both of us."

He slipped the news clipping back into his billfold resigned to do whatever necessary to find and ace the cousins, even if it was the last thing he ever did, otherwise Pop could be a dead man . . . maybe the family, too.

"And it'll be damn soon."

Uttering a sigh, he slid off the seat, rose and started for the door, convinced of Montego's intention, but resolute, feeling he must act, do something, anything, to get to the lousy cousins.

Aware Montego abruptly was on his tail, Haley swore inwardly.

Damn it—don't spook him. Calm down—gotta look like I'm going along freely—throw Mike off. Then make my damn break.

On the broad sidewalk, Haley sought escape, seeing everything and nothing at the same time, aware that Montego could drop him in a flash should Haley make the wrong move. He studied the traffic to his right. No, he would make his move after they were on Cherokee, fewer cars to dodge through. Montego wouldn't shoot, but he was lightning fast.

I've gotta be faster!

Montego, glad he had unbuttoned his collar, strode alongside Haley, nearest the curb, keeping pace, smelling his sour fear. Montego focused on Haley's hands, they were flexing.

When they crossed Cherokee and turned north toward their unit, Haley went curbside to Montego's left.

It was obvious that Haley wanted to kill Brunetti and Simeti. Their deaths didn't bother Montego as long as they happened in the line of duty—but it meant Haley needed more time.

It meant that Haley might do something drastic.

He's gonna make a break. Don't do it, Neall.

Montego blocked out the street noises making them a white noise.

"The meatheads could be anywhere," Haley grumbled.

297

Sensing Haley's increased tenseness, Montego stayed light on his feet. They strode along the east sidewalk past several oncoming pedestrians.

Suddenly, Montego felt an ominous energy nearby, a vibration, his spine tingled—evil stalked. He sensed it with a visceral certainty.

Glancing around, he tightened his left arm against the cumbersome Python. It hung like a cold black snake against the thin white cloth clinging to his damp skin. He drew in a deep lungful of night air, easing it out trying to slow the thumping inside his chest.

More vibrations—physical this time.

Footfalls—much heavier than falling leaves.

He quickly stepped behind Haley, just as his partner twirled toward the street.

Grabbing Haley's collar and twisting clockwise, throwing Haley to the pavement, Montego spied a skinny body, an arm out, rushing up behind them. Flames flashed, *pfitting* noises sounding through the white noise.

Montego freed his Python as he dropped over Haley's prone body.

The Colt Python spit loudly repeatedly.

Nino Simeti was lurching toward them, shouting, "Va fa in cul—" He fell face-forward onto the concrete—his silenced gun slid into the gutter.

More flashing, more spitting—but from a distant shadowy figure. Piercing blows slammed into Montego.

"Ungh-ungh."

Vision is blurring . . . aim low, squeeze . . . a shadow . . . gone. . . .

From above he saw his body floating in a placid pond. . . .

Neall Haley couldn't break away, he'd struck the pavement too hard and the ear-shattering blasts from Montego's Colt revolver were deafening.

Ears ringing painfully, Haley glimpsed Simeti's head smacking the sidewalk. Haley strove to gain his magnum, but was pinned by Montego.

Then, more flames flashed from farther away, nearer the corner.

Mike Montego's body convulsed and dropped atop Haley.

Finally wresting his S&W loose, Haley spotted the distant shooter under the bright neons. He had him in his line-of-sight, but terrified people scurrying about obscured the moving target.

Beak Brunetti whirled around the corner.

Gone.

Chapter 63

Haley tried to twist free, to give chase, but Montego had his jacket collar in a death grip. Haley spied the spent Colt Python on the sidewalk near an expanding dark pool—blood flowed from his partner's chest. A gurgling breath sounded.

Mike's alive!

"Someone call an ambulance," Haley yelled to no one in particular. "Now, dammit! We're cops—my partner's been shot."

He glanced at Nino Simeti to ensure he wasn't moving as he used pinpoint pressure to Montego's wrist until his hand released its hold.

Getting free, Haley jammed his revolver home and yanked out his handkerchief. He pressed the wad of cloth against the surging liquid.

Too close to his heart.

Montego's body jerked. His eyelids flickered open, his bloody lips parted. Another airy sound spilled forth bringing tiny orange-red bubbles.

Haley put an ear closer and heard a gasping, "They dead?"

"You got them, partner." Haley drew Montego to his chest, hearing, "Protect your dad—good man. . . . Your mom, Missy . . . Lissa, too. . . . Sorry . . . forgive me, Nea. . . ."

"Stay with me, Mike! You can make it—*you've got to.*"

Haley clasped Montego more tightly.

"Tonto!"

Montego's body folded against Haley, crushing his very being.

In just a few explosive seconds a ponderous mental millstone had transformed into an emotional burden too heavy to bear. Haley's leaden heart banged against his soul. Angst filled him with remorse.

He rocked and wept, grieving for a man he hadn't allowed himself to get close to. The cop in his arms had performed the ultimate assignment to protect his partner. When Chief William H. Parker heard his version of events, Officer Michael Dane Montego would receive the highest honor an L.A. cop could achieve: the Medal of Valor.

A screeching. Haley raised his head. Through teary eyes, he spied KW Deal and Bobby Diaz jumping from their prowler.

KW rushed up. "Ambulance is on the way!"

"We were a block away," Bobby D said, excitedly. "Heard shots and people screaming 'call an ambulance—a cop's been shot.' We damn well called. One'll be here ASAP—keep the pressure on his wound, Haley."

KW secured Simeti's wrists behind his back, following policy to handcuff all suspects regardless. None were considered dead until a deputy county coroner made it official.

Haley glanced at Simeti. "He's dead, Dealer."

"Not Tonto?" Bobby D sped over, kneeled and touched Montego's neck. "Uh-uh. Got me a pulse—faint, but it's there."

Haley prayed that he was right.

Bobby D hand-wiped at the blood dribbling from Montego's mouth just as an RA unit skidded to a noisy stop nearby.

Soon, Montego, on a mobile stretcher, was rolled into the rear of the rescue ambulance.

Haley swiped at his moist cheeks with renewed hope. He stared at the tan van pulling away, wishing it God's speed. Emotionally, he rode with his tough, blue-eyed partner. Wildly urgent up-and-down keening, like a wailing lament, tugged at what was left of his grief-stricken heart.

He listened until the shrill siren died in the night air. He prayed fervently that a physician in green scrubs wouldn't be scribbling today's date and time on a document to indicate that his partner was DOA.

"Oh Mike." Haley moaned. He sat sideways on the prowler's seat, his feet flat on the asphalt, agonizing over his guilt.

Brad Kozier came up and gripped Haley's sagging shoulder.

"Just heard a radio dispatch, Mike's hanging on."

An angel's voice sang in the night air.

Haley stood and bear-hugged his boss-friend. Then sobbed.

When Detective-Sergeant Nick Karos asked Haley for a summary, he gave his self-promised statement, avoiding any mention of the true events leading up to the face-to-face with Brunetti and Simeti. Instead, Haley explained that Brunetti must have been pissed about Montego busting his nose weeks earlier during his arrest and apparently was getting even.

Haley completed his story saying, "Mike, spotting the meatheads coming up behind us, knocked me down, covered my ass, took their slugs while putting five into Simeti—his last round was fired at Brunetti."

"You found Simeti's suppressed forty-five there in the gutter." He pointed, then dabbed his coat sleeve to his eyes. "Brunetti had a semiauto—he was in my sights—couldn't shoot—people all over the damn place."

The interview completed, Haley stared at the dark coagulating pool, his partner's blood. Not far away, next to the gutter, lay Simeti, now a lump beneath a thin gray blanket. The corpse would stay there, a grim reminder, until the deputy coroner finished his field investigation.

Haley turned away, his insides a twisted, aching hollow.

Sergeant Kozier still standing by, asked, "You all right, Neall?"

"Not really. . . . Yeah, I'm fine, Brad—thanks to Mike."

Lieutenant John Cowland approached them.

"The coroner found five bullet holes in the corpse, and we found blood drops around the corner. Montego's sixth round must have connected. Brunetti is wounded."

Kozier said, "I'm going with Cowland to make the notification."

"I'd like to go along. . . . Mike saved my life." To his very core, Haley felt a painful guilt for his partner's critical condition.

He shuffled to the lieutenant's black-and-white and dropped onto the back seat. Agony for the unsuspecting parents nearly overwhelmed him.

En route, Brad Kozier turned back to look at Haley.

"Neall, you might want to take off your coat before we get there."

Haley followed the direction of Kozier's focus and saw the blood—too much of it.

Tears fell, mingling with the dark-red stain that fast became a blur.

Chapter 64

Haley slogged into the supervisors' room and dropped onto the swivel chair by the Analytical Officer's desk. An eerie quiet shrouded the station. He picked up the telephone and dialed slowly, rubbing his throbbing head, but unable to ease his heartache.

"Lissa. Sorry if I woke you—we had a shooting."

"Neall!"

"I'm fine—Mike was shot—he's critical." His breath caught upon hearing her groan. His eyes welled, again. "Are you up to meeting me here at the station?" He cleared his throat. "Soon?"

"Oh yes, Neall."

"I'll be in front, hon."

While trying to collect his emotions, KW entered. His eyes were bloodshot, a line grooved between his eyebrows. He put a hand on Haley's shoulder and nudged him gently. "What happened out there?"

Haley told how it had gone down, limiting his remarks to the actual shooting. KW grunted and left the room. Haley went upstairs to the dicks' squad room and after being given Brunetti's arrest photo by the night-duty detective, he went to a nearby desk phone and dialed 9 to get an outside number.

"Pop—it's me—sorry to wake you—there's been a bad shooting—Mike was shot."

"No—how bad?" His pop's raspy voice came across intense.

"Mike's damn critical—Leonardo Brunetti and his lousy cousin, Nino Simeti, attacked us on the street—Simeti's dead, but Brunetti is on the run." Haley eyed the small mug shot of The Beak. His nose was bandaged.

"What hospital?"

"Central Receiving—Sixth and Loma Drive. Lissa and I are driving to Manhattan Beach to get Mike's girlfriend, Julie. We're going to take her to the hospital."

"I'll see you there, son."

"You don't—" Haley caught himself. Pop was that type. "Just keep your eyes out for Brunetti. He'll want to finish what he started—I'll explain later, Pop." He hung up and went outside to wait for Lissa.

When she drove up, he went to her; they embraced, both trembling.

"I'm so sorry, Neallie." She pulled him tighter. "Thank God you're all right."

"Hon, Mike saved my ass." Tears tumbled. His arms stayed around Lissa until he felt more calm.

Releasing her, he locked the Porsche then went over and climbed behind the wheel of her Pontiac. The radio was playing, *Lonely Teardrops*.

They drove to Julie's apartment. He parked in front. At the window, a lace curtain moved aside. He quickly went to the door, his badge in hand and knocked, Lissa close beside him.

The door edged open.

"I'm Mike's partner—"

Julie flung the door wide. "Where's Mike?" She looked past them and cried, "No! She sank back. Neall reached out, but Lissa was quicker. Two strangers held each other in a heartwarming embrace.

"Mike's alive—but critical." He realized that Julie had jumped to the worst conclusion. "We're here to take you to the hospital."

Julie broke loose and, untying her robe, hurried to another room.

Haley took Lissa's hand and they stepped outside. The beach air blended with his salty tears. He turned to look out at the Pacific, thinking how Lissa's tenderness with Julie showed her special strength. The feeling enveloped his soul. He squeezed Lissa's hand.

"Hon, go in and ask Julie if you can drive her car—you don't mind following us?"

"Of course not. I expect such thoughtfulness from you, Neallie." Lissa went into the apartment.

Haley sat with the small gathering in the hospital corridor: Lissa, Julie, Helen, Montego's mother, her husband, Steve, and Haley's mom, pop and Missy.

Near daybreak Sergeant Joe Whitehead appeared and said in a high gravelly voice, "Mike's finally out of surgery. Doctor Robert Morgan says it went well, but our boy had a narrow brush. Three bullets were removed. His pericardium was nicked, a lung punctured, and his liver partially damaged. All in all I would say he's a very lucky young man."

Montego's mother, gasped and quickly placed a hand on her chest. Her husband, his arms crossed, looked like he didn't know what to do.

Julie grabbed the tall sergeant's arm. "Thank God, thank God."

Haley, rising to his feet when Whitehead appeared, felt lightheaded. Overcome with relief, he found a chair and plopped. Lissa sat beside him and put a hand on his knee.

Mom, Pop and Missy joined them. Pop's put his arm across Haley's shoulders.

Their closeness comforted him, but it couldn't assuage his guilt.

*   *   *

Brunetti locked the door after Goochie left. He went into Simeti's bedroom while replaying the night's events in his mind:

He and Simeti had tailed the bulls to the restaurant and waited for them to come out. It was supposed to be a silent hit after the bulls were in their car, but his crazy cousin had to get anxious and make his stupid yelling charge.

Blue-Eyes was damn fast—his loud fucking rod scared everyone; and a slug had slashed Brunetti's neck.

Another damn inch and it would've been bye-bye Big Leo!

He was on the sidewalk across the boulevard before he'd felt the burning and touched his neck. The blood on his hand scared him. He'd pressed his handkerchief over the wound, then he'd bought a ticket at the Egyptian Theater kiosk using his free hand to finger bills from his pocket. He'd kept his bloody side away from the window.

In the restroom, he'd squatted in a toilet-stall feeling queasy, until the blood quit seeping.

When he'd finally split the theater, he'd gone straight to Simeti's Hillview pad and called Goochie. He'd told her to catch a cab and also get some medical stuff for a cut he had.

She'd dressed his neck, and then she satisfied his raging boner.

Now he needed to be damn smarter. . . . Think things through.

Grunting, he poured himself three fingers depth of Grappa.

Blue Eyes is fuckin' dead—good. Nothing like a dead cop.

He threw back his head and drank. "Ow." His neck burned like hell. He poured another triple shot and dropped onto the sectional couch.

Now for the bull kid, 'n' then the yellow fuck—Pinky Sancia.

Fuck what that suave-ass chump, Pio, might think about the cop hit. He was a loser. But Momo would be damned pissed.

Can't be helped—a vendetta is a fuckin' vendetta.

Chapter 65

Haley appeared in Municipal Court Tuesday morning. It didn't matter that he was on RFD status, or how tired he was. He had spent the last 36 hours at the hospital while Montego stayed in a drug-induced sleep.

However, traffic court duty called—an old ticket was being fought.

The judge, an attractive blonde, liked cops, especially motor cops in their blue breeches and knee-high boots, but the shapely divorcée was an absolute stickler. Officers arriving in her courtroom one minute past the appointed hour got "cannonball-ized," a play on the judge's surname.

Lissa had followed Haley to his home where he had changed. He'd given her his blood-stained suit to take to the cleaners, kissed her, and then endured the rush-hour traffic. He got to Municipal court barely on time.

Montego's heroism was the talk of the courthouse. Thankfully, only one person, Eagon Quinn, knew Haley was the *saved* partner, and he'd just flagged Haley to join him in the coffee alcove. He knew Quinn from the veladas, and recently heard that Montego and Quinn were longtime friends.

It explained where Montego's inside information had come from.

They shook hands and Quinn said, "I dropped by CRH an hour ago, just missed you, Haley. I'd like a few words, if you've got a minute."

"I've got time, Counselor. Miss Iron Pants moved my case back." Haley sensed Quinn's serious tone and followed the man out to the patio where fewer people mingled.

"Call me Eagon—may I call you Neall?"

"OK, Eagon." Haley found a folding chair and sat, as did Quinn.

"Neall, I've known Mike most of his life, so I want to hear first hand exactly what happened on Cherokee Monday night."

Haley could see that Quinn was suspicious about something and believed when Montego was fully recovered Quinn would learn the truth, hopefully not everything—but Brunetti's vendetta seemed a certainty.

"Eagon . . . I'm living with a ton of guilt."

Quinn grasped his arm. "Just let it out, son."

"You sound like my pop." Haley, mildly amused, felt an eyelid ticcing. He paused then explained about ignoring the directive to avoid the mobsters. He described how Beak Brunetti had accosted him, saying, "Brunetti believes my pop killed his dad back in the 'thirties."

Haley noted Quinn's surprised look. "The lousy meathead has a vendetta with my pop that he's intending to satisfy—but he's got the wrong man." He didn't continue when he saw that Quinn was about to speak.

"Neall, I know about the vendetta—what I did not know was that your father might be Angelo Sancia. That's a bit of a stretch, me thinks."

"My pop is *not* Pinky Sancia—and before you ask, I've told him— Pop just laughed it off."

"And now you've got a situation with Brunetti because he believes your *Pop* is the so-called Purple Hand?"

"That's it. And he's been having what he called 'fun 'n' games' ever since. . . . He's been trying to make me into a damn hit man. Of course I've refused, but it got Mike concerned 'cause he'd seen me with Brunetti— and he also knew that I had faced Preston with a packet of compromising photos that I had—ask Mike about the situation with the councilman."

"I heard about the compromising photos from my old partner."

"Oh. Anyway, Beak Brunetti must've had a wild hair up his ass, because he and his lousy cousin, Nino Simeti, tried to run us over outside the Hollywood station."

Haley noted Quinn's surprised look.

"That pissed-off Mike. He said we should see the cousins, so we did. It so happened we found them together at the Villa Capri. Mike told them if they had a problem to face him man-to-man."

"That sounds like Mike."

"Yeah, but I believe it brought on The Boulevard ambush. We were leaving Musso's and the meatheads came up behind us firing away. Mike, pushed my ass to the ground, protecting me—he took the slugs, but he dumped Simeti, and wounded Brunetti." Haley paused to light up a Camel.

Blowing out smoke, he said, "I didn't really expect the bold way they came at us, but I was certain there'd be a confrontation, except I'd pegged The Beak to be more an in-your-face type asshole."

"Neall, Brunetti would never have faced you men man-to-man. I know his type. He could not conceive of putting himself into a neck-risking situation without the odds overwhelmingly in his favor. You've seen it— he's a back-shooter. And from what you've told me, it sounds like he stayed back and let his cousin act as his shield."

"Yeah. . . . I suppose the meathead did at that."

"What surprised me a bit, Neall, was the gunsels even shooting at you men. Mafiosi families reputedly leave the police and DAs alone, not to

306

mention reporters. They don't like the high-profile trouble it can bring." Quinn looked about the patio. "So what did you mean by 'a ton of guilt'?"

"I never told Mike about the hold Beak Brunetti had on me."

"And you feel you put Mike in danger because of that? Well, let me say this: life's too short to waste time sodden with guilt about what you should or should not have done in a given situation. Learn the lesson and move on—I've had to."

Quinn's words helped put things into better perspective for Haley. "Forward, march, huh, Counselor?"

"Yes. Mike chose to take the bullets to save you, and I am damn thankful the boy's alive." Quinn moved his hand to the back of Haley's neck and shook him gently.

Then Quinn retrieved his briefcase. "When Mike is feeling up to it, maybe on Thanksgiving Day, I want your team *and* your better halves," he smiled, "to enjoy a sail on my ol' Chris-Craft. I think we all have something to be thankful for."

Quinn rose and they clasped hands.

Haley, completing his testimony on a traffic stop he'd made months earlier, drove to Central Receiving and parked in the rear lot.

Entering the Fire and Police Ward, he strolled to Montego's room. Montego was asleep, his mother was sitting bedside. Haley remained nearly an hour, all the while hoping his wishful thoughts were being conveyed subliminally to his unconscious partner.

Before heading home, Haley detoured to the station wanting to talk to Alex Strait. Passing Gower Street he gazed up a the "Hollywood" sign high on Mount Lee. He remembered the hot summer days as a youngster, crawling through the prickly scrub with his brother and oldest sister, following rabbit and coyote trails up to the base of the world-famous 50-foot-tall metal-fabricated letters that had read "Hollywoodland" back then.

He imagined that Montego had done the same when he was a boy.

So long ago, yet Haley felt small again, but with an Atlas-sized weight now on his shoulders. Instead of the world, the burden he carried was his past actions and how they had severely hurt his partner.

He thought of Missy and his fear of nearly losing her; it helped him cope with the hit on Armanno. But the single blond hair—*mine*—found in the Ford sedan gutted Haley.

Could it ever be matched?

Yeah, If the lab boys knew I was a suspect—and Mike knows.

Chapter 66

Haley worked the Porsche into a spot on Cole Place, then he slogged up the back stairs to the locker room, even though Quinn's words had helped, Haley was unable to ease the angst he felt.

I should've told Mike a lot sooner about the lousy meatheads.

After changing into a pair of faded Levi's, a light-blue polo shirt, and slipping into his bomber jacket, he returned to his sports car hoping that Nancy might have information about The Beak's whereabouts.

Stepping into the sunny courtyard at The Palms Motel, Haley aimed for Room 8. He was about to knock when he saw his once-upon-a-time sexy girlfriend shimmying toward him on the narrow pathway.

She spotted him and quickly closed the distance, brushing a dry palm frond away from her bouffant hairdo. Concern was written on her artfully made-up face.

"Neallie, I've been trying to reach you—I went to the police station but they said you were at the hospital. I thought it was you who'd been shot, but the cop at the counter told me it was your partner—did I know him?"

"You saw him the night we busted Brunetti. The lousy meathead and his damn cousin almost killed Mike."

"Ooh, no. I'm sorry—how is he . . . Mike?"

"Critical, but he'll make it." Haley knocked a Camel from a pack.

"I'm glad you're all right. Is that why you're here—to tell me?"

"No—I'm here to ask you if you knew where Brunetti might be."

Nancy glanced about the sunlit courtyard. "Let's go into my room."

Inside, she sat on the bed and pulled off her pink cardigan while snapping chewing gum. She flicked her tongue and wet her ruby-gelled lips. Her puckered smile glistened like a round July birthstone on smooth ivory.

"Leo called me late Monday night. He wanted me to get some bandages and come to his cousin Nino's place at the Hillview Apartments. When I got there I saw his bloody neck. It looked really awful. He told me he'd been in a bar fight at the Continental, but I knew better."

"Is he still around?" Haley lipped the cigarette.

"Nah. He has a couple of jobs to do before he splits for Chicago."

"What's Nino's apartment number?" Haley clenched the Ronson.

She told him while leaning over and switching on the new bedside lamp. Sitting up, she unbuttoned her white-nylon blouse. She wore no bra.

He had to make this quick. They weren't in high school anymore.

"Where's Pio—I need to settle something?" He fired up the Camel.

"Dante just left the restaurant—he was having coffee with Mister Momo, but now he's over at the Capri having a late lunch with Virginia." Nancy tugged her blouse loose from her skirt. "Gotta tell ya, Neallie—Dante is in a really rotten mood . . . prob'ly something Momo told him. That ugly man didn't look too happy, neither."

Haley pocketed the Ronson. "Can Pio be trusted?"

"I think so, sweetie. Virginia's told me Dante considers his word—how did she say it? 'Once given, it's platinum. If he makes a promise, that's it.' Leo's told me pretty much the same thing—and he doesn't like Dante."

She pulled open her blouse.

He blew out a stream of smoke. "I've gotta go, kiddo."

"Ooh noo—reeally?" Her heavy breasts bounced freely when she sprang off the blue coverlet, arms out, lips puckering.

He turned his head quickly—her kiss landed on his cheek.

She finger-wiped away the red residue with several strokes.

"Sweetie, if you're seeing Dante, you'd better watch out."

Minutes later, parked on the rise a half-block north of Yucca, Haley locked the S&W and shoulder rig in the glove box. After removing his jacket, he secured the sports car and strode down the cracked sidewalk toward the Villa Capri and Dante Pio. This would not be a leisurely stroll like he and Montego had done. This brief meeting was for the Haleys, and for Montego. Haley didn't know what to expect, and seriously doubted the capo would divulge anything, but regardless what the underboss knew or did not know about The Beak's vendetta, the Haley family was off limits.

Leonardo Brunetti was Ice Cop's alone to deal with.

The smooth-looking capo regime was at a table along the far wall sitting cozily with the tall brunette, Virginia, who today, wore a bright red pillbox hat. The color matched her gloves. A pair of swarthy-complexioned thick-necks stuffed into dark pinstriped suits slouched at the table between Haley and his well-dressed target.

"Show time," he breathed out venomously. Dante Pio's pissed look verified what Nancy had told him. Haley focused on the twins; he didn't expect the tag team to use their muscles unless Pio wanted them to.

Haley saw the capo mouth something to his soldiers. The "hefties" swiveled their heads, eyeballed Haley, and clambered to their big feet. Their thick forearms "Cagneyed" up their pleated trousers, then folded over their beefy chests.

"Holds it where you're at, buddy," the closer hefty growled. He and his scowling look-alike blocked Haley from the capo's table.

The chattering in the room dropped to a low buzzing.

Haley stopped a tactical space from the overgrown James Cagney pretenders and stared at the underboss.

"Don't make this difficult, Capo Pio. I only want a private word—if you're gentleman enough to hear me out. Tell your boys to step aside."

Dante Pio scrutinized him; a thin scar curving from his left ear down along his jawbone added a sinister touch to his urbane looks. A grossly large marquis-shaped diamond ring adorned his left pinky. He made a show of being disinterested and tapped his fingers on the white tablecloth.

Haley bided his time, even though adrenaline coursed through him.

The low buzzing in the room had stilled.

An eternity passed before Pio spoke. "Make your damn speech."

Haley stepped closer. The toad-faced hefty twins stiffened.

"I've heard you people don't mess with police, but your imported muscles, Brunetti and Simeti, have violated the rule. And now my partner's lying in critical condition because of those lousy meatheads. Simeti's ass got buried—but you know that. What I'm telling you, Capo, is the way it's going to be—Leonardo The Beak Brunetti is all mine."

Pio slid his hand next to his wineglass, the diamond facets caught a distant light, arcing a "thousand-star point" rainbow across the table linen.

"Officer Haley, right? No one tells me what to do." Pio eyed Haley coldly. "But whatever that stupid crumb did was of his own damn doing. The Beak's no longer my concern."

Haley stayed alert to the hefties shifting movements an arms-length away, while he focused on the underboss, trying to read his rigid face.

Dante Pio grasped the stemmed wine glass.

"I suppose you know what Brunetti believes about your old man?" Pio sipped the white wine, now seemingly amused, smirking slightly.

The hefty Cagneys fidgeted about. Haley eye-pinned them.

"Yeah, supposedly he's Angelo Pinky Sancia, a lousy meathead who some people call The Purple Hand." Haley's low voice leveled coldly.

"Capo—my pop is *not* Pinky Sancia." Wanting to believe his own words, Haley realized he sought confirmation from a man who should know.

Do I really want to know?

"That's what I told The Beak," Pio's tone turned even more caustic. He set down the wineglass, sneering. "The crumb never saw your old man close-up. And missing a damn pinky finger means nothing." Pio eyed the sparkling ring on his pinky.

Haley, eased out a breath, but sensed a pulsing anger emanating from the capo. Apparently, Sam Momo Giancana had given Pio bad news. Haley wouldn't mind if Giancana made Pio's time on earth damn short.

Dante Pio continued, "The Beak bought into what his fool cousin told him. Personally, I'd go even odds that Sancia bought it during the war. Anyways, I don't care if your old man is or was the damn Jews' so-called Purple Hand." He sneered. "That's ancient history." Pio's diamond-ringed hand now rested on the courtesan's nearest black-gloved one.

Virginia's striking eyes fixed on Haley.

He shot the smooth-acting underboss the iciest glare he could make.

"I've heard that your word once given is pure platinum. So tell me, Capo, that whatever happens to Beak Brunetti will have no repercussions from you, or your boys—agree, and we'll be cool."

Haley now considered that Pio's anger was due in part to the cousins' stupid caper. Their cop-shooting action, a mob no-no, meant bad notoriety. The capo might agree, because doing so would be good business. Yet, there was no real guarantee that the meathead's word was sacrosanct.

So be it.

A siren shrilled in the distance. Haley's heart skipped several beats. Somebody in the kitchen must've called for the blue-suits.

Dante Pio arched a black eyebrow and glanced at the main entry. He didn't appear to be happy about talking to more cops.

"I don't give a good goddam what happens to the big crumb. The Beak's too damn much trouble—I never want to see his stupid cop-shooting ass again." Pio eyed his two soldiers and shook his head slightly. His signal kept the twin hefties at bay.

Pio returned his cold gaze to Haley. "Your ass stays out of my life, Haley, and you've got my solemn word."

Haley nodded, turned about, and forcing himself, to be casual, tread toward the rear. Once outside the kitchen door, he raced to the Porsche, hearing screeching tires a half-block behind him.

His next stop was to the Hillview Apartments on The Boulevard. He strapped on the shoulder rig, holstered the magnum, and twisted into his brown leather jacket. He didn't expect The Beak to be inside, but still. . . .

Haley entered the building and went directly to Simeti's second floor apartment. He listened at the door for a minute. Hearing nothing, he tried the handle. To his surprise the door opened.

The Beak must've left in a hurry.

As Haley had suspected, the apartment was vacant. An empty bottle of Grappa and several sticky tumblers were on a coffee table along with a *Playboy* magazine opened to *Miss October*. Stale cigar odor accosted him.

In the bathroom he found a sink plastered with black, wiry hair, a bloody towel, a soiled gauze strip, and wadded gobs of adhesive tape.

He left the apartment, drove to the station, and parked on Wilcox. Quick-stepping into the corridor, he headed for the detectives' squad room.

Rosy Rosenbloom called to Haley as he passed the front desk.

"*Khaver*—tell me Mike's gonna make it." Rosy looked worried.

Haley gave him Joe Whitehead's latest report.

"*Vunderbar.*" Rosy pounded the high wooden countertop.

Haley smiled and turned toward the main stairs and glanced to his right as he passed the narrow side hallway. He spotted Strait opening the outside door and chased after him.

"Strait—you heard anything more about Brunetti?"

Alex Strait, looking back, held the door open. He appeared haggard. A sudden gust flipped his striped rep tie over his right shoulder.

"How's Mike doing?"

Haley stepped outside and told him.

Strait remained silent, but his relief showed in his hazel eyes.

"Have you any leads on Brunetti's whereabouts?" Haley asked.

"Haven't located the big prick, yet," Strait sighed, "but we did impound his fancy Cadillac Biarritz. We found it parked on Lanewood." Letting the door blow shut, Strait snatched his narrow necktie and pulled it down. "Also, we found an old black-and white snapshot in Mister Simeti's billfold. I'm heading down to PAB now to get it enhanced and copied."

"Can I see it?" Haley sensed his voice was an octave above normal.

Strait paused, then he opened his leather briefcase, and retrieved a small, faded print with dog-eared edges clipped to a file folder with "SIMETI" printed on it. He handed the snapshot over.

Haley viewed the scratchy image of a fedora-covered young man standing closest to the camera. He looked to be unaware that his picture was being taken. Handwritten on the backside: *Pinky Sancia, 193*—the last part was smudged and illegible. The man had similar features to Pop, but Haley felt certain that even enhanced a positive identification could not be made.

He handed the photo back.

"Thanks, Strait."

Alex Strait opened the door, but stopped and eyed Haley intently. "I'm sorry about what has happened." He hesitated. "I'm glad you're safe, Neall, and I'm tremendously pleased that Mike is on the mend." His striped tie flipped over his shoulder again from a strong gust as he turned away.

Haley strode back to the Records room and asked the stenographer if he could use her telephone. She twirled the black instrument toward him.

Scanning his pocket address-book, he found the number he wanted.

"Dealer—Haley here. I'm going to look for Leonardo Brunetti, and I know you've got some street connections. If you've got any info I can use, I'd appreciate it."

"Shouldn't take me long, Neall."

"I'll be at the front desk—call me." Haley liked KW Deal. The man didn't ask stupid questions.

An anxious period passed before Rosy handed Haley the telephone.

"For you, Haley."

"Neall—checked with the manager of the gym where the dirty pictures first showed," KW said. "Where Brunetti and another dude made a visit. Came in separate vehicles: a yellow Caddy Biarritz convert, and a new T-Bird, cherry red, with a black landau top."

"Good stuff. Word is, Brunetti's heading for Chicago, but he might risk a run by Central Receiving to try another hit on Mike—maybe try for me, too," *and even Pop, given the chance*, "being I was a wit. . . . Also, Dealer, he's got a neck wound and I believe he's shaved his ugly head."

"Get lucky, Ice Cop—for Mike's sake—and, watch your own ass."

Chapter 67

Leo Brunetti pulled Simeti's red T-Bird into a Union 76 a block north of the Santa Ana Freeway on Excelsior Drive in Norwalk, about twenty miles southeast of L.A. He told the attendant to change the oil, and lube the Thunderbird, ending with, "No hurry, I'll pick it up tomorrow morning."

He had just come from a department store where he'd bought a couple of polo shirts, socks, underwear, and an off-the-rack sports coat. His bloody suit-coat and dress shirt were wrapped in a plastic bag inside Simeti's Samsonite suitcase along with Brunetti's leather toilet-articles case and the morning purchases.

He'd located a travel agency and now held a one-way ticket to Detroit, leaving the next morning on an early flight from Frisco. He'd told Goochie Chicago, but she didn't need to know the truth. By late afternoon he'd be on the highway going north to the Bay Area. But first things first.

He tramped from the Bird to the motel across the street feeling he fit the neighborhood good enough. He wore casual clothes and a Yankees' baseball cap. He put on his dark sunglasses, stuffed several fives into his front pocket, and entered the motel. His activities had him dragging.

Not enough sleep—too much shit going on.

A pimpled punk slid a registration card at him, his sneaky eyes fixated on Brunetti's bandaged neck. "Cash or credit?"

Brunetti scratched out a name and shoved the card back at the punk with a five dollar bill for a one night stay. He grumbled, "Car accident."

"I need your license plate number."

"I told you I was in a car accident. Now gimme a corner room facing north." Brunetti displayed an extra fin.

The kid, glancing around, snatched it.

Outside the office, Brunetti dropped a quarter into a slot and lifted out a newspaper. He carried it and the suitcase to his room. The corner spot provided the expected view of the T-Bird parked at the service station.

He shoved an overstuffed chair in front of the window, tossed the blue baseball cap onto the bed, and flopped down next to it. His head ached like a bitch and his neck burnt like hell. He opened the paper and scanned the article about the plainclothes cop, Michael D. Montego, getting shot in Hollywood and being in critical condition at Central Receiving Hospital.

That the bull was alive shook Brunetti, but not as much as the mug shot of him above the fold.

Sumbitch. All 'cause Nino got crazy again. Got his ass killed, 'n' me damn near, too. . . . All them people running, screaming. If Nino hadda just slowed hisself, we coulda taken out both bulls. Speakeasies woulda kept things nice 'n' quiet. Nobody woulda been any the wiser—'n' I wouldn't hafta leave town. Fuckin' Nino.

Brunetti tossed the newspaper on the floor, undressed, and eased into bed. The mug pix showed his bandaged nose but not his shaved head. That was something.

*   *   *

Early the next morning, Wednesday, Haley slipped out from under the bed covers, padded to the bathroom and completed his morning ritual, finishing with a glass of cool tap water. Nancy's words rang in his head. The Beak still intended to satisfy his damn vendetta.

Beak, make me your top priority—because I want your hairy ass.

He called Kozier and learned that the lieutenant had approved the 1.18 Commendation Report. *That was quick.* The report was now with the Awards and Decorations Board. The deputy chiefs heading the seven bureaus would decide whether or not Montego merited the Medal of Valor. To receive the highest award was not a given. Chief Parker would be told that the Mafia was involved, and that could be the seal of death. Still, a cop saving a cop's life—damn hard to ignore.

Cradling the receiver, Haley looked out the bay window checking for gray squirrels, but his mind's eye visualized wasting Beak Brunetti.

Dante Pio had cut "the big crumb" loose, obviously to create distance from the shooting. The best part of the meet with the capo was learning that he didn't think missing a pinky finger meant anything. What Pio thought and what Brunetti believed meant Haley wasn't dealing with the damn Mafia. Thank God.

He dialed the PPSI number.

"Pop. I told you I had something more—well here it is." Haley felt compelled to rush his words as if there was no time to lose.

"Angelo Sancia killed Leo Brunetti's dad, he has a vendetta. Your bad heart kept me from telling you—I should've. Damn! It just dawned on me—he knows where you live—I don't know how I forgot about that—too

315

much has been going on—Pop, I'm sorry. Stay extra alert. I'm heading to the hospital to see Mike. I'm thinking that Brunetti will go there—make another play in revenge for his cousin. You need to know if he's not driving a rental, he might be in a new red T-Bird—it has a black Landau top."

"Yes, you should've told me—but thanks for the heads up, and I did see the mobster's mug in the *Times*. I doubt his nose is still bandaged."

"Yeah, I saw it, too. The bandage *is* gone, but Mike's shot hit Brunetti in the neck. Also, I found where the meathead spent the night, and from what I saw, I think he shaved his head—Pop, be damn careful."

"You too, son."

Haley hung up. Talking shop to Pop was easier than he'd imagined. *Like it'd been talking about Lissa. Why didn't I do it weeks ago?*

*　　*　　*

Brunetti awoke and checked the bedside clock: 10:25 AM. He crawled out of the sack and went to the window. He spotted the T-Bird in the station's lot and studied the surrounding area. It didn't look like any bulls were staked on the car.

He showered, re-bandaged the oozing wound on the right side of his neck, and dressed slowly. He grabbed the Samsonite, left the motel and made his way circuitously to the service station, checking for hidden bulls.

Feeling things were cool he keyed open the T-Bird and cruised the area until he located a diner.

After gobbling down two cheeseburgers and fries, he sat back, and drank several cups of coffee. It was time to settle the score for his old man.

Hasta be easy. Fuckin' Sancia's pale-assed kid's gotta be going to that hospital to see his chump blue-eyed pal, Montego. He's first up.

Getting directions from the waitress, he headed for a sporting goods store and found what he wanted: a Model 77 Winchester, a Leupold scope, a box of .22 caliber rounds, and a pair of wax earplugs. From there he rolled into L.A. and topped off the gas tank. With the directions he obtained, he drove to Central Receiving Hospital where Blue-Eyes hopefully was dying.

Brunetti couldn't find a spot close enough to give him a good view, so he parked farther up the hill behind the small hospital. He waited and watched. Although the tree-lined street was quiet, he gave up the idea of going inside and putting Tonto *Montaygo* to sleep, permanently.

Too damn many bulls coming and going in the parking lot below.

316

The Purple Hand

Yeah, Neallie Baby, you're first—'n' Pinky, you're fuckin' next.

Brunetti reflected on his two months in L.A. and Momo's planned move on little DeSimone's turf.

I'm gonna miss that. Gotta lay low in Detroit, give the boss some time to cool his nuts, then back to the windy city for me.

Brunetti thought of Coochie Goochie's bouncy knockers; his roscoe swelled. Damn, he could use her services now. He imagined her naked body grinding on top of him, her big tits banging his face. He rubbed his boner.

A space 200 feet or so away from the rear of the hospital opened up. Letting go of his stiff joint, he kicked over the T-Bird's motor, and grabbed the spot.

Once re-parked, he eyeballed the area.

Come on, Leo—calm your ass down—Damn, wish Nino was here.

The Bird's swing-away steering wheel feature was damn cool. He moved it 18 inches to the right to give him enough room to maneuver. He slipped the scope into the grooves on the rifle, removed his sunglasses, and studied the street. Then he did a practice aim. From the uphill location, he could watch the entry to the visitors' parking lot. He laid the rifle on his lap. The shot would be loud so he stuffed the wax plugs into his ears.

When it's done I gotta split the scene rapido.

He loaded the Winchester, then checked the Beretta's magazine and homed it. He shoved the piece under his left thigh for backup.

Next, he took out his handkerchief, polished the scope's lens, then the sunglasses. Before slipping them on, he checked the dash clock: 3:30.

Gotta have me a quick smoke.

He lowered the side windows, lit up a fresh Dutch Master, and drew in, savoring the tobacco. Twenty minutes passed, he took a last drag on the stubby cigar, tossed it out, and settled into a slouch. He felt more at ease. He pulled the Yankee cap's bill lower to shield his eyes from the sun's rays.

Damn, his neck burned like hell . . . he still felt fucking drowsy. . . .

Shoulda put more medicine on my neck . . . but first . . . gotta take care of Neallie Baby—

"Hey, Beak! Gonzo! Roust your big ass!"

Brunetti, jarred alert by a muffled voice, felt a sharp pain below his left ear. Pissed for dozing, he tried to sit up, simultaneously letting his left hand slip to the Beretta pistol, but the sound of a hammer cocking by his ear froze him.

Shit—a fuckin' revolver—gotta be a damn bull!

317

The hot electric currents shooting into his brain from the cold steel jammed into his neck fucking hurt like hell.

The voice sounded vaguely familiar, even through the earplugs. He tried to see who the fucker was, but the baseball cap and sunglasses had slid onto his nose, blocking his vision.

Who the fuck am I dealing with? How the damn hell was I found? Fuck. Nino's damn T-Bird—stupido, stupido, Leo!

Brunetti's fingers finally found the pistol's butt beneath his left leg.

Gotta free the damn gat—stall this bull muthafuck.

"Who the hell are you—what the fuck do y'think you're doing?"

He blinked his eyes rapidly. They had blurred from the painful steel screwed into his neck. He couldn't see shit, but he understood the menacing words:

"I'm *The* Purple Hand, clown, and I'm killing your skanky ass."

Pa's killer! Pinky Sancia—fuck me—I'm in deep shit.

He'd never been cornered before—always he'd had the damn edge.

Not this time, Leo.

Brunetti's bladder sprang a leak.

Madre di Dio!

Never—fucking never in his life—had the damn shakes rattled him like now. He couldn't help his damn self. He was scared shitless, literally.

Wet heat flooded his groin area, soaking through to the rifle laying useless on his lap.

His bunghole busted loose.

Damn—Leo!

He smelled like a back alley full of cat shit in Hell's Kitchen.

Papa, Papa—help me—I'm only here for you! I don't wanna die.

Desperately, he yanked up the Beretta.

Suddenly he was muscling the pistol for control.

The last words Leonardo Brunetti spoke: "Oh fuck me."

The last words he heard: "Never shoot a cop—not in LA."

Chapter 68

Haley rushed into the hospital corridor and saw a group outside Montego's room. KW Deal stood next to a large black man. Lissa was sitting beside Julie. She quickly rose and they embraced. He looked through the doorway. Montego appeared to be sleeping. His mother sat at his bedside.

Turning, Haley patted KW's shoulder, "Dealer, you're looking good." And to Julie, "What have you heard from Doc?"

"Mike woke earlier. He was groggy from the Demerol, but doctor says given time he's going to be his old self."

"Tonto back on the job kicking butt—that's great." Haley smiled. A guilty load lifted.

"Doctor Bob Morgan's the best." KW jostled Haley's shoulder as KW's free hand swung toward the man beside him whose massive arms were a shade lighter than his polo shirt.

"Neall, meet Russell Smith—my father-in-law's assistant."

The muscular man extended his large hand. "Call me Smitty."

"He grips more like a bodyguard." Haley grinned. "You must be the gym trainer who found. . . ." He paused, glanced at the women then continued, "Heard you had a run-in a while back with Beak Brunetti and his meathead cousin. Right?" He noted Russell Smith's intense look.

"One and the same." Smith winked, then glanced at KW.

The five of them made small talk.

Minutes later, Haley's pop came up and gave him a strong hug. To his surprise, his pop kissed Lissa on both cheeks before he peered into Montego's room. Then he went to Julie. "How's our boy doing?"

She reiterated what the doctor had told her.

Haley introduced his pop to KW and Smith. They shook hands.

"Pop, you're wearing a clean shirt. A slow day?"

"Can't be visiting with pipe putty all over me." His pop grinned. "You look fairly starched yourself, son." He turned to Lissa. "Your doing?"

She eyed Haley wistfully. "Not yet, Lonn."

Haley wanted to say "Soon," but too much had happened.

Just then, Whitehead called out to KW who quickly moved down the corridor to join the gray-haired Medical Liaison Officer.

Haley, realizing that during KW's recent stay a good friendship had developed with the sergeant, felt a slight recurring pang, but what he overheard the sergeant saying: "That Thunderbird listed on the Hot Sheet has been located by a patrol unit on Loma—just up the street," sent Haley racing alongside KW toward the rear exit.

Hearing footfalls behind him, Haley glanced back. Pop and Smith were close on his heels.

The four men came to a stop up the hill where a black-and-white was angled across the roadway. Farther up the road, a new red T-Bird was parked. Two uniformed officers had the street blocked off both north and south with red-spitting flares.

Haley went to the nearest one and flashed his badge.

"What've you got?"

"A bloody stiff with several holes in what's left of his head—stinks like shit. Haven't touched a thing. Downtown homicide has a team rolling."

Haley went with KW to the driver's side door, Smith and Haley's pop behind them.

"He's *not* kidding." KW quickly pinched his nose.

Haley looked inside the car briefly then spun toward the uniform.

"Did anyone see anything?"

"Nada," the patrol cop said.

"Unbelievable." KW backed away, exhaling audibly.

"Nasty looking."

Haley, hearing his pop's raspy voice, looked back. His pop was staring coldly at the dead Leonardo Brunetti. Turning, Haley saw Smith watching them both, his no-tell poker expression fixed as if set in concrete.

When Pop and Smith bid their goodbyes and headed down to the parking lot, Haley and KW waited at the squad car for the detectives.

KW shifted about on his feet. "Messy. Wrists bound to the steering wheel like that—a real twist." He chuckled, then said, "Going back to the hospital—gotta call Kozier, explain why we're gonna be late for muster."

KW did an about-face and strode away.

Haley dropped out his last Camel and lit it.

Brad will understand.

He was taking a last drag on the cigarette when Nells and Strait arrived. Haley stayed by the black-and-white while the detectives conducted their investigation.

Eventually, Strait, pulling off his painter's mask, went to his sedan.

The Purple Hand

Haley, anxious to hear Alex Strait's thoughts, moved to join him, the smell of menthol wafted as he got closer.

He heard Strait on the mic calling the dispatcher for the coroner.

Strait re-hooked the handset and grasped a clipboard from the seat.

Haley noticed a business card for The Steel Bar Gym attached to it. *Missed that. When did the card find its way inside the T-Bird?*

Forcing his breathing to even out, he said, "Brunetti had the ideal spot to snipe a cop. He could've taken me out when I entered the hospital."

Strait gave him a questioning look. "Yes, you were an eye-witness that night. . . . You might well have been the prick's target."

It was mid-morning the next day, Thursday, when Haley parked his Porsche behind The Steel Bar Gym and headed for the rear entry. He found Smith out on the main floor spotting a heavyweight type who was bench-pressing a plate-loaded Olympic bar that Haley would never attempt to lift.

"Haley. You joining us?"

"No way, Russell—I'm here to talk to the gym's *new* owner."

Smith, grinning, helped the lifter rack the long bar. Coming around the bench, he touched Haley's shoulder. "Join me." He led the way to his office.

Haley noticed the black-plastic card holder on Smith's desk and took a business card from it.

"Owner/Trainer. How long've you been passing these babies out?" He watched as Smith lounged back on his swivel chair.

"A while. Didn't know when I'd have the bucks for this place— wanted them on hand when the time came."

"On hand?" A prickly sensation attacked Haley's spine. He sat.

"Yeah, on hand." Smith eyed him steadily.

Haley let out a tremulous breath. "Yesterday, when we all ran to the Thunderbird, what do *you* remember seeing?"

Smith studied him while he swiveled the chair slowly.

"A smelly piece of scum slumped to its right with a bandaged neck, a bloody shaved head with a crater on top, and a twenty-two scoped Winchester on piss-and-blood-stained trousers—oh, yeah, and a Yankees' baseball cap."

Haley was aware that Smith had arrived at CRH before him.

"How did you happen to be at the hospital—did you know Mike?"

Smith's focus stayed on Haley. He continued his slow swiveling.

"Met Mike through Dealer. I was at City Hall helping my boss, Councilman Forrall, celebrate the defeat of the booze bill. The boss asked me to pass on his concern about the condition of his son-in-law's partner, Officer Montego."

Smith stopped swiveling when the phone rang.

"Black Smith's Gym, Russell Smith here—please hold." He placed his hand over the mouthpiece and eyeing Haley, said, "I phoned Dealer. He asked if I would meet him at the hospital. When I got to Central Receiving, he hadn't yet arrived."

Smith stayed focused on Haley. His stone-hard gaze over a slight smirk etched into Haley's psyche.

"Neither had you . . . as I recall."

Haley pressed down on his knees while tightening his butt muscles.

"Did you happen to see anything unusual?"

"Nope." Smith tilted his head toward the phone receiver. "Mind?"

His self- assured manner and quiet tone captured and calmed Haley. *Russell Smith would make a damn good LA cop.*

The Purple Hand

Chapter 69

It was early afternoon on Friday when voices awoke Montego. He looked about trying to place where he was. A moment passed before he got himself oriented; he remembered a twilight awakening when a nurse had drawn his blood. He'd muttered that his pain was a 7 on a scale of 1 to 10, responding to her question. She gave him Demerol, soon he was fuzzily high.

Seeing Strait talking to Whitehead by the doorway, Montego called, "Joe, Uncle Alex." His throat was dry, but they'd heard him and came bedside. His beach pal carried a clipboard with a yellow legal tablet on it.

"Good to see you looking so handsome, Mikey." Whitehead studied him. "You've had a rough go, but you're a tough one." He winked at Strait.

"Tough he might be—handsome? I cannot in all good conscience corroborate that comment." Strait tweaked his baby handlebar mustache.

"Give him his due, Alex." Joe Whitehead arched an eyebrow. "Mikey, do you feel up to a little cop talk with this sartorial detective?"

"As long as his questions aren't filled with multi-syllabic words."

Whitehead chuckled, then went to the other patient in the room.

Strait pulled up a metal chair. "I'd like to get your statement— that's if the hopeful TMA is up to it." He sat.

Montego cleared his throat. "I could use a bit of water first, if you don't mind, Uncle Alex—please?" He pointed toward the pitcher on a table.

Following several draws of water, he related what he recalled, starting with the moment he and Haley had crossed Cherokee Avenue.

Montego ended saying how he saw himself floating on a pond. Then, taking in more water through the straw, he waited for questions.

Strait, however, put down his clipboard.

"That sums it up adequately, Mike." His voice cracked slightly. "Are you up to hearing what I've determined?"

"I know I shot Simeti. . . . Don't know what happened to Brunetti."

"You nearly dropped that cowardly cop shooter on the spot. Apparently your last slug nicked his neck. Mister Simeti expired on the scene . . . and Mister Beak is dead . . . now—rather revolting, too. He was shot just up the street from here—squatting in a red Thunderbird. It can be assumed that the big prick was intending to finish what he had started. Nonetheless, someone, probably two *someones*, got to the nasty man first."

323

Montego, letting out a long breath, searched Strait's haggard face. "Two someones? Mind doing a bit of explaining TMA?"

"Not at all. Mister Brunetti's demise was quite vile. His wrists were bound to the steering wheel with three-eighths inch copper tubing—similar to how we found Mister Armanno. But the corpses were entirely different."

Montego felt a chill.

Strait pocketed his blue mechanical pencil.

"Anyway, in Mister Brunetti's case, a single round entered under the jaw, exited through the top of the skull, and embedded in the headliner. Likely fired from a nine-millimeter Beretta we found—it was the fatal shot. Four smaller holes, also in the head, were fired from a twenty-two Minx we located on the floorboard—it was wrapped in a small canvas bag. . . ."

Montego felt another chill. He remembered, when he'd given Haley the Manilla envelope with the sex photographs, seeing a small canvas bag in the Porsche's storage compartment.

". . . The dearth of bleeding from the twenty-two slugs indicated they were post-mortem." Strait tweaked his baby handlebar mustache. "And the Minx was suppressed. . . . The canvas bag might have been used as a wipe-down rag—it had blood smears on it."

Strait set the clipboard with the lined yellow legal pad on the bed. "Also, we determined the Minx was been fired from the passenger side."

Montego drew up the last of his water. "Two shooters—huh?"

"Yes, more than one individual did mess with the crime scene . . . there also was a reddish imprint below the prick's left ear, like a gun barrel had been pressed hard against the flesh—the dimensions of a thirty-eight."

Strait, steadying the straw, filled Montego's paper cup with water.

"I found a business card in a blood-spattered Yankees' baseball cap behind the driver's seat. I surmise that the cap was atop Mister Brunetti's head and was blown off. Beside brain matter, there was a single bullet hole through it." Strait grasped his clipboard. "Why the business card was there, I can't say—it belonged to a weight-lifting gym on Jefferson."

Montego hesitated briefly. "The Black Smith's Steel Bar Gym?"

Strait's hazel eyes half-lidded. "Yes, as a matter of fact."

"Beak Brunetti had been there to threaten the new Councilman—Rudolph Forrall owns, or he did own, the place."

"Interesting." Strait finger-smoothed his mustache as if considering the ramifications of what he'd just heard. "That's the establishment, but it indicated a Russell Smith as the owner." He made a notation on the tablet.

The Purple Hand

*   *   *

It was late afternoon when Haley went to Central Receiving Hospital and spoke to the attending nurse. He learned that Montego was doing well, and that he had received numerous visitors, including a Detective Strait.

Haley had mixed feelings entering Montego's room. His partner, eyes shut, lay on one of four beds. Two beds were made up. Another patient occupied a bed diagonally from Montego's. A tall vase of mixed flowers with a mock firefighter's ax was on the table by his bed.

"Tonto, you awake?" Haley asked softly.

Montego's heavy lidded eyes cracked open.

"Neall . . . good to see you." His voice was thick.

Haley handed over a paper cup with water and a straw, then he slid a chair to the bed and sat. Unexpectedly, he gushed, "Mike, you saved my damn ass," tears welled, "and nearly lost yours doing it."

"Neall . . . you gotta know . . . I was gonna take—"

"Yeah, I know." Haley swiped at his eyes. "I'm damn sorry about all of this." He glanced across the room at the other patient, he appeared to be asleep. "I was trying to get your help to take out Brunetti and Simeti."

Montego sucked up some water then set the cup on the side table. Grimacing, he squiggled up on the bed. "Grab that handle, if you would," he pointed at the foot of the bed, "and raise this end a bit, please, amigo."

Haley found the L-shaped handle and stopped cranking when he heard, "That's good, thanks." Satisfied that if he spoke in a low voice the other patient wouldn't hear, he leaned closer. "Heard you talked to Strait."

"Yep."

Montego's look and his intense eyes nearly wilted Haley's resolve. Feeling drained, he sagged. "Then he knows the whole story?"

"Nope."

Haley jerked up. "But you know about Beak Brunetti?" He glanced at the other patient. The bedridden fireman was snoring.

"Alex Strait said it was 'rather revolting.'"

"It was—had to've happened within minutes of my getting here."

Montego studied him for a moment, then slowly a smile emerged on his sallow face. "Thanks for dropping by, partner."

Haley smiled too, slightly. "Dealer and his Herculean friend, Smith, also were here. . . . Pop came a while later."

"Quite a group. I do appreciate it." Montego seemed visibly moved.

"Yeah, we've all been checking up on your brave ass, every day—Mom and Missy, even Russell Smith. He said he was paying his respects on behalf of Rudolph Forrall." Haley looked around then asked, "Strait happen to mention that he found a Steel Bar Gym business card in the T-Bird?"

"Yep—and I guess no one knows how it got there."

"Yeah—it had me curious, too—it was Smith's card. Showed him to be the new owner. I went to see him yesterday. He told me that he'd had the cards for 'a while.' The Beak must've taken one when he was at the gym threatening Forrall. The card could've been in the T-Bird for some time—or maybe it fell free when The Beak's body slumped over."

"Smitt—Smith's gotta be a good guy if he's Kay Dub's bud."

Haley felt shaky. "Yeah, he is . . . What else did Strait have to say?"

"He was curious about the blond hair he found in Armanno's rental car." Montego quickly looked at the side table and snatched the paper cup. "I suggested that it could've been in there from a previous driver."

Haley chilled. "Mike, know this, I did *not* ace Armanno! I swear—"

"What?" Montego's eyes widened. Expected shock flashed, then a look of questioning relief slowly spread over his pallid face.

"I intended to, got stopped—and you never did ask me if I did it."

"I know . . . and you never actually copped to it—"

"I told you, I was in the back seat of the Ford behind Armanno. What I didn't tell you, was that the rear door suddenly flew open and a man wearing a dark ski mask C-clamped the back of my neck and grabbed Armanno's gun, growling, 'Outta here, Beak's mine, now—go—scram!' Hey, I wasn't shooting anyone by then—I damn well *scrammed*."

Montego studied him. "No idea who the growler guy was, huh?"

Haley, feeling fright shooting through him, knew he needed to be convincing.

Keep your damn eyes on Mike and don't you dare blink.

"No idea." Desperate to be believed, Haley eased out a sour breath. "But believe me, I was damn well relieved."

Not really—sick and dismayed was more like it.

Montego looked dubious. "You didn't see another vehicle nearby?"

Yeah, I saw a vehicle—a light-gray van!

"I did not—and I still don't know who the hell jumped my ass. Mike, the sun was low—it blinded me—and I was damn scared. Crap, a Sherman tank could've been blocking the road and I'd've missed it."

"Some story." Montego continued eyeing him steadily. "Neall, who would want to hit Joey Armanno besides you?"

My only hero.

"Maybe Pio—if he got wind of Armanno's caper he could've sent an enforcer to waste the hitter for being stupid. Let's face it, the capo doesn't control his boys—look at Brunetti and Simeti for crying out loud."

Montego nodded. "What might've happened to Missy sickens me. And your right, it would've meant bad press, and Dante Pio doesn't need that . . . I suppose he could have ordered it."

After adjusting his position, his focus re-centered on Haley.

"Strait said Brunetti's wrists were bound with three eighths-inch copper tubing. He claimed it looked like 'Paulie the plumber's work'—I was surprised when he said the same thing happened to Armanno."

Haley coughed turning away. "Gotta quit the damn cigarettes."

Montego feeling a bit of pain, watched Haley depart. His coughing reaction to the copper tubing comment was surprising, and confusing.

Reaching for the telephone, Montego dialed a memorized number.

Minutes later, homing the receiver, he stared out the large window. Drowsiness came as his mind worked over all the information he had taken in that afternoon. Myriad questions arose as he dropped off:

Who had jumped Neall and killed Joey Armanno? Possibly another goon like Neall had suggested? The copper tubing makes Lonn a suspect—and, it's doubtful that Neall has the hand strength to have done the deed. Lonn is capable, but doing it in front of his son? Neall had seemed surprised when he heard about the tubing.

So how did the Armanno hit go down. . . ? Ah—it happened on a Thursday—pie-baking day. Lonn could've been at the school to pick up Missy and spotted Neall in Armanno's car. Lonn could've followed Neall and taken over. It's understandable that Neall wouldn't divulge anything that might hang his father.

Armanno was killed for attempting to hit Missy. But Brunetti . . . ? Did Dante Pio find out what the huge goon was planning and had him hit to stop him from finishing off two cops—one a victim-witness to the shooting—me? The other, his partner, and also a witness—Neall?

Montego stirred while in dreamland but his mind remained active:

The Mafia has it ways. Like when they'd brought in help during the booze war in Detroit. Could Lonn be The Purple Hand? If he is, what can be done about it? Who would want to do something about it? It's unlikely any warrants, if there were any, exist for Angelo Sancia—and less chance of any ever being filed in L.A. With the cousins dead, Beak's vendetta ends.

Montego's thoughts fast-forwarded, reaching for an understanding:

Why were Brunetti's wrists bound with tubing like Armanno's? Had Lonn seen Brunetti staking out the hospital and ambushed him?

Or did Lonn spot his son at the red Thunderbird and take over— like he could have with Armanno? Twice? Pretty coincidental. But Alex had said more than one person had "messed with the crime scene."

Montego stirred again, then he slipped back into his musing:

Three firearms had been involved, Alex said: one threateningly—a thirty-eight caliber; a second one fatally—a nine-millimeter semiautomatic; and a third, fired post-mortem, probably in revenge—a twenty-two caliber Minx.

Alex believes Brunetti was jumped in the T-Bird and a gun barrel the size of a thirty-eight jammed into his neck. Alex also believes Brunetti, reacting, yanked up the Beretta accidentally killing himself—but with help. Alex added that the "culprit" holding the thirty-eight could've knocked the Beretta pistol aside or grabbed Brunetti's left wrist or hand.

In either case, the fatal shot came from the Beretta.

If it was Neall, using his service revolver would have nailed him; still, the slugs fired post-mortem from the Minx could've been his doing. Alex had mentioned that the small pistol and its silencer were untraceable.

What about the canvas bag . . . was it the one in the Porsche. . . ?

Maybe Neall saw his dad make the kill, spotted the bound wrists, then, to confuse the crime scene, fired the Minx post-mortem four times into The Beak's skull.

What if the opposite occurred? Lonn saw Neall firing the Minx and thought he'd killed Brunetti? Afterward, he deliberately confused the scene by using the copper tubing to copycat the Armanno hit. Risky, but to save his son—? Yet if Neall had wrestled Brunetti for the Beretta, why would he go around and shoot him again with the Minx? Not realistic.

The thirty-eight-sized circle on Brunetti's neck. . . . Whose gun?

Montego semi-awoke when the day nurse lifted his left arm to draw blood, but his twilight thinking continued:

Who got the drop on Brunetti?

He came wide awake when the nurse whispered, "He's sleeping."

Opening his eyes Montego saw Smith's toothy smile.

"Damn, if Tonto's not almost his cinnamon-colored self, again."

Montego eased forward letting the pillow from behind his head drop to his low back for support, it help ease the heaviness in his chest.

"Smitty, thanks for coming here, amigo." He paused for a moment. "I called you because I'm darn confused. I need a bit of info."

Smith leaned against the bed. "Ask away my friend."

"Detective Strait told me your new business card was found by Brunetti's body. I remember seeing a box of cards in your Bel-Aire the day after Brunetti and Simeti threatened Rudy. I doubt you gave Brunetti one—so how did your card end up in the T-Bird?" Montego had made and effort to sound matter-of-fact.

"The gonzo might've gotten it from Riffelano . . . when Baldy came by the gym with the Manilla envelope."

"I don't recall seeing the new cards on your desk at that time."

"Maybe Brunetti snatched one the day he threatened Rudy."

"I thought you said Rudy was jumped? Brunetti would've had to be inside your office after that . . . and you told me the 'clowns' took off in separate cars—a yellow Caddy and a red T-Bird."

Smith's expression sharpened.

Montego grasped the paper cup, drank some water, and set it back.

"I figure you just happened by, saw the Thunderbird, and dropped your business card inside—right?"

Smith's dark eyes bore into Montego's questioning ones.

"The snazzy red Bird stood out like a damn lit-up Christmas tree—I'd seen it before at the gym, remember?"

"Yep . . . so Brunetti was dead when you—"

"He was. Pleased me, too." Smith, biting his bottom lip, edged up.

"OK, here's the skinny, Tonto." His eyes glistened. "I was on my way to see your tight-ass buns when I spotted the Bird and the mess inside. At the time, I thought it would be cool to drop my calling card inside—let it subtly be known to those *few* who cared that my boss and I appreciated it."

Montego felt a stabbing pain, but covered it with a smiling sigh.

"Detective Strait also told me that Brunetti shot himself fighting for control of the Beretta. He said the guy Brunetti struggled with likely held a thirty-eight revolver in his right hand. . . . The threatening guy must've had a powerful left-handed grip, while his right held a thirty-eight rev—"

"Spice pal," Smith cut in, his large hand resting on Montego's arm. "Let it go. The damn clown killed his own felonious ass."

Epilogue

Mike, wearing only white Laguna shorts, sat with his mentor on the open bridge of the 54-foot Chris-Craft cruiser. The bright Thanksgiving morning sun rising in the east teased a deep blue into the topsy-turvy sea as the billowy clouds floating overhead began to scatter. The breezy ocean air was comfortably warm. He drew in a long wonderful breath. Following surgery, his heart had stayed in sinus rhythm, his lung had healed, and the scabs had fallen off the bullet wounds. And there was no more pain.

Julie and Margaret "Margie" Janes, Eagon's attractive secretary, were below preparing tuna salad sandwiches. KW and Yolanda were on the aft deck with Neall and Lissa. Roy, sitting with them, enjoyed playing with a "rescued" brown-and-white-spotted mongrel puppy, "Kelli O'Brody."

Mike watched the greenish waves between them and the distant isthmus of Catalina where the sky met the uneven earth hidden in a mist. The surface gave up sprays that caught the sunlight with myriad sparkles while cresting the bow and moistening his skin, refreshing him with a taste of salt. He looked down noting how the glow on his legs brought out his natural skin tone, but the tan shade had lightened, as had his weight.

The past weeks had been painful, especially when he'd cut back on the Demerol. The drug had made him feel "way too good." He'd sensed how it could become addictive. For sure, it had affected the thoughts he'd wrestled with about the Haley men, but finally resolved to his satisfaction.

Mike recalled the afternoon he awoke and saw a pumpkin with numerous dyed turkey feathers protruding from it. Bad Bobby D was one of many cops, including The Furry Clam Diggers, who had dropped by. It pleased Mike how the law enforcement family supported each other.

Mother had visited him daily, staying long; Steve joined her twice, but left within a few minutes. Irene and Missy came each Thursday, after Missy was out of class, with a freshly baked pie. Neall complained he'd been coming so often that he'd been forced by hospital rules to cut back on his chain-smoking, but Mike believed Ice Cop truly wanted to quit.

Since all of the Haleys were now safe from Brunetti's vendetta, Neall seemed more relaxed. He had even taken on a bit of color.

The Konos, Yoshi and Kenny, also had visited Mike daily. Still, Yoshi had insisted that Mike come by the dojo when he was released. He had wished for "Michael-san" to sit with them and to share an inner calm. Yoshi had said it would promote a healthier healing.

Last night, Mike had gone to the Kono's home. Before he left the dojo, he'd told the elder, "Sensei, thank you for guiding me to my haragei—it helped my spirit . . . it kept my body alive."

Mike gazed up at the sky. The sea breeze blew his hair back.

It's going to be a glorious day.

Eagon, holding the helm, reached out and tapped his shoulder.

"Mikey, we're clearing the shipping lane so I'm going to give you a try at being skipper on the bridge." He pulled down on the brim of the white captain's hat to shade his reddened face from the sun's rays.

"You're trusting me?" Mike faked disbelief.

"As long as you hold a steady course." Eagon squinted in a manner letting Mike know he'd caught onto his act as he drank from a clear plastic tumbler. "Don't want Roy falling overboard."

"I've one question, Eagon. If you were to represent the person who fired the four deuces into Brunetti's brain cage postmortem, what would your defense be?" Mike swigged a mouthful of Budweiser and set the can in a gimbals.

"Plead him to self defense." Eagon had a wry look, but suddenly he had trouble sipping his drink and burst into laughter.

"From a dead man?" Mike's laugh was cut off by an abrupt belch.

After a few seconds he said, "I guess you'd get your client off too." He realized that Eagon knew that mutilation of a corpse was a crime but not one the County Prosecutor would think worth trying in the Brunetti case.

"What if your client admitted to holding a revolver to the goon's neck when he shot himself?" Smitty's "Let it go" comment still echoed.

Eagon winked. "You've had a tough go, Mikey—forget the dead gunsel and enjoy this little cruise. We should have a most pleasant sail even though the sea's a bit active."

"Yes, *a bit.*" Clearing his mind, Mike nodded back to his right. "Abaft to starboard—porpoises." Dark gray sea creatures were dancing over the foamy wake.

Dancing.

He thought about his tango-dancing dad leaving him to grow up fatherless. Mike realized he wasn't alone in that regard. KW also had not enjoyed the love of a father—and Smitty and Kenny, as boys, had lost theirs to separate wars. Neall enjoyed a dad's love and almost had lost it.

Eagon twisted to watch. "They'll stay with us for awhile."

"They're circling the boat."

"Having fun." Eagon shaded his eyes. "See their wide smiles?"

Mike also smiled, about everything. He thought about the women in their lives and the ones they had to lean on. He had Julie, Lonn had Irene, Neall had Lissa, and Eagon, the ruddy bachelor, had a serious thing going for Margie who was as pretty as her voice had sounded.

Roy had been a large part of Eagon's life, and he would continue to be so; the female puppy, Kelli, helped to fill the vacant spot in the retired detective's, now a law firm investigator's, life.

"Keep the big lady on course, Mikey. I'm going below."

Eagon's words brought Mike back to the open bridge. He knew his mentor preferred to stay out of the sunlight and to steer from the cabin when he was the helmsman, rather than from topside—and Margie *was* in there.

Mike grasped the king-spoke on the wheel of the heavy cruiser and sensed the pressure on the rudder. The grand vessel slowly responded to his slightest turn, rising and dropping, moving to the off-rhythm of the constant waves. He loved it, and the whipping air added to his enjoyment.

"OK, I've got the hang of this gal—I'm ready to try her muscles."

Eagon used the intercom to tell the women in the cabin below, "We're throttling up, ladies." And to Mike, "Run her up five knots, Skipper. Remember, you're moving twenty-nine thousand pounds of mahogany."

Mike momentarily stared at the several chrome-rimmed gauges. "Knots? All right, Counselor, where's the darn knot-meter?"

The sunrays glinting on Eagon's light-blue eyes almost hid his jolly and florid expression. He pointed. "Watch that tachometer and run it up to twenty-two hundred rpm."

Mike, shaking his head, clenched the chromed knob and pushed forward, increasing the power. The bow rose higher as the speed built.

Exhilarated, he maintained the faster clip, listening for countless heartbeats to the slapping of the rippling waves against the ocean-going hull. When he eased the knob back, it slowed the twin diesels until the tach showed 1000 rpm and the bow dropped.

He heard a soft bubbling resonance to stern.

Eagon apparently picked up on Mike's cocked head. "What you hear aft is called silver-heels," he said, grasping the side window framing. "Happens when she's slipping through the water."

Silver Heels—the actor who played Tonto. Is he putting me on?

"Now give us a couple of tacs and treat our pretty lady smoothly, Mikey. . . . Just like making love."

Mike, grinning, followed instructions. He made several changes in direction, then heard, "I think you've got it. Take her to fifteen hundred and keep our girl steady. Slow her some if you wish, we're in no hurry. Dinner at the *El Patio* restaurant on the island isn't until three."

Eagon put a hand on Mike's shoulder.

"Keep holding the wheel I have some news. Wayne Nells' vacancy in Hollywood Homicide has been filled by a fellow already working the second floor—he's moving over from the burglary squad."

"Expected that." Mike visualized the pipe smoker. He could almost smell the aroma of sweet tobacco mixing with the ocean breeze.

"Bucky, however, is pleased with you. He got Captain Whitaker to enter your name for the dicks on the next Transfer Order, but Parker nixed it—thinks you need to learn to follow orders and stay clear of the Mafiosi." Eagon lowered his cap to shade his eyes.

"Thought the Mafia didn't *operate* in LA." Mike cast a sideways glance while he worked the king-spoke.

Eagon grinned. "Time to take over the helm—"

"Lunch time." Julie, at the base of the bridge ladder, held a food basket. The long tails of her lavender blouse were tied below her breasts. White cuffed-shorts set off her lightly suntanned legs.

Eagon said to Mike, "I know Strait's seat is available, but forget it for now. Slow down a bit, son—you'll make it upstairs. By the bye, I heard you *are* getting the Medal of Valor—Parker relented."

"Eagon, I simply reacted instinctively—I'm no hero." Mike didn't bother to explain what was going on at the time. Eagon knew of his concern regarding Neall.

Stepping back, Eagon cast Mike a wink as he waved his freckled hand at two gulls eyeing the wicker basket as he helped Julie climb topside.

She sat beside Mike.

"Enjoy, kids." Eagon touched his hat brim and started down the ladder. He stopped, a gleam in his eyes. "I wonder if Brunetti's killer knew it was Halloween?"

"Hey, you're right." Mike abruptly realized that Brunetti's body *had* been discovered on the eve of All Saints' Day.

Eagon glanced at Julie before he gave Mike a mischievous grin. "The gunsel's mitts were swollen."

"Yep, Alex told me The Beak ended up having purple hands."

Mike conjured up a picture of Alex, half-smirking and tweaking the tip of his prized baby handlebar mustache while enjoying describing the gruesome scene in elaborate detail.

It immediately brought the thought of Lonn to mind, but days before Mike had made up his mind to let the whole matter go. A father fiercely protecting his family—heck, it simply felt just.

For sure, the Haley men have tested my resolve.

He watched Eagon bend and kiss Julie's furrowed brow before he continued down the ladder and disappeared into the cabin.

Mike believed he now had the entire story about the two mobsters' deaths, likely more than Alex Strait, the *professional* detective, had. Mike had teased Alex about having become a pro. In response, Alex had wanted to relinquish his TMA title. Mike adamantly had refused to accept it, saying, "There's only one Toughest Man Alive—you Uncle Alex. You're the original."

Mike held the big cruiser steady, allowing it to crease a foamy path through the watery expanse. The seagull couple eyed the beer. He snatched the Budweiser, finished it off, and eased the throttle down to 700 rpm.

Gazing out at the vast horizon, he could see the southern end of the narrow 22-mile long island. Its ridge now seeming to rise out of the mist.

Below, Mike saw KW's arms around Yolanda, the sleepy puppy, Kelli, snug in hers. Roy, facing the cabin opening, was waving a plastic tumbler, toasting Eagon and Margie. Julie was watching the seagull pair flying in for a closer look at the food basket.

Beyond the birds, Mike observed a lone pale cloud riding a warm westerly wind heading toward a dark cloud. Then, as if colliding with a cold wind, it swirled into an ominous dark face. Goose bumps prickled his arms. He eased his grip on the king-spoke, letting relief rise up his arms and into his shoulders.

Eagon had advised Mike that in time both the emotional pain and the troubling doubts about Neall would dissipate and become tolerable. Perhaps acceptable. But it didn't matter now. There partnership was ending. Neall had said he was being transferred to Ad Vice, and that Nancy Gooch was going to be his snitch.

The Purple Hand

The skipper of Administrative Vice ought to be very pleased, having a Hollywood prostitute who was familiar with the Italian mob as a confidential informant.

Turning back to the horizon, Mike touched his left pinky finger. "Nuchidu takara," he said.

"What, Mike?" Julie asked, her fingers now circling up his inner thigh. She obviously was enjoying the sailing experience, for sure he was, along with her familiar impish touching.

"Life is the most precious thing."

The sea breeze brought moisture streaming from his eyes, tickling his ears.

"Yes it is, Tonto," Neall called out from the foot of the ladder.

"So is forgiveness," Lissa added, her face beaming up at Neall.

Mike's blurred eyes held his partner's icy gray ones. Unheard words passed between them. Loyalty came to mind.

Neall must've told Lissa the truth! She's forgiven him. True love.

A feeling of loneliness suddenly tugged at Mike's heart.

But today isn't Sunday, mi amigo.

He blew out, realizing what he had been unable to grasp till now. He reached down and pulled Julie to her feet, casually glancing at Neall who was down on one knee. Mike swore that Ice Cop was slipping a sparkling diamond onto Lissa's ring finger.

The porpoises squealing their high-pitched songs blended with the droning twin diesels making unique music in the balmy mid-morning air.

Desire surged within Mike. He released the king-spoke letting the yacht slowly tac to starboard. It pitched and yawed over the irregular swells.

Wildly flying strawberry-blonde tresses teased his nose. Smiling, he drew Strawberry Gal close, her breasts crushed against his bare chest.

He tasted her parted lips and heard her throaty purring.

Love stirring with lust floated in the swirly ocean air.

Hasta luego. . . .

Waid Woodruff

Author's Final Note:

Little Frank DeSimone was the L.A. don at the time of this novel having succeeded Jack Dragna in 1957. Frank DeSimone was known widely by the various crime families to be a cream puff. He ruled L.A. from 1957 to 1968, an uneasy period for him. Perhaps a bad omen was his becoming boss right after being caught in the Apalachin mob conference raid in New York.

When DeSimone learned that he was on Mafia boss Joe Bonanno's hit list along with several other crime family leaders including New York's Tommy Lucchesi he was shaken. He also had become aware that "Bananas" Bonanno had moved much of his interests west and was operating part-time out of his Arizona estate.

Insiders admitted that DeSimone had become a recluse, afraid to be seen in public; never going out at night. Meanwhile, the L.A. crime family was becoming known as the "Mickey Mouse Mafia," a hark back to the Mickey Cohen era.

When DeSimone died in 1968, his underboss, Nick Licata, took over. He was no more effective than his predecessor.

Licata had been close to Dominic Brooklier, who was big in porno and various forms of extortion. Try as they might, the two failed to take over the bookmaking racket in southern California. (Dante Pio's character was drawn from these two mobsters.)

And, they were unable to control the independent criminals and gamblers working the southern California area. As a result, Nick Licata's influence waned rapidly.

The Chicago and East Coast crime families, who recognized L.A.'s weakness, moved in on a number of rackets—even though such a maneuver was supposed to be against Mafia rules.

Nick Licata died in 1974. He was no Godfather.

Dominic Brooklier was "ratted" to having ordered the fatal hit on "The Bomp" Bompensiero in 1977. Actually, he was keeping Bomp on the telephone thus enabling the hitters to get to him.

Although he was acquitted of that murder conspiracy, he was later convicted along with several other L.A. crime figures on racketeering and conspiracy charges involving extortion of bookmakers and pornography dealers. Brooklier died of a heart attack while in a Tucson prison in 1984.

The Purple Hand

The author served as a sworn officer on the Los Angeles Police Department for over twenty-one years. He patrolled Hollywood Division in 1961-2, 4, and again as a field sergeant 1969-71. He completed his law enforcement career as the Officer-in-Charge (OIC), Lieutenant II, of the Sexual Assault and Domestic Violence Unit in Robbery-Homicide Division.

He has earned his BS, BSL, MPA and JD degrees.

"Writing this story has been a nostalgic experience. I enjoyed it immensely. The personalities of many officers I knew were blended into several of the characters, but they are not necessarily representative of the characters' acts. Readers who worked the L.A. streets as police officers during the period of this tale might find their memories 'stimulated.' Maybe, they will find themselves reminiscing, perhaps with their old partners . . . those who are still around, as have I. *Hooray at last. . . .*"

All readers will get a taste of what "the good old days" were like. The author resides with his wife, Barbara, and his 97-year-old mother, Gladys. She retired from the Los Angeles Fire and Police Pension System as the Executive Assistant Manager in 1973. Their family home is located on the Wild Rivers Coast of southern Oregon. They are owners of a popular Mexican eatery, Pancho's Restaurante y Cantina, in Brookings located on the inland side of North Highway 101, south of Harris State Park.

They market their legendary salsa in local food stores, and on-line.
Website: panchosalsa.com

Waid Woodruff

Acknowledgment

This novel would never have been completed without the loving support of my beautiful wife, Barbara. Her love, patience, and understanding—awesome. And I know she will be there when I strike the keyboard to begin a new story: *Shades of Blue*.

The critiques I have received—too numerous for me to give proper credit—battered my ego, for sure, but none were malicious, and all were helpful.

www.ingramcontent.com/pod-product-compliance
Lightning Source LLC
Chambersburg PA
CBHW071046250626
47159CB00002B/387